Addicted to You

BETH KERY

writing as

BETHANY KANE

BERKLEY SENSATION, NEW YORK

THE BERKLEY PUBLISHING GROUP
Published by the Penguin Group
Penguin Group (USA) Inc.
375 Hudson Street, New York, New York 10014, USA

USA | Canada | UK | Ireland | Australia | New Zealand | India | South Africa | China

Penguin Books Ltd., Registered Offices: 80 Strand, London WC2R 0RL, England
For more information about the Penguin Group, visit penguin.com.

ADDICTED TO YOU

A Berkley Sensation Book / published by arrangement with the author

Berkley Sensation Books are published by The Berkley Publishing Group.
BERKLEY SENSATION® is a registered trademark of Penguin Group (USA) Inc.
The "B" design is a trademark of Penguin Group (USA) Inc.

For information, address: The Berkley Publishing Group,
a division of Penguin Group (USA) Inc.,
375 Hudson Street, New York, New York 10014.

ISBN: 978-0-425-26682-3

PUBLISHING HISTORY
Heat trade paperback edition / June 2011
Berkley Sensation mass-market edition / August 2013

PRINTED IN THE UNITED STATES OF AMERICA

10 9 8 7 6 5 4 3 2 1

Cover photo by Getty Images.
Cover design by George Long.
Interior text design by Kristin del Rosario.

Acknowledgments

I'd like to acknowledge my agent, Laura Bradford, and my editor, Leis Pederson, for their continued support and encouragement. Thanks to Lea and Mary for the beta reads—your help is always invaluable. I especially want to send out a huge thank-you to my readers. I so appreciate you.

One

No one in their right mind would want to visit him, so the sound of knocking at his front door took him by surprise.

Maybe it was Sherona Legion? But he'd warned the only viable candidate for visitation for miles on end—curvy, kind Sherona—about visiting him on this godforsaken hilltop. Who knew what he'd do to her, the state he'd put himself in? Of course, Sherona'd taken Rill at his word for a year and a half, so he couldn't imagine who was trying to barge in on his drunken, morose solitude now.

He was so caught off guard by the phenomenon of someone visiting that he briefly reverted to his old self—his civilized self—hastening to answer the door.

He was a big man, so when he tripped on the useless little rug in the entryway, he crashed to the wood floor with the impact of an ax-felled oak.

He rolled over and sat up, curses blistering his tongue, the savage Rill Pierce once again fully in evidence.

"My, my. How the mighty have fallen," she said from above him.

He glanced up in midprocess of ripping the frilly rug in half, his blurry-eyed gaze encountering long legs and curving hips. Nope, this was *definitely* not Sherona Legion. His eyes lingered in a lap he'd like to spend the next twenty-four hours in without pause.

He grinned.

There was good reason he'd warned away Sherona Legion. In his drunken state, his usual tight controls on his baser nature had evaporated. It was precisely why he'd made a vow long ago not to drink to excess around women.

No real woman existed like the one in front of him in Vulture's Canyon, Illinois. Rill was left with the intoxicated conclusion that a sex angel had been dropped on his doorstep, and God had packaged her in a tight tank top and even tighter jeans. If there was a deity looking out for him—something Rill seriously doubted, considering he was sin personified—then said omniscient being would know how he loved nothing more than a woman in jeans that hugged every tight curve.

He unglued his eyes from the tempting juncture of shapely thighs and looked up. He grinned like the town idiot when he saw a glorious spill of brown and gold-streaked hair and thrusting breasts pressed snugly against white cotton.

"Well, well, well . . . what have we here," he mumbled thickly. He reached and ran his hands over the back of the woman's thighs. His cock lurched when he encountered her tightly encased buttocks.

He'd finally gotten drunk enough to hallucinate. He was getting *good* at this wastrel business.

"Rill, what are you—"

She abruptly stopped talking when he kneaded her two round ass cheeks in his palms. His face hovered next to paradise. It was amazing what a guy who had no future and who daily tried to forget his past might consider heaven, but there you had it. He closed his eyes and inhaled, catching the scent of cotton mixing with the subtle spice of woman.

No, it wasn't just his whiskey-soaked brain. It wasn't just

the fact that he hadn't inhaled the scent of pussy in his nose in a god-awful long time. Drunken hallucination or not, his angel was sweet.

He kissed her with an open mouth at the bottom of her zipper.

She gasped.

"And here that doctor was preaching to me about rehab," he mumbled. "You're *just* what the doctor ordered—least you would be if I didn't have a wanker with a rod up his ass takin' care of me. Come 'ere."

He spread his hands on her hips, liking the way he encompassed all those tight curves in his grip. He pulled. She fell onto his lap and thighs with a cock-tugging thud. He buried his face in fragrant hair and soft, firm breasts and nuzzled. Inhaling her scent was like breathing in a potent opiate. He could get lost in this unexplored territory—

Lost . . .

"Rill . . . what the hell are you doing?"

Did angels stun, because that was exactly how his sounded. He turned his head, drowning in the arousing sensation of wedging his face in the valley of delicious breasts.

"I'm enjoying my hallucination to its fullest," he mumbled as his hands came up to cradle those firm breasts. He held her against his face and twisted his nose in a fleshy nirvana.

His angel snorted.

"You're not hallucinating. You're hammered. There's a difference."

She'd sounded derisive, but he'd heard the telling tremble in her voice when he pressed his lips against a distended nipple.

"One and the same, if you can get drunk enough," he muttered.

He cupped one ass cheek and rode her jeans-covered pussy against the ridge of his cock. She inhaled sharply and froze. He knew why. A powerful jolt of lust had torn through him as well. He'd thought his cock had been tamed with a combination of whiskey and his own hand for the past eighteen months, but he'd thought wrong.

It had just awakened, and not with a whimper but with a bang. In a matter of seconds he'd been transformed by the power of volatile need.

His thumb stroked the peak of a breast. He grunted appreciatively when he felt the button tighten. He wasn't surprised she wore such a flimsy bra. She was supposed to be his fantasy, after all, and Lord knew he preferred women wearing very little, if anything, over their breasts. At least in the privacy of his mind that was his preference. In real life, he'd prefer they covered up and kept the beast in him from rearing its head.

Drunken delirium or not, he was going to love every minute of letting the beast out of its cage. Tomorrow would come soon enough, and he'd be plunged into the abyss once again. But that moment wasn't now, thanks to this hallucinatory, blessed angel. He moved his head and slipped a stiffened nipple between his grinning lips. His smile faded at the sensation of turgid flesh against his laving tongue.

"You're stiff as a bullet," he muttered a moment later. He wanted that flesh served up raw on his tongue. Nevertheless, he forced himself to still, his nose pressed against supple, fragrant flesh. "Do you want me to do this more?"

"What?"

"Do you want me to stop, or do you want me to see to the other one?" he clarified in a tight voice.

Her breathy whisper felt like a caress along his cock. "I don't want you to stop."

He moved hastily.

"Rill!" she cried out when he suddenly shoved her tank top over her head. She sputtered against cloth, and he jerked the garment off her. He whisked aside the flimsy satin of her white bra, unveiling bountiful pale flesh capped by a fat, erect nipple. He paused, recognizing true beauty even with the feeble tool of his whiskey-pickled brain.

"Aw, baby," he whispered. His cock throbbed hard enough to make him wince when he saw how his whisking breath made her nipple peak beneath it. "You're so pretty."

Something between a whimper and a moan leaked out

of her throat when he wrapped his lips around her nipple. His tongue moved like the fingertips of a blind man reading the secrets of the universe in braille. He learned every tiny bump with fascination. He coaxed the center nubbin until it pressed like a hard little dart against his laving tongue.

When he drew on her, it was as if he had also drawn that sexy, surprised cry from her lungs. Power and lust stabbed at him. Heat rushed into his prick, and he once again rocked her against his straining erection. Her ass cheek filled his palm. He was inundated with the scents of sex and flowers and the sensation of ripe, soft flesh. Heat penetrated her clothing and his own, resonating from her pussy to his cock.

He ground her down on him and rotated his hips, grunting when she gyrated against him in return.

Arousal reared up, a beast about to pounce. The feeling was so powerful, it sobered him for a very brief moment. He'd long ago schooled himself against the charms of nubile flesh and inviting smiles. Lord knew he'd been offered more of that fare than a normal man.

Rill hadn't been a normal man, though. He'd made a point of that.

He blinked and a dark pink nipple came into focus. It was a rose-tipped delicacy, glistening wetly atop soft curves of mouthwatering flesh. A snarl shaped his lips. A need to mate, hard and fast, swelled dangerously in his blood. He leaned down and latched onto the nipple. Distantly, he recalled her other sweet breast, and he couldn't resist the temptation.

Her fingers clawed into his hair when he shoved aside her bra and sucked on her other nipple.

"You let your hair grow," he heard her say through his haze of greedy lust.

He continued to feast on firm, responsive flesh. Did she know him? Was that how she knew that he'd shaved his head for the past couple years? He doubted it. As a film director—an *ex*-director—plenty of people had seen him on television and in entertainment magazines.

Besides, if he'd ever come face-to-face with a woman

like this, he would have remembered. She was too sweet to be real. She melted on his tongue. He drowned in her scent and flavor. His balls pinched tight. He reluctantly withdrew his mouth from her breast.

The necessity for haste jolted through him like an electrical shock. He jerked up his hips and she fell off him, long hair spilling over her face.

"I'm sorry, baby," he mumbled as he rolled on his hip and came up on his hands and knees. When he got there, he paused for a few seconds, willing his world to stop spinning.

"Rill . . . are you all right?"

"No worries," he mumbled as he slowly, carefully stood, putting his hands out for balance as though he were on a lurching ship. "I may be shit-faced as an Irish sailor on payday, but I'm in fine fucking form."

"Charming," he heard her say dryly when he grabbed his cock through his jeans and grimaced. He could tell by the tone of her voice that his angel thought he was being crude, but in reality, he'd been trying to alleviate the stab of lust that went through it when he noticed her shapely legs encased in tight denim and supple, calf-length leather boots.

His vision blurred as he held out his hand to her. She got up on her own, however, which indicated he'd hallucinated some brains along with all that firm, ripe beauty. Most likely, he would have stumbled and brought both of them down on the hard wood floor. She stood, her hair falling in a riot of waves and curls around her shoulders—a fucking glorious display. The tendrils reached her waist. He stretched his hand farther, longing to touch the burnished strands.

"Come on," she said, grabbing his hand firmly in her own instead. "I'm taking you to bed."

"Now you're talking," he agreed with drunken earnestness. He staggered after her down the hallway to his bedroom, his eyes glued to the beguiling curve that led from her waist to her hip. He couldn't wait to peel those jeans off and expose the rest of that golden apricot-hued, juicy flesh.

In his drunken state, fantasy and reality melded. One

second, he'd been in the hallway leching over his angel's ass, and the next, he was in the bedroom pulling her back in his arms and nibbling at her neck, the fragrance of her hair and skin deepening his intoxication. He bent and pressed her ass against his erection. She squirmed.

"Rill Pierce, behave."

Instead of stopping, his mouth grew hungrier on her neck. He felt the vibrations of her soft, helpless moan against his lips.

"You don't want me to behave," he growled against her ear before he pressed his mouth to her neck. She shivered in his arms. He could feel her pulse, throbbing quick and strong beneath his lips. "Your heart is racing."

"That's because I'm trying to throw a six-foot-three drunk Irishman off me," she said acerbically. But he heard the tremor in her voice; he knew what it meant. And, no—it wasn't drunken wishful thinking, either. She'd slowed her wriggling in his embrace. She molded against him like she couldn't stop herself from feeling his shape.

He opened his hand at her lower belly, his third and fourth fingers spreading down to her mons. He liked how much of her compact body he could encompass with his hand. His actions didn't strike him as forward or inappropriate, only right and natural—soft woman against hard man. He pulled her closer, holding her hips captive.

She went completely still in his arms.

"I may be drunk, but I'm not an idiot. Don't tell me you don't feel that," he said gruffly, referring to the palpable heat that emanated from both of their groins, daring her to deny the obvious. His voice had gone hoarse with acute desire. Something about her scent and the feeling of her satiny, warm skin beneath his hand was turning him into a horny satyr. Sure, her body was a fine piece of equipment, but he'd thrived in a profession where breathtaking women abounded. It wasn't her soft skin and lush curves that were making him crazy.

Or at least it wasn't *just* that.

"I don't think . . ."

"Stop thinking. Just feel," he entreated in a whisper next to her ear. "That's what I'm doing, and I haven't let myself feel much of anything for two years now. Have pity, beautiful."

If he didn't feel her wet, sleek flesh surrounding his cock very soon, he suddenly doubted for his sanity. Not that doubting his sanity wasn't a daily occurrence these days, but on this occasion, the possibility of losing his mind felt frighteningly close.

He placed one hand on her chin and pushed it gently, urging her to twist her face toward him. He plucked at her lips. Even though she didn't kiss him back immediately, she didn't turn away, either. He closed his eyes and nibbled at her. It was like trying to coax a flower to open for him. Rill loved the art of kissing—at least, he did when he wasn't shit-faced with his cock ready to burst.

He reined in his lust, willing her to respond as he shaped their mouths together tenderly, and then with increasing fervor as the sensation of her pervaded his awareness. His brain may be taking a bath in alcohol, but he recognized her premium flavor nonetheless.

Something swooped up from his chest to his neck until it tightened like a clawed hand on his throat. It took him a second to recognize the sensation as blinding need.

"Open up, baby," he growled. "I've waited for this for so damn long."

When her lips parted, he swept down on her, drinking her nectar thirstily, letting her taste course through his blood and flesh, allowing it to drown out his memories by a means exponentially more effective than whiskey.

She made a sound in her throat that he couldn't completely identify when he began to unfasten her jeans with fingers that had grown fleet from an onrush of distilled lust. Had it been surprise he'd heard in her tone? Arousal?

Or uncertainty?

He didn't know, and he didn't care.

He groaned gutturally as he kissed her—well, ravaged her mouth, in truth—while he shoved down her jeans and one hand rose to caress the smooth skin of her hip and ass. Lust raged in him at the evidence of all that sweet female flesh.

It'd been so long.

The way he felt, he might have been a sixteen-year-old boy first dribbling jeans off the girl of his wet dreams, not a thirty-six-year-old man who had known his share of fame and accolades, the touch and desire of many women, the love of a wife whom he'd failed, in the end . . .

. . . the black void of loss and self-doubt.

Rill was too familiar with all those things.

The flickering thought galvanized him. He shoved her panties down next to her clinging jeans, and then regretfully interrupted their kiss. She wasn't so hesitant in her response now; she'd been kissing him back with a fervor and heat that nearly equaled his own, tangling her tongue with his, twisting her face farther over her shoulder to get a better angle on his penetration. He ducked his knees and dragged her jeans and panties down to her shins.

She cried out in surprise—or possibly distress—at his clumsy seduction. He was back to reassure her in a second, biting gently at her lips and then penetrating the warm, wet well of her mouth again. He wanted to kiss her forever.

He knew fucking her would prevent him from doing that.

He needed to do both.

When he heard her moan, deep and aroused, as she pressed her bare ass against a cock that was fit to pop, Rill found he couldn't take any more. If he didn't get inside this tempting creature, he was going to take a trip to the asylum sooner rather than later.

He continued to kiss her, his hunger mounting uncontrollably, as he tore at his button fly. He impatiently shoved his jeans and then his boxer briefs down over his thighs. He fisted his cock and broke their greedy kiss with a hissing sound.

"I'm gonna come right in my hand. I can't take any more of this."

He had a fleeting image of her delicate profile through

tendrils of curling hair. Her lips parted in surprise. He placed one hand on her hip, rubbing her in a soothing motion. Despite what he'd said—despite the need for over-whelming haste—he remained unmoving for a moment, his gaze glued to the sight of a compact, round white ass with just a hint of a peach-tinted glow. He tested that flesh with one hand. Her skin was as soft as a flower petal, the flesh firm and succulent.

"Don't make me wait," he whispered, leaning over and nipping at an earlobe. "I want you so bad I think it's cutting at me from inside out."

He felt her hesitate, and for a split second, he knew misery.

But then she brushed her ass against his erection in a beckoning gesture. She bent at the waist.

"That's right. You *are* an angel. Put your hands on the bed," he said thickly as he moved behind her.

Who in their right mind named a town Vulture's Canyon? Katie Hughes wondered as she peered out her front wind-shield at the forlorn-looking buildings that comprised down-town Vulture's Canyon, Illinois. She'd seen quaint-looking downtowns circa the 1930s, both in her road trips around California and on Hollywood movie sets. But Vulture's Can-yon's storefronts appeared much older. She stared at the Dyer Creek Trading Company as she passed and wondered if she'd gone through a time warp back to the 1800s. A humid September evening and the soft, hazy lavender fall of twilight only added to the surreal feeling. The sensation of being lost in time was so complete that she gave a little sigh of relief when she saw the door of the Legion Diner open and a teenage boy step onto the sidewalk wearing a rock band T-shirt, jeans and tennis shoes.

The kid gawked at her as she approached. Katie gave him a wave, sympathetic toward a young man's admiration of sex on wheels. It was embarrassing to admit, but she'd had a similar adolescent longing when she'd bought the shiny black Maserati. Maybe she'd always treasure the feeling of the open road and a fast ride surging through her veins, but at least she'd learned a measure of shame over her crush on sleek, mechanized power. She was a thirty-year-old woman, after all, not one of this kid's classmates.

Something squirmed inside her belly when she recalled the look of incredulity and vague disgust on the manager's face when Katie had whipped into the parking lot of the soup kitchen to volunteer for service a few months back.

Note to self: don't show up for philanthropic service in an expensive car; it reeks of self-disgust and the need to fill the empty hole of a useless life.

Katie shoved the depressing thought aside and smiled when the teenager dazedly waved back at her. She hit the brakes and waited while the kid walked toward the curb with a stride that was all long, scissoring legs and arms. She recognized his awkwardness and felt a rush of warmth toward him. She lowered the passenger-side window.

"Hi," she called. "I'm Katie."

"Uh . . . hi," he replied, his deep voice spiced with a slight twang. Southern Illinois was a whole different world from the northern part of the state. She saw him inspect her car, and then her, with brown eyes that looked curious, but also slightly alarmed, as though he thought she passed for normal, but hadn't entirely discounted the possibility that an alien had just glided into Vulture's Canyon in a Maserati.

"What's your name?" Katie asked.

His Adam's apple bobbed when he swallowed. "Derek Legion."

"Hey, Derek. Could you tell me where I might find Eagle Perch Road?"

"Yeah. Just keep going straight through town, pass Dyer Creek and take the first right you come to." He crouched slightly to get a better look at her. "You're not going up to the Mitchell house, are you?"

"Yeah, I am. You know Rill Pierce?"

Katie thought she read a hint of belligerence in the kid's expression, making him look older than he had just seconds before. "I know who he is. He manages to come down the hill a couple of times a week. Sees to the necessities," he added, glancing pointedly across the street. Katie turned her head and saw where the boy was looking: the Last Stop Tavern.

She straightened in the car seat. She wasn't surprised at the boy's subtle judgment of Rill, but it still made her uncomfortable nonetheless.

Rill had practically been adopted by the Hughes family since he'd come to southern California from Ireland to attend UCLA. That had been almost twenty years ago. People usually gravitated toward Rill. Grandmas adored him and little boys begged him to rugby-tackle them. He could make a female of any age marvel at the wonder of her womanhood as she experienced the delicious contrast of her own sexuality and Rill's easy charm and rugged good looks.

Things must be even worse than she'd thought if Rill's behavior in the small town could cause this nice-seeming kid to glower so darkly.

She thanked Derek, assuring him that Rill was a long-time friend when he asked her if she was *sure* she should go up to the Mitchell place alone.

Twenty minutes later as she leaned over Rill's mussed bed and stared blindly at the wall while his cock slowly carved into her flesh like a hot knife through melting butter, Katie distantly realized she should have heeded the boy's warning.

Two

⁓≫

I've waited for this for so damn long.

Katie'd still had the capacity to refuse Rill until he'd muttered those words. Forget that what he'd said was probably forgotten in his whiskey-addled brain the second after he'd said it. Never mind that she was nothing more to him in those seconds than a willing female who would ease his pain, if only for a few short moments.

He'd spoken *her* wish as if it were his own.

It wasn't his wish, of course. If an angel had, indeed, dropped on his doorstep and offered him one wish, Katie knew what he'd wish for, and it wasn't her. His cock had just been doing the talking for him tonight. Since his wife, Eden, had died, Rill had existed in almost constant torment. Katie found that she had no interest in denying him a few moments of pleasure and forgetfulness.

Not that her acquiescence was completely altruistic.

She shook with excitement as she leaned over that bed. Rill may not know her from a fantasy conjured up in his drunk mind, but Katie was stone-cold sober. She gave her desire to him in the same way she would offer him a bandage if he'd come to her bleeding.

She stood with her rear end in the air, her hands on Rill's mattress. The thick head of his cock probed her entry. The scent of him rushed into her nose: a hint of spicy soap, the lingering salt of his sweat . . . the musk of his come.

It should have turned her off, to know that the man of her fantasies hadn't washed his sheets in weeks . . . maybe longer. She was typically fastidious about her boyfriend's hygiene. What if Rill'd had sex with a parade of faceless females in this bed before that moment?

But it was Rill, and instead of allowing the thought to dissuade her, she spread her thighs an inch and sent her tailbone higher.

She bit her lower lip to suppress a cry when his cock sank several inches into her pussy. It was like harboring the *Titanic* in that narrow, burbling creek she'd passed on her way up the hill.

When he made a sound that was a mixture of choke and grunt, she exhaled shakily. The cry she'd trapped in her throat leaked out against her will.

"Shhhh," he soothed. "Your pussy is as tight as the rest o' you."

She clamped her eyelids closed at the sound of his Irish accent. It always became thicker when he drank, not that Rill had ever been a big drinker before Eden died.

It was bizarre to hear his familiar voice saying something so intimate . . . so *illicit*.

Emotion and pounding sensation overwhelmed her as he stroked her hip and ass soothingly with one hand in the type of gesture she fully identified with Rill. The fact that he held her other hip firm and steady while he worked his cock into her struck her as both bizarre and wildly arousing.

He began to pump, gentle but insistent.

"God must save pussies like this for dying men."

She jerked up, stopping only when he grunted and prevented her from moving farther with both hands at her hips.

"What the hell is that supposed to mean?" she demanded over her shoulder.

He thrust and his cock drove into her body. Katie gasped. Her hands dropped once again to the bed, bracing herself instinctively for the coming storm.

"Just being overly dramatic. It's why I never could have been an actor," he said in a choked voice. He withdrew and plunged into her to the hilt.

"Oh, *God*," Katie moaned. His cock was harbored deep, deep inside her. Did drunk men get this hard? He was hot, too. Was he feverish? She swore she could feel his heartbeat throbbing at the very core of her.

"All right?" he asked. She blinked. His voice had sounded very Rill-like all of a sudden, concerned and gentle.

She didn't have the ability to speak with his cock lodged so deep in her person, so she just nodded.

He began to fuck her. Her vocal cords froze. He stroked her hip with one hand as though in reassurance, but the rest of his possession was purely primal.

"Aw, you've got a pussy so tight you're gonna squeeze the life out of me, every . . . last . . . drop," he mumbled, pumping his hips to emphasize his words. Katie's mouth gaped open as sensation overwhelmed her. Rill was as lustily loud in the midst of his pleasure as she was silent. The deep, throaty sounds of his groans as he thrust in and out of her filled her ears; he grunted in satisfaction each time his balls slapped against her ass.

Katie would have loved to show Rill Pierce that she was an experienced, sexy woman. But she couldn't do much of anything at that moment but allow pleasure to slam into her, each successive wave more powerful than the last. She'd never been filled in the way Rill filled her. He ducked his hips slightly when he pumped into her, straightening slightly when he withdrew, creating an extra jab of stimulation that had her clit sizzling.

Previously, Katie had jadedly believed that the G-spot was an urban legend perpetuated by *Cosmopolitan* magazine.

Rill taught her different.

He spoke to her while he fucked her, and what he said had Katie rolling her eyes back in her head in mounting arousal. Sure, Rill's films were known for raw language. The knowledge that he actually *talked* like that at times was just as eye-opening as the rest of this unexpected experience.

He held her hips tighter and lifted. Katie squealed when her boots came slightly off the floor. Her hands faltered on the mattress, but she caught her weight on her elbows. Both of them shouted when he plunged his cock into her at the new angle.

"Oh," Katie yelped.

"Aw, yeah, that's good," Rill growled as he withdrew until just the head of his cock was lodged in her pussy. Katie gritted her teeth, knowing what was coming. He held her hips captive in his hands and pounded his cock into her from head to balls. She squealed at the impact of him massaging that magical spot deep inside her. Orgasm loomed. He held her lower body at his mercy and slammed into her with rapid, shallow thrusts.

Katie pressed her cheek to the mattress and shuddered in climax. Through her haze of swamping pleasure, she distantly heard Rill.

"You're so fucking *hot*," he gasped, pausing with his cock fully sheathed. He grunted in pleasure, and Katie knew he felt her orgasmic convulsions. His low growl sounded a little dangerous.

She shrieked when he resumed fucking her, fast and furious. Within seconds, she felt his cock swell, the sensation sending a powerful shiver of ecstasy to ripple through her flesh. He thrust into her one last time, the strike of their perspiration-damp skin sounding like the sharp pop of a firecracker.

Katie opened her eyes wide. Rill placed her feet back on the floor. She felt his body going rigid as orgasm blasted into him. His strangled grunt morphed into a pressured shout. His penis jerked inside her. She grimaced, her vagina instinctively clamping around him as he came. His muscles tightened and loosened again and again as he climaxed.

When his convulsions lessened, he leaned over her, his jagged pants blending with her soughing breath.

"Sweet Jaysus," he groaned almost incoherently.

"*He's* got nothing to do with it," Katie mumbled. When he'd spoken, she'd felt the warm vapor of his breath on the back of her shoulder. She glanced back when he began to move his mouth as he panted, caressing her with his lips. Her pussy tightened around him again. He groaned against her shoulder blade. The sensation of his cock lurching deep inside her—and the resulting surge of heat in her pussy—brought reality crashing in on Katie.

"Rill?"

"Yah?" he mumbled as she shifted his hips slightly, stroking her with his sated penis.

"That's enough."

"Who says?" he slurred against her shoulder.

"*I* did," she emphasized. The beginnings of panic began to flutter in her belly. She pushed up off the bed. Rill grunted when she attempted to push his weight off her. He straightened and his still-formidable cock slid out of her body.

"Spoilsport," he accused. Katie stood and nearly fell on her face as she tried to turn. She cursed and bent to reach for the panties and jeans binding her shins. She straightened a moment later, spitting her long hair out of her face, and paused.

Rill had already fallen into bed. He lay on his back, his head on the pillows, torso twisted, and his feet hanging off the mattress. His eyes were closed, but Katie noticed how pale he looked beneath the shadow of his dark whiskers.

"Rill . . . are you going to be sick?"

"Course not. What'd you think I am? An amateur?"

Her mind flashed back to just moments ago when pleasure had splintered through her flesh. One thing was for certain: Rill Pierce was no amateur at making love. Even in his drunken state, he'd been utterly in control . . . masterful. Katie steeled herself against the powerful memory.

"I think you're going to be sick, that's what I think."

His arm dropped from where it'd been resting on the pillow. His muscles went lax.

"Always the doubter, eh, Katie?" he mumbled, his accent so thick she'd barely understood him. He nestled his cheek into the pillow and passed out.

She went very still at the sound of her name on his tongue. It'd been the first time he'd acknowledged her all evening. Had he known her all along? she thought incredulously. She instantly vetoed that idea. It was just the casual camaraderie of their conversation there at the end, their typical taunt and tease that had made him think of her—Katie Hughes—before he'd passed out.

Before that, she'd just been a warm, willing body—a role Rill never identified with his best friend Everett's little sister . . . or with his wife's best friend.

For a few seconds she just stood there, undecided about what to do. She was paralyzed by her disbelief of what she'd just done. She'd just had sex with her best friend's husband. It didn't matter that Eden had died. Years of conditioning herself to a neutral role, of holding back when it came to Rill, suddenly struck her in a forceful rush. She'd been on a mission of friendship, and within a matter of several minutes, her entire world had changed.

If she got in her car and drove away, chances were he'd never remember she'd been there. The idea tempted her.

You came here for Rill, another part of her brain scolded. Just because she'd screwed things up by giving in to an infatuation that had lasted since she was teenager didn't give her the excuse for fleeing the scene of the crime. Not when Rill needed help.

Not when Rill required saving.

She bit her lower lip, her gaze roaming over Rill's body and lingering on his groin. His cock was moist and softening, but still firm and beautifully shaped. Her pussy tightened with desire. Her cheeks heated.

Good God, she was staring at a man who was dead drunk and she was getting turned on.

She stepped forward determinedly. He shifted in his sleep and mumbled something when she gingerly lifted his feet off the floor. Katie froze. When he once again began to breathe rhythmically, she swung his long legs fully onto the bed with effort.

She cased the scene for remaining incriminating evidence. Luckily his feet were bare, so she had only minimal trouble jerking his lowered jeans and underwear off his legs and feet. There was no way she could get his shirt off without risking waking him. She compromised by tossing the blanket over him.

He probably would assume he'd started to undress for bed and fallen on the bed in his drunken state, unfinished.

She hurriedly re-dressed in the hallway and exited the house. She recovered her leather carryall from the front seat of her car. On her cross-country trip, she'd grown into the habit of stowing the bare necessities in the shoulder bag for the night instead of taking her large suitcase into the hotel for the nine or ten hours she'd spend there.

A hot shower didn't completely restore her composure following what had just happened, but it helped. Afterward, she unpinned her hair and let it fall around her back and shoulders. Her reflection in the filthy vanity mirror over the sink looked a bit desperate.

Had it really happened? Had Rill Pierce really just been deep inside her?

And why the hell had she allowed him to come inside her?

Rill'd had an excuse, of sorts, for his impulsive idiocy. Not a *good* excuse maybe, but a comprehensible one. He'd been drunk.

Katie had no excuse, or at least not the sort of excuse a grown woman should claim when she knew better.

At least the chance of getting pregnant wasn't huge. The timing would have been off. It was little consolation, everything considered, but Katie'd cling to that threadbare comfort for now.

She wandered through the house, inspecting her surroundings fully for the first time and trying to quell a rising sense of panic.

When she'd pulled up to the "Mitchell place" earlier, she'd seen a classic American beauty of a house that had been neglected and fallen into disrepair. The home nestled in the midst of towering oak and maple trees. The foliage had started to turn despite the lingering summerlike weather. The vivid hues of the turning leaves against a muted lavender sky had looked a little surreal to Katie's city-dulled eyes.

The house where Rill had gone into exile had three gabled dormers on the second floor and an enormous wrap-around porch. The home possessed excellent bones, Katie decided, even if its faded and chipped painting and a few broken porch posts did give it a sad, forgotten air.

The interior was much the same, she discovered, as she walked through the kitchen, which featured appliances that at one time in their history had been white, and a chipped linoleum floor, but also handcrafted maple cabinetry, wainscoting and trim. She scowled at the crumb-covered counter and the sink filled with dirty dishes—mostly glasses left over from Rill's drinking.

The next half hour was spent restoring some order to the kitchen and scrubbing the appliances until the pure white was once again revealed. She picked up the nearly finished bottle of Jameson Irish Whiskey on the counter and poured the remainder in the sink. She closed the cereal box she found and headed for what she'd come to suspect while cleaning was the pantry door.

"Brilliant," she exclaimed a moment later as she peered into the pantry. She stood next to the closed bottom half of a double Dutch door. The top part of the door was open, revealing a plethora of delightful handmade bins, drawers and shelves inside the pantry. She entered and found three unopened bottles of whiskey along with very little else on the handcrafted shelves, aside from another box of cereal and a mousetrap.

The man was determined to kill himself, she thought grimly. The realization sent a jolt of fear through her, just as it had earlier when she'd leaned over that bed while Rill worked his cock into her.

God must save pussies like this for dying men.

"Dying man, my ass," she mumbled heatedly. She

marched over to the sink and poured the rest of the whiskey down the drain.

Afterward, she inspected the living room with the tattered but comfortable-looking furnishings and magnificent carved oak fireplace. A snowy version of the local news played on the ancient-looking television set. Katie shut it off, wandered around the rest of the first floor and walked out onto the front porch.

How the hell had Rill ended up here?

How had she?

She became aware of a dull ache between her thighs, an undeniable reminder of what had just occurred. Was it possible to forget it had happened? Rill had gotten inside her mind and spirit long ago. Allowing him into the final territory of her body had been a mistake. Anyone could see Rill had nothing to offer a woman since Eden had died.

Except for his cock, that was.

The ache in her sex seemed to slowly expand to her belly. The loud chorus of birds and tree frogs she'd heard when she pulled up earlier had ceased. All was quiet now that darkness had fallen. More stars than she'd ever seen in her life winked at her from a vast midnight-blue dome. Some kind of animal—a coyote?—howled eerily in the distance.

She suddenly felt very small and insignificant standing there in the midst of the Shawnee National Forest, an alien in a strange land . . . an exile.

Her thoughts again strayed to what had happened in Rill's bedroom. Her core clenched with arousal at the memories of the impulsive tryst even as her gut tightened with regret. Or maybe that hollow pain was hunger? She hadn't eaten anything all day except for a breakfast sandwich at a drive-through outside of Kansas City.

Her backbone straightened.

What she needed was some food in her stomach, an opportunity to regroup after this. . . unfortunate turn of events.

"Should be the title for the story of my life," Katie mumbled.

She dug in her jeans pocket for her keys and headed for her car, thinking all the while that the sleek Maserati appeared as out of place and ridiculous in these surroundings as she felt.

A basset hound sat in the entryway of the Legion Diner. It looked up at Katie beseechingly with drooping brown eyes, but remained on its haunches and didn't try to enter with her through the open door. The interior of the Legion Diner looked as worn and weary as the rest of Vulture's Canyon, but the smells wafting out of it made her stomach growl. Four pairs of eyes examined her when her boot heels clicked on the black-and-white-checkerboard tile floor. Katie picked the warmest gaze and sidled toward the woman behind the counter. She took a seat and tossed her Lena Erziak handbag on the barstool next to her.

"Hi," she greeted the woman, who held a coffee cup in her hand. She had auburn hair, brandy-colored eyes and a figure that put Katie in the mind of a young Jane Russell. She glanced over her shoulder and saw a gray-haired man in his late fifties, his mouth frozen in midchew, watching her with frank suspicion from beneath shaggy eyebrows.

"Evening," the woman behind the counter said. She had a light, musical voice, and while her stare was frank, it didn't strike Katie as rude or inhospitable. "What can I get you?"

"What's good?"

"Everything." The female glanced down over Katie. "Nothing low-cal, though."

"Great. I could eat a deep-fried horse."

The woman looked amused in a patronizing kind of way, which Katie found mildly annoying. She surveyed the handwritten menu on a whiteboard next to the grill. There was the usual diner fare, but also the not-so-typical: meat loaf with mashed potatoes and gravy, $3.00; cheeseburger with French fries, $2.75; vegetarian sandwich on seven-grain bread, $3.00; loaf of homemade bread, $2.00 . . .

Cut, $6.00?

Cut? Perhaps it referred to a steak? Katie thought. The prices were right out of the 1970s. Whoever heard of a steak for six dollars?

"I'll have a double cheeseburger with the works, onion rings and a large chocolate shake, the thicker, the better," Katie said.

"You got it," the woman agreed levelly as she turned to start making Katie's meal. She continued to speak to Katie with her back turned as she pulled some items out of a refrigerator. "I guess my little brother isn't crazy after all."

"Excuse me?" Katie asked.

The woman glanced over her shoulder. "My little brother, Derek."

"Oh . . . Derek Legion . . . the boy who gave me directions," Katie said, finally connecting the dots. "You're his sister? Do you own the diner?"

The woman nodded as she tossed a couple hamburger patties on the grill and kicked the refrigerator door shut with one foot. "Name's Sherona. Sherona Legion. Derek was telling me some tall tale about a movie star visiting Vulture's Canyon. I didn't believe a word of it," Sherona said as she lowered a metal basket of onion rings into sizzling oil, "but here you are."

Katie looked around, but the other three people in the diner were even less likely candidates than her. "Movie star? *Me?*"

Sherona smiled as she flipped open the freezer and removed a carton of ice cream, moving around the small space like a dancer doing a familiar routine. "Well, Rill Pierce was a director, after all, and Derek said you were on your way to see him."

She noticed Sherona's musical voice had suddenly gone neutral and disinterested. *Too* disinterested? Katie glanced down at her lap. She'd showered, but some women had a sixth sense when it came to sex. Who was she to say Sherona couldn't smell Rill on her?

Katie didn't like to consider the fact that she might be instinctively sensing the same thing about Sherona Legion.

Out of the corner of her eye, Katie noticed the muscular

guy wearing the fatigues seemed to tense and lean his ear
closer at the sound of Rill's name on Sherona's tongue. She
scanned Sherona's voluptuous figure and scowled. Why
couldn't Sherona Legion cooperate and look like the other
scruffy, disreputable characters in the town diner?

"Rill Pierce *is* a director," Katie corrected shortly. She
took a drink of the ice water Sherona had poured for her
from a chilled metal pitcher. "One of the greatest screenplay
writers and directors of our time. He's just going through a
rough patch right now, that's all." One of the three men
behind her—Katie thought it might have been the survivalist
guy wearing camo—snorted. Katie glared over her shoulder
before she continued. "And I'm no movie star. I'm a tax
attorney from Beverly Hills."

Or at least I was.

She scowled. Why did people always make a habit of
declaring their identity by telling strangers what they did
for a living, anyway? What did that really tell anyone?

"You're not here visiting Fordham, are you?"

Katie started at the sound of the accusing question coming from behind her. She swiveled around on the counter
stool and planted her prized pair of Loeffler Randall Kit
boots squarely on the lower rail. The gray-haired guy was
still staring at her like she was a cockroach.

"Fordham? Who's that? No. I'm here for Rill Pierce," she
said.

The man's scowl told her Rill was nearly as low a recommendation for an acquaintance in Vulture's Canyon as this
Fordham guy.

"What kind of a vehicle *is* that?" He nodded his head
toward the window and the curb where she'd parked her car.

"That's a Maserati GranTurismo."

"Derek says the insides are filled with soft, cushy leather,"
the man said before he took the last swig of his coffee and
smacked his lips. "I reckon you weren't doing taxes for the
destitute, riding around in a monstrosity like that."

"Shut it, Monty," Sherona said wearily before she flipped
a switch and the blender roared to life.

"You got an issue with sports cars?" Katie challenged once the noise from the blender ceased.

"I've got an issue with trouble," Monty told her point blank. He opened up his newspaper and put it in front of his face, making it clear the conversation was over. Katie's gaze shot defiantly over to the man in the farthest booth, a dark-haired, very thin male in his early thirties wearing a baseball hat that looked as if he'd found it at the muddy bottom of Dyer Creek. The hat couldn't quite contain his large ears, which stuck out like two flesh handles from the sides of his head. Her irritation at Monty's rudeness immediately softened when she saw the man regarded her with the manner of an eager puppy.

"I think it's an amazing car, Miss . . ."

"Hughes," Katie supplied. "I'm Katie Hughes."

The way the man hurried out of the booth made Katie glance around to see if there was a fire. Her eyes widened when he rushed her, the flaps of his torn plaid shirt flying out around him.

"Slow down, now, Errol. You'll freak the girl out."

Sherona's bark had the effect of a hose-down on a rioting crowd. Errol stopped midstride ten feet away from her, staggering back a step. He held out his hand shyly. Katie squinted at the tiny model airplane he offered.

"It's the *Spruce Goose*," Errol said in the manner of someone imparting a great gift.

"Errol," Sherona interrupted with kind exasperation, "Ms. Hughes probably doesn't like airplanes as much as you. Remember how we talked, about how your model planes are your special thing? Now . . . do you want another helping of biscuits and gravy?"

"No, I'm full," Errol said as he lowered his hand, disappointment dimming his prior enthusiasm.

"Actually, Errol, I *do* like planes," Katie consoled. "My dad is a distant relative of Howard Hughes. Do you know who he is?"

Errol looked floored.

"*Errol,*" Sherona warned quietly, but Errol resumed his

former rush at Katie. At first, she thought she was going to be tackled, but then the gangly man hauled up short and sufficed to shove the model plane near her face, talking all the while with the rapidity of machine-gun fire.

"Howard Hughes is one of the greatest aviators in history. He designed this, the *Spruce Goose*. He set tons of air-speed records. You *know* him? You know Howard Hughes?"

Katie's eyeballs crossed as she focused on the painted wooden plane an inch from her nose. She inhaled and gently put a hand on Errol's wrist, encouraging him to lower the projectile.

"We're a pretty distant offshoot of the family. I doubt Howard knew we existed. I don't think I was even born yet when he died. So . . ." Katie attempted a smile at the child-man once he'd reluctantly lowered his arm and backed off a bit. "The Hercules is a favorite of yours, huh?"

"You know the *Spruce Goose* is the H-4 Hercules?" Errol shook his head, his dazed expression assuring Katie he was in the midst of ecstasy. He turned toward an amused-looking Sherona. "She *knows* the *Spruce Goose* is the H-4 Hercules."

"I see that, but Ms. Hughes is going to eat her dinner now," Sherona replied. There was a clinking of china and the rattle of cutlery. "If you're done eating yours, you run on, now, Errol. You know what I told you about hovering around people when they eat."

"Yeah, okay." Errol backed away, his brown eyes still glued to Katie. "You probably know the *Spruce Goose* is the Hercules because you're related to Howard Hughes."

Katie picked up the ketchup bottle on the counter and shook it, inhaling the delicious aromas wafting up from the grill. In her cross-country trek from Los Angeles to Vulture's Canyon she'd eaten some truly disgusting meals, but the Legion Diner smelled promising.

"Actually, I know about it for the same reason a lot of elementary school kids in Southern California know it. We took a field trip to Long Beach to see the *Spruce Goose*."

She paused in shaking the ketchup bottle when she noticed Errol vibrated where he stood.

"You *saw* the *Spruce Goose*?"

Katie glanced at Sherona uncertainly. "Well . . . yeah."

It apparently was the wrong thing to say. Errol abruptly charged out of the diner like a startled cat. Katie stared after him, her jaw hanging open.

"Don't worry," Sherona said when she noticed Katie's shell-shocked expression. "His father used to be an air force pilot, and Errol learned his love of airplanes from him. They used to assemble the models together. Poor man passed away when Errol was so little, he had no way of knowing his son was born with a brain that would make him obsess about planes to the exclusion of everything else in life, including basic self-care and hygiene." Sherona sighed and turned to pull the onion rings out of the fryer. A minute later, she efficiently slid Katie's plate onto the counter. Katie remained in the same position when Sherona returned with a frosty milk shake. Sherona must have noticed her bemused expression.

"Well, go on. Eat your food. Errol won't hurt you. I thought they had plenty of different people in California. Why should it surprise you to find someone like Errol in Vulture's Canyon?"

Katie flushed. "I'm not surprised," she mumbled. She was feeling pretty fed up with Sherona Legion and her weird diner before she took a bite of her hamburger and groaned in ecstasy.

For a burger like this, she could forgive Sherona murder.

Just as she was scraping her last onion ring through the remains of the ketchup on her plate, the diner door opened. Katie glanced over, wondering if Errol had returned. She did a double take at the man who entered. He walked up to the bar and flashed her a grin, highlighting a dimple in his right cheek. His face was deeply tanned and his light brown hair was cut in a short, John Kennedy–esque fashion, the bangs combed back in a thick wave. His expensive-looking casual clothing gave Katie the impression he'd just left the golf course. It was a little strange to try to picture the mani-cured lawns of golf in the midst of this wild forest, almost as strange as imagining this man as a resident of Vulture's Canyon.

"You wouldn't be the owner of that beautiful car, would you?" he asked.

Katie couldn't help but glance back at Monty. Sure enough, the older man was scowling at her over the edge of his newspaper. He flipped it back up, covering his face, but Katie sensed him listening like a hawk.

"I'm Miles. Miles Fordham," the man said before Katie had a chance to reply.

"Katie Hughes."

"What can I get you, Miles?" Sherona asked, her tone brisk, but polite enough. Miles Fordham didn't look like the type that a business owner would choose to insult. Sherona sure didn't seem to be too in love with the guy, though, Katie observed.

Fordham glanced down at Katie's plate. His gaze trans-ferred quickly enough to her body, however. Katie did a mental eye roll as he cased her out from boot to eyelash. "I'll have what Katie had. She looks like she enjoyed it, and whatever it was, it sure is sitting well on her. May I ask what brings you to our quaint little town, Katie?"

"Rill Pierce," she replied matter-of-factly after she'd washed down her onion ring with a swallow of her milk shake.

Saying Rill's name caused a wave of regret and mortifica-tion to sweep through her. For a few seconds, the memory of what had happened up at the Mitchell place seemed too bizarre to be a reality. The trip into town, the unfamiliar environment and the strange people had the effect of turning her earlier visit to Rill's into a dream.

The tenderness between her thighs told her different. She dug in her purse and pulled out a scarf, which she defiantly wrapped around herself, hiding her breasts from Miles's gaze.

She held up ten- and five-dollar bills. "Will that cover it, Sherona?"

"Just the ten'll do. I'll get your change," Sherona replied.

"Don't bother," Katie said as she laid the bills on the counter. "It was worth every penny. Well . . . be seeing you."

"Wait. You're not going so quickly, are you?" Miles asked with a laugh. "I haven't had the chance to ask you to the club while you're visiting Vulture's Canyon."

"Club?" Katie asked as she got off the barstool.

"The Forest River Golf Club and Marina. It's right on the Ohio River. I've been trying to get Rill to stop by for ages now."

"Rill hates golf," Katie said with a smile as she passed. "He's more the rugby or American football type."

Miles turned and started to follow her to the door. *Tenacious bastard,* Katie thought with a trace of exasperation. He was a nice-looking guy, but Katie's head was too filled with Rill at that moment—Rill slowly poisoning himself to death with whiskey; Rill touching her, kissing her . . . claiming her. She couldn't attend to another man's advances at the moment.

"The Forest River Club is about much more than golf. The Shawnee National Forest is truly God's country. We have a world-class restaurant, the marina, areas for rock climbing, camping and rappelling, plus some stunning trails, both for hiking and horseback riding."

Katie was about to tell him to send her a brochure when he continued.

"We're right on the verge of getting a gambling license from the State of Illinois for a boat on the Ohio River."

Monty slapped his paper down on the table in front of him so hard Katie thought he'd swatted at a fly.

"Marcus . . . calm down," Sherona warned in a low voice from behind the counter when the muscular guy wearing the camo pants suddenly stormed toward them. For an anxious second, Katie thought he was going to eviscerate Miles Fordham with some kind of bowie knife secreted in his pants, the way he was glaring at him. She exhaled shakily when Marcus stormed out of the diner instead, loudly rattling the bells over the door with his departure.

Lovely choice of town, Rill, she thought.

Obviously, the prospect of a casino on the Ohio River near Vulture's Canyon wasn't a popular topic for some residents.

Not any of my business, Katie thought. She gave a ruffled-looking Miles a look that was half-apologetic, half-"well, that's my cue to be on my way."

"I better get back to Rill. He'll wonder what's keeping me. Nice meeting you all," Katie said before she dashed out the door.

She plunged into the humid night. When she'd driven down the hill from Rill's place, she'd grown used to the darkness. But coming out of the bright diner onto a street that was lit only by two distant, dim streetlights made her blink in slight disorientation.

She didn't glance back at the diner as she started up her car and whipped around in a U-turn, but she had the impression she was being watched through the windows.

She hit something just in front of her right-hand wheel.

Thunk.

Katie yelped and broke hard when she caught sight of Errol's pale face going down in her headlights.

Three

At eleven fifteen the following morning, Rill awoke to the impression his cell phone ringer was burrowing like a twisting screw through his right temple. It made no sense, of course, because a sound couldn't possibly pierce skin and bone. It sure as hell felt like it could, though. After a blessed moment of silence it began to burble again.

He didn't have Internet up here on this remote hillside, but if he did, he'd download a funeral dirge to replace that frickin' cheerful ringtone.

He poked his hand around on the bedside table, trying to locate the obnoxious object. His arm was cocked back to hurl the phone against the wall when he blinked and brought the name of the caller into focus.

He hit the receive button.

"Katie?" he demanded roughly. The inside of his mouth felt like he'd gargled with ooze from a toxic spill.

"Rill! It's about time you answered the phone. You've got to get down here right away."

He sat up in bed, alarmed. Katie Hughes didn't get riled

easily. "What do you mean I've got to get down there? Down *where*? What's wrong?"

"You've got to come down here to the hospital."

"*Jaysus*. The hospital? Who's hurt?" Rill demanded, now fully alert. Katie sounded okay. Who could be sick? Everett? Stanley or Meg Hughes, Katie's parents? Had there been an accident?

"It's Errol. I hit him with my car. Several ligaments in his right knee were torn or strained."

Rill swung his legs over the side of the bed and groaned when a wave of nausea struck him. Christ, just how shit-faced had he gotten last night? He fuzzily recalled watching a movie on one of the local networks last night— What had it been? *The Shining*? He recalled a crazed Jack Nicholson saying his famous line—"Here's Johnny!"—but everything was black after that.

And what the hell was Katie talking about?

"Who's Errol?"

"Errol Banks. The guy who carries around the model airplanes and lives in a shack down by the river?"

Rill's eyes crossed. For some reason, Katie Hughes, who was one of his closet friends from his life in California, was talking about Errol, a resident of his new life—such as it was—in Vulture's Canyon.

Errol was the mentally disabled guy who wandered around rambling about airplanes.

Rill must still be drunk.

"Where are you, Katie?"

"At Prairie Lakes Hospital."

He abruptly stopped rubbing his burning eyes. "Prairie Lakes . . . *Illinois*?"

"Yes, I'm here, just a few miles away."

"What do you mean, you're here?" Rill barked.

"I'm here. In southern Illinois," she said slowly and loudly, as if she thought she was talking to a hyperactive three-year-old. "I drove here to see you. And I hit Errol Banks on Main Street in downtown Vulture's Canyon and injured him. They had to do outpatient surgery on his knee early this morning. You've got to get down here right away, Rill. Errol has been cleared to go, but I have to pay for his treatment, so bring your checkbook. They won't take a credit card from me, and apparently the one ATM in the hospital is busted. I can't find another one in this little town. I've got to pay the bill before they let us go and I don't have enough cash or a checkbook."

Rill stood, scowling when he realized he wasn't wearing any pants.

Jaysus. Katie Hughes. Everett's little sister. Gorgeous, smart-mouthed, vibrant Katie.

Katie *in a crisis*.

It was like inviting a cache of fresh dynamite into a slowly burning house.

Just what he needed right now.

"Okay. Okay, I'm coming," he mumbled. He staggered into the hallway, not entirely sure if he was awake or sleeping. The nailing pain in his right brow seemed too real to be a dream, however. "But, Katie?"

"Yeah?" He heard the tremble in her voice and pulled up short in the middle of the hallway.

"What are you doing here?"

"Why the hell else would I be in this godforsaken place, Rill Pierce? I came to save you."

There was a short pause. He heard her sigh and suddenly saw her clear as day in his mind's eye, the vivid green eyes, the wild tumble of golden ringlets and waves. He'd directed Katie's brother, Everett Hughes, in six of his films. It'd always fascinated him how Everett and Katie shared a face, and yet the impressions of the two were polar opposites. Everett epitomized male good looks, while similar features on Katie comprised the essence of vibrant feminine beauty.

In Everett, Rill had found that rare combination in an actor; he was respected by other men and adored by women.

A sickly worm of suspicion wriggled around in Rill's gut when he considered Everett. He quickly tried to dismiss the sensation.

Of course Eden had never lusted after Everett Hughes.
Everett was his best friend, for fuck's sake. Or had been,
before Rill took a sabbatical in these woods, a sabbatical
that may end up lasting for the rest of his life.

His head swam. Nausea swept through him.

He needed to focus on the moment. Katie Hughes was
on the phone, and she needed help. That was all there was
to consider.

He struggled to bring Katie's image back into his
mind's eye.

Katie and Everett may have represented polar opposites
on the spectrum of male and female beauty, but Katie's
delicate features were often cast in an expression of pure
stubbornness, just like Everett's. Katie didn't sound too sassy
through his phone receiver, though. No, she sounded beat.

He resisted an urge to blurt out that she was a little fool.
No one in her right mind would *choose* to be in his company.
But now wasn't the time to chastise her for barging in on
his misery. Whether he wanted her there or not, he would
never leave Katie hanging in a pinch.

"Are you okay, Katie?"

"I'm fine. I wasn't hurt."

"All right. Give me forty minutes."

"Thanks, Rill," she said before the line went dead.

Rill stood there in the bathroom staring at his cell phone
for several seconds. A shiver of unease had coursed down
his spine when he'd heard his name on Katie's tongue.

"What in the hell did you do to your hair?" Rill accused
by way of greeting.

Katie spun around from where she'd been reading about
the rules of sanitary hand-washing on the hospital waiting
room bulletin board. She stared at Rill for two heartbeats . . .
three.

His hair looked strange and yet right at once. Several
years back he'd shocked them all—his wife, Eden, most

notably—by shaving his head. But Rill had just laughed at
their surprise. What was hair to a man like Rill Pierce?
Better off without the crap. Pain in my ass, Katie recalled
him saying with a wicked grin.

He had a mess of dark hair, but the strands were finer
than she'd remembered. It'd felt dense yet silky when she
ran her fingers through it last night. That thick crop of lustrous hair contrasted markedly with his bold male features
and insouciance in regard to his appearance.

No wonder he'd shaved it off. He probably resented any
suggestion from the magazines and tabloids that he even
remotely resembled a Hollywood pretty boy.

He'd cut himself while shaving and stuck a tiny square
of tissue on his right cheek to staunch the blood. For some
stupid reason, the sight made tears well up in her eyes. She
ducked her head and picked up a curl that hung to her waist,
flicking at it impatiently. "It's just a temporary color rinse.
I wanted something different, so I darkened it. It's already
fading."

"I don't like it at all."

"Don't hold back, Rill."

He returned her scowl. His brows drew together slowly,
and she wondered if the emotional upwelling she experienced showed on her face. He beckoned with his hands.

Katie flew into his arms.

"Hey, Shine. It's not so bad, is it?" he crooned from above
her, his voice gruff and lyrical. Katie was five foot four on
the days where she could hold her head up high, which
hadn't been very often, in recent history, anyway. Her cheek
pressed just below Rill's nipple line. He felt good—hard and
male. He smelled even better, like soap and clean male skin.
Hearing him call her "Shine" had caused a fresh wave of
misery to surge through her. It'd been his pet name for her
since she was a teenager, a shortened version of "sunshine."
When she'd reached her senior year in high school, he'd
shortened it to "Shine," explaining soberly that she'd out-
stripped the light of a single sun.

He'd teased her a few times since, saying he could never put her in one of his films because his lighting director would never let him rest for ruining everything he'd ever learned about his profession.

Full of it, that was what Rill Pierce was. But in the sweetest kind of way.

"Hey," he murmured.

She leaned back when he placed his hand at the side of her head. When she looked up at him, Katie abruptly became aware of how blue his eyes were, how thick his lashes were . . . how her belly pressed against the fullness between his thighs. Everett, Eden, Rill and Katie had been friends for years now. She'd hugged Rill countless times. She'd never had cause to feel ashamed hugging him before.

She stepped back now.

"You said Errol's knee was injured. Is that all?" he asked.

Katie nodded and furtively wiped at an errant tear. "Yeah. They did outpatient surgery on it this morning to fix a torn ACL. The doctor said he would be fine, but he has to take some anti-inflammatory medicine and use a passive motion machine every day. He'll start outpatient rehabilitation in a week or so."

"It could have been a lot worse." He seemed uncertain when another tear spilled down her cheek. "What *is* it, Katie?"

She bristled at the sound of him saying her name. *Ka-tie.*

"Have you ever hit a man with your car before?"

"Can't say I have. Hit a bull when I was filming *Pamplona*, though. Ruddy thing did more damage to the truck than we did to it."

Katie laughed, even though she was feeling far from mirthful. "Well, it's awful. I might have killed him. And Errol's so . . . He's so . . . like a . . ."

"Like a child."

"Yeah," Katie whispered. She met Rill's eyes. "He'd run back to his house to get more model planes. He wanted to show me. It was so dark on that street after I left the diner. I never saw him until I'd hit him."

"It could have happened to anyone. Vulture's Canyon becomes a dead man's land at night. And Errol acts on impulse. He should have known better than to run in front of a moving car."

Katie sighed. "Well, it's done. I'll have to pay for his hospital stay and his rehab. He doesn't have any insurance. He doesn't have a car, either. I'll have to drive him to all his appointments," she added, not realizing the truth of her words until that moment.

"I'll be driving him."

Katie glanced up in surprise at Rill's resolute tone. "Don't be ridiculous. *You* didn't hit him."

"That may be, but Errol will likely require rehab for weeks on end. There's no way you're staying in Vulture's Canyon that whole time."

Katie straightened to her full height. "Who says?"

"I do." He seemed to reconsider his bluntness. "I can imagine Morgan and Watkins might have a say in the matter as well."

"I've taken a vacation from Morgan and Watkins," Katie said, referring to her former employer, a large law firm that did taxes for the rich and famous.

"You took a vacation and came to *Vulture's Canyon*?" Rill asked incredulously.

"I told you I did."

"That's just stupid."

Anger rose from her belly to her brain like mercury in a thermometer stuck in boiling water. "Don't you call *me* stupid. I'd say what you're doing these days is way off the idiocy scale, so I guess you can put up with *me* for what's left of your miserable life."

Katie paused when she saw how the color left his face, but she didn't relent. Suddenly, the idea of this beautiful, talented man wasting his life felt like a personal affront, like a slap to the face. It surprised her a little to realize she shook with emotion. Or perhaps it was some culmination of the bizarre events of the past fifteen hours and a sleep-deprived brain that was finally getting to her.

"You're not going to chase me off like you did Everett, Rill," she said in a quiet, vibrating voice.

His lips flattened in irritation. "I wouldn't be too sure about that, Katie. You haven't seen how I live."

She swallowed convulsively. There it was: proof positive that he definitely had been too drunk to recall her being at his house last night, let alone remember what they'd done. A feeling of mixed relief and sadness swooped through her.

She stepped toward him and tilted her chin up, meeting his glare. "You call what you've been doing the past eighteen months *living*? We both know you're flirting with the opposite, Rill. It's gonna stop here and now, too."

"Oh, yeah?" he asked belligerently. "How do you know that?"

"Because Eden would be ashamed of you. I figure you just need someone to remind you of that."

His eyes flashed in fury at the mention of Eden's name; his jaw clamped tight. Katie recoiled slightly in her own skin, the evidence of his hurt paining her as well. She stepped back.

"Did you bring your checkbook or not? I'll pay you the cash I have and drive into Carbondale tomorrow to get the rest. Errol's itching to get back to his house, and I sure could use some sleep."

His right eyelid flickered, indicating that while Katie might be willing to dust off her hands and move on from her little outburst, Rill was still angry.

"You can come up to my place and get rested up for your drive back to California. You're not welcome here, though. I want you gone as soon as you're rested," he said stiffly.

She stalked past him toward the nurses' station, wondering why having Rill say out loud what she already knew with perfect clarity could hurt so damn much.

Rill made a phone call before they left the hospital. Katie heard him telling the person on the other end about Errol's injury. Fifteen minutes later, they dropped a tired, pale-faced Errol off at his house and left him in the care of a woman in her sixties who was dressed like she was on her way to a

Grateful Dead concert. Her name was Olive Fanatoon, and once Katie got past her hippie apparel, she realized she was a sweet, soft-spoken lady.

"Is Mrs. Fanatoon a relative?" Katie asked Rill as they walked out to their cars. Katie and Errol had followed Rill to Errol's. The tiny house itself was in disrepair, but it was ideally situated on the serene, thickly wooded banks of the Ohio River.

Rill shook his head. Katie could tell by the way he didn't make eye contact that he was still irritated at her. "No, but she's taken care of Errol on and off since he was a baby. Every adult in Vulture's Canyon, and most of the teenagers as well, takes turns watching out for Errol, but Olive pitches in more frequently than most."

"Do you take a turn?" she asked as she reached her car.

Blue eyes flashed at her. "No. I don't belong to this town."

"Right. Silly of me to ask. You've got much more pressing matters to see to, like drinking yourself into oblivion, for example," she said as she flung open her car door.

She pulled out of the dusty dirt road that led to Errol's and onto the rural route, her wheels squealing on the blacktop. She imagined hauling ass up to the Mitchell place and finding a shower and a place to sleep before Rill even had a chance to make his way through her dust.

It galled her to have to pull over and wait before she hit the main road, because she'd recalled why it was so critically important for Rill to believe this was her first time visiting his house. She couldn't traipse up the hill like she owned the place.

Tears burned in her eyes when he barreled past her in his sedan without a sideways glance. She couldn't help but contrast his cold aloofness with the scorching memory of him pressed to her backside, his mouth hungry and hot on her neck, his gruff whisper in her ear . . .

Open up, baby. I've waited for this for so damn long.

She shivered despite the heat of the early autumn day. *Holy shit. Can't you even console an old friend without ruining everything?*

For a few seconds, she felt like something volatile was going to burst right out of her chest, but then she sniffed and determinedly pulled her car onto the road. So what if on an impulse she'd quit her job, driven across the country, run over a town resident whom she'd now have to provide for medically with a quickly dwindling bank account, fucked the man she was supposed to be consoling and then offended him by speaking his dead wife's name out loud?

"At least you've got your health," she muttered grimly before she turned onto the main road and started up the hill where Rill lived.

Four

~~~

By four o'clock that afternoon, Rill was ready for a drink. He'd been confused and worried by Katie's initial phone call, infuriated when she threw her sauce in his face at the hospital and on low boil since she'd hauled an enormous Louis Vuitton suitcase up the front porch stairs and burst through the screen door.

"Don't bother to help. *Really.* I've got it," she snarled as she rolled the monstrosity of a suitcase down the wood-floored hallway. The noise she made was loud enough to wake the dead. Rill leaned against the counter, silently fuming as she opened door after door in the downstairs hallway, knowing full well the only other bed in the house was upstairs. When she'd opened up the last door, and he heard the suitcase clacking down the length of the hallway, he cursed under his breath and charged after her.

She said nothing when he grabbed the suitcase and stomped up the stairs. It was hot and sticky in the dormer bedroom, so he flipped on the window-unit air conditioner before he tossed Katie's suitcase onto the bed. It bounced up six inches before it settled.

"The shower up here doesn't work. You'll have to use the downstairs bathroom."

He'd been hyperaware of the sounds of her moving around the house since that moment of rude welcome. Her presence there bothered him more than Everett's visit several months ago, and he'd been perturbed enough by Everett being in Vulture's Canyon.

For some reason, he kept matching up the image of Katie in his mind to the sounds in the house. He saw the bounce of her long, lush curls when he heard her quick step on the stairs; he imagined the scowl on her face when she walked into the bathroom and noticed the state of it.

In the silence that followed, he clearly pictured her unbuttoning her jeans and peeling off tight denim to expose the juicy, succulent flesh of her hips and ass.

When he'd realized the direction of his thoughts—when he recognized he'd trained an ear down the hallway, eager for more cues of what she was doing in the privacy of the bathroom—Rill grabbed a bottle of cold water from the fridge and stomped out the back door.

He really was turning into a degenerate.

An hour later, he felt more than a twinge of guilt when he recalled how pale her face had been when she'd followed him upstairs to that hot dormer bedroom. It was *Katie*, for Christ's sake; sweet, generous, brave Katie, whose inner flame had always drawn him. She may have been completely misguided by thinking she should come to Vulture's Canyon to save him, but her heart was in the right place.

Katie's heart was always in the right place.

He ran down the hill to the market in Vulture's Canyon while she napped. They didn't have much at the Dyer Creek Trading Company, but there was enough to get by in a pinch. He figured he should at least feed the girl after she'd rested and before he politely sent her on her way.

While he was placing pasta, pasta sauce, rice, fresh-baked bread and cereal in the pantry, he noticed his whiskey supply was gone.

His regret over the way he'd treated Katie earlier dissipated in an instant.

He'd thundered halfway up the stairs, ready to haul Katie's butt out of bed and give her a piece of his mind, when it suddenly struck him what he was doing. He pulled up short and plunged back down the stairs. His shirt fell to the kitchen floor. He shucked off his socks and hiking boots at the foot of the back stairs. His jeans were left in the grass about halfway through the backyard.

The water in Dyer Creek was probably at its warmest temperature of the year, but it was still cold enough to make him grit his teeth when it came up around his balls and then his belly.

His head went in next, and damn if it just wasn't what he needed. He kept his head underwater until the incendiary fantasy of strangling a good friend because she'd gate-crashed his solitude and bogarted his whiskey slowly receded. When he pulled his head out of the cold, clear water, he heard a loud shriek and a choking noise.

"What the hell'aw you doing?" he bawled.

Katie paused, thigh deep in the water, and spit a tendril of hair out of her mouth, her green eyes wide in disbelief at his question. "What does it *look* like I'm doing?" she yelled at the same time she winced and yanked up a foot, nearly losing her balance. The rocks may well be smooth in the creek bottom, but they were plentiful. "I'm trying to save a crazy man from drowning himself! *Rill?*" she asked, staring at him like he truly was the lunatic she'd accused him of being.

Rill blinked, realizing too late he'd been gawking at her breasts through the thin fabric of the tank top she wore.

He wouldn't have been a guy if he hadn't noticed before that Katie possessed beautiful breasts, large in relation to her compact body, but high and firm. It'd never shamed him before to consider Katie attractive, because he knew admiration was as far as his attentions would ever go. He knew that because he'd set a firm limit on himself, and when it came to sex, Rill was steadfast in his self-imposed limitations.

It was one of his only true virtues.

First, Katie'd been Everett's little sister, and decent guys were careful about respecting that sacred domain. Then she'd been Eden's best friend.

Besides, Katie wasn't his type. She was a force of nature: a whirlwind, a golden beach that stretched for an eternity, a gypsy-spirit in designer jeans.

She looked downright indecent standing there in all her splendor, a majority of that pale gold skin exposed to the sunlight, her hair falling in wild curls. His hands prickled with a need to grasp that glorious mess, to tangle his fingers in it. Her breasts heaved, her nipples clearly outlined against nearly nonexistent fabric.

Rill experienced a potent surge of lust followed by a pang of shame. The shame wasn't enough to block out a desire to pick Katie up, lay her on the banks of the creek, strip her bare and consume her with the hunger of a wolf who hadn't fed in months.

His lurching cock tugged at his conscience. God. He'd thought he'd successfully quieted the animal inside him, but apparently all he'd done was strengthen it with his abstinence. Lust tore through his veins like a potent drug.

"Go inside, Katie."

She blinked. Even to his own ears, his low command had sounded ominous. She opened her mouth, just like he knew she would. Katie couldn't keep her mouth shut if a torpedo streaked straight toward her head. He stepped toward her.

"Inside."

This time he'd gotten the message across in spades. She turned abruptly in the chilly water, cried out in surprise, and went straight down. He caught her before her chin hit the water, but the rest of her was submerged. He heaved and she came out of the creek with a loud sucking sound and a squawk.

"Jaysus," he fumed at the feeling of a wet, stiff-nippled breast pressing against his bare chest. He marched out of the creek and through the yard with Katie in his arms, his gaze trained on the house, refusing to look at her as she commanded him to put her down.

Blood roared in his ears and pounded into his cock. Why, he had no idea. Katie Hughes wasn't his type. She *wasn't*. Rill preferred quiet, elegant women. He'd had enough of blatant, earthy sexuality from his mother, who had dragged him from one man's house to another when he was a child, their rent paid by his mother's spread thighs.

Not that Katie was like his mother. She wasn't at all. He was just worried *he* was.

In the distance, he heard shouting in his ear, but he existed in a thick fog of impenetrable lust and fury.

It infuriated him to hold a wet, nearly naked Katie in his arms and consider his mother. He was *not* like her. He may drown his sorrows in alcohol when the mood struck him, but unlike many of his friends and coworkers, Rill had never been ruled by his prick. *My fucking, aching, chubbed-up, traitorous prick,* he added to himself furiously.

The cry Katie made when he tossed her onto her bed in the dormer bedroom finally pierced his anger.

She lay on her back, her elbows propping up her upper body. She stared up at him with huge eyes, her breasts and belly heaving in agitation, her legs parted. Wetness gleamed on her smooth skin. He stood over her at the side of the bed, breathing heavily, watching as her gaze lowered over his torso.

He was hard enough to pound nails with his cock, and there was nothing he could do to stop her from seeing it. His boxer briefs clung to him like a second skin. Rill didn't need to look down at himself to know his erection was about as obvious as a servicing bull's.

He jerked his gaze off the sight of her tiny, thin, wet shorts clinging to a well-trimmed triangle of pubic hair and outlining succulent-looking sex lips. He should be shot point-blank just for thinking about what he wanted to do to her in that volatile moment.

Her expressive eyes told him that she knew he fought with his baser instincts. The hint of anxiety he saw in irises that were the color of a newly opened, green leaf caused a wave of self-disgust to flood him. When he pointed at her, his hand shook.

"I want you out of this house, Katie."

He turned and stalked out of the room without another word.

The night passed, and then another day, and still Katie couldn't get Rill to sit down and speak with her. His withdrawal left her feeling even more anxious than she had been after the creek incident.

And after having sex with him, of course.

On the morning after her arrival, she'd left when Rill disappeared into the woods. She'd driven down to Errol's house to check on him. Once she'd assured herself that he was properly using the passive motion machine they'd given him at the hospital, which helped to keep his knee joint limber while he began to heal, she headed back to the hill.

Instead of isolating himself in the woods this time, Rill had taken refuge in his bedroom.

She'd spent the better part of the day making the place livable again. The house really was nice once one got rid of a year and a half's worth of the dust and grime of Rill's depression. She'd been making the beautiful wood mantel gleam with furniture polish and considering what she could make them for dinner when she heard Rill in the hallway.

"Rill?" But he never answered her call, just headed out of the house. Katie had heard his car start up before she reached the screen door.

Almost two hours later, she waited in the shadows of the wraparound porch sitting on a rusty wrought-iron chair. Darkness had just fallen, slow, silent and all-consuming. The creatures in the trees and fields had ceased their clamorous communications. The dim kitchen light barely penetrated the thick shadow of night.

Had Rill found her presence in the house so disturbing that he'd left town, perhaps? What if her being there had made him more desperate . . . more impulsive, and he'd done something crazy and dangerous?

She stood. She'd promised herself she'd wait until nightfall before she went to try to find Rill. The time had come, but uncertainty stilled her feet. He would only resent her more for seeking him out . . . for treating him like he was a delinquent fifteen-year-old. No matter how much she wanted to, Katie couldn't *make* Rill see reason.

She couldn't force him to snap out of his grief.

Helplessness didn't sit well in Katie's belly.

She heard a vehicle's motor in the distance. Her heart pounded into overdrive when she saw headlights cast on the grove of trees that lined the road.

The car door shutting sounded abnormally loud in the still night. A dog in the far distance must have thought so, too, because it started barking a warning.

She assumed Rill didn't know she was there as she listened to his heavy footfalls on the steps and front porch. He paused a few feet away from the screen door, though, his head lowered.

"What am I going to have to do to get you to go, Shine?" he asked quietly.

"I'm not going," she replied softly. Firmly.

He sighed. With a hitch in her chest, Katie realized he *had* known she was there. Somehow. He hadn't been talking to himself. When he didn't respond, Katie took several cautious steps toward him.

"Are you drunk?" she asked bluntly.

"No."

"Where'd you go?"

"Down t' the pub," he replied.

"I thought you said you weren't drunk."

"Jaysus, Katie. I didn't even finish my second beer. I hardly think it qualifies." He turned and plunked down on the top step.

Katie approached and sat at the opposite end. She swallowed, trying to tamp down the unpleasant feeling of helplessness lurching around in her gut.

"You don't really think the people who care about you are going to stand idly by and watch you kill yourself, do you?" she asked.

"I'm not trying to kill myself," he muttered. "All I want is to be left alone."

"You're self-destructing, Rill."

"I'm living alone because I *choose* to. I pay rent. I'm not breaking any laws by getting myself good and ossified once in a while. I can't see how *you* have a say in it one way or another," he said, frustration heavily lacing his tone.

Katie bit off her aggressive reply. She took a deep breath and stared up at the night sky. A low cloud cover obliterated the light of the stars.

"How did you ever end up in this place, anyway?"

For several seconds, she thought he wasn't going to answer.

"My plane got grounded in St. Louis during a storm on a trip from New York to Los Angeles," he said quietly after a moment. "I got off the plane, rented a car and drove." She saw the shadow of his hand going up in a vague wave. "This is where I ended up."

"An eighteen-month-long layover?"

He shrugged.

"You said you'd been coming from New York. Had you been visiting Eden's grave in New York?"

Katie saw him tense.

"She was my friend in addition to being your wife, Rill. I'm not going to go around refusing to say her name. That's no way to honor her memory. Is that where you'd been? Before you came to Vulture's Canyon?"

"Yah," he replied, almost inaudibly, after a moment.

Katie had been to the cemetery in the Hudson River Valley where Eden Pierce had been buried. Eden had been visiting her parents while Rill was filming in London. She'd been driving home from a meeting with an old school friend when a sleeping truck driver veered across the centerline, hitting Eden's car. She'd spun out of control and flipped into a deep ravine at the side of the road.

They said she'd still been alive for several minutes, but pinned against the seat and the steering wheel. The bloody fingerprints on the window, the smashed door and the handle indicated she'd been trying to get out before the air in her collapsed lungs ran out.

"I miss her, too," Katie said softly.

"You don't know what you're talking about, Katie. You don't know what's happening inside me."

Her chin tilted up defiantly, but inside, she felt herself wilting. His grief seemed insurmountable at that moment. Was she delusional, thinking she could actually help him when he obviously didn't want it? She suddenly knew that the unbearable burn she felt in her chest—an explosive, frightening feeling—was precisely what Rill experienced in the silence; it was a sympathetic pain.

She was a little horrified when a thought struck her and laughter popped out of her throat. Rill glanced over at her sharply.

"What?"

"I was just thinking . . . she would have hated this place. Eden. Remember how you were filming in that pitiful little town outside of Dublin and she and I flew over to visit? She took one look at the accommodations and insisted we stay in the city and drive to the town every day."

Rill's clamped jaw made Katie sure she'd gone too far once again, but the pressure in her chest wouldn't allow her to stop. She was compelled . . . or hysterical, one of the two.

"I'm not saying she was a snob," she added nervously. She screwed up her face and tried to hold Eden's image in her mind's eye, the glossy brown hair, the kind gray eyes, her elegant, expressive hands. They'd been roommates in college for two years, and Katie had always been envious of Eden's hands and her long, graceful limbs.

"She actually wasn't snobbish at all," she continued, "but I always pictured Eden in refined places, like libraries or conservatories or art galleries. The first time I visited her at her job at the Hammer, I thought . . . *perfect*. She belongs here," Katie recalled, referring to Eden's position as a collector at the Armand Hammer Museum of Art. "She was like a piece of fine china. I could never really picture her in the country."

"She was a lady."

Katie started at the abruptness of Rill's gruff voice.

"Yeah," she whispered. Both of them sat for a moment in silence. "What was the name of that godforsaken town where you filmed in Ireland?"

"Malacnoic. She *really* didn't belong there. She was right to want to stay in Dublin."

"I sort of liked it."

She chuckled when he glanced over at her. The dim light from the kitchen allowed her to see his wry expression.

"I *did*. It had its charm."

"Malacnoic is about as charming as a clatty old whore. I should know. I was born there."

"What?" Katie asked, sure she'd misunderstood him.

"You heard me," he said evenly, his face once again turned in profile.

"But . . . you never mentioned it to us. Did you ever tell Eden? Or Everett?"

"Everett knew. Couldn't keep it from him. Most of the crew and cast ended up at the pub with me after we were done filming for the day. I paid most everyone in Malacnoic—including five-year-olds—a small fortune to keep it quiet that I grew up in that town. Didn't want the press to get ahold of it. What?" he asked when she made a miffed sound.

"You might have told Eden and me. It would have made the visit more interesting. Don't even *tell* me your family was nearby that whole time."

"My mother lives in the country, or at least she did at the time. My uncles were in prison while I was filming. They're usually on a one-year-in, three-month-out cycle," he said darkly.

Katie frowned. She'd never before heard him make mention of his uncles, and he was always closed-mouthed about his mother. He had once told her he'd never known his father. "Still . . . you'd think you'd have taken your wife to meet your mom."

He shrugged. "Like you said, Eden was like a piece of fine china. I didn't want to dirty her by exposing her to my ma."

Katie just stared at his large shadow for a moment, her mouth hanging open. There was so much she didn't know about Rill Pierce, so much *nobody* knew. Sometimes it seemed he'd just sprung into existence when he'd arrived in Los Angeles. His brilliance as a writer and director was widely acclaimed, his intelligence nearly palpable when one looked into his incising gaze. Before Eden had died, he'd always been the first to laugh, the quickest to get off a witty barb aimed at one of his friends. He'd been the epitome of insouciant male charm, a bad boy with a heart of gold, a lighthearted jester always ready to use his films to poke fun at people who took themselves too seriously.

And all along, this darkness, this turmoil, had existed at his core. Of course it had. Katie had known it all along, this hidden side of Rill. Deep inside, she'd sensed it, even if it hadn't become completely obvious to her until that moment. It wasn't just Eden's death that had turned him into this tortured soul. Sadness and fury had been a shadow on Rill's face since the first time she'd set eyes on him.

It was the contrast of that shadow with his heart-stopping smile that made Rill so attractive. The sparkle in his blue eyes was so magnetic because she'd sensed a different gaze, a dark, lost one just beneath it.

She sighed heavily. For some reason, the pressure in her chest eased some. She joined Rill in studying the thick blackness of night.

"How's Everett?" he asked after a moment.

"He's fine. He's furious you're allowing Kevin Battershea to direct *Ellen Drake*."

"I didn't pick Battershea. The studio did."

"The only reason they were looking for another director was because you refused to direct your own screenplay. You and Everett can't stand Kevin Battershea. You always say his films are like *shite* dipped in syrup," Katie said, imitating Rill's accent.

"I told Everett I wouldn't be offended if he took the part. He shouldn't have turned it down. He loved that part," Rill said, his flat tone nearly silencing his lyrical accent.

"He doesn't want to work with Kevin Battershea. He doesn't want to be there seeing him butcher your film first-hand," Katie exclaimed heatedly. It irked her—alarmed her—to see Rill so disengaged from a topic that used to consume him.

"I'm staying," she said suddenly.

"I don't want you here, Katie."

"You don't want sobriety, either. You *want* to throw a brilliant career to the dogs. You want to chuck your whole damn life away. Call me an idiot, but I'll trust my judgment over yours at the moment."

It gave her a strange sort of satisfaction when she saw his expression tighten with anger. Anything was better than that eerie, flat detachment.

"And I suppose you're the goddess of wisdom, leaving your job and driving across the country to save a drunkard. No offense, Katie, but I'd hardly cast you as a Florence Nightingale."

She rolled her eyes. "As if you'd do a film about Florence Nightingale."

"T'at isn't the point," he spat. "You don't know what you're getting yourself into. I'm not the man you used to know. I'll toss you out on your ass if you try and stay."

"I'll come back."

"That'd be when the real trouble starts, then."

She started at the impact of his low growl in the darkness, then immediately hoped he hadn't seen her trepidation. She stood and straightened her backbone.

"I'll take my chances. No one has ever said *I* was made of fine china." In the corner of her vision, she saw his head whip around at her words.

Katie walked into the house, leaving Rill to stew in his darkness.

Five

He wanted to bring himself off in the shower. The images that kept rising in his mind in graphic detail, however, were the same images that he'd forbidden himself to associate with his aching cock.

It was three o'clock in the morning three nights after Katie had arrived. Rill hadn't touched whiskey in nearly seventy-two hours, a rare occurrence. His temporary abstinence had *nothing* to do with Katie Hughes sleeping upstairs.

Or maybe it did. He was too restless, too grouchy and bitter to settle down and get comfortable in the numbness of a good shit-facing.

His hand seemed to have a mind of its own, joining in a conspiracy with his prick against his brain. He found himself standing in the spray of warm water and running his hand along the engorged shaft, rubbing his thumb over the sweet spot on the underside just below the head with increasing speed. When he closed his eyes, the image popped up as clear and close as if he sat in his private viewing room in Los Angeles: the wet, translucent material of cotton sticking to Katie's skin, the round globes of her breasts heaving up and down as she gasped for air . . . the expression in her wide green eyes.

She'd been as aroused as he'd been. The knowledge had shot through him like a plunging lance as he'd stood by the side of Katie's bed. But there'd been a hint of anxiety there, too.

And damn it if his reprobate genes weren't finally expressing themselves full blast, but that combination of raw heat spiced with a tad of wariness had been haunting him . . . plaguing him.

He could perfectly picture himself yanking off those tight little shorts and burying his face between Katie's thighs. The level of tension in her body was such that she'd vibrate like a tautly drawn string beneath his strumming tongue. She'd taste like honey and musk, like sex distilled. He'd coat his tongue and throat in her essence and let the wild riot take over his brain and body.

When he held her down and worked his cock into that tight little pussy, it'd be like diving into a vast orgy of need. Katie wasn't the type of woman you could take in half measure. One taste of her, and he'd have to consume her completely. Frequently. He'd make her ache, but he'd take her again and again anyway, his cock demanding he find surcease in her body . . . anywhere.

Anyhow.

His rapidly moving arm slowed. He opened his heavy eyelids and water droplets shot into his eyes. The realization that he'd been picturing sticking his cock into Katie's ass— *Katie Hughes*—made him let go of his erection as though it'd burned him. The heavy head dropped, the shaft extending at a downward angle. His balls pinched, needing to be emptied.

Requiring it.

"Bloody hell," he muttered under his breath, cowed by shame. His affinity for sexual fantasy hadn't been this vivid since adolescence.

He viciously twisted the shower knob.

The cold water succeeded in diminishing his erection

minimally, but damn it all if it wasn't a monster again by the time he pulled on a pair of clean boxer briefs. He avoided looking at his reflection in the mirror. Katie had cleaned it, just like she'd cleaned everything else in this bloody house.

Rill had much preferred not being able to see himself so clearly.

Fuck, he thought as an almost untenable wave of frustration and self-hatred rose up in him. It stunned him to know that his sexual needs hadn't really been snuffed out by grief and whiskey. Apparently the only thing that had spared him was his self-enforced isolation from females. Sure, he'd occasionally run into an attractive woman in the past year and a half. He'd more than half considered taking up Sherona Legion on the subtle invitations she made with her soft, inviting touches and promising glances.

But Rill had always kept a distance from Sherona, even though he was probably closer to her than any other citizen in Vulture's Canyon. She was undemanding, warm . . . a good listener. Not that Rill ever said much. He'd spent his share of nights down at the diner, the only other occupant besides Sherona. She didn't seem to mind his morose silence, just kept the hot coffee coming.

Now, in hindsight, he wondered if he'd been a fool not to let off some steam with Sherona. If he had, he might not have become so ludicrously horny at the sight of an old friend.

It was frickin' pitiful.

His hand had sufficed for his sexual urges for the last year and a half. No . . . Longer than that, he reminded himself grimly. Depression and a raging libido didn't tend to go hand in hand.

He'd bought two bottles of Jameson earlier. They were still in the trunk of his car, sorely tempting his pornographic brain and temper-tantrum-throwing cock. For a split second, the image of filling up the bathroom sink with whiskey and sticking his prick straight into it flashed in Rill's mind's eye.

He laughed under his breath. Made sense, in a bizarre way. He wanted his damn cock to shut up and give him some rest. But there was no way around it.

He'd have to knock out the monster by swallowing the poison.

Jaysus, he thought grimly as he stalked out of the bathroom. And Katie had crowed that she'd come there to save him.

Katie woke up in the middle of the night, freezing. She rose from bed and turned off the air-conditioning unit. The temperature must have dropped during the night. Technically, it was autumn, but summer just didn't want to abdicate her throne this year. Maybe autumn had finally ousted her tonight, Katie thought sleepily as she felt around at the end of her bed for her robe. Her throat was dry. The water in the dormer bathroom appeared to be completely shut off. Maybe she'd hire someone from Vulture's Canyon to come up here and make it functional again. It was going to be a pain to stumble downstairs every time she had to pee or get a drink—

"Rill? Where are you going?" she called out a few seconds later when she stepped over the threshold of the kitchen and saw him walking out of the house. He'd been so elusive for the past few days, catching sight of him suddenly took her by surprise. If he kept it up, she'd be more likely to see Sasquatch in these woods than Rill.

He paused in the process of opening the screen door. Katie's eyes widened when she fully registered the image of him. He was wearing only a pair of boxer briefs. Smooth, naked skin gleamed with moisture. His wet hair stuck up in odd angles all around his head. His long legs were dusted with dark, crinkly hair. His skin wasn't tanned, but Rill was black Irish, to be sure. His complexion carried the olive tone of some distant Roman or Spanish ancestor who had settled in Ireland.

Her gaze caught and remained glued on his crotch. He was turned in profile. His cock and balls were a heavy package barely constrained by white, stretchy cotton.

He just stood there, apparently as frozen to the spot as she was. It took her stunned brain several seconds to realize she'd been staring . . . and that he'd never replied. She pried her eyes off the compelling vision of his cock. His muscular abdomen was beyond flat; it was slightly concave below his ribs and powerful chest and shoulders.

"You haven't been eating properly. . . . You've been starving yourself. I bought groceries today. I wish you'd let me cook for you," she mumbled through a dry throat. She couldn't think of what else to say, standing there in the presence of his flagrant male beauty.

Her skin prickled as he continued to pin her with his gaze, still not moving. He studied her with such intensity that Katie nervously glanced down at herself. She pulled her robe closed when she saw how exposed she was in her typical sleepwear—cotton boy short briefs and a tank top. Her nipples pinched even tighter beneath the weight of the extra layer of fabric. Perhaps her slight grimace at the sensation roused him, because he stirred.

"What I do and what I don't do are none of your business," he said harshly before he walked out and the screen door slammed behind him. She rushed after him.

"*What . . . ?* Are you truly crazy, walking out there in the middle of the night, wet and mostly naked?" she shouted through the screen. He must have gone over the edge, she thought. The temperature really had dropped overnight. Where was he going? She heard a rattle of keys and burst onto the porch.

"Rill? You're *not* driving anywhere. Have you been drinking?"

"No. But I'm planning on it," he replied, a dangerous edge to his tone.

She stuck her hand out, trying to find the stair railing. In the distance, she heard a popping sound and a noise like a rustling paper bag. She jumped when the trunk of his car slammed shut, shattering the silence of the night.

"Rill?" she asked when she saw a large shadow moving in the blackness. He came toward her—fast. She backed up the stairs anxiously, bumping into the screen door. She turned around and opened it.

"I'll make a deal with you, Katie," he said when he caught the closing door and followed her into the house. She noticed he carried what looked like two bottles of liquor in a paper bag in one hand. Figured.

"What?" she asked, edging backward toward the lit kitchen.

"You stay the hell out of my way and keep your mouth shut."

She came to an abrupt stop next to the stove and eyed him disdainfully. Well, it began that way, until she once again noticed his heavy cock straining against white cotton and followed the thin strip of dark hair that rose from beneath the low waistband of his briefs and kissed his taut belly button. The beguiling trail disappeared, but it teased Katie's gaze upward to a powerful chest, where dark hairs were again in evidence, albeit not thickly, just above Rill's nipple line. Katie had formerly had a preference for a hairless chest, but she decided then and there that the sight of a real man—such a flagrantly male specimen—had completely reformed her.

Well, Rill had.

She wanted to touch, to run her fingers through that crinkly hair, to make a tactile feast out of the smooth skin and hard muscle just beneath it.

When she realized she'd completely forgotten to be defiant in the midst of her drooling, she straightened and crossed her forearms beneath her breasts.

"That doesn't sound like a 'deal' to me. It sounds like a proclamation. What do I get out of it?" she challenged.

He took another step toward her . . . close enough for her to see the gleam in his eyes. She didn't look down, but she was highly aware of his cock straining between them. It was a little like trying to stand on the beach and ignore a tsunami roaring toward the shore. She resisted an almost overwhelming urge to retreat when he leaned down and his face came less than a foot from her own.

"What do *you* get out of it? You stay out of my fucking

way, and I won't turn you over my knee and spank your ass fierce hard."

Her clit twanged. Air burned in her lungs until she finally released it. The roots of her hair prickled in rising fury.

"I'd just like to see you try it," she muttered darkly.

He smiled. It hadn't been what she'd expected him to do, but suddenly that grin was there: slashing, compelling . . .

Dangerous.

She backed away, stumbling when her hip hit the edge of the counter.

"I'm not leaving," she whispered.

He glanced down pointedly to the bulging front of his briefs, his smile already a memory.

"Do you see that? If you stay here, you're gonna end up under me. Is that what you want? Is that what you came here to do, Katie? Destroy our friendship?"

"*No*. That's not what I set out to do. But if it comes down to a choice between our friendship or you? Like I said, *I'm staying*. Go ahead. Fuck me. Your friendship means *shit* to me if you're dead, anyway."

Out of the corner of her vision she saw his heavy erection lurch next to stretchy cotton. Her clit throbbed between her thighs in full sympathy, but her muscles remained as unrelenting and tense as his. He hissed under his breath, his accent too strong for her to catch the words. One thing was for sure: whatever he'd said, it'd been foul . . . and it'd been hurled at her.

She didn't move when he stormed past her. He slammed his bedroom door so hard the wood floor rattled beneath her bare feet.

"Well, there you have it. The lines are drawn," she said out loud to the empty kitchen.

Even though she'd sounded brave enough, it was a lie. She just stood there, waiting for her zapping nerves to quiet and the clamor of alarm and arousal to shut off in her brain. When the adrenaline of their confrontation faded, guilt started to seep into her consciousness—regret for pushing

Rill when he seemed so vulnerable . . . guilt for having officially spoken the words out loud to her onetime best friend's husband.

Go ahead. Fuck me. Your friendship means shit *to me if you're dead, anyway.*

She closed her burning eyelids. *I hope you can understand, Eden. It's true . . . I'm doing it for me. But I'm doing it for him, too. I can't let him follow you. I won't.*

She waited, listening to the voices of her past, listening to her own conscience. Slowly, a sense of steadiness came over her, if not peace.

Somehow, she thought Eden would understand.

Six

Rill prowled around on the front porch, his gaze pinned to the road.

Where the hell had Katie gone?

It was going on suppertime, and he hadn't seen her since he'd rolled out of bed at eleven this morning. He'd made a point of avoiding her since she'd arrived in Vulture's Canyon, so it wasn't really a surprise that she wasn't here. Every time she'd run out for an errand in the past several days, though, she'd left him a little message on a pink sticky note: *Ran down to check on Errol and pick us up some veggies* or *Off in search of some glass cleaner. This house would be so much brighter if there wasn't an inch of grime on the windows.*

He'd grown accustomed to those little notes when he'd reenter the house from one of his walks or when he'd venture out of his bedroom after hearing her car rev up in the front drive. He'd convinced himself that he couldn't care less about where she was or what she was doing. The absence of a little pink note today told him differently, however.

What if his rude, surly behavior had successfully gotten rid of her?

The possibility wasn't as gratifying as he'd imagined it would be.

He'd been so disturbed by the prospect of having finally chased her away that he'd hurried into the bathroom. He'd been relieved to see some of her toiletries arranged neatly on the counter. He'd inhaled the clean, fruity scent clinging in the air for reassurance.

The fragrance of Katie's hair.

His brow had crinkled when he'd had that thought, because he couldn't recall why he'd immediately recognized the scent. He hadn't been close enough to her to breathe it as deeply as the memory that flashed at the edges of his memory. His nose had been surrounded in silken coils. . . .

He'd suddenly reverted back to wishing she'd left. She was ruining everything. He wanted his life—or lack of a life—back. Didn't he?

Fact was, Rill couldn't decide what it was he wanted.

He'd considered going down to the diner. Sherona would make him something tempting. Maybe if she gave him that warm, inviting smile, he wouldn't refuse the offer this time.

Yeah . . . that was what he should do, he decided. He should drive down to the diner. This time he wouldn't politely refuse Sherona's overtures. Why should he? He'd let her take the edge off. There was a tight, uncomfortable pressure in his balls, a sensation that wasn't being adequately assuaged with his own hand.

It wasn't just his cock that was bugging him, though. He felt edgy, like he wasn't at home in his own skin.

It was all Katie's fault.

He wandered into the kitchen and made himself a sandwich, forgoing sex and home cooking without ever making a conscious decision to do so. Afterward, he took a long, strenuous walk. He rambled around a lot in the forest. His hikes distracted him. Navigating the sometimes-challenging paths cleared his head. The fragrance in the forest today had been rich and peaty.

When he returned, he went to the side of the house to the woodpile. A definite chill had entered the air. Fall had finally arrived. He only dimly recalled last autumn in Vulture's Canyon. It'd been as though he'd been color-blind. Today, the vivid colors of the trees blazed against the clear, cornflower-blue sky, the vision scoring his consciousness.

He hauled a load of firewood into the house and stacked it near the fireplace. Last year, he'd rarely lit a fire. It was too difficult, and it wasn't as if he'd been capable of enjoying lazing around by a cozy blaze.

Where the fuck was she?

He tired of pacing on the front porch, looking for her car in the drive. He entered the kitchen and pulled a pot out of the cabinet and filled it with water in preparation for making pasta.

He'd tried to call her three times over the course of the afternoon, but she apparently didn't have her phone turned on. Either that or these hills obliterated the signal. Phone coverage around here could be spotty at times.

It would be getting dark soon. Katie may fancy herself a hotshot driver, but she'd grown up a city girl, used to wide, perfectly paved roads, multiple lanes and well-lit streets. The twists and turns on the narrow forest roads and the pitch-black hills reminded him of driving in Ireland, which could be downright perilous for those not accustomed to it.

She'd likely get herself killed playing speed racer on the forbidding, dark hills.

Thinking about car crashes made him think of Eden, of course. He thought of what Katie had said several nights ago about his wife hating Vulture's Canyon if she ever saw it.

Katie'd been right. Eden would have hated Vulture's Canyon. She would have been very polite to the residents, but privately found them ignorant and strange. Why in the world would they stay in a place like this? He recalled her saying something similar of the people of Malacnoic, the village where he'd been born. Her face had been shadowed with amusement, but also puzzlement. Eden couldn't understand how people would choose to isolate themselves from culture and facilities of higher learning.

When it came to Malacnoic, Rill shared Eden's opinion. Vulture's Canyon wasn't much better, but at this point in his life he'd learned to appreciate the value of a place where you could lose yourself. One couldn't forget the past in a place like Los Angeles, where reminders and regrets were constantly leaping up to pummel you in the face.

The pasta was finished and drained. He tried to call Katie a fourth time as he paced around in the front yard. Maybe she was purposely ignoring him. Probably pissed at him for his frigid hospitality and rudeness.

Good.

He'd go inside, have a drink, eat his supper and then call Stanley and Meg Hughes. True, he didn't particularly want to talk to Katie and Everett's parents. He respected Stanley and Meg a lot, thought of them as family since they'd welcomed him into their home during his college years at UCLA. It'd be awkward, talking to the friendly couple after so many months of isolation.

But Stan and Meg needed to know about their daughter's latest flighty adventure. This was just another in a long series of impulsive decisions for Katie—like the time she'd threatened to drop out of college when she was a freshman to join the Peace Corps or the time she decided to completely redecorate her apartment in furniture rehabbed from trash in garbage dumps (Rill swore the glass coffee table retained a subtle odor of pickles).

Maybe he'd even drop a hint to the Hugheses that Katie wasn't safe there with him.

That'd motivate them to call Katie and talk some sense into that stubborn brain of hers.

He built a fire and sipped at a glass of Jameson on the rocks. The drink didn't mellow him, though, so he poured another once the logs caught flame. All the while, he had a sinking feeling the whiskey wouldn't numb him like it had in the past.

Piss won't do the job anymore, he thought bitterly.

It hadn't since Katie had come to town.

He turned on the light in the pantry and just stood in there for a moment, staring at the mostly empty shelves. For a brief second, the image in front of his eyes struck him as surreal. Where the hell was he? What was he doing, standing in a musty pantry that looked as if it'd been built in the American Civil War?

It was as if some old, foreign film clip had been sutured into two sides of the movie that was his life. He stood there, his hand frozen in the motion of reaching for a jar of pasta sauce on the counter. Nausea suddenly rose in his belly; vertigo caused his vision to swim.

For a few seconds, he was terrified.

He abruptly put his hand on his cock, grimacing when he squeezed with his fingers. Perhaps it was a strange thing to do at such a disorienting, existential moment, but he was just a guy. If there was one thing a man knew was real, it was his cock. He grasped onto that thread of lust, that bright flare of the familiar.

He ripped at his button fly impatiently and struggled with his clothing. All the sharp arousal he'd experienced so unexpectedly yesterday at seeing Katie, all the need, roared through him in a potent flash. He slammed shut the pantry door and fisted his cock.

He'd thought of himself as a dead man walking. The sudden surge of sap flowing through his veins, fast and hot, both alarmed and confused him.

His head fell back and he groaned in mixed misery and pleasure as he stroked himself. He didn't even bother to try to shove the illicit images and fantasies out of his brain this time. It was either fall into the dark abyss of meaninglessness or grab onto the one remnant of his humanity that remained intact in him.

He reveled in all that he shouldn't, imagining what it would be like to bend Katie over at the waist and bare her ass, what it would be like to slide a finger into her warm, tight slit, to coat himself in her abundant juices . . . to push his cock into a pussy that'd squeeze every memory from his brain . . . every last drop of come from his boiling balls.

She could make him forget. He knew she could. If he got lost in Katie, the memory of how he'd disappointed Eden as a husband might fade, the sadness of losing her, even though he'd known deep down at that point their marriage was over.

Katie might be able to help ease the grief of knowing what died inside Eden's womb along with her.

The fantasy was so realistic he felt himself cresting after only a couple dozen jerks on his supersensitive cock. He was panting and gritting his teeth, already at the vinegar strokes despite the fact that he'd practically just begun. In some distant part of his brain, he knew the explosion that was about to erupt out of his balls had been building since he'd seen Katie standing there so uncertainly in that hospital waiting room . . .

. . . maybe sooner.

He groaned gutturally as pleasure swelled in him.

"Rill? Is that you?"

His fist paused midstaff on a near-to-bursting cock. He opened his eyes and stared at the closed double Dutch door, breathing heavily.

"Rill?" he heard Katie ask, her voice closer to the pantry door now. He stood unmoving, every muscle in his body strung tight, his cock throbbing in his hand. Her voice had trembled slightly when she spoke his name. She must have heard him groaning.

She had to know what he was doing in there.

"Don't open that door, Katie," he warned.

He stood utterly still, his body straining, his mind hyperfocused, like a man with questionable balance who suddenly found himself poised on the high wire. His ears strained to make out Katie's movements. The silence seemed to roar in his head.

His heart lurched in his chest when he saw the knob move on the lower half of the double Dutch door and the soft click of the latch slipping out of the catch.

"Don't, Katie," he demanded, but that wasn't really what he meant. He wondered how she'd known that when the lower half of the Dutch door swung outward, the top half remaining closed.

He watched, his misery and sharp arousal rising, as Katie went to her knees.

He could see her full, shapely breasts pressed tight against an indigo tunic that she'd belted with a braid of leather. Her untamed mane of hair hung loose, curls and waves abounding. She'd said the color she'd put on it wasn't permanent, and he was glad to see gold shining through the brown, the dye having faded further with her morning shower. He saw the lower half of her face—the delicate chin, the lush lips. She placed her hands on her thighs, the gesture striking him as prim . . . subservient for some stupid reason. Katie was hardly the submissive type.

Every ounce of his attention was focused on her mouth when it moved.

"Come here," she said softly.

His cock lurched in his hand.

He staggered toward her, hating himself but recognizing the sheer impossibility of refusal. Besides, he was at the breaking point of arousal.

He came close, feet just an inch away from her knees. She didn't move away, although she must be able to see him at this point. He placed one forearm against the top of the closed Dutch door, bracing himself. He leaned toward her.

Her lips parted.

He watched, spellbound, as he used his hand to brush the flaring tip of his cock against her lower lip. She remained immobile, allowing him to spread a thin coat of pre-come on her mouth.

His groan felt like it was ripped out of the depths of him.

Her tongue came out, pink and quick, wetting the head of his cock. An uncontrollable shiver of excitement rippled up his spine. Her lips enclosed the rim in a tight clamp while she licked eagerly, giving him the impression she wanted to press his taste deep into her, like she was doing a rubbing etching with her tongue to find patterns on his dick. Her carefulness, her obvious hunger—the sheer strength of her tongue—drove him nuts.

She sucked, and there was no other direction for him to go but forward in that volatile moment. The arm that braced him on the top of the double Dutch door bent at the elbow. He thrilled to the sensation of sliding against her wet tongue, of being surrounded by her sultry heat.

He'd been so primed before that it was almost too much for him to bear. He nearly shamed himself further and came on her tongue then and there. Only his greed for her, the desire to relish in the moment, helped him to hold back.

She pushed forward with her head. Several inches of his cock filled her mouth, but he knew the top part of the door stopped her from ducking forward too far. He stepped toward her, so that his feet bracketed her knees, and leaned into her, watching from above as his dick slid between pink lips. She moaned softly, and he clenched his eyes closed as the vibrations from her vocal cords buzzed into his flesh.

Friction—the need for it overwhelmed him. He pumped and grunted at the sublimity of it. Delicious jolts of pleasure shot up his spine. His ass tightened again and again as he thrust, but she kept up with him stroke for stroke, bobbing her head with as much range of motion that she could without hitting the barrier of the door with her forehead. Wet, sucking sounds intermingled with his grunts of pure pleasure.

He transformed into an animal in those precious seconds, a creature that lived only to vanquish its hunger and survive another day.

The top of his head fell against the closed portion of the door. He wanted to keep his eyes shut, to keep up some semblance of a barrier between himself and Katie. The truth was, he was about to explode, and he hated that reality almost as much as the fact that he couldn't control his need to surrender. The moment was too fraught with tension and sharp pleasure, too laden with emotions he wished he could strangle into silence.

But how could he quiet this need?

He opened his eyes slowly and watched through narrowed eyelids as his thick, veined flesh plunged into Katie's
mouth again and again. When her hands came up and lightly
touched the backs of his naked thighs, he once again shut
his eyes and bit his lower lip. Hard. Something about her
gentle, tentative touch contrasting with his furious thrusts
and her shockingly strong suction had nearly made him
come once again.

Jaysus, if this had to happen, why couldn't he have had
the capacity to enjoy it more, at the very least? It didn't
matter what he wanted, though.

This was way beyond him.

He wanted to go deeper. He didn't care in those volatile
moments if it was sweet, beautiful Katie Hughes's mouth
he desecrated; he just wanted this fucking torture to end.
The top part of the door restrained him somewhat, making
it impossible to plunge as deeply as he desired.

He groaned desperately and pressed closer to both Katie
and the door. When she twisted her head and tugged at his
cock with her mouth, he knew she was trying to lower her
head beneath the barrier of the door and take him deeper.

He reached down and grabbed at a handful of hair at her
nape, holding her head immobile for his rampaging cock,
but also prohibiting her from taking him into her throat. She
pulled against his restraint, her mouth tugging on him even
more strongly, and he tightened his fingers.

"Nah, Katie," he growled, but he submitted to his hunger
in his own way.

He pushed his chest against the upper part of the door
and thrust madly, causing the catch to rattle. Only the first
half of his cock pierced her mouth at its farthest point. He
craved more but, at the same time, thanked God Almighty
for the limit of the barrier between them.

The banging sounds of his chest against the door, his
blistering curses and grunts of pleasure hailed down around
them like sharp projectiles. He held her head firm, limiting
her ability to pleasure him, but he existed in a haze of taut

bliss, nevertheless, as he made free with her sweet, sucking mouth. His upper body battered at the barrier between them, but the top half of the door held firm.

He clutched her soft hair tighter and thrust as deep as he could go. He felt her recoil slightly, but then she was bobbing her head over him, taking him fast and furious.

Everything went black.

A roar of desperate pleasure scored his throat as he came. His entire body went rigid as his climax consumed him. In some distant part of his brain, he realized it wasn't stopping.

Why the hell wasn't it stopping?

Pleasure kept racking him in waves. Semen kept ejecting from his balls like he'd stored it under pressure for years.

He opened his eyes a moment later—an eternity later. His upper body was pressed flush against the top part of the double Dutch door. His head was turned, his cheek pressed to the white-painted wood as he gasped for air.

For a weird, mind-pulsating moment, he wondered if he lay prone on a hard floor. Then Katie twitched her tongue and his eyes rolled back in his head. He shivered at the sucking, muscular movements of her mouth and the quick caresses of her tongue as she cleaned him of his come.

He just stood there, smashed up against the top of the door by the force of his greedy lust. She continued to suck him. Even when he was utterly spent, she explored him with her lips, mapped out his contours with her tongue. It sent little electrical jolts through his sated, overly sensitive flesh.

He should move. He knew he should move. But what, precisely, should he do? Where should he go?

What the hell should he say?

Her hand came up and cradled his balls softly.

"Jaysus, Katie," he moaned in mixed misery and arousal—a fresh arousal, forbidden to him in all new, even more complex ways than from that first surge of incomprehensible, wild lust. She slid him out of her mouth and kissed the crown chastely.

"Shhh, Rill."

His thigh and ass muscles tightened at the sensation of her breath brushing against his moist cock. He fantasized about letting her bring him off again. Why not?

He'd already crossed the line, hadn't he?

But what he wanted to do most in his fantasies was open that door all the way and remove the partial barrier between Katie and him.

"No," he stated harshly.

He pushed himself off the door, not really sure where his reserve of strength came from, seeing how it was so glaringly absent just moments ago. He wouldn't allow himself to glance up as he hastily pulled up his underwear and jeans.

When he finally did look, it was to see that the opening at the bottom of the double Dutch door was empty.

She'd gone.

Why the hell had he bothered stopping himself from opening that door all the way and taking Katie in the way he craved? he thought bitterly. He'd doused himself in alcohol daily.

Might as well drown in self-loathing as well.

Seven

Four days later, Katie sat on a stack of floor mats in the Prairie Lakes Hospital physical therapy gym. Errol's physical therapist was hot. Katie knew this, but recognized his attractiveness like she might a dreary work duty. She knew she should have some sort of reaction to his warm glances and sexy smiles. Instead, she was consumed with what it'd been like to have Rill Pierce's cock convulse in orgasm in her mouth . . . what it'd been like to have him give himself to her.

Even if he *had* given himself in half measure. Even if he *obviously* hadn't really wanted to surrender. Even if they'd hardly spoken since then.

Katie had joined league with Rill in his avoidance efforts. It was amazing how two people could coexist inside a house and never catch as much of a glimpse of each other, if they had their minds set to it.

At least he was eating the meals she made him. Not *with* her. But she'd noticed that the meals she prepared for him and covered with plastic wrap were disappearing from the refrigerator for the past few days. Small comfort, to know he wasn't starving himself to death like he had been. In addition, Katie didn't think he'd been drinking, either. Drunk people weren't as quiet and elusive as Rill had been lately.

She forced herself to focus on Errol's blond, svelte therapist—Dave Portland—when he approached her.

"I did an assessment on him. He's strong as a horse, so that'll really help him recuperate," Dave was saying. He stood in front of her, his slim hips outlined in dark blue cotton surgical pants, his broad shoulders encased in a sky-blue hue. Had he winked when he finished speaking? Katie's brain was too preoccupied to fully interpret flirtation.

What did flirtation matter to her?

Rill wouldn't know the meaning of flirtation if it socked him in his gorgeous, scowling mouth.

Forget about how he'd interpret a woman going down on her knees for him and sucking for her life. She'd never done anything like that before, never been so hungry for a man. It'd been like some kind of void had opened inside her, a hole she hadn't known existed until she'd tasted Rill on her tongue.

Now this thing had happened between them. Sure, it'd happened on that night she arrived as well, when he'd bent her over that bed and worked his cock into her until she'd screamed in pleasure. But Rill had been drunk that night. He didn't have the memory searing his consciousness like Katie did. Knowing that he didn't recall it had made it easier for her to look him in the eye. Well, *somewhat* easier. Not that she'd had much of an opportunity to look into Rill's eyes much since coming to Vulture's Canyon.

But four days ago—that'd been different. Rill hadn't been drunk. Somehow she knew Rill had been stone-cold sober when he'd traced her lower lip deliberately with the tip of his cock and anointed her mouth with his semen. If he'd been drunk, she wouldn't have felt his ambivalence so acutely.

"So . . . are you related to Errol?" Dave the physical therapist asked.

"Hmmm?" Katie asked as she licked her lower lip distractedly. When she realized Dave's expression had gone rigid as he followed the movement of her tongue, she straightened and stood, donning her professional manner.

"No. No, we're not related at all."

"She ran me over," Errol stated bluntly as he hobbled up to them in his crutches, still wearing the baseball cap that made his ears seem to poke out even farther from his head than nature had. Katie had been able to make out the letters beneath the dirt today: US AIR FORCE. The hat must have belonged to Errol's dad. She wondered if he ever took it off. She grimaced apologetically at Errol's bald statement, but Errol didn't seem upset. He hadn't seemed angry, in fact, ever since she'd hit him with her car. His lack of vengefulness, his bland acceptance of his incapacity, only increased Katie's guilt.

"Her uncle is Howard Hughes. He flew planes, like my dad," Errol told Dave.

"Not an uncle. Just a distant relative. You ready to go, Errol?" Katie asked.

"Yeah."

"Will you be here for Errol's first rehab appointment?" Dave asked Katie eagerly.

"Er . . . sure. I'm bringing Errol to all his appointments."

"You hungry, Errol?" Katie asked him fifteen minutes later just before she hit the turnoff that would lead either to town or to Errol's riverside shack.

"Yeah."

"How about if I buy you a burger from the diner to take home with you?"

"Yeah," Errol repeated. When he wasn't talking about airplanes or his dad, Errol was pretty laconic, but not in a dull way. In fact, his placidity and comfort with himself, no matter where he was, was something Katie had begun to admire about Errol. If only *she* could be so comfortable in her own skin.

She parked her Maserati across the street from the Legion Diner. In the distance, she saw Derek Legion and a couple of his friends crossing the street. Their adolescent laughter and deep voices bounced off the brick walls of a desolate Main Street. Katie waved. Derek returned her wave, but halfheartedly. He didn't look too happy for some reason.

As she and Errol crossed the street, a sarcastic voice started cracking off in her head. *Coward. You're just going to the diner in order to avoid Rill for another hour. Did you come here to help him, or to make an art out of avoiding him? You're scared to face him.*

And why shouldn't she be humiliated to look him in the eye? What in God's name had possessed her to get down on her knees like that when she had guessed what he'd been doing in that pantry. There weren't many men who would have refused such a bald-faced offer in the midst of a vulnerable moment.

She'd taken advantage of him. That was what she'd done.

"Hey, boy," Katie crooned to the mournful-looking hound dog that sat outside the diner door. He looked hopeful when Katie leaned down and put out a hand to pet him. She halted abruptly when Errol uttered one word.

"Fleas."

They entered, and Katie immediately saw Rill. She paused in surprise. He sat on a chair in the middle of the diner's open floor. A white sheet had been placed beneath his chair and clippings of dark brown hair lay on top of it. Sherona Legion froze in the process of making a snip with some scissors, Rill's hair between her forefinger and second finger. Her legs straddled one of Rill's long, bent legs.

Her huge breasts were just an inch away from Rill's face.

The sound of bells jangling as the door shut brought Katie out of her shock.

"What are you *doing*?" Katie asked incredulously.

Snip, snip, went Sherona's scissors. "Giving a haircut," she stated blandly.

Rill still hadn't turned his head to look at her as Sherona continued to trim his hair. Katie glanced from the whiteboard

menu above the grill and back to Sherona and Rill. The *Cut
$6.00* had meant a *hair*cut?

"You can't do that," Katie exclaimed. "That's . . . that's
unsanitary!"

"Katie," Rill growled menacingly. He gave her a sideways
glare without turning his head. Her humiliation mounted at
his tone. He'd sounded like an older brother, exasperated by
the antics of his annoying little sister in front of a girlfriend.
What was more, she'd come to learn recently that his accent
got stronger not only when he was drinking, but also when
he was angry.

Rill's Irishness was largely in evidence at the moment.

"I clean up every single hair," Sherona said. "My place
always passes inspections with high marks for cleanliness."

"Katie's going to buy me a hamburger to take home,
Sherona," Errol said, all the tension in the air and visual
daggers being hurled around utterly lost on him.

"Just give me a few seconds and I'll get you two set up,"
Sherona said. She lifted one long leg and swung it over Rill's
knee. When she took a step and straddled his other knee,
practically putting Rill's eye out with a nipple, Katie thought
she'd seen enough.

"Come on, Errol. We'll get dinner somewhere else."

"Ain't nowhere else to go but the diner," Errol said
matter-of-factly. He set his crutches against the counter and
sat on a stool. He removed a model of a B-52 bomber from
his pocket, examining it closely while Katie continued to
stare at Sherona shoving her breasts in Rill's face. Her blood
pressure must have shot up because her heart began to pound
uncomfortably loud in her ears.

In a bid for self-preservation, she tossed her red Chanel
cocoon bag on a barstool and sat down next to Errol, blocking the incendiary view from her eyes.

"What are you getting?" she asked Errol.

"A hamburger. That's what you said."

"You don't have to get a hamburger, Errol. That was just
an example. You can get whatever you want." *Just not the
haircut,* Katie thought irritably as she examined the menu.

Whoever heard of doing haircuts inside of a diner? Vulture's Canyon was a loony bin without walls. She noticed Errol looking at her, clearly confused by her statement. She sighed.

"Yeah, a hamburger sounds good," she agreed.

"Can we get a hamburger patty for Barnyard?"

"Bernard?"

"No," Errol corrected. "*Barnyard*. The dog."

Katie recalled the resigned-looking dog that seemed to be a permanent fixture in front of the diner. "Sure, we can get Barnyard a burger, too. Doesn't he have an owner?"

"Not really," Errol said. "Everybody in town gives him food. He's like me. When you take me home, do you want to see my model airplane collection again?"

"Yeah, okay," Katie replied, feeling a little saddened by Errol's casual reference to being similar to a dog.

She dared to look over her shoulder and breathed a sigh of relief. Sherona had stepped away from Rill and he was standing up from the chair, brushing clippings off his broad shoulders. He strode toward the counter and sat down next to Errol. His actions surprised her, given his newly ingrained habit of avoid versus approach when it came to her.

Katie resented Sherona for making his dark, glossy hair look so combed and tame. She also envied her for the chance to furrow her fingers through it without restriction.

Exactly how many times a week, Katie wondered, did Sherona Legion furl her fingers through Rill's hair while the last thing on her mind was a haircut?

"Have you guys been to the hospital?" Rill asked Errol, cutting through Katie's bitter thoughts.

Errol nodded. "Dave is my physical therapist."

"How'd it go?"

"Dave said I was as strong as a horse. My knee hurts bad." Errol held up the plane and showed it to Rill, who inspected it soberly before he nodded.

Katie grimaced. "It does, Errol? You didn't say it hurt before."

Errol shrugged and swished his hand, making the model plane zip through the air.

"We need to get you home and get your foot elevated." She glanced at Rill and noticed he studied her. For some reason, his shorter hair made his eyes look even more electric blue than they usually did.

"Errol's physical therapy couldn't have lasted all day. Where else have you been?"

She bristled at his tone. What right did he have to know her schedule when he had barely spoken a word to her in a week plus and didn't even *want* her in Vulture's Canyon?

"I drove over to Carbondale this morning and found a health food store so I could stock up the pantry." She paused when Sherona approached behind the counter, tying an apron around her voluptuous figure.

"You didn't have to drive to Carbondale to find a health food store, Katie. Vulture's Canyon has the co-op that provides all the goods for that store. Didn't anyone tell you?" Sherona asked when she noticed Katie's bemused expression. "We have a small farm and a co-op run by most of the residents in Vulture's Canyon. We grow everything from vegetables to nearly every grain under the sun. Errol can show you on the way home. It's not far from his house, down by the river. Now, what can I get you two?"

"A hamburger and French fries," Errol replied without looking up from his airplane.

"I'll have the same. Along with a large chocolate shake and a slice of cherry pie. Make it to go, will you? What's wrong with you?" she asked Rill when she noticed he shook his head and laughed.

"Health food?" Rill asked derisively, referring to what she'd said earlier. "Since when does Katie Hughes eat health food?"

"Ever since I came here. We have to do something about your health. I saw what you were surviving on before I came here. You're malnourished. I've been working on getting you healthy again. Don't tell me you haven't appreciated it," she warned with an anxious sideways glance. "I've noticed you've been eating the meals I've made you, even if you haven't eaten them in my presence."

"I didn't say I don't appreciate it." He seemed undecided, but then continued gruffly. "I do. I appreciate what you've done to the house, too. It looks great. I . . . I haven't had a chance to tell you."

Katie stared at him, openmouthed. Where had this come from? She didn't get a chance to find out, because the bells over the entrance rang loudly and what looked like half of the population of Vulture's Canyon entered—Katie counted five of them in all. Among the new arrivals was the disapproving, gray-haired Monty holding the hand of none other than Olive Fanatoon.

Olive grinned from ear to ear when she saw Errol, and immediately came over to chat. With Errol's tendency for being monosyllabic unless he was talking about airplanes, it took Olive about two seconds to determine that Errol was "good" and that his visit to the hospital had been "fine." This being clarified, Olive turned her attention to Katie. When Katie told her about her trip to Sowing Your Oats, the health food store in Carbondale, Olive had replayed Sherona's surprise.

"Vulture's Canyon is the central supply for health food in southern Illinois, southeastern Missouri and western Kentucky," Olive exclaimed.

"I didn't know about the co-op until just now. Do you work there, Olive?" Katie asked.

Olive nodded. "Yes, and over at the Trading Company as well. Have you been to the Trading Company yet?"

Katie shook her head.

"You should stop by. Vulture's Canyon is the home to many fine artists." She gave a smile of hopeful acknowledgment to Rill, who pointedly looked away. "The Trading Company is where we sell our wares. Sixty percent of all the proceeds for our sales of art go to Food for Body and Soul, a charitable organization with the goal of stamping out hunger and malnourishment in rural families in the Midwest and the Appalachian regions. Most of the funding for Body and Soul comes from the co-op, though."

Rill has landed himself smack-dab in the middle of a

hippie commune, Katie thought with a rising sense of fascination and amusement.

"Sixty percent? But . . . how do you all make a living?"
she asked Olive.

"It doesn't take much to get by in Vulture's Canyon. Our
needs are few, and most of our food comes from the farm.
We could donate more proceeds and time, but we haven't
been able to spread the word about Body and Soul as much
as we'd like to help the organization grow. We have no one
to really advocate for us with the government, the press and
so forth. None of us are very good in the public eye," Olive
said a little sadly. Katie knew it was uncharitable to think
it, but Olive's news didn't exactly surprise her. From what
she'd seen so far, the residents of Vulture's Canyon were a
bunch of misfits.

"Oh, here's your dinner." Olive nodded toward the counter where Sherona had just set a large bag. Olive's brow
creased in confusion when she saw the animal fat from the
burgers already creating a stain on the side of the paper sack.
"You know, Sherona does have some amazing healthy items
on the menu. Her vegetarian sandwich with guacamole,
Monterey Jack cheese, red onion and sprouts on homemade
seven-grain bread is amazing."

"Great, thanks. I'll have to try that next time. Sounds
like something Rill might like."

Rill had seemed to make a point of excluding himself
from her conversation with Olive by facing the counter, but
he glanced at Katie and rolled his eyes when she said that.
Katie ignored him. Who was he to make fun of her for her
junk food diet when he'd lived off cereal and whiskey for a
year and a half?

"So . . . are you and that man an item, Olive?" Katie nodded her head significantly at Monty, who was now sitting in
a booth with another man she recognized as the camo-
wearing, tattooed guy with the army haircut who was in the
diner the first night she'd arrived. Hadn't Sherona called
him Marcus? He was wearing jeans and a white T-shirt this
evening, but Katie still thought he was likely one of those

survivalist people who stockpiled enough supplies to live through an apocalypse and believed the government was responsible for everything from the swine flu to tracking individuals through electronic sensors in dollar bills.

"Monty?" Olive asked. "Yes, he's my common-law husband."

"He doesn't like Maseratis," Katie said before she tried to take a sip of her milk shake and couldn't, because it was so thick. Awesome.

Olive laughed. "Did he tell you that?" She threw Monty an amused look over her shoulder. His shaggy eyebrows went up when he saw Olive's glance. Katie also noticed that the survivalist guy was busy watching Sherona as she did her graceful dance of food preparation behind the counter. When he wasn't staring at Sherona, he was throwing visual grenades at Rill's back.

Note to self: don't be so tough on camo-man. Perhaps he and Katie had something in common, namely that it made their blood pressure rise to see Rill and Sherona anywhere near each other.

"Sorry about Monty," Olive said, still smiling when she turned back around. "He's a social worker and this is one of the poorest counties in the state. He sees a lot of needy people and poverty on any given day. He tends to be a bit harsh in his judgments because of that."

The milk shake didn't seem so interesting to Katie anymore. She set it down on the counter, suddenly feeling self-conscious when she noticed Rill watching her from the corner of his eye.

Rill had always seemed to notice when she was embarrassed in social situations. It was one of the many reasons she loved him. Everett would blunder on like a typical male, clueless about her emotional state. Too many times to count, though, Rill had changed the subject with a segueing joke or a self-deprecating story, giving Katie a chance to regain her emotional footing. She used to appreciate his keen observance, but now she had reason to curse his sharp eyes.

She hopped down from the counter when Olive said good-bye.

"Come on, Errol. I'll take you home. We've got to get that knee on ice."

"I guess since you have your *health food* dinner, you won't be back at the house for supper?" Rill said as she threw some bills on the counter.

Katie started to give a flippant reply about already having plans before she met Rill's gaze and was caught. Their eyes locked only for a few seconds, but suddenly it all came back to her: the taste of his come on her tongue, how she'd struggled to keep up with his abundant emissions . . . the poignant sound of his climactic groan, like his soul was being ripped out of him with a giant hook.

She couldn't quite interpret his expression. What in God's name was he thinking of her, after what she'd done . . . after what *they'd* done? She hated herself for allowing it.

She wanted to do it again.

Awkwardness had never before been a part of her and Rill's relationship. Now it seemed like the main component. What if she'd ruined their friendship forever?

And why had he decided all of a sudden that he wanted to talk to her?

She carefully refolded the paper bag and tried to master her anxiety. "I suppose I could still make you something with the supplies I got today. . . . What about rice pasta with an olive oil, basil and garlic sauce and some steamed asparagus?"

"I'll pick up something here at the diner, but I want to talk to you later," he said pointedly.

Katie glanced over at the statuesque Sherona. She was busy taking Marcus's order, and he looked like he wanted to eat her more than anything on the menu.

"Fine by me," she said briskly as she picked up the paper bag, doing her best to disguise her swelling nervousness. She'd hated avoiding Rill, but suddenly she wished they could go back to living in separate corners of the same house. Something told her that whatever he had to say wasn't going to be good.

"I'll be up the hill in an hour or so," she said.

She marched out of the diner, Errol trailing after her. If Rill wanted to be fed by Sherona instead of her, well, more power to him. Chances were, Sherona was a lot more stable, grounded—she threw the paper bag in her hand a dirty look—and *healthy* for him than Katie was.

Eight

The first thing she noticed when she drove up to the Mitchell place was the smoke curling out of the chimney. Rill had built a fire for the past few nights, but he appeared to be doing it solely for Katie's benefit. Every time she cautiously entered the living room, he was absent, leaving her to stare gloomily at the cozy fire in solitude.

Katie had no doubt about what Rill wanted to say. He was going to tell her they'd crossed the line. She'd gone too far. She'd ruined their friendship forever.

He was going to throw her out on her ass.

He looked up when she entered the kitchen. He stood by the counter. The glass he was filling with diet soda nearly overflowed before he glanced down and righted the bottle. He wore a pair of faded jeans and a dark blue collared shirt. Rill always had been able to wear jeans better than any man she knew.

"Do you want some?" he asked, holding up the soda.

"Yeah, okay." Her awareness of him ramped up exponentially as she stared at his strong forearms sprinkled with dark hair while he prepared her drink. It was so strange to relate to Rill like this, to feel this awkwardness and straining tension.

He handed her the iced soda and nodded toward the living room. Katie followed him. Something felt as if it were coming to life in her belly and squirming around to get out. He sat on the worn sofa, and Katie perched on the edge a foot away from him. A friendly fire crackled in the fireplace, but the cozy ambience did nothing to still her nerves. She opened her mouth, figuring she should be the one to speak first . . . to apologize for the other night, but Rill cut her off.

"I called Morgan and Watkins today."

Katie paused in the action of raising her soda to her mouth. Shock coursed through her at hearing Rill say her former place of employment. It'd been the last thing she'd expected him to say. "You . . . you did what?"

"I called Morgan and Watkins. I've met your boss, Steve Fedderman, at a couple parties at your mom and dad's house. Did you forget that?"

"*Forget* it?" Katie sputtered. "I've had no reason to think about it one way or another, let alone forget it."

His mouth twisted slightly in dissatisfaction at her answer. "Fedderman told me you handed in your resignation at Morgan and Watkins three weeks ago. You just became partner last year, Katie. Are you mad, quitting a job after you worked your ass off for years?"

Katie just stared, at a total loss for words.

"When were you planning on telling me you'd quit your job?" Rill asked intently.

"I . . . There hasn't been a chance. We've hardly talked since I arrived." She blushed when she recalled what they *had* found time for.

"I called your mom and dad, as well."

She felt like all the blood rushed out of her head. "You didn't tell them, did you? About my job?"

"About your *lack* of a job, you mean? What were you thinking, quitting your job like that and driving halfway across the country by yourself?" he demanded.

"Don't accuse *me* of being irresponsible," she retaliated,

pointing a finger at him. "You're the one who hasn't had gainful employment for eighteen months now. If I want to take a couple months' sabbatical from work, that's *my* business."

"You made it my business, as well, when you showed up on my doorstep, Angel."

Katie went very still. Her breath burned in her lungs. Something had flashed in his eyes when he'd said . . . *showed up on my doorstep, Angel*. For an anxious few seconds, she thought he'd remembered what'd happened the first night she arrived. He'd never called her an angel before that night, and never had since. Her alarm faded when she noticed Rill seemed irritated and confused, but not suspicious.

"You told them, didn't you? My parents?" she asked grimly.

"I can't believe you've kept Stan and Meg in the dark about this."

"Did you tell them about Morgan and Watkins or not?"

He gave her an annoyed glare and then took a sip of his soda as though he were trying to cool off his temper with the frigid beverage. "No, I didn't. But I told them you were in Vulture's Canyon. I told them I didn't want you here, but you wouldn't listen to me."

"What did they say?"

"Your father just laughed," Rill muttered under his breath. When he noticed Katie's small smile of triumph, irritation flared in his eyes. "He laughed until I told him a woman wasn't safe here in this house with me."

"*Safe?*" Katie uttered before she snorted. "I'm sorry for having to tell you this, Rill, but you're starting to have delusions of grandeur in regard to your foulness. That bathroom might have been a threat to my health before I cleaned it, but that's the only risk to my safety I've encountered since coming to Vulture's Canyon, unless potentially catching Barnyard's fleas counts."

He leaned forward, his elbows on his knees, clearly astonished. "And what about the other night?"

"I'm the one who took advantage of you. Not the other way around."

He gave a bark of incredulous laughter. "So that's the way you feel about it, is it?"

Her spine straightened. "Yeah, it is. You were vulnerable and I . . . I used that to my advantage."

He shook his head slowly, his blue eyes gleaming in the firelight. "You've been my friend for sixteen years now, Katie—Everett's little sister. And I let you suck me off through a half-closed door."

The words seemed to hang in the still, warm air, dark, incendiary . . . arousing. Katie inhaled slowly, trying to ease the band of tension that had tightened around her chest.

"I'm still your friend, Rill," she whispered.

"Friends don't want to fuck each other blind."

"You mean . . . you mean you want to?" she asked in a quavering voice.

"What d'ye mean?"

"Fuck me. Blind."

"That's not even the half of it, Katie. Not even a fraction," he rasped. For a few seconds he looked so furious Katie was sure he was going to strangle her. The gravid tension in the room was so thick it felt difficult to draw air.

"Well . . . then why can't we? We're both adults."

A puff of air popped out of his lungs. He shook his head and put his glass on the coffee table.

"Is there someone else?" Katie asked slowly when he placed his forehead in his hand and didn't respond.

"Someone else?" Rill repeated bemusedly, lifting his head.

"Are you sleeping with someone?" she said through her teeth, irritated by his confusion. This was Rill Pierce, one of the most gorgeous, talented, virile men on the planet, as far as Katie was concerned. Surely he shouldn't be so dumbfounded when she asked about his sex life. The idea of Rill being celibate was just . . . ridiculous. True, he'd never flaunted his sex life, never brought a parade of females to the Hughes house while he was still a bachelor. Her assumptions had more to do with what Rill *was* than anything she'd ever witnessed. He epitomized masculinity. He practically oozed sex from his pores.

He rolled his eyes. "Vulture's Canyon doesn't exactly provide a wide variety of choices in that department."

"You're not sleeping with Sherona?"

"*No.* Maybe you haven't noticed, but I'm not really up for wooing a woman at this point, Katie," he snapped.

His frustration must have overcome him because he sprang up from the couch and began to pace on the far side of the coffee table. "I told you from the very beginning you don't understand how I live. You don't get what I've become."

"I get what you *wish* you'd become!" Katie spat, standing and facing him. "You wish you were a robot. You wish you didn't have any feelings at all, so you convince yourself that you don't. You drown your grief in alcohol. You avoid people who care about you. You don't care about your friends; you've abandoned your work and the people who rely on you. You pride yourself on your detachment. You claim not to give a damn about the people in this town, even. But you're not cold and aloof, Rill; you're just running. You're scared that if you take a moment and really focus on the loss of Eden, your grief will swallow you up whole. So you've come here to the woods to hide, and meanwhile your grief gets the better of you even as you try and escape from it. It binds you like a prisoner. *That's* what you are, Rill. You're a prisoner in these damn woods, and you're the jailer as well."

He'd stopped pacing midway through her rant and now stared at her, his face glazed with shock, his mouth hanging open.

The words had flared out of her in one fierce, leaping blaze, but now that she'd said her piece, she felt empty . . . deflated.

"I won't let you destroy yourself," she said quietly. "I know Eden meant everything to you—"

"You don't know what Eden meant to me," he interrupted darkly. "You don't know why I'm here in these woods."

"What?" she asked sarcastically, her fury flickering to life if not blazing like it had a moment ago. "You're the only one on this planet who knows what it is to love someone? You're the only one who feels they're in a living grave because they've lost that person?"

"You don't know the meaning of love," he shouted. "You don't love anything but your fast car and purses so expensive they could support a starving village for a year. You're a child. . . . You're a fucking little girl, coming here and telling me how to live my life. *You*—preaching to *me*. Someone who quits her job on a whim and hauls ass halfway across the country for no good reason—"

"I'm thirty years old, Rill," she interrupted, her voice trembling with fury. "I'm not a little girl. And I came here with *very* good reason."

"A grown woman wouldn't suggest something as ridiculous as us fucking each other." His mouth slanted into a harsh line. "It'd spoil everything. Our friendship is probably already in ruins."

"Then I guess the only direction we can go is forward."

For several seconds they faced off in straining silence, both of them breathing heavily.

"I think you're scared of touching me because you know it won't be sterile and safe," she challenged.

"Cut your crap, Katie," he muttered, his accent thicker than refrigerated molasses. He stared at the fire before he shut his eyes as though the flames had scalded them. "If you stay here, I'm going to have you soon enough. I don't think I can control it. I'll take my fill of you, too. I don't think you have any idea what that means, the state I'm in."

She slammed down her glass of soda on the table hard enough to make the liquid splash onto her hand. "At least if you were fucking me blind, you wouldn't be drinking yourself into a grave."

She didn't glance back at him as she stalked out of the room. At that moment, she couldn't stand to look at Rill Pierce a second longer. She vibrated with anger.

How dared he accuse her of not knowing what love was?
How dared he accuse her of coming here on a selfish whim?
How *dared* he?

He stood beneath the spray of frigid water and reached
for his drink. It was his first drink of the evening, and Rill
knew it'd be his last. Neither a cold shower nor whiskey
could dampen the memory of Katie sitting there in the fire-
lit room. He was learning from solid experience Katie wasn't
expunged easily from his mind, period.

She'd been wearing some kind of stretchy gray skirt that
hit her at midthigh and those supple leather boots that drove
him nuts for some damn reason. The mild autumn had persisted. Her smooth legs had been bare. She'd looked as sinful
as an unmade bed when she'd strutted into the diner this
afternoon wearing that godforsaken skirt and a tight T-shirt
that she'd knotted at the hip, her long, shapely bare legs on
display for all the world to see.

When she'd sat down on the couch in the living room,
the skirt had risen on her thighs. He'd resented the fact that
he needed to talk with her about something as serious as
her quitting her job—not to mention what he'd allowed to
happen the other night—and all he could concentrate on
was the tempting V between her legs. He knew firsthand
the type of nonexistent underwear she wore.

All he could consider was how close he was to paradise.

Well . . . then why can't we? We're both adults.

He clamped his eyelids shut as lust shot through him at
the memory of her speaking the words. She was such a wild
thing, such a gypsy child. She didn't know what the hell she
was doing, offering herself to him like that.

She's not a child, a voice in his head reminded him, a
greedy voice that he associated with his stiff cock. *She's a
grown woman. She knows the consequences. It's her choice
to make.*

He shut off the water but he didn't get out of the tub

immediately. He stood there with his hand on the handle and his head lowered.

She didn't know the consequences, but he wasn't so sure he did, either. Maybe that was what made him so wary about touching Katie Hughes.

None of it mattered. None of his self-recrimination; none of his self-doubts. He'd have her. Maybe he'd be able to control his hunger once he touched her, but nothing . . . nothing could keep him away from her at this point.

He didn't bother to quiet his steps on the stairs. Best she knew he was coming. She might have heard him breathing it was so quiet in the old house, and his lungs were heaving choppily from acute anticipation.

The dormer bedroom was swathed in pitch blackness. There was a tiny green light next to the bed—probably a clock. Rill used it to navigate through the room. He heard the sheets rustle and knew she was awake before he reached for the bedside lamp. He stifled a curse with effort when the dim light came on.

She lay on the bed naked, her hair spread out around her torso like an opened cape. She looked serene but watchful as she inspected him.

For two seconds, he almost turned and walked away. This was much, much bigger than he'd expected, and he'd bargained on plenty.

"While I'm here with you, don't plan on touching anyone else," she whispered.

He swallowed thickly and nodded. He couldn't have spoken if he tried. The realization that her naked beauty had nearly brought him to his knees made him glance away in order to save himself. His gaze landed on the scarf she'd worn twisted around her neck with artistic carelessness earlier. Her eyes moved, but her head remained immobile when he picked it up and stepped toward the head of the bed.

"Give me your wrists," he said gruffly.

Uncertainty flickered across her beautiful face. Not fear, thank God, just confusion.

"You have to let me be in control of this, Katie. It's the only way I can do this thing."

Her facial features tightened when he said that . . . *this thing*. He couldn't even bring himself to put into words what was happening between them. She slowly lifted her arms above her head, the motion making her back arch slightly. He ripped his gaze off the vision of her round, pink-tipped breasts rising in the air, tempting him. She didn't say anything as he bound her wrists together firmly. He gently pulled her arms farther over her head and used the scarf to restrain them to the wrought-iron headboard. He stepped back.

It was a little hard to look at her, she was so beautiful at that moment. For a few seconds he just stood there, a mortal in the presence of unearthly beauty, a worshipper at a shrine of sex and voluptuous pleasure.

"Don't," she whispered when he reached for the lamp.

He ignored her and plunged the room into darkness.

"Spread your thighs," he ordered through a throat that felt as if hands were wrapped around it, squeezing. He knelt between her opened legs. He reached, his hands encountering the satiny smooth, warm flesh of her hips. Her subtle scent reached his nostrils. His cock throbbed viciously next to his thigh. He hadn't bothered to put on underwear after his shower, but had merely thrown on his jeans and partially buttoned them before he'd come up the stairs to do this deed. As a result, his cock was trapped down his left pant leg. It felt like a hot poker burning the skin of his thigh, stretching the fabric of his jeans tight.

He lowered his head, a bee drawn to honey. He placed his lips on soft pubic hair and inhaled her scent. She whimpered. She was aroused. The cream on her labia moistened his mouth before his tongue gathered it.

He went rigid with need, like he was an animal that had just caught the hint of prey in the wind. She stiffened, too. He used his hand to open her labia wider, exposing the sensitive kernel of flesh hidden within the folds.

She gasped his name when he plunged his tongue into that forbidden fruit. When her taste fully registered in his brain, he was lost. He closed his eyes and ate her with savage abandon. Some part of his brain was exquisitely attuned to the sounds she made, to every nuance of tension in her sleek body. He sucked gently and stabbed at her clit without mercy with his tongue, but when her cries became desperate, he softened to a caress, gliding his tongue over that swollen flesh until she quivered like a leaf held fast to a branch during a wild storm.

He ran his hands from hip to belly to ribs, relishing every shiver, coaxing more out of her. It was intoxicating. Not just the taste of her sweet juices running down his throat, the entire idea of possessing Katie, of evoking those sexy little cries from her throat, of creating the uncontrollable quaking in her muscles, of tempting her pussy to give him more of her addicting cream. He twisted his face slightly, stimulating her sensitive tissues, glorying in how wet she was.

He wanted to thrust his finger into her slit. She'd be tight and warm . . . all creamed up for him. The thought made his cock jerk in his jeans, demanding freedom, demanding its due. But he knew if he slid his finger into that welcoming little clasp, all control would be gone.

If it wasn't already.

Katie was like a wildfire. She'd snatch him with her delicious heat, pull him in like a moth to the leaping flames. She was a thousand times more addictive than whiskey. It was the reason he'd insisted upon tying her up. This was an ordeal as it was, to give in at least partially to his raging lust. If he had to endure her hands all over him at this stage of the game, he'd forsake everything. He needed to set some ground rules. He needed to *stick* to those rules.

He was *not* a slave to lust. He may share his mother's and his uncles' and a whole shitload of other Pierce ancestors' wastrel genes, but he was different.

Instead of allowing himself to experience the delicious core of her heat, he turned his face and sucked her clit between his lips and teeth. Gently, he bit, determined to show her that even though he'd been too weak to resist her potent allure, he *would* be master of this situation.

But when he felt her body go rigid, when she screamed as pleasure gushed through nerve and muscle . . . when he felt her warm juices surge from her slit against his chin, Rill doubted he'd mastered much of anything.

Her climax was delicious, not just the taste of her flooding his senses, her catchy, surprised gasps and whimpers, the delicate convulsions that wracked her taut body. He couldn't stop himself. He lowered his face and plunged his tongue into her pussy again and again, drowning in that sweet font, anointing himself with the essence of Katie.

Her trembling muscles sagged into the mattress and her climactic cries segued to anguished groans. He realized he was still drinking from her thirstily, exploring the narrow confines of her drenched slit with avarice.

When he recognized his greediness, he lifted his head, panting heavily. His face was slick with her juices. He wanted to slide his cock into her and ride her into submission. A feral need to utterly possess her, to even make her hurt a little, to force her to share in some of his sharp anguish, overwhelmed him.

He stood clumsily next to the bed.

"Rill?" she asked between pants for air.

He opened his mouth, but he couldn't think of what to say. So he yanked at the knot restraining her wrists, turned and walked out of the room. If she said his name again, and he heard the vulnerability and disorientation in her voice, he wouldn't be able to control what he might do.

Downstairs, he rushed into the bathroom and shut the door. Without turning on the light, he put his back to the door and fumbled with his jeans. His cock felt leaden. He jerked at it, his actions nearly as violent and desperate as Rill felt at that moment.

He'd held her hips in his hands and served her pussy to his marauding mouth. She'd jerked like a plucked harp string when he'd bitten her clit gently. Then she'd been shaking beneath him, helpless and beautiful.

He groaned in agony when he started to come. It hurt. All of it. It hurt that he'd crossed this line with a friend because of his innate degeneracy, but it hurt being alone in the world, too. Hurt like hell. He couldn't decide what felt worse, the numbness or this sharp pain of need.

It hurt the most shooting his seed onto the cold tile floor instead of in Katie Hughes's furthest reaches.

Nine

When Katie woke up the next morning the house was empty. Rill's bedroom door was wide-open, a sure sign of his absence, since he religiously kept it closed when he was in there.

She wandered into the sun-dappled kitchen, feeling grouchy and exhausted after having slept a total of three hours. A bit difficult to sleep after the man of your dreams plays your flesh like a maestro and then turns around and walks out of the room.

What did it mean? Had he been unsatisfied with her?

Stupid question. He must have been. How else did his behavior make any sense? If she'd pleased him, he would have taken his own satisfaction. He would have wanted more of her, just like Katie thirsted for more of him . . . the feeling of his skin sliding beneath her palms, the sensation of his mouth moving over hers, the experience of holding him in her arms while he shuddered in pleasure.

He'd denied her all that, although he'd given her a pure, distilled blast of bliss.

Rill was trying to make it abundantly clear that the only

thing he could give her was pleasure. He was highlighting the unnaturalness of them becoming sexually involved by walking away after sharing something so intimate.

If that was what he was trying to prove to her, he'd failed. Katie couldn't imagine anything more total and natural than her body's response to his touch.

She'd come downstairs last night for a while after he'd left her bedroom, determined to speak with him, to tear down the barrier he'd erected by tying her up to the bed and eating her until she hardly knew where or what she was except a quivering mass of pleasure completely at the mercy of Rill's tongue. The house had been dark and his bedroom door closed by the time she'd finally worked up the nerve to descend. It couldn't have been clearer that while he might exchange sex with her, he wasn't willing to do something as intimate as sleep with her.

She'd gone back upstairs, undecided whether she was more heartsore or furious. The combination of her volatile emotions had been a key ingredient for a serious dose of insomnia.

While she was making coffee, she heard the sound of gravel popping beneath tires. Her heart leapt. Rill would have no choice but to face her in the full light of day. She smoothed her hair—hopeless cause—and tightened the sash of her short robe. She couldn't resist racing to the front door when she heard the sound of a step on the front stairs.

Her heart sank in disappointment when she peered through the shut front door window and saw Miles Fordham approaching, wearing a pair of jeans, a button-down blue shirt and a well-cut blazer.

"Hi," she said a little bemusedly when she opened the door before he had a chance to knock on it.

He looked surprised by her sudden appearance, and then pleased. A little too pleased, Katie thought as she tightened her robe yet again as Miles inspected her.

"Well, I'll be," he murmured appreciatively when his eyes finally found her face again. "The man who wakes up to see the vision of you every morning would be blessed indeed."

"He'd have to be blessed to put up with me in the morning," Katie replied with a frown. Miles gave her a helpless look and then grinned. She relented and smiled back. He really did have a charming smile.

"Are you looking for Rill?" Katie prompted.

"No. I came looking for you."

"Me?" she asked in surprise. She motioned with her hand and he followed her into the house. She opened up a cabinet and held up a coffee cup with a questioning look. Miles nodded.

"I thought I'd stop by and see if you were interested in a drive. It's going to get warm again in a day or two, but today is the perfect fall day—chilly, but nice in the sunshine. The foliage is gorgeous out at the club grounds."

"Are you trying to court me, Miles?" she speculated casually as she poured both of them a cup of coffee.

He seemed a little taken aback. "Yeah, I guess I am. It's not a crime, is it?"

She raised her eyebrows thoughtfully and handed him his coffee. "Not a crime, no. It's not a very wise thing to undertake, though."

"I see. Your affections are otherwise engaged, is that it? Who is he?" He glanced around the house. "Don't tell me it's Pierce."

"What if it was?" Katie asked, scowling.

Miles shrugged. "He just doesn't seem like ideal boyfriend material, that's all."

Katie gave him a wry glance and let her eyes move over the sexy wave in his light brown hair and his casually elegant attire. "And you're what good boyfriend material is made of, I suppose."

He laughed a little disbelievingly at her cheek. "Well, even if I was, I wouldn't say so."

"Why not?"

"Because modesty is just one of many traits of a good boyfriend."

She laughed.

It was on the tip of her tongue to turn him down, but then she glanced out the window onto the brilliant day. It'd be depressing to sit in this empty house and wonder where Rill was. A horrible thought struck her. What if he didn't come back? His car was missing from the driveway. He'd disappeared off the map eighteen months ago. No reason he couldn't do it again if she'd pushed him too hard.

"Katie?"

"Hmmm?" She focused on Miles with effort. "Oh, right. Sure, a drive would be nice. Errol doesn't have to be in physical therapy until next week, so my day is pretty free, although I should stop by later and make sure he's keeping that leg elevated," she muttered to herself as an afterthought.

"Excuse me?" asked Miles, looking politely confused.

"Oh, I ran Errol Banks over in my car," Katie replied in a preoccupied manner. "Can you give me a few minutes to get ready?"

Miles laughed. "Take your time."

Katie knew she was being ridiculous, but she couldn't stop herself from sneaking into Rill's bedroom before she got in the shower. It surprised her to see that he'd not only put clean sheets on his bed, but made it. Was that a possible sign that he'd abandoned her? She breathed a sigh of relief when she saw clothes in the closet along with a pair of tennis shoes and dark brown leather hiking boots.

Rill hadn't left Vulture's Canyon for good. Not yet anyway.

They sat at the best table in the Forest River Restaurant. From her seat, Katie had a spectacular view of the dining terrace, landscaped grounds and, in the distance, the wild beauty of the Ohio River Valley. The colors of the trees were so bright it hurt her eyes a little to look at them. The terrace was bathed in golden sunshine and nearly filled with golfers and other diners who didn't mind the bite of autumn in the air.

"It's beautiful," she murmured before she took a sip of the cool, dry white wine Miles had ordered along with their lunch.

"You're looking right where I plan to put the boat," Miles said, nodding toward the sparkling river in the distance.

Katie glanced over at him and smiled. He'd been a pleasant enough companion for the past two hours. A little full of himself, but nice. The tour he'd given her of the surrounding countryside and then the lush grounds of the Forest River Country Club had been relaxing. Fortunately, Miles's favorite topic of conversation was himself and his business ventures, which was just fine by Katie. She didn't particularly want to talk about herself.

Plus, it was kind of relaxing, not to be with someone who asked her a slew of questions either about her celebrity brother, Everett, or Rill, who was just as renowned in his own way.

"The gambling boat, you mean?" she asked idly, toying with the rim of her wineglass. "There isn't a huge population around here, is there? Where will you get your customers?"

"St. Louis is only forty minutes away." Miles tore his gaze off her circling finger on the glass and nodded toward the terrace. "Three-quarters of those men out there are from the St. Louis area. They drive up on Fridays and stay for a weekend of golf and relaxation. I hired a good portion of my employees from the St. Louis area, as well. The people around here are ignorant, for the most part. They don't have the polish to work in this type of establishment. Once the gambling boat opens, people will come from miles away for an exciting vacation in Mother Nature's embrace. Las Vegas can't offer a man a view like that—"

Miles's explanation was cut short when the waitress arrived with their food.

"Thanks, Debbie," Miles said after she'd placed their lunch before them. He gifted Debbie with the kind of smile that had long ago lost voltage in Katie's world, but apparently still had them buzzing in the vicinity of Vulture's Canyon. Miles continued when Debbie walked away. "My lawyers should have the final approval from the Illinois Gaming Board for the boat by next spring, so I went ahead and started construction. See that over there?"

Katie turned in the direction where he pointed, seeing a portion of the large construction site that snaked out onto the grounds. She'd already noticed the building project next to the club when they arrived earlier. Miles had informed her it was the location of his new grand hotel.

"That'll be where the walkway leads from the hotel directly out onto the boat. Customers won't even know they passed from land to water," Miles told her smugly.

"Nice," Katie said politely before she placed a forkful of salad in her mouth.

Miles chuckled. "You don't seem very interested, Katie."

She took her time chewing and swallowed. "I'm not much for gambling. Not with money, anyway."

Miles leaned forward slightly, his hazel eyes gleaming. "What *do* you like to take a gamble on, Katie Hughes?"

"Just the little things, like my future."

Miles chuckled, clearly thinking she was joking. Katie didn't mind.

"So I heard a rumor you were a tax attorney," he prompted.

Her mouth was full, so she just nodded.

"Can I hire you to do some consulting? I could use a good tax attorney in my corner."

She considered while she swallowed and took a sip of wine. It was a tempting offer. Her savings wouldn't last forever. But she had other things in mind for her future—the gamble she'd referred to just now.

"I'll pass," she said with a friendly smile. "I don't do the type of tax work you probably need, anyway. I might be looking for work, depending on how things work out for me in Vulture's Canyon, but you'll need a specialist, with all the tax issues that come from the gambling operation."

"If you're looking for work in this area, you'll end up having to come to me anyway."

She gave him an "excuse me?" look at his overconfidence. He chuckled.

"I'm just telling it like it is, not bragging. There aren't many men in this area who could afford to pay a high-class Los Angeles attorney like you."

"Actually, I'm thinking of getting out of the tax business."

"You're kidding. Why would you want to do something like that?" he asked, amused, as he reached across the table and grabbed her hand in his.

Katie found his attitude incredibly condescending. Miles Fordham didn't know anything about her. What right did he have to be surprised at her choice of career even if she told him she planned to join the space program?

Someone touched Miles's shoulder, saving Katie from his patronizing flirtation. She gently pulled her captive hand back. Miles was too preoccupied to notice. His eyes widened with male appreciation when he looked up and saw the woman standing next to him. Katie continued to eat her salad as she studied the new arrival curiously.

"Amber. Well, aren't you a sight for sore eyes," Miles complimented, his gaze roving over the tall, curvy red-head wearing a wool skirt, leather boots, a matching belt and a soft-looking angora sweater that clung to generous breasts. One thing was for certain: whoever this woman was, she didn't do her clothes shopping in any stores Katie had spotted as of yet in southern Illinois. When Amber twisted slightly in her heeled boots, Katie was reminded of a six-year-old showing off her new party dress to Daddy. Whoever Amber was, Katie decided as she chewed a cherry tomato, she couldn't be much older than twenty or twenty-one.

"Katie, I'd like you to meet Amber Jones. She's the new hostess at the restaurant."

"Nice to meet you," Katie said.

Amber's return greeting wasn't quite as warm, but Katie couldn't really blame her. The girl obviously had a thing for Miles, the way she was staring at him like he was a rock star while they exchanged small talk.

"Well, I'd better get back to work," Amber said breathily

after a moment. "Will I see you at happy hour at the lodge bar tonight?"

"Sure. Maybe I'll be there."

Amber grinned and sashayed away from the table, apparently satisfied despite Miles's ambiguous response. A dose of Amber must have dislodged the topic of their former conversation from Miles's brain. He resumed his meaningless banter about his plans for the hotel and boat, and Katie nodded politely once in a while, which seemed to be a sufficient enough response for Miles.

It wasn't bad at all, Katie decided as she sipped the last of her wine. The food and wine had been good; the sun radiating through the pane of glass had warmed and relaxed her. She watched idly as Amber seated a group of businessmen on the terrace and lingered to chat and charm them. One of them stroked her hip in a gesture that went beyond flirtation. Amber wasn't put off, however, given her seductive smile.

After lunch, Miles asked her if she'd care to see the latest renovations he'd done on the house he'd had built on the club grounds, but Katie politely refused, explaining that the two glasses of wine had made her a little tipsy.

"All the more reason for you to come to my house and check out my hot tub and heated pool," Miles told her suggestively.

"All the more reason for me *not* to," she replied with a warm smile.

As they reached Miles's car, Katie was surprised when he abruptly let out a stream of invectives. It wasn't that she wasn't used to cursing—Rill, for instance, had a repertoire of curse words that only an Irishman could acquire—but Miles hadn't said so much as "hell" since she'd first met him.

She hurried around to the driver's side of the car to see what he was staring at with such fury.

"Both tires. Slashed," he said.

"Damn," Katie mumbled. "Who would do something like that?"

"Take your pick," Miles said bitterly. "Any one of those Vulture's Canyon hippies or the illiterate coal miners from the hills might have done it. There've been little incidents in the past—plenty of them. Idiots wouldn't recognize progress if it stabbed them in the eyeball."

"You mean the person who slashed your tires doesn't want you to put in the gambling boat?"

"That's exactly what I mean." He got on his cell phone and snapped out an order for some employee to call Sheriff Mulligan. He was in such a tiff, Katie felt a little uncomfortable. She was relieved when he told the same employee to bring another one of his cars around so he could take Katie home.

Despite that nasty bit of business, thanks to the two glasses of chardonnay, she was in a much better place to meet up with Rill later that afternoon. She saw him immediately when they pulled up to the house. He wore jeans, a red T-shirt, a flannel shirt and a pair of work gloves and walked around the corner of the house with a huge stack of logs in his arms. He came to a halt in the yard as she thanked Miles and got out of the passenger door of his BMW sedan. As she got closer to Rill, she noticed the storminess in his blue eyes and the rigidity of his facial muscles.

"What the fuck do you think you're doing?" he demanded as Miles turned his car around and headed back down the hill.

What the feck do ya t'ink yer doin'?

From the sounds of things, Rill was *not* in a good mood. Surprise, surprise.

"I went out to lunch with Miles," she said with a shrug.

"You went to lunch with Miles," Rill repeated sarcastically. "That man is reviled by every citizen of Vulture's Canyon and every coal miner in the employ of the Black Velvet Mines. Fordham is fixing to change everything about their way of life by installing that gambling boat. Do you *plan* on making life hell for me, Katie, or does it just come naturally to you?"

"Why should *you* care what the people of Vulture's Canyon think of Miles Fordham? He's okay. And it's not like you sympathize with the people in this town. *I'm not a part of this town*—isn't that what you said the other day?"

Rill made a sound of deep disgust and stalked toward the front porch on long legs. Katie pursued at a jog, not finished with her argument. She tripped on the first step and caught herself from falling flat on her face by using Rill's back as a brace, causing him to drop a log. It clattered loudly on the wood steps.

"Did Fordham get you drunk?" he asked incredulously, pausing on the stairs.

"No, I did that myself," Katie mumbled, righting herself. She slung her bag on her shoulder and picked up the log. When she noticed Rill's blazing eyes, she added, "Not *drunk*, just a little tipsy. We had wine with lunch."

"You had wine with lunch."

Her sigh was filled with asperity. She took another log off the pile in his arms in order to lessen his load. When she tried to take another, he shifted his arms, preventing her. She gave him a condemning glance.

"Is that all you're going to do? Repeat everything I say and give me dirty looks?" she asked.

"Put those logs back on here."

She frowned at him and did what he said, putting the logs back in his arms. He stomped up the stairs. Katie let him go this time, made a pit stop in the bathroom and then cautiously entered the living room a few minutes later. Rill glanced over at her from where he knelt before the fireplace.

"I would have preferred to have lunch with you, but you were nowhere to be found when I got up this morning," she said quietly.

He'd been about to say something, but her honesty made him pause. He threw the last of the kindling sticks he held in his hand into the growing fire and stood.

"I was hiking in the woods," he said gruffly. "I do that a lot."

Katie removed the jacket she'd been wearing, tossed off her flats and settled into the corner of the couch, drawing up her knees. "Your car was gone."

He shrugged. "There are hundreds of hiking trails around here maintained by the forest preserve. Sometimes I drive to the park entrances and try different ones. Other times, I just wander around here."

"Does it bring you any peace?"

"No, not really. Something to do, though."

He didn't move to join her on the couch, but he didn't walk out of the room, either. The living room was cast in shadow despite the brilliance of the fall day outside. Katie could see the gleam of his eyes from beneath a lowered brow as he studied her. When Miles had arrived earlier, she'd showered and thrown on a pair of skinny jeans and a frilly little button-up blouse, and tempered the superfeminine effect with a sleek belted jacket. She hadn't once thought about how she looked when she was with Miles, but she felt hyperaware of how she might appear to Rill. It suddenly occurred to her that Eden had always been dressed impeccably in conservative suits and elegant tailored blouses.

She couldn't help but feel Rill must find her appearance lacking.

His forehead crinkled. "What are you thinking, Katie?" he asked slowly.

"I was thinking it blows my mind. I don't understand it. You must be bored to tears living here." It wasn't a complete lie. She'd been wondering about that very thing even though she hadn't been thinking it at the moment he'd asked. "Are you at least writing?"

He exhaled and stepped toward her. Katie gave an inner sigh of relief when he walked around the coffee table and sat on the center cushion of the couch, his thigh just inches away from her toes. For a few tense seconds, she'd been sure he was going to walk out of the room and abandon her once again.

"I haven't written a word since I came here."

"Why not?"

He shrugged, the movement bringing her gaze down to his shoulders and chest. He looked delicious in denim, red cotton and flannel . . . rugged and so male she could practically taste the pheromones he exuded on her tongue. She was overwhelmed with a need to touch him, but something stilled her hand. Maybe it was the voice inside her that kept reminding her repeatedly that she wasn't what Rill wanted. Not really.

You're not his type. You're not like Eden.

"I haven't got any ideas for a story," he said, his voice carrying that flat, empty tone that Katie hated. She breathed deeply and felt a glimmer of satisfaction when his eyes flickered over her chest.

"I haven't seen a computer anywhere. Don't you have one here?"

"Yeah," he muttered, glancing away from her breasts.

"Well . . ." She paused and gave a wide yawn. The heat from the fire had started to warm her. "Why don't you at least set it up, make yourself a work space? It'd at least create an atmosphere for the *possibility* of writing."

When he didn't say anything, Katie thought he'd dismissed her advice just like he did everything else she offered him. She sighed dispiritedly and laid her cheek on the arm of the couch. He turned at her defeated sound.

"Why are you here, Katie?" he asked her yet again, his tone a mixture of irritation and puzzlement.

"I told you," she mumbled groggily.

"Why did you quit your job?"

"I hated that job," she said impulsively.

His mouth dropped open in surprise. "I thought you loved it. You said you did. You always had such great stories to tell about those weird old Hollywood movie stars. I always pictured you wandering into some Gothic Hollywood mansion and meeting up with Gloria Swanson–type *Sunset Boulevard* loons, telling them how they could save a buck or a million on their taxes."

She shifted her head and stared at the fire, not wanting Rill to see the tears that sprang into her eyes. Why was she always trying to convince the world she was so happy and fulfilled when she wasn't? Once she'd begun the role, it was so difficult to break out of it. She'd had no one to blame but herself for her typecasting. She'd wanted to do something different with her life for years now—something *meaningful*—but it was so damn difficult not to play the role everyone expected of her. Even when she volunteered for charities, she couldn't get it right, coming off like a spoiled Hollywood golden girl who assuaged her guilt by sacrificing a pittance of her time to the needy.

Maybe part of her identity was associated with being an affluent, educated white woman from Southern California, but she was more than that. She *was*.

Why wouldn't anyone believe her?

"Katie?" Rill asked in a quiet, firm voice.

She turned her chin reluctantly and met his stare. One of his eyebrows crinkled in concerned puzzlement when he saw the tears in her eyes.

He reached for her.

She couldn't understand why she felt this compulsion to cry when it felt like heaven to rest her cheek on Rill's hard chest while his hands moved up and down her arms and over her back, soothing her. Katie just stared at the fire and absorbed everything Rill offered her: his compassion, his strength . . . his heat.

"I'm sorry," she mumbled wetly after a few minutes. "I don't know where that came from."

"Yeah, you do," she heard him say, his voice rumbling straight through his flesh into the ear she pressed next to his chest.

She lifted her head and looked at him in surprise. "You mean aside from the two glasses of wine?"

He gave her a hard glance and stretched, hooking a box of tissues sitting on the end table with his finger.

"Why don't you just tell me about it?" he suggested as she wiped her face with a tissue.

Despite the tempting invitation, Katie hesitated. She knew what she wanted to do with her life—in a general, very vague sort of way. The thing she most dreaded was the reaction she'd get from her friends and family, and Rill counted as both.

He had once, anyway, Katie thought as the earthshaking memory of him consuming her with single-minded intent last night in the darkness smashed into her awareness. Something shifted in his expression and she wondered in a flash of panic if he'd recalled those volatile moments at the same second she had.

It was all so confusing. Just because her own life was chaos, did she feel some inner need to throw everyone else's life into disarray, as well? Not that Rill's life was running like clockwork, but Katie surely wasn't making things any smoother for him with her presence.

"I . . . I'm thinking about changing careers. My work isn't very fulfilling," she said, desperate to deflect that sudden hard gleam in Rill's eyes, wild to ignore the way her right breast was crushed against his ribs, how she could feel the rise and fall of his chest as he breathed. She pressed her face against his sternum.

"I know you think I'm a mess," she said in a choked voice. For a tension-filled moment, he didn't speak or move. Her head rose as he inhaled deeply.

"I don't think you're a mess, Shine," he said quietly. She clamped her eyes shut to suppress a flood of emotion when she felt his hand move in her hair. "I think you're impossible, and I don't know what the hell I'm going to do with you, but I know from firsthand experience you don't even begin to qualify as a mess."

She couldn't hold it in anymore. She gasped for air and shook. Rill just held her and touched her hair while she cried out the past few years of uncertainty and self-doubt.

When her tears had quieted and she'd succeeded in soaking Rill's T-shirt, he placed his large, open hand on her back. She felt the heat of his palm soaking down through her blouse. She wasn't sure how to interpret the gesture, but she

sensed he wanted her to look up at him and knew she was
right when he spoke.

"I need to talk to you about something, Katie."

She remained completely still. It struck her that he was
going to tell her to leave again, and not in the self-destructing,
bitter manner she'd grown used to since arriving in Vulture's
Canyon, but in the old, sweet, thoughtful Rill way. It terrified her to consider it. She'd have no defense against a *kind*
rejection.

When he didn't speak again, she took the coward's way
out, and fell asleep in his arms.

Ten

~∽~

The sensation of Katie's even, slow breath lulled him until Rill, too, drifted off into sleep. He wasn't sure how long he was out of it, but when he awoke, he had a hard-on that was difficult to ignore. He sat there on the couch with an armful of soft, fragrant woman and wondered how he could have gone for so many years without having this profound of a physical reaction to Katie. He grimaced as he tried to shift into a more comfortable position without waking her, but his erection continued on its merry way.

His cock must be making up for lost time.

Lost time, he thought disgustedly. The only thing lost between Katie and him except for the old security of their friendship, the once-familiar structure of their relationship.

He'd been planning on telling her when he saw her again that he'd thought things over and come to a crucial conclusion. Things weren't irreversible. They'd crossed the line, but the line was still within their vision. They still could creep back over it to their separate territories. Sure, it'd take some effort, and effort required energy and care, and those were two resources Rill had been in short supply of lately.

But he'd decided on his long hike in the woods today that he'd dig deep. He'd try to salvage the friendship, because Katie was worth it. He'd been resolved on the matter until he'd seen Katie step out of Fordham's car. The brown rinse she'd put in her hair had nearly vanished. Sunlight turned her long mane into a living crown and cloak of incandescent, shifting golden waves and curls.

If there was such a thing as a wild angel, its halo and wings might resemble Katie's hair and sunlight combined.

When it dawned on him that she'd been out with Miles Fordham, anger had transformed his beneficent intentions to make things right with Katie. What was she trying to prove, anyway? Suggesting to him last night that they sleep together and then traipsing off with that tycoon-in-the-woods Fordham, whose smiles looked like they'd been air-brushed by a photographer?

His anger had turned to a dull roar as he'd watched Katie march toward him.

Had she let that asshole touch her?

The incendiary thought struck Rill again as he sat on the couch holding Katie while she slept. He told himself it was a natural reaction to be annoyed at the idea of Katie going out with Fordham. If Everett had stayed long enough in Vulture's Canyon—if Rill hadn't been so foul to him and allowed him to stay on—Everett would have disliked Miles Fordham as well.

Everett hated almost all of Katie's boyfriends. At the very least, he was highly unimpressed. None of them was good enough for Katie.

His brow crinkled as he tried to recall if Everett truly *had* disapproved of Katie's boyfriends or if it'd been Rill doing the disliking. . . .

Katie rustled in her sleep. Her hand dropped to his lap. Rill jumped like she'd prodded him with a red-hot poker. Katie lifted her head from his chest and mumbled something unintelligible.

"Jaysus," he hissed under his breath as he braced Katie's

shoulders with his hands and carefully eased his body around her. Her eyelids had fluttered open when he'd jumped, but they'd quickly drooped once again.

She was in some territory between sleep and consciousness when he carried her up the stairs. He gritted his teeth when she put her arms around his neck and pressed her supple, sleep-softened body against his chest. His heartbeat thundered in his ears and throbbed in his cock.

He'd broken out in a sweat by the time he laid Katie on her made bed, and it wasn't because the room was hot. She'd opened a window before she left with Fordham. The air in the dormer bedroom felt cool against his heated skin. Her eyes were open, watching him as he straightened and looked down at her, but the sweet, slightly dazed expression on her face made him think she was still existing in the muzzy, warm embrace of sleep. She reached and caught his hand with her own.

"Come to bed, Rill," she whispered throatily.

He swallowed, but the knot in his throat remained.

"I was going to tell you earlier that it'd been a mistake. We can still go back, Katie," he croaked.

"I don't want to go back," she said simply.

"I do."

But despite his words, he didn't move.

She just stared up at him, her eyes keeping him pinned to the spot even though his conscience willed him to move. It surprised him a little to see his hand cradling her jaw. His skin looked dark in contrast to her pale gold hue; his fingers seemed large and blunt—poor instruments for exploring the delicate angles and exquisite softness of Katie's jaw and cheek.

He pressed his thumb into her lower lip, testing its plumpness. He met her gaze and saw her heat.

The next thing he knew, he was unbuttoning her blouse, the frilly little flounces that decorated the placket tickling at his fingers. She reached beneath his opened flannel shirt as he leaned over her, her eager caresses making him lose his concentration.

"Where's the scarf?" he asked bluntly, standing and glancing around her room.

"Rill, *no*," she murmured as she came up on her elbows. Her blouse gaped open, giving him a glimpse of curving flesh tightly encased in a shimmering champagne-colored bra. He tore his gaze off the arousing sight and walked over to the bureau where he found the scarf.

"If we don't do anything more than we've already done, maybe it'll be okay," he said grimly, holding up the scarf, a question in his eyes. Katie looked bewildered.

"What are you talking about?"

"I mean if we keep a cap on this fucking thing," he growled, "there's a chance we won't have to . . ."

"What?"

"Lose each other," he grated out between a clenched jaw.

"You're not going to lose me," she whispered.

"I am. I think I already have, but I'm such a selfish fuck, I still want to taste you again," he said bitterly.

A tear rolled down her cheek. She held her hands together and raised them above her head. He glanced away, the evidence of her sadness and the arousing image of her putting her hands up to be bound making him feel like he straddled a razor's edge.

It'll be okay. It'll be okay, he told himself repeatedly as he bound Katie's hands to the wrought-iron posts of the headboard. *It'll be just like last night, and you kept it under control then.* He hadn't yet fallen into the degenerate pit where his relatives lived, where carnal desires and selfishness ruled his very existence.

He'd never been seriously tempted by another woman when Eden had been his wife, when just the thought of her calm, elegant presence could quench a random attraction almost immediately. But Eden wasn't here anymore; the woman he'd believed Eden to be had *never* been there. She'd been an illusion he'd created in his mind from his own needs, his own fantasies.

He spread Katie's blouse wide, baring her smooth torso. His hands shook slightly as he unhooked the front clasp of her bra and peeled the fabric off her breasts. He paused, his hands at the sides of her body.

This isn't like last night all, he realized with a growing sense of desperation. Last night he'd been able to shut off the lamp, but he couldn't turn off the late-afternoon sunlight that streamed through the window . . . couldn't remove his gaze from Katie's full, creamy breasts.

They looked vulnerable somehow, rising from the plane of her chest . . . tender, succulent . . . easy prey for the beast that raged inside him.

She must have been affected by his stare because she stretched taut and twisted in her restraint, shifting the firm globes of her breasts slightly. His cock jerked in his jeans. He grimaced and unfastened the first several buttons of the fly, giving himself some much-needed room.

"Don't move, Katie," he demanded through a clenched jaw.

"If you won't let me touch you, I wish you'd get on with your business." He glanced at her face when he heard her pressured hiss. Her cheeks were stained a delicate pink. Her light green eyes shone with a mixture of irritation and arousal.

This was most *definitely* not like last night.

She pulled on her restraint again and shifted her torso, jiggling her breasts. His fingers were suddenly ripping her jeans open. She must have felt some measure of his haste because she lifted her hips, making it easier for him to jerk her jeans and champagne-colored panties down her legs and off her feet in a rush.

He looked down at her when he'd finished. She spread her thighs and whispered.

"Hurry."

But he was already on his way. He knelt between her legs and slipped his hands over smooth hips, cradling her buttocks. Instead of leaning down over her, he lifted her to him and served her to his mouth.

If last night had been wild, this was a frenzy.

She jerked her hips so hard as he thrashed her clit with his tongue that he strained tight to hold her in place for his consumption. He ran his tongue up and down the nerve-packed flesh repeatedly, and each time she quaked uncontrollably and wriggled. It was like holding a squirming creature in his hands and trying to perform a delicate piece of surgery. Her wildness sent him into a fever pitch, but he couldn't get a good angle on her.

He swatted a taut ass cheek in warning, but his action seemed only to throw Katie into a heightened state of excitement. She keened and jerked in his grasp. He growled into her flesh and spanked her again, this time more firmly. But only when he grabbed her legs and tossed them over his shoulder, holding her thighs in place, did he successfully immobilize her.

He buried his face in her pussy, finally free to drink her cream without hindrance, to evoke every shiver of pleasure from her taut flesh that his hunger required. She shrieked and came a minute later. He held her at his mercy, pressing firmly with his tongue, vibrating her while she shook in climax. From the sound of her screams, his forced stimulation while she came was powerful enough to border on pain, but he wasn't in a mood to show her mercy.

Katie'd been torturing him ever since she'd strutted into Vulture's Canyon. It wouldn't kill her to feel a little of the discomfort of this godforsaken lust.

He wasn't finished even when the shudders in her flesh eased. He put his hands on the backs of her thighs and spread them wider. She gasped when he curled his tongue and sent it high into her drenched slit. His eyelids opened heavily. She watched him while he searched greedily for more of her essence. He closed his lips on her, his tongue stuck high up in the sweet, creamy core of her. He sucked with the ridge of his upper lip pressed tightly against her clit. Triumph and lust roared through his veins when he felt her tremble against him.

He closed his eyes, the sight of her face gleaming with perspiration and arousal overwhelming him. When she began to thrash against him like she had before, he held her with one hand at her hip up to his mouth and swatted her bottom, not hard, but repeatedly, the sounds of his palm striking taut flesh popping in his ears. When her frenzy only increased, he lifted his head.

She made a sound of protest between a groan and a shout. "Keep *still*," he ordered.

He regretted the pained expression on her beautiful face—the discomfort of the abrupt cessation of pleasure.

He buried his face again between her thighs to atone, agitating her clit briskly with his tongue. Even though she forced herself to stay still, he spanked her ass several more times, sensing that the sensation excited her nearly as much as it did him.

He knew he was right when she went rigid and shook again in climax as he thrashed her clit with his tongue. Sensation flooded him. He saw red as he felt Katie shaking against him and her juices coated his tongue and throat. The sound of her screams and his own palm firmly striking a plump buttock entered his ears in a sharp, arrhythmic cacophony.

He set her hips on the bed. The periphery of his vision had gone fuzzy and shadowed, but Katie was sharp in focus, the image of her scoring his consciousness, burning it with her sheer vibrancy.

He ripped at the remainder of his button fly, shoved and fumbled, finally jerking his cock out of his boxer briefs.

He was possessed. He couldn't breathe.

A paroxysm of pleasure ripped through as he stroked his aching length, a convulsion of unbearable grief. His own hoarse shout cleaved through the thick cloak of his arousal.

Rill blinked open his eyes to the vision of his cock shooting an arc of semen onto the smooth harbor of Katie's belly. It seemed to burn as it seethed out of his body. He'd needed to be rid of the scalding fluid. His body tightened and he ejected more . . . and more. He grunted each time he jerked his cock and more spilled onto the growing semen pool on Katie's heaving belly.

In the last convulsions of climax, he shifted. He groaned in agony as he shot the final drops of his thunderous orgasm onto the dark gold pubic hair of Katie's mons.

So close.

His body shuddered again, but his balls had been utterly emptied. He fell forward, catching himself with his hands next to Katie's body, his eyes shut, struggling to regain his equilibrium. He felt a little like he'd been clocked in the head from an unsuspecting blow.

"Rill?"

Katie's whisper penetrated his awareness. He slowly opened his eyes. He couldn't describe the expression on her face as she looked up at him. Wary? Uncertain? Stunned?

She *must* be stunned. He'd been like a madman in those final moments, completely and utterly at the mercy of strangling lust.

He glanced down Katie's naked body, pausing when he saw his semen wetting her abdomen and pooling in indention of her belly button. He moved quickly, hoisting his body off the bed and jerking up his underwear and pants. Even though the bathroom off the dormer wasn't functional, there was a box of tissues on the sink counter. He returned to Katie and sat on the edge of the bed. He avoided her stare as he dried her belly and then untied her.

"I'm sorry," he said gruffly as he released her wrists. Her arms were falling back to the bed, but they paused in midair.

"Are you?"

His gaze flickered over her face. Her springtime eyes, golden hair and vividly pink cheeks created a vibrant palette of color. He'd thought it before, and he thought it again a hundredfold seeing a postorgasmic Katie; he wished he could put her image on film.

All of it except the doubt on her face.

He placed his fingertips over his shut eyes, blocking out the image of Katie's uncertainty. Or maybe that was his own wariness he saw reflected on her beautiful face.

"I don't know why I want you so much," he muttered brokenly.

In the seconds that followed, his eyes remained closed, but he sensed her rustling on the bed.

"You make it sound like a crime," she said eventually. When he pried his eyes open, he saw that she'd pulled the comforter around her. He was glad she'd covered herself.

He hated that she had.

There was something so elementally right about Katie's nudity. Now that he'd seen her full glory exposed, it struck him as almost a crime to hide it.

But of course he was thankful she had. She was more of a temptation than he was prepared for, broken as he was.

"It's not a crime," he muttered.

"It disappoints you that you want me," she whispered. "Because I'm not Eden."

His chin jerked around. "*No.* That's not it."

A prickly sort of uncomfortable silence fell between them. She'd pulled herself up into a sitting position, her legs crossed beneath the comforter. She held her blouse closed over her breasts. He realized she felt vulnerable in front of him. He wanted to comfort her, but he felt just as confused . . . just as exposed by his blind, naked need.

She inhaled shakily. Rill sensed her resolve to try to make sense of the situation, to put it into words.

"Has it been hard for you . . . when you get aroused by another woman since Eden died?"

Her matter-of-fact tone annoyed him. He didn't want to sit here and analyze why he went crazy every time he touched her. He certainly didn't want to discuss why he'd avoided relationships ever since Eden had died.

"No," he replied edgily.

"Why is it so terrible to want *me,* then? Why am *I* so objectionable?"

He gave her a disbelieving glance. "How could you think I find you objectionable? You know what just happened."

"You made love to me, and it seemed as if you liked it so much, you lost control a little bit. What's so awful about that?"

"I wasn't making love to you, Katie," he snapped. He felt beleaguered and cornered. "I love you as a friend, but I wasn't making love to you. *That's* what's wrong, if you're so bent on knowing the truth of it. *Now* are you happy?"

Her face went rigid. Beneath the two spots of vivid color on her cheeks, she went pale.

"Get out of here," she said in a low, dangerous tone.

Rill opened his mouth, wanting to take back his words. He felt as if he'd just reached across the bed and slapped her out of spite. Knowing he'd blown it, and that there was nothing else he could say or do at that moment to make Katie understand what he couldn't comprehend himself, he stood and did precisely what she'd asked him to do.

Eleven

Katie just sat there in the bed for five minutes after Rill walked down the stairs. She felt both overly aware of her body and distanced from it as well. It seemed that every nerve throbbed in a dull ache, as if Rill's attack had come from pummeling fists over every square inch of skin and not from a dozen words.

Don't be so dramatic, she thought irritably as she tossed aside the blanket and scurried out of the bed. *He didn't attack you.* He just . . . just . . .

Told the truth.

It was the truth that was making her feel like she'd just received a beating, but that pain was 100 percent in her head. Rill had made her scream in pleasure. If she experienced some residual psychic pain following what had happened, surely she had only herself to blame.

Rill had warned her beforehand.

She grabbed some clean clothes and opened the dormer bedroom door. She paused at the top of the stairs, straining to hear where Rill was in the house. It was quieter than a grave down there.

She quickly showered, dressed and combed her hair. Much to her relief, she didn't catch a glimpse of Rill when she made a dash out the front door. What she needed was some speed to sort things out in her cluttered head.

The days were growing shorter, Katie realized as she pulled out of the long driveway and onto the rural route. The narrow, black road surrounded by somber, towering trees, their vibrant colors washed out by the thinning light of the sinking sun, the seamless cool-blue sky overhead—all of it suited her dark, desperate mood.

I love you as a friend, but I wasn't making love to you. That's *what's wrong.*

The nerve endings beneath her skin seemed to throb feverishly with a dull ache at the memory.

She switched to the "manumatic" and got the Maserati into sixth gear on the straightaway portion of the slope down the hill. She drove on the twisting country roads without conscious thought, searching for stretches of road where she could feel the engine roaring at full throttle beneath her, where she could fly, unhindered by her doubts and insecurities.

It was twilight by the time she pulled into the river road where Errol lived and then turned down the long drive that led to his shack. An older-model but well-tended Honda Civic sat in the driveway. Olive answered the door with a cheerful smile. The older woman's kindness sent a glimmer of warmth through the numb chill that had come over Katie as she tried to evade her demons on the twisting, tree-lined roads.

She sipped chamomile tea and chatted with Olive as Errol watched an old episode of *Hogan's Heroes* on the black-and-white television that sat on the kitchen counter. Slowly, her confidence started to seep back into her spirit.

"I was wondering," she began slowly as Olive poured some more hot water over her tea bag, "where you and Monty live? There's something I'd like to ask him."

Olive's pale blue eyes widened in mild surprise. "You want to speak to Monty?"

Katie nodded.

"Well, he's here. He's down on Errol's dock, fishing," Olive explained, waving toward the kitchen door. "He always says they bite best at nightfall."

There was barely enough light left in the sky for Katie to locate the dock. She tiptoed on the weatherworn boards as she made her way to the still figure of the man sitting in a lawn chair at the end of the dock. She supposed the cantankerous Monty would have no problem scolding her for scaring all the fish clear to Kentucky with her city ways, so she was extra careful in her approach.

Much to her surprise, he didn't even glance around when she eased down on the dock next to him. Katie whispered.

"I'm sorry for . . ."

"Shhhhh," he warned softly.

Katie gave him a glance and then peered into the wide, flowing river, trying to see what Monty was studying so intently. After several seconds of silence, during which Katie was starting to get impatient, Monty finally spoke.

"He's gone," he growled as he began to reel in his line. "Little bastard probably nibbled away all my bait and never touched the hook."

There was just enough light left filtering through the trees on the western horizon for Katie to see Monty had been right. His hook was bare. He cursed without heat, removed the hook and set his fishing pole aside.

"Sorry if I chased him off," Katie mumbled.

"It's not your fault. I know that devilfish. He'd been playing with me for fifteen minutes before you walked on the dock."

It suddenly struck Katie that he probably didn't know who she was. It was pretty dark out here, and he'd never fully looked at her. Besides, why would he expect *her* of all people to come sneaking up on him while he was fishing?

"It's . . . er . . . me. Katie Hughes."

He gave her a swift glance. "Thanks for informing me."

"How'd you know it was me?" she asked, gleaning from the sarcastic edge to the older man's voice he'd known who sat next to him the whole time.

"Heard that monstrosity of a car of yours roaring down the road from three miles away."

Katie flushed. She really had been gunning it, and she was learning quickly that sound traveled eerily far through these silent hills.

"I came to see how Errol was doing." She let her boots drop down over the side of the dock, figuring Monty wouldn't mind since he was no longer fishing.

"What'd you come out *here* for?" Monty asked bluntly.

"To talk to you." She hesitated. "Is Monty short for Montgomery?"

"You came out here to ask me that?" Monty growled.

"No, I just was wondering."

"It's short for my first, middle and last names," he admitted brusquely after a pause. "Montrose Montague Montgomery."

Katie glanced over at him in surprise, barely making out the outline of his prominent nose and overhanging brow in the darkness. "Your parents must have had a sense of humor."

"My parents," he replied briskly, "didn't have a funny bone in either of their bodies."

"Huh," Katie mused.

A cricket began to squeak loudly. It sounded so close, it might have been just feet above Katie's head. She glanced back. The thick forest of trees seemed to stare back at her like silent, dark sentinels. Katie shivered.

"I have three different men's names—my dad's, my grandfather's and a great-uncle's. My grandfather and great-uncle were decorated officers in the army," Monty said after a pause.

"What about your dad? Was he in the army, too?"

"No."

"Oh, I was just wondering."

"Wondering *what*?" Monty asked. She heard puzzlement and a trace of irritation in his gruff voice, but he must have sensed there was something she wanted to ask him. Monty obviously wasn't one for small talk.

"How someone like you ever became a social worker."

"What do you mean, *someone like me*?"

"I don't know," Katie said, throwing up her hands in exasperation. "Just . . . how *did* you? What kind of a degree did you have to get?"

"I have a master's degree in social work."

"Oh," Katie replied pleasantly. *Now she was getting somewhere*. She leaned back on the dock, trying to seem casual.

"What kind of schooling did *you* get?" Monty countered.

"I went to law school and then got my master's in tax law. So . . . where'd you get your degree from?"

"What is this? The inquisition?"

"No. What's so terrible about me asking where you got your education?"

"What are you sniffing around for?" Monty snapped.

Air popped out of her lungs. "I just asked a question. There's no need to be rude." When he didn't speak for several seconds, and she sensed his frank suspicion, she sighed.

"I was thinking about going back to school. I'd like to do something where you can . . . you know. Help people."

Then it came, the snort of derisive laughter she dreaded hearing. Well, she'd just have to get used to being ridiculed. One day, people wouldn't laugh.

"*You*. Want to be a social worker?"

Katie straightened her spine and glared up at him in the chair, even though she knew he couldn't make out her defiance in the dim light. "I want to do something where I make a difference. And yeah . . . social work was one of the fields I was considering," she said defensively.

"You'd never last," Monty said bluntly. She heard a metallic sound and knew he'd opened the tackle box she'd seen earlier next to his chair.

"How do you know?" she asked. "You don't even know me."

He made a scoffing sound that told Katie loud and clear he thought he knew enough. The cricket's solo chirps seemed to intensify to a screech in the silent seconds that followed.

"You really want to make a difference?" Monty asked after a moment.

"I really do."

"Meet me Sunday morning at the diner. Eight o'clock."

"Okay," Katie agreed. She waited expectantly, but Monty didn't appear to plan on telling her anything else. She stood and started to carefully make her way back on the dock when Monty called out to her. A small flashlight blinked on.

"Here. Take this," the older man said.

Katie accepted the flashlight with a word of thanks. She could tell by his tone that Monty didn't take much stock in her proposed career plans, but she had to start somewhere, didn't she? If she was thwarted every time someone gave her an incredulous look or laughed at her, she'd never get anywhere.

Before returning to Rill's house—something she was definitely dragging her feet about doing—she found the entrance to the co-op. Olive had told her the store would be open for another hour or so. She was amazed at the variety and quantity of food offered on the farm. She stocked up on cartons of fresh vegetables, fruit, rice and freshly baked bread.

Everything was dark and quiet when she pulled up to Rill's at a little past eight in the evening. Rill's car was still parked out front, but the house felt empty to her. Where had he gone? He seemed to make a habit out of disappearing into thin air.

She flipped on the light in the kitchen. The warm glow seemed to chase away some of her feelings of alienation and uncertainty. She put away the groceries she'd bought and removed some meat from the freezer. She'd prepared a salad, including some juicy tomatoes from the co-op, and was broiling two large steaks when she heard the back door open and close.

Leave it to the scent of cooking beef to call a man home, she thought wryly.

She was a little nervous by the time she spied Rill's large shadow moving toward her from the darkened living room, but she was determined not to show it. She put two plates on the counter.

"Hey," she said, her gaze flickering over him. His dark hair looked windblown. "You been walking?"

"Yeah."

She had a vivid impression of them both studiously ignoring the chartreuse bull elephant in the room and resisted a hysterical urge to laugh. "I made you a steak. You hungry?"

He shifted uneasily on his booted feet. His expression was guarded, but also . . . pained somehow.

"You okay, Rill?" she asked softly.

"I'm fine." He came into the kitchen and made himself useful, getting silverware, glasses and napkins, while Katie removed the fragrant steaks from the broiler. Feeling awkward but determined, she asked Rill where he wanted to eat. They usually ate separately, but Katie wanted to halt that routine before it became a habit. He shrugged and nodded at the small table situated near the front windows.

The food had been good, but the conversation had been stilted and terrible, Katie reflected as she took her last bite of salad. Each of them tried twice to bring up a safe topic while they ate. Every time, their attempts seemed to be sucked into the vacuum of straining silence.

Katie had to admit, the fact that Rill'd tried, at least, had meant a lot to her.

When the awkward silence continued even as they both cleaned up in the kitchen, Katie decided she'd had enough. She was still hurt by what Rill had said upstairs. Confused. Pissed. Why did *she* have to be the one to offer the olive branch? By the time Rill had scraped the broiler clean and she'd dried it and put it away, Katie'd had enough.

"I'm going upstairs," she said quietly.

"No, Katie. Wait," he said, turning around from where he stood at the sink. She froze in her retreat and met his gaze fully for the first time that evening.

"I . . . want to tell you something," he began gruffly.

"What?" Katie prompted when he winced and glanced away.

"I'm not sure."

"Fine," she said abruptly. "I'm going upstairs, then."

"Wait a second," he said in a low but insistent tone. "Do you think this is easy for me?"

She looked at him, her eyebrows raised in sarcastic expectation. His jaw moved as though he were chewing on a rock.

"I'm sorry," he said, as if he'd just spit the rock out of his mouth.

It didn't satisfy her. Not in the least.

"For what, exactly?" she asked bluntly.

He glanced at her in surprise. "For . . . for letting it happen."

She turned and started out of the room.

"Wait . . . Katie?" he called out.

"What?" she asked, turning so quickly her long hair whipped into her face. She pushed it back impatiently. "Do you think you're telling me something I don't already know, Rill? Jesus. You can't even put it into words."

His nostrils flared in anger.

"I'm trying to apologize for 'putting it into words.' I shouldn't have said what I said before. I shouldn't have done what I did."

"Fine. Apology accepted. If that's what you want to call it." Katie added the last under her breath before she turned again and started to head for the stairs.

"Don't walk away from me, Katie."

"Why shouldn't I?" she asked, spinning around once again at his quiet but commanding voice. "You seem to find my presence unsettling somehow. I told you before I knew that. I'm *still* not going. You can apologize all you want. By the way, you should work on that hangdog expression. Pick up some tips from Barnyard, because your acting is *terrible*."

His eyes flashed dangerously. "I'm not acting, you little . . ."

"What?" she asked aggressively. "Child? Nuisance? Convenient piece of ass?"

He expression went rigid. "I was going to say *idiot*, you little idiot."

Her chin went up. She crossed her hands beneath her breasts. He inhaled in exasperation when he took note of her defiance.

"Can't you see this is a mistake? You don't *belong* here, Katie."

"Oh, yeah? When's the last time you got shit-faced?"

His expression flattened. Katie zoomed in for the kill.

"The night I got here, right? You've been sober going on two weeks now. So you know what that tells me, Rill? For this moment in time of my life, this is *exactly* where I belong." She jabbed her finger down at the chipped linoleum floor. Incredulity flickered over his rugged features.

"That's your plan? To drive me so nuts that I can't even find any peace in a whiskey bottle?"

"Peace," she repeated sarcastically. "The only reason you were so calm is you were too drunk to feel anything else."

"You're not my type, Katie," he bellowed abruptly, startling her. It took a second for the sting from his words to fully settle, but when it did, Katie was galvanized.

"You think you're telling me something I don't know? What precisely is it that you find unappealing about me? Come on, don't be a coward. Just say it!" She stepped toward him in a challenging gesture.

"You want me to say it?" he shouted.

"That's what I said, isn't it?"

He glanced down over her, burning her with his gaze. "You're too obvious, with your short skirts and tight jeans . . . all that hair. Everyone has got to drop what they're doing when Katie Hughes blows into a room like a sexed-up whirlwind. What are you trying to prove, tempting a man until he goes and does something he's bound to regret? Why can't you just give it a rest, Katie?" He made an angry slashing motion with his hand. "I can't frickin' think straight when you're around."

His words seemed to hang in the air like the vibrations of a struck gong, making her ears ring.

"Oh, I see," she said, her voice trembling. "I'm too much of a slut for you, is that it, Rill? I'm not ladylike enough. I'm not soft-spoken. I'm not *Eden*; isn't that right?" She spun around, suddenly compelled. She started flinging open drawer after drawer, rattling utensils and tableware.

"I don't think you're a slut, for fuck's sake. . . . What are you doing?" Rill asked from behind her, sounding pissed off and bewildered.

"You think I'm too flagrant, is that it? Well, *fine*," she spat viciously. Her hands settled on the handles of an aged pair of gardening sheers. She grabbed a handful of curls above her shoulder and opened the scissors.

"Jaysus fucking Christ."

He grabbed the hand holding the sheers in an iron grip. Katie just moved the hunk of hair over to where the scissors were. Rill cursed lividly and held the wrist gripping her hair, as well. His grip tightened uncomfortably on the hand holding the scissors.

"Let go of them, Katie, or I swear I'm going to turn you over my knee," he warned in a low, vibrating, thickly accented voice.

She jerked extra hard the wrist of the hand holding her hair and broke free.

"You little . . ." He closed his arms round her, forcing both of her hands down to her sides. She had to let go of her hair, but the scissors were still clutched in her hand a few inches away from her thigh.

"Drop those fucking scissors," Rill demanded.

"No." She struggled in his hold, but he held her fast, her elbows pinned to her sides. *"God*, I hate you, Rill Pierce."

But it was a lie. The realization that it was she—Katie—she loathed at that moment made her growl in pure frustration. She dropped the scissors to the floor and let her leg muscles go slack. Rill let out a stream of curses as they both toppled off balance. He was so large, and she was so small, however, that he almost immediately righted himself. He swung her into the air and began to walk to the living room with a long-legged stride, Katie's back pressed to his front and her booted feet flaying the air in front of her.

"Put me down," she shouted, but Rill's anger seemed to even exceed her own. She caught a glimpse of his rigid features and fiery eyes when he hoisted her upper body with his arms and draped her thighs in the crook of his elbow. He sat down on the couch, holding her struggling, squirming body in his lap, one forearm holding her down like a steel bar at her middle back.

"I don't believe you," he grated out furiously as he pushed her skirt up. Cool air tickled her naked thighs. He smacked the bottom curve of a buttock when she tried to slide off the end of his knees onto the floor, and then hauled her back up onto his lap. Her heart beat wildly in her ears in rising anticipation, and sure enough, his palm came down again, smacking her other buttock.

"Stop it! How dare you," she squealed when he spanked her again. Her muscles were pulled so tight as she struggled that the smack of skin against skin sounded like gunfire going off in the still room.

"How dare *I*? You were going to *cut off* your fucking hair!" Rill boomed above her. He sounded personally affronted. He made a sound of impatience. Katie went still for a moment when he grabbed both sides of the bikini briefs she was wearing and shoved them into the crack of her ass, exposing her buttocks.

"No!" she cried out when he held her firmly and raised his left hand. Her entire body tightened as he began to smack her bottom repeatedly. The blows weren't hard, but they stung. She wiggled beneath his hand at her back, trying to avoid the steady reign of spanks by making her ass a moving target. But Rill didn't seem to mind; in fact, her desperate squirming seemed to amplify the rate of his spankings.

"Stop it!" she screamed finally between pants.

When he did, indeed, cease for a moment, Katie came up on her elbows and spit her hair out of her face. Tears wet her cheeks; not tears of pain, but tears of anger and humiliation.

Her mind kept going back to those blistering moments in the kitchen when Rill had been pointing out her imperfections. Her bottom smarted from his spankings.

The bastard. Katie could only imagine how pink her ass was.

She'd noticed he'd pinkened it when he'd been eating her last night as well. The memory sent a flush of heat through her pussy, making it tingle nearly as much as her spanked ass. *Everything* started to buzz pleasurably down there.

She started when Rill placed a hand on her burning right buttock. He was so large that he held the whole thing in his hand. Beneath her lower belly, she felt his cock leap and swell in his jeans.

She craned her head around and glanced warily at his face. An intimidating snarl shaped his firm lips. His eyes blazed. Good God. She'd been right in thinking he appeared to be taking her haircutting attempt as a personal affront. He looked as insulted as if she'd just spit in his face. A feeling of shame burrowed into her awareness.

He said nothing, but he lifted his forearm from her back and placed his hand at the back of her head. He pushed until her forehead hit the couch cushion. Katie lay there in his lap, her breath coming in jagged pants, her eyes wide in anticipation as he slid her panties down to her thighs.

He began spanking her again, but this time it was different, and both of them knew it. She didn't sit still for this, either, but her wiggling wasn't entirely for the purpose of escape. She found herself waiting for the friction of his popping palm, getting excited by the taut smacking sound and the resulting prickling sensation in her flesh.

Besides, when she squirmed, she traced the contours of Rill's straining cock with her flesh.

The smacking sounds filled the room as he spanked her again and again. Finally, Rill grew tired of her frantic movements.

"Hold that ass still, Katie, or I'll hold it still for you," he muttered tensely.

Katie bit her lower lip and moaned. Her pussy was

wet. She could feel the air licking at her moist, sensitized flesh. She couldn't believe she did it, but instead of just holding still, she raised her ass in the air for him, making herself a target for his hand. He made a growling sound, low and ominous, and Katie raised her bottom another half inch in the air.

He spanked her with rapid, firm strokes. Katie tried to stop herself from moaning, but she wasn't entirely successful. As if he'd considered the sounds exuding from her throat an invitation—which perhaps they were—he released his hold on her back and spread his palm over the lower curves of both of her ass cheeks. He pressed up slightly, exposing her pussy.

He plunged a long, thick finger into her slit.

She heard his stunned curse as if through several feet of insulation. Most of her awareness focused on the sensation of him moving his finger in her pussy. She pumped her hips to get the friction she needed. She felt so hot, so damn horny, that she distantly wondered if her whole body would incinerate with a loud pop and a sizzle.

After enduring a minute of her thrashing, Rill gave a low growl of frustration and swatted her bottom again.

"Keep still."

Katie forced her muscles into immobility, but it was hard to do with Rill's finger lodged high up in her slit and her hot flesh seemingly melting around his penetration. She whimpered at the effort. Perhaps he took pity on her, even in his angered state, because he began to massage her clit while he finger-fucked her briskly.

She broke in orgasm. Jolts of pleasure tore through her. The sound of flesh smacking flesh rang in her ears as Rill stimulated her pussy and popped her ass with his palm.

It was really too much. Katie wasn't even sure what was happening, entirely, a moment later when Rill heaved his body to the edge of the couch.

"Oh!" she cried out in disoriented surprise when suddenly Rill stood and she was flying upward in the air. "What . . . the hell . . . are you doing?" she asked brokenly in confusion when for a second she was airborne. She fell back neatly in Rill's arms a second later, this time facing upward. She stared up at him in shock, her body still vibrating in anti-climactic pleasure.

He'd just flipped her in his arms like a pancake on a skillet. Rill's face looked rigid and strained above her. Was he still furious?

"If you don't know the answer to that, Katie, you're a lot stupider than I thought."

Twelve

The living room and the hallway soared past her vision. When he reached his bedroom, he lowered her to a foot above the bed and let go. He was already working her panties and skirt over her leather boots before she'd settled from the bounce on the mattress. He seemed fixed and determined. By the time he'd grabbed the hemline of her blouse and jerked it over her head without unbuttoning it, flinging it onto the floor carelessly, Katie realized with a thrill of excitement that Rill wasn't mad at her.

He was in a fever pitch of arousal.

He whipped off his flannel shirt and tore his T-shirt over his head, exposing a broad chest with a smattering of dark hair and powerful, flexing shoulder and arm muscles. He bent to tear at his laces, kicking off one boot impatiently. Katie started when he kicked and the other leather hiking boot hit the wall with a thud.

"Take that damn bra off." His blue eyes flashed at her, causing Katie to sit up as if she'd been shocked. She reached around to unfasten her bra. Excitement pooled in her belly and spread like a wave of heat to her pussy when Rill reached for his button fly.

He stood after jerking off his jeans and boxer briefs. She paused, her bra unfastened, her hair spilling around her and her booted feet planted on the mattress. Had she thought he'd been in a fever of arousal?

More like a frenzy.

For a split second, neither of them moved as Katie stared at his cock protruding from his body. Had he really gotten that inside her before? It looked thick and heavy . . . flagrantly beautiful. Her fingers itched to touch him, to hold that long column of vibrant, sensitive flesh in her hand . . . to feel Rill's life force throb beneath her fingers.

But Rill seemed to have something else in mind.

He lunged for the bedside table and opened a drawer.

"Scoot over a little on the bed."

Now that Katie had seen the evidence of his arousal manifested in flesh, she understood his brusqueness. The idea of being polite seemed ludicrous in the presence of Rill's wild eyes and straining erection. She wiggled over on the mattress, giving him room. She stared wide-eyed as she watched him efficiently roll a condom on his cock.

He tossed a pillow against the wooden headboard of the bed and came down on the mattress in a sitting position, stretching his long legs in front of him. He reached out his arms toward her.

"Come here, Katie," he prompted in a thick accent.

Katie rose on her hands and knees and crawled toward him, her gaze flickering to his condom-covered cock. It lay against his taut belly while he sat. The condom was thin and stretched very tight. His balls looked round and very full.

A frisson of wariness mingling with excitement shivered up her spine.

"Don't you dare look at me like that," Rill whispered roughly. "You're the one who wanted this, Katie." He reached and grabbed her shoulders. He pulled her toward him, his hold firm but gentle. Katie moaned when he slid her onto his lap and she felt his hair-sprinkled, rock-hard thighs whisk against the backs of her legs and wet, aroused pussy. She kicked him inadvertently in the leg during the maneuver.

"I'm sorry. I should take off my boots," she moaned.

"You're not going anywhere"—he lifted her hips with what seemed like effortless ease, even though his muscles bulged, and nodded down at his cock—"except right there. Go on, Katie. Show me this is what you really wanted."

She bristled a little at the dark challenge in his tone, but the lust buzzing in her body trumped her irritation by a long shot. Her gaze flickered to Rill's blazing eyes as she reached for him. His expression grew even tauter when she closed her fingers around the turgid shaft of his cock and lifted it off his body. He held her off him as she shifted him into position.

Katie pressed the head of his cock to her slit and let out a whimper. She could feel his heat through the condom radiating into her flesh. In the seconds that followed, gasps, moans and growls filled the air along with Rill's taut instructions. Slowly, her body gave way to his steely hardness, melting around him, welcoming him, harboring him fast.

When he was halfway into her body, Katie became aware that she was shaking. She glanced up, and saw Rill's perspiration-damp, clenched face a half a foot away from her own. He stared fixedly at the staff of his cock penetrating her pussy. Every muscle in his body was drawn tight enough to break.

It was *Rill* who was shaking; she was feeling the vibration and thought it'd been her own trembling. A wave of compassion went through her. She put her hands on his bulging pectoral muscles, bracing herself, and leaned down close to his ear.

"It's okay, Rill. Give in to it," she whispered.

She gritted her teeth and pressed down, willing her body to take him completely. A shout ripped out of her throat, but it was Rill's guttural groan that filled her ears. He sounded lost.

She sat in his lap, his cock lodged deep inside her body. The pressure of harboring him was intense, bordering on pain.

He flexed his hips up slightly and Katie moaned. The

pressure bordered on pleasure, as well. Increasingly, the slow burn dominated her consciousness. Every nerve in her vagina seemed to be firing with excitement at the hard stimulation of Rill's cock.

He shifted his large hands to her buttocks and squeezed her flesh around his penetrating penis. Katie's mouth fell open in a loud gasp. He held her completely at his mercy. Rill made a choked sound like he was suppressing a violent explosion. For three seconds, he didn't move, his dark head lowered, his chin on his chest, Katie's flesh squeezing his throbbing cock.

She sensed he gathered himself.

He looked up, and she saw that hard, focused gleam in his eyes had returned. His biceps, shoulders and pectoral muscles flexed in unison. Katie rose over his cock. They bulged even larger as he lowered her carefully, clamping his jaw as he did so. Her mouth already hung open, so when she started to keen, there was nothing to dampen the incredulous sound. When her thighs and ass hit his lap with a brisk pop, Katie braced herself with her knees on the mattress and hands on Rill's shoulder. She joined him in mounting the supreme friction.

"Is this what you wanted, Katie?" Rill rasped between grunts as his cock moved like a well-oiled piston in her pussy and Katie gasped loudly. She was quickly learning that it was hard to hold much in when Rill's cock was inside her, including air or any semblance of self-restraint.

She threw him a glance that was half anger and half pure lust as he ground her hips down in his lap and then lifted her again as though she weighed about five pounds. It should have intimidated her, how much physical control he held over her. Instead, it aroused her so greatly that she wondered if she'd sprouted a thousand times more nerves in her body.

"Yes," she told him defiantly. She drove her hips down with extra force, making their skin smack together with a whapping sound and her eyes roll back in her head. Who *wouldn't* want this?

"I thought I told you to take off that damn bra," Rill

managed between grunts as he lifted her and drove her down on his cock again. Katie glanced down at herself while Rill's cock throbbed deep inside her. The light coat of perspiration on her skin had caused the satin cups of her bra to cling to her breasts like a second skin. Rill watched her as she hastily snatched at the garment and peeled the fabric off her breasts. Her nipples were stiff from arousal. They'd deepened in color from the normal tea rose color to a pinkish red.

She felt Rill's cock lurch inside her and whimpered. He slowly transferred one hand to her middle back. For a moment, he just held her, his long fingers nearly spanning her waist, his cock embedded deep inside her and his eyes fixed on her breasts. Then he began to brush his hand through her hair, pushing the portion that hung over her shoulders behind her. When he'd gathered her hair, he gripped a large portion of it in a fist at her neck.

Even though she knew what he planned on doing, given that hot, ravenous look in his blue eyes, her pussy squeezed his cock in mounting excitement when he leaned forward and nudged a nipple with his lips, as though he wanted to feel her texture with that sensitive skin. He must have felt her tighten around him because he growled, his blazing eyes fixed on her breasts. Katie gasped when he pulled gently on her hair, forcing her head back slightly. She sat there on the staff of Rill's cock, her chin tilted back and her back arched, her breasts thrust forward like an offering.

"I tried to stop it," he said in a pressured whisper, so that Katie felt his breath against the stiff crest of a breast. "Now it's too late. I'm going to have to consume you, Katie."

A whine leaked out of her throat when he bent forward and slid the tip of her breast into his hot, hungry mouth.

Rill had long known he possessed a proclivity for carnal decadence, a potential for degeneracy. He was like a child in a family of heroin addicts who makes a solemn oath to never touch the stuff for fear of transforming into a slave to the drug. Of course, sex wasn't a drug, and he damn well hadn't lived without it since he was fifteen years old—the last year and a half being the exception to the rule. But he'd always made a point of tempering his desires . . . controlling them, always wary of the beast that resided within.

Rill had much better things to do with his life than to become addicted to sex. Or at least he used to.

As he sat there on that bed, however, with his Katie Hughes skewered to his lap and her firm, luscious breasts just inches from his mouth, Rill realized something crucial. He was *going* to fall. It was inevitable. Katie had seen to that. And if he was going to abandon all wisdom and lose himself in that pit of decadence, he was going to dive in face-first and revel in every damn moment of it.

He leaned forward and inserted a nipple in his mouth. Just like he'd known she would, she melted on his tongue. He closed his eyes and listened to Katie's low, sexy whine while his tongue laved a pebbled nipple and he sucked on prime female flesh. In a moment of greedy lust, he released her hair and scooped her breasts into both hands, planting his face between all that glory, shifting his mouth back and forth between two dark pink, distended nipples . . . drowning in need.

She shifted restlessly in his lap and Rill abruptly became aware of the uncomfortable ache of his cock. He transferred his hands to her ass and began to move her over him with subtle strokes; up on the staff of his cock several inches, back down in his lap, a delicious slight tug forward before she rose over him again and back an inch on the downstroke. Her pussy was so tight the whole thing would have been a lost cause if she wasn't also wetter than a man's hottest fantasies. One second he was carving through her clamping channel; the next she was melting around him, squeezing him in an eye-crossing embrace.

Taut, fluid friction at its finest, Rill thought mindlessly as he moved his mouth over her thrusting breasts, relishing in firm flesh, kissing, licking, biting . . .

Devouring.

She clutched at his shoulder with one hand and his head

with the other. Her moans and catchy sighs were like an audible intoxicant. Rill dug his finger into the dense, supple flesh of her ass, sending a silent command for her to ride him more strenuously. She responded immediately to his touch, reading his mind, her cries of arousal piercing through the wild tattoo of his heartbeat pounding in his ears.

Sweet, tight, vibrant, wild . . .

"Katie," he groaned, his voice muffled against a soft breast. He used his grip on her ass to pound her down on his cock with increasing force and rapidity. His heartbeat amplified until he distantly wondered if he'd pop a blood vessel.

He'd die an ecstatic man, he thought grimly. His arm muscles felt as if they'd rip clean through his skin, they flexed so hard as he fucked Katie for all he was worth and Katie returned the favor. He existed in a world of taut pleasure, fueled by the sexy sounds of Katie's cries, the vision of her breasts bouncing rapidly before his seeking lips, the sound of their skin smacking together . . . faster, faster, faster . . . until the edges of his vision went black.

He stilled her frantic hopping in his lap and held her in place while his mouth closed over a nipple. His arms wrapped around her waist, holding her captive against him. He sucked hard, triumph mingling with soaring lust when he felt her body shudder in his embrace and the walls of her pussy clamping and convulsing around him.

His cock lurched viciously inside her. Her nipple popped out of his mouth. He roared as he came.

It felt so blessedly good it hurt, but this pain was different from what he'd suffered last night. Tonight he experienced the pain of total surrender.

He'd thought he was lost when he'd staggered blindly into Vulture's Canyon more than a year ago, but Rill had been wrong. That'd been a mere detour, a bizarre drop down the rabbit hole.

Lost? He hadn't known the meaning of the word until he'd died a small death while he was buried, hard and fast, inside Katie Hughes.

Thirteen

❧

She finally caught her breath and found herself draped over Rill's body like a heated, melting confection. Her face was pressed near the hairline on his neck, her lips against his ear. His scent pervaded her—sweat, soap, musk and some unnameable fragrance that reminded her of the hills and green fields, as if all the rugby tackles of Rill's youth had hammered the fresh smell of grass subtly into his skin.

She pressed her mouth to his hairline and wetted the tip of her tongue with his sweat. She'd never known a man to show so much raw, focused strength during lovemaking. Now that she was no longer in the intoxicated throes of orgiastic pleasure, the memory of his power amazed her . . . awed her.

She dropped her head and glided her lips over a perspiration-damp shoulder, giving the hardworking muscle its due. When she bit, she found his flesh dense and succulent.

His cock twitched inside her. Katie felt his hand move and grasp the hair at her nape. With a sense of growing wariness, she straightened at his silent bidding and met his eyes. Her lungs began to burn as he pinned her with his solemn stare.

"Now it's done," he said.

She exhaled with a gasp at the sense of finality in his tone. It'd been as if he'd just spoken after they'd committed a murder together. She thought of the way he'd criticized her there in the kitchen, of his mixed desire and repulsion in regard to her.

"No, don't . . ." She whimpered in protest when he lifted her off his cock.

"I had to. The condom." He grimaced, and Katie realized his withdrawal hadn't been any more pleasant for him as it had been for her. It was a small consolation. Her spirits rallied slightly, however, when he pulled her closer until she straddled his lower belly and the tips of her breasts pressed against his chest. He opened his hand along the side of her head, and Katie was once again stunned by his largeness. He cradled her entire skull so effortlessly.

She glanced up at him. What was he thinking? Her hand rose and she mirrored his hold on her, furrowing her fingers through his dark, silky hair and palming his head.

"I know you aren't happy about it, Rill," she whispered.

His nostrils flared slightly. "I don't know what I am about it. You scramble my wits, Katie."

She looked away, mortified by the memory of what he'd said in the kitchen. *Everyone has got to drop what they're doing when Katie Hughes blows into a room like a sexed-up whirlwind. What are you trying to prove, tempting a man until he goes and does something he's bound to regret?*

"But like I said," Rill continued gruffly. "It's done. There's no going back now."

He nudged her slightly and Katie responded, swinging a leg over his body. Her heart seemed to sink like a stone to her belly as she watched him stand next to the bed.

"I'll be right back," he mumbled.

She realized he was flushing the condom. In the seconds of his absence, she began to feel uncomfortable . . . exposed. Rill made her feel beyond desirable when he was hot and aroused, but when he wasn't, she couldn't help but feel that he found her disappointing somehow.

Inadequate.

She heard the bathroom door open. Her eyes popped. He was returning. She was completely naked, but still wearing her Kit boots. She reached to whip them off, but it was too late. Rill's step was just outside the door, and she didn't want to be found fumbling around clumsily on the bed. She hastily pulled her long hair around her shoulders and drew up her knees. Her heart found the wherewithal to begin beating out a rapid warning in her ears despite all the hard work it'd done in the past hour.

Rill stepped into the room, a long, breathtaking landscape of brawn, sex and naked skin. His short, dark hair was tousled and sticking up at odd angles, just the way she liked it. The whiskers darkening his jaw looked sexy as hell, and had felt even more so slightly abrading the tender skin of her breasts. He started to reach for his bedside table and gave her a quick glance.

He froze, his hand outstretched.

Katie's eyes widened when she saw the way his brows drew together. This situation sucked. What was he thinking? She had no freaking idea what to expect from Rill in that awkward moment. She had no clue what she was supposed to do. Try to knock some sense into his thick skull? Get up and leave? Scream in frustration over his stubbornness?

He pulled on the drawer, reached and withdrew something. He dropped a box of condoms on the table. It sounded like a small bomb exploding in Katie's brain. He stood by the side of the bed, naked and magnificent, and examined her through narrowed eyelids.

"I told you not to look at me like that, Katie."

"Like what?" she asked edgily.

"Like you think I'm the big bad wolf or something. You're the one who started this. Why'd you cover yourself?"

"I . . . I wasn't sure what—"

"I told you," he interrupted quietly. Katie wished she could identify the expression on his face. She wished she wasn't flailing around in confusion like a newly blinded person. "It's done. You started this. There's nothing left for it now." A small, bleak grin pulled at his lips. "I'm going to wear you out, Katie. Now . . . move your hair." His eyes flickered down over her body. Did his gaze stick on her boots for a split second? He glanced back up to her face. "Please," he added gruffly.

Katie managed to shut her gaping mouth. "Are you still mad at me?" she asked cautiously.

He seemed to consider and shrugged. "Every time I think about you trying to cut your hair off I feel like turning you over my knee again. What the hell were you thinking, Katie?" he asked, incredulity and his accent heavily spicing his tone.

What t' hell were you t'inking, Kai-tee?

A flash of indignation straightened her spine. "What should you care if I cut it off? You'd just told me you hated it."

"*Hate* it? I never said I hated it. It's the most beautiful mess of stuff I've ever seen in my life," he scowled. "I *love* your hair."

Katie stared in shock.

"I may love it, but I want it out of the way at the moment," he said as he placed one knee on the bed and looked down at her, waiting. His posture struck her as thrilling for some reason . . . dominant and possessive. Katie sat up and swept her hair around her shoulders. His nostrils flared as he raked her body with his gaze. Katie noticed that his long, flaccid penis lengthened and swelled slightly. When she looked back at his face, she saw that he'd been watching her examine him.

"Lay back, Katie."

She leaned against the pillows slowly. She trusted Rill implicitly, but this determined, hard side of his character that she'd discovered upon arriving in Vulture's Canyon confused her. What should she expect? She'd already allowed him unprecedented liberties with her person. He'd restrained her, spanked her . . . owned her. Katie'd been restrained before during sex; she used to have a boyfriend who fancied handcuffs upon occasion. But it'd been just a mild stimulant, evoking nothing even remotely similar to the sexual arousal she experienced in submitting to Rill's demands.

Consequently, she might have been watching Rill as he came toward her on hands and knees *precisely* like he was the big bad wolf.

He straddled her, his hands a few inches from either side of her head. Even though he was on his hands and knees, he covered nearly her entire body.

He slowly started to lower over her, his eyes rapt on her face. Katie's breath caught in anticipation when his warm flesh brushed against her nipples, then molded against her ribs and belly. He pressed her into the mattress, holding her captive beneath his weight. And in a million years, she'd have never guessed what Rill would do next.

He kissed her softly . . . no tongue . . . just brushing, questing, firm lips. He sandwiched her lower lip between his, then the upper; he molded her to him and taught Katie the miracles that could be evoked from a concentrated focus of nature and a talented mouth. Her body softened and heated beneath the power of that kiss. He nipped at her lower lip and then slicked the tip of his tongue over the spot, as if to soothe her.

She stared up at him between heavy eyelids when he stopped. His penis had stiffened along her thigh and hip.

"I've wanted to kiss you for days. I keep dreaming about it," he admitted gruffly. He looked at her lips, his eyes glittering blue crescents beneath heavy lids. "Your mouth ought to be outlawed. Every time I think about how you got so good at giving head, I think I might break something. That's right, open up," he rasped when she prepared to protest.

His tongue slid between her lips. Her indignation vaporized beneath his heat. He explored her thoroughly and leisurely, as if he had all the time in the world despite the growing ache at Katie's core and her increasing focus on the smooth, stiff rod of his cock pressing against her thigh. Rill didn't seem entirely unaware of it, either. Every once in a while—far too infrequently for Katie's desire—he shifted his hips slightly while he devoured her mouth, getting pressure on his balls and stroking the heavy column of cock against her skin.

Perhaps the thing that got her craziest was that Rill allowed her free rein over his body while he melted her with his kiss. Katie greedily detailed strong back muscles, discovering every ridge and indentation between bones. For a taut, delicious minute she tangled her tongue with Rill's while she squeezed his ass. She couldn't help but remember the hundreds—no, thousands—of times she'd coveted Rill's ass in a pair of jeans. Now that ass was hers, she thought as she tested the dense muscle gently with her fingernails and then filled her palms again with curving, dense flesh; she couldn't get enough of the sensation. No wonder he could fuck with such a sublime mixture of control and force when he had these powerful muscles to do his bidding.

Rill growled softly in her mouth when she pushed down on his ass, pressing his erection tightly against her skin. It might have been a sound of warning, but Katie continued, greedy for her fill when he'd denied her in their former electric but too-brief encounters. Her fingertips explored curiously in the furrow beneath his buttocks, liking how Rill's muscles tightened and his kiss became more demanding.

After several moments of this sensual torture, Katie's bones felt like they'd been liquefied right along with her pussy. She became desperate, pressing her mons against Rill's hard body to get an indirect stimulation on her clit. It struck her as both satisfying and unsatisfying at once. Rill paused in his wicked stirring in her mouth when she twisted her upper body beneath him, stimulating her aching nipples against the crinkly hair on his chest.

He lifted his head. Katie's eyelids opened sluggishly, hating the sudden absence of his upper body and mouth. He put his hands on her waist and slid her down on the mattress several inches, breaking her possessive hold on his ass.

"Come back here," she whispered, craning her neck up, craving his mouth back on her own.

He grabbed her forearms and lifted them. She scowled
when he pinned her wrists above the pillows.

"You're a little hedonist, do you know that?" he
murmured.

"Is that another criticism?" she asked as she tried to pull
her wrists free from his gentle but ungiving one-handed
grip.

"It's another fact," he said grimly, before he leaned down
and began to own her mouth again. He kept his chest a few
inches off her breasts this time, leaving the distended peaks
without any stimulation. Her breasts felt swollen and achy,
her skin hot and prickly. She required pressure, friction . . .
release.

Her pussy was so wet she could feel moisture gathering
on her inner thighs and along her perineum. She'd likely
leave a damp spot on Rill's sheets. The thought sent a jolt
of irritation and thwarted longing through her. She groaned
desperately in Rill's mouth and wiggled her hips against his
body, beckoning him to put her out of her misery.

He responded by bringing up his knees and bracing his
upper body on one hand. He remained like that on one hand
and both knees, leaning down and kissing the daylights out
of Katie. He finally sealed their lips and lifted his head an
interminable amount of time later. Katie tried to glare at
him, but it was difficult through eyes that had crossed from
his kiss.

"Do you mind telling me what the hell you're doing?"
she asked, craning her head up off the pillow. He wouldn't
relinquish hold of her wrists in the slightest.

"Kissing you. I told you I've been thinking about doing
it for days," he said, unsmiling. His gaze flickered down
over her naked body. "I've been thinking about doing a lot
of things. Guess I won't rest until they're all done."

"I'm about to spontaneously combust down here, so do
you think you might get on with it, then?" she asked breathlessly. She was so busy eating up the sight of him. His cock
hung between them. She could see a swollen blue vein popping beneath the surface. Suddenly, a different sort of hun-

ger overcame her. She licked her lower lip and craned up farther.

"Let me suck—"

"Keep your mouth shut for once, won't you, Katie?"

She stared up at him, taken aback by the harshness of his tone. He seemed a little surprised by it himself. He closed his eyes for a second and breathed deep, apparently trying to calm himself. When he opened his eyelids, he transferred her captive wrists into the opposite hand and reached between her thighs.

Katie's eyes sprung wide when he worked his thick forefinger between her labia and began agitating her clit, bull's-eye fashion. She heard a clicking noise as he moved briskly against her lubricated flesh.

"Ohhh," she cried in delighted surprise.

"You're so wet," he growled.

"You make it sound like a crime." She moaned and thrashed her head on the pillow. It felt delicious. Heat flooded her cheeks. Her clit sizzled beneath his expert manipulations.

"If it's not a crime to drive me straight over the edge, it ought to be."

But Katie barely heard him. She was too busy gushing in orgasm.

He watched, every fiber in his being focused on the image and feeling of Katie as she shook beneath him. When her orgasmic shudders and the thrashing of her hips against his finger began to wane, he placed his hand over her entire outer sex, the ridge of his palm against her clit. He massaged her tender pussy briskly, evoking a surprised cry of delight out of her throat and more orgasmic shivers from her body.

Now that he'd succumbed to it, he couldn't help but wonder how long this greedy hunger would last.

He released Katie's wrists while he lunged for the bedside table. "We're going to need more condoms. A lot fucking more."

She paused in her panting. In his fever to get inside her

again, he hadn't realized he'd spoken his thoughts out loud. It surprised him that he felt every bit as hard, every bit as excited, as he sheathed his cock once again. *She's like Viagra in leather boots*, Rill thought grimly as he straddled her once again.

He bent her knees farther and pushed on her shins. He caught a glimpse of her glistening, pink pussy. His cock lurched. She gasped when he unapologetically arrowed his cock tip into her slit. She was so hot and wet, he glided into her, but only with effort. He had to apply a firm, steady pressure with his flexing hips. He watched his cock stretching her delicate tissues until he was lodged in her at half-staff.

He glanced up when he heard her moan.

"Are you sore?" he asked thickly.

She shook her head on the pillow. "No. No, it feels so good."

It was all the permission he needed. He let the fever overtake him once again. He'd denied it while he'd kissed Katie's sweet mouth and she'd wiggled beneath him and run her hands all over his body. He'd survived it while she'd shuddered beneath his hand and her abundant juices anointed his fingers.

Damn it if he was going to hold back a second longer. It'd been why he'd made sure she'd come before he got inside her. He wanted to see pure lust shining in Katie's green eyes, but he sure as hell wasn't in a mood to deny himself a moment longer. He ignored her hoot of protest when he gathered her wrists again, holding them down on the pillow behind her head. He drove his cock all the way into her and grunted in sublime pleasure. She surrounded him like a tight, wet fist.

"I could die in this pussy," he mumbled between clenched teeth.

"I wish you wouldn't say stupid stuff like that."

"Shut up, Katie," he replied distractedly as he began to pump.

Somewhere in the back of his mind, the realization struck

him that the thought of *this*, of being buried in Katie's pussy, had been taunting at his consciousness for the better part of two weeks. Yeah, he wanted to bury his face in her lap and live off her sex juices, and yeah, the thought of having his dick in her mouth plagued him so greatly that he'd almost had a heart attack when she'd started to suggest it a few minutes ago.

But *this* experience—he withdrew and plunged his cock back into her muscular channel, grunting in supreme satisfaction—was what had been plaguing him, haunting him. He'd become obsessed with getting his cock back into her. . . .

The thought evaporated as he thrust and drove into Katie again and again. He kept one hand on her leather boot, keeping her spread wide for him while the other kept her arms restrained. It not only was a prerequisite to restrain Katie—her small, eager hands drove him nuts—but it made him horny as hell to do it as well. He reveled in the experience, holding her down on the mattress, completely at his mercy while he fucked her with increasing force and rapidity. When his pelvis began to strike the backs of her thighs, making taut, brisk whapping noises, Katie joined in the cacophony. Little surprised *oh!*'s of pleasure popped out of her throat with each smack of flesh against flesh.

It sent him into a frenzy of lust.

"Kai-tee," he warned ominously. She was determined to turn him into an animal. His balls ached with the need to come. Her pussy pulled at his helpless cock like a hot, sucking little mouth. He released her wrists so that he could put both hands on supple leather. He pushed her knees back to her shoulders and reared over her.

"I'm starting to like these fucking boots almost as much as I do your hair," he grated out before he began to pound into her like a piston going at full throttle. The headboard clacked loudly against the wall and Katie began to keen like a steam whistle. She was small and compact, but damn if she wasn't strong. Her hips moved in a fluid, forceful synchrony with his strokes, her precision such that his eyes rolled to the back of his head. In a desperate bid to win one more second of this wild ecstasy, one more moment of control, he grabbed her hips and stilled her frantic bucking. His biceps flexed hard as he brought her to him, again and again.

He served her pussy to his cock in precisely the manner he'd fantasized about doing for tortured days and nights. It was every bit as decadent as he'd imagined, he thought as he watched himself plunge into her repeatedly.

The fantasy was topped a hundredfold when he heard Katie shout, and he felt a rush of liquid heat around his cock. Her vaginal walls clamped him tight.

It was too much. His balls pinched in a crisis of bliss. He let go with a guttural groan. His orgasm scalded him, as if his semen had reached the boiling point in his testicles and was ejected with explosive force.

A pleasure-infused moment later, he dropped those accursed sexy leather boots and fell down over her, bracing himself with his arms and panting like a madman.

"You're going to kill me," he accused without any real heat, busy as he was trying to recover from being turned inside out by cyclonic sex. She breathed heavily, but her gaze was solemn as she looked up at him.

"No, I told you. I'm going to save you."

He made an exasperated sound and withdrew from the tight, warm channel of her pussy with a wince. He came down next to her on his side and rolled her into his arms, her back to his chest. She curled up to him like a cat craving body heat. Her hair was everywhere, Rill thought as he brushed a silky curl away from his mouth. *Bloody glorious nuisance.* He grabbed a handful of it and pressed the mess of golden waves to his lips and nose.

"I still can't believe you almost cut this off," he said in a low voice as he released it and smoothed it across a curving hip. *Tried* to smooth it. It was like holding something soft and alive against a warm, silken curve. He couldn't decide which sensation he liked better: Katie's skin or her hair.

She turned her head so that he could see her delicate profile, the rosy color of one cheek and an arching eyebrow.

"Careful, Rill," she whispered. "You'll make me think you like something about me."

"If I liked you any more, you'd be at risk of being eaten in one bite."

She chuckled and turned her head on the pillow. "I thought you didn't want me to compare you to the big bad wolf."

He shifted his palm over her lower ribs and waist, capturing the vibrations of her laughter, once again appreciating how much of her body he could span with one hand. Her scent enfolded him, the light, clean, fruity smell from her hair, the subtle, addictive fragrance he'd come to prize that seemed to release from her skin when she climaxed.

It struck him as surreal, what had just occurred. This was Katie who fit the curve of his body like a seed snuggled within its shell. This was Katie he'd just fucked like he thought it was his last volitional act on earth.

I told you. I'm going to save you.

But who would save Katie from the distrust . . . the *dislike* Rill had acquired for the world since Eden had died?

Fourteen

Katie had nearly fallen asleep, feeling drowsy and content in the circle of Rill's arms. She was roused after several sleepy minutes, though, when she felt him trying carefully to extricate himself from their embrace.

"You live here, Rill," she murmured sleepily. "If you're considering doing a fuck and dash, you're out of luck. I'm in your bed."

"I'm not trying to get away," he said. "I just need to get rid of the condom."

She opened her eyes into slits and glanced back at him while he got out of bed. Her gaze was snagged by the small, sexy smile that curved his lips. A pleasant rush of warmth settled in her lower belly and pussy when she recalled those delicious minutes she'd spent under the magic of Rill's mouth.

"If you can manage to part with those boots, you could take a shower with me," he suggested quietly.

She grinned. "I think I can manage that. I usually only sleep in my boots for special occasions like this one."

His bark of laughter took her by surprise, but it was his hand swatting her ass that made her spring up like she'd been goosed. She rolled over on the bed and retaliated by doing the same to him, spanking a dense, hard buttock. She saw the flash in his eyes and started to back away immediately, laughing the whole time. The devil spark in his blue eyes, that naughty grin—those were things she associated all too much with the Rill she knew and loved. He caught her by the ankle when she tried to scoot off the bed. He yanked. She slid toward him along with the majority of the bedding.

"No, no . . ." she protested between jags of laughter. She squawked when he flung her over his shoulder. He smacked her butt again and headed toward the door.

"Quiet, woman. You'll have all the wolves in a three-mile radius howling at the front door."

Katie was laughing so hard she barely had air to protest her ignominious position. Despite his boisterous play, Rill set her down gently enough in the bathroom and even left her to her own devices as she pinned up her hair.

Once he'd started a steam going in the shower, he came up behind her where she stood at the bathroom sink. Katie met his eyes in the reflection of the mirror.

"How many of those damn things do you have to use to pin up that stuff?" he asked, his gaze following her actions with interest.

"I'd appreciate it if you stopped calling my hair 'stuff,'" she managed around the large bobby pin she'd stuck in her mouth.

He caught a rebel tendril at her neck and ran it between his thumb and forefinger, watching in fascination when it coiled again as he released the tension.

"There's even more of it than I thought . . . before having touched it, I mean," he said gruffly.

Katie went still in the process of inserting a pin when she saw the expression on his face as he studied the errant curl. A second later, she thought she'd imagined it when he turned and pushed back the shower curtain.

"I've wanted to do this for more years than you probably care to know," Katie told him a minute later.

Rill glanced up from where he'd been watching her work up a lather on his chest beneath searching, sensitive fingertips.

"*Don't* tell me you wanted to get naked with me in the shower since you were fourteen years old," he said, a smile in his voice. "That really is more information than I want to know."

Katie laughed. "No, I did not want to take a naked shower with you at some innocent age." She continued her discovery of his body, worshipping every nuance of bone and muscle. When she brushed a fingertip over a nipple, thrilling to the way the flat, dark brown disc beaded beneath her, her smile faded.

Rill, naked and wet with warm water, was no laughing matter, after all.

"But I've wanted to touch you for a while now," she admitted huskily, her eyes still on his stiffening nipple. She inhaled slowly, searching for courage.

"In fact, I've wanted you for years."

He placed both his hands on her shoulders. Katie continued to stroke him with a soap-lathered hand in the silence that followed, too intimidated to look up at him. Actually, too scared to breathe, given what she'd just admitted. When he didn't respond for what seemed like an eternity, she glanced up. Her mouth fell open when she saw the stiffness of his facial muscles.

"Are you serious?" he asked.

"I . . . Yes," Katie mumbled, confused by his intensity. "Does it really surprise you?"

He didn't speak, just stared down at her, unmoving. The water hitting the tub floor started to sound like a loud crashing noise in her ears.

"You say this has been going on for years?" Rill clarified.

Katie glanced away from his penetrating stare. "Is that so terrible? I never acted on the attraction, obviously. Not while . . . Eden was alive." She said the last hesitantly, not sure how Rill would take the mention of his dead wife while they stood together naked in a hot shower. "I know this isn't easy for you to talk about, but it's not easy for me, either."

"I had no idea," he said starkly.

She looked up at him, surprised. *"None?"*

He shook his head slowly.

For some reason, his admission deflated her. Was she so substandard as a female that a man like Rill couldn't sense her desire, no matter how hard she tried to mask it? Was she *so* "not his type" that Rill never had even considered her as an attractive woman who admired him . . . wanted him?

His expression had grown grim. Damn. Why had she spoken when all had been going so well between them?

"What's wrong?" Katie asked slowly.

He shook his head and turned, letting the warm water rinse the soap off his body.

"Don't tell me you drove across the country like this because you have some kind of a crush on me."

His words seemed to echo around in her skull like her brain had suddenly vacated it and left an empty, hollow space.

"Crush? Why do you say *crush*? What? I'm incapable of any meaningful feeling? The extent of my emotional range is a *crush*?"

"I didn't mean that," Rill replied, but Katie didn't like the way he averted his gaze.

"Well, what it is that you're saying, exactly? Because I'm pretty sick of being cast as the perpetual teenager in a *fucking* John Hughes film!"

He turned to her, obviously shocked by her explosion of anger.

"I only meant that I suspected there was some other reason for your impulsivity in driving all the way here from California. That's all. I knew you weren't telling me the whole story." Something seemed to occur to him and he straightened. "Jaysus. Don't tell me you drove all the way out here because you *planned* on this happening." He waved significantly between their naked bodies.

Katie's scalp and spine tingled with fury.

"I told you why I drove here: because you're my friend, and I love you, and I couldn't stand the thought of you here all alone, destroying yourself."

He nodded his head slowly. "And you thought offering me your body might be a way to jump-start me out of my funk, is that it?"

Anger sent her blood to a low boil. "I didn't come here with the intent of seducing you. But what if I had? Are you upset about the idea of my intentions, or are you more upset that us getting together possibly *could* be the thing to kick some common sense into that thick head of yours?"

For a moment they faced off while the steam rose around them. A shadow of uncertainty flickered across his face. He swallowed thickly, and Katie wondered if he was about to apologize. The man certainly knew how to shove his foot in his mouth. She wasn't to find out Rill's intentions, however, because at that moment a man shouted from the kitchen.

"Rill? Katie?"

Her eyes sprang wide.

Rill's expression flattened with shock.

"It's *Everett*," Katie hissed incredulously.

Five minutes later, Katie came downstairs from the dormer bedroom to greet her brother. She felt somewhat more composed for his unexpected presence than she had standing nude and furious in the shower with Rill. Rill had whispered to her to wait in the bathroom while he went out to meet Everett.

She'd taken one look at Rill's initial shocked, and then, grim expression as they stood there in the shower and knew they wouldn't be greeting her brother arm in arm.

She followed the sound of low male voices onto the front porch. The air felt crisp and cool on cheeks that were still warm from steam and phenomenal sex. Everett turned at the sound of the screen door squeaking open. Her brother grinned at her, white teeth flashing in the dim light.

"What are you *doing* here?" she demanded as she returned Everett's hug.

"I could ask the same of you," Everett replied. The hall light illuminated his handsome, classically cut jaw and smiling mouth as he stepped away from their hug. He wore jeans and a white button-down shirt. Golden-brown whiskers darkened his jaw. He'd pulled a gray newsboy hat down low over his brow, shadowing his upper face. Everett loved hats, and had a vast collection of them. Most people assumed it was an affectation, but Katie knew he wore them to hide what was perhaps his most famous feature—his tousled blond hair. He wore it relatively short, but in the front, around his face, it was so light that it caused double takes from a hundred feet away.

Not that Everett needed any help in the garnering-attention department, Katie thought grumpily. She and Everett had always been very close. She knew that most of the women alive on the planet would sacrifice their firstborn to be near Everett Hughes.

Katie's reaction to her brother's presence at that moment was quite the opposite of the general female population's.

"I came to see after Rill, that's all," she replied briskly, avoiding glancing at the tall, brooding shadow to the right of her. Rill's latest accusation—that she'd come here with the mercenary purpose of seduction in order to flip him out of his funk—still smarted and stung. She gave her brother a wry glance.

"What? You couldn't trust my judgment, either? Is that why you're here?" she asked sourly.

Everett looked politely taken aback. "Retract the claws, Katie. Mom and Dad told me about you coming out here, and I thought I'd come join the two of you. Rill's my friend. You're my sister. I needed a vacation. These are beautiful woods. What's so shocking about me coming for a visit? I need the fresh air."

"Haven't you got anything better to do?"

"Not really," Everett said pleasantly. "Haven't you?"

Katie's fake smile melted into a frown.

"Rill's made it clear how he feels about visitors. We'll just have to cheer him up a bit, make him remember why he should appreciate us," Everett blathered on amiably. Katie gritted her teeth. Her brother was playing the part of a cheerful, perennially clueless friend to perfection. Give him an English accent, have him say *old chap*, and he might be reprising his BBC role as the handsome, lovable, doltish aristocrat in *Lord and Butler*. Everett was an excellent actor, but Katie could see through this particular role perfectly.

She couldn't tell if Rill was sweating it or not, but he needn't worry about whether or not Everett knew what they'd been doing before he arrived. Everett knew, all right. He must have picked up some message in Rill's call to her mother and father; some code a parent couldn't quite catch. Hadn't Rill said something stupid to her father like Katie wasn't *safe* in the house with him?

The awkwardness of their delayed greeting likely only confirmed her brother's suspicions.

"There's not enough beds in the house," Rill said.

"It's a good thing we Hughes have skins thicker than a walrus, or we might actually get our feelings hurt by all this rudeness," Everett said.

"Speak for yourself," Katie mumbled.

"What's that?" Everett asked.

"Nothing." *Great,* Katie thought. That flat, lifeless quality was back in Rill's voice. Next thing she knew, he'd be back to hitting the bottle. Katie didn't need to see Rill's expression to know that he definitely did *not* want her to pipe up and tell Everett that he could have her bed, as she'd be all too happy to join Rill in his.

"No problem. I'll take the couch," Everett continued. "I slept on it last time, anyway; remember, Rill? There was no heat up in the upstairs bedroom. So . . . what have you two been up to?"

Katie sensed the sparkle in her brother's eye, even though her view of his upper face was obscured by his hat. Rill's shadow went entirely still at Everett's question. Rill's obvious unease in this situation made Katie want to kick one of the intact posts on the front porch railing.

"You're timing is impeccable, Everett," she said.

"That's what I've been told," Everett replied lightly, ignoring her sarcasm. "So what about it, Rill? I've had a long trip. Why don't we go down to that little pub down in Vulture's Canyon and get a beer so I can unwind a little."

"Everett," Katie exclaimed in disbelief. "Rill hasn't been drinking lately. What are you trying to do? Ruin everything?"

"Aw, Katie, give it a rest. He just wants to talk to me. Maybe I've got a word or two for him, as well," Rill said woodenly as he clomped down the front steps.

Katie glared flaming knives at her brother, but he only smiled.

"No worries, Katie. Leave it to me to take care of him."

"If you're his caretaker, we might as well purchase his casket now." She sighed when Everett smiled and gave her a peck on the cheek. "Don't do anything stupid, Everett. The last thing he needs right now is a drinking buddy," she whispered when he remained with his head bent. "He really has been doing better."

"I just want to talk to him, that's all," Everett said softly, all signs of his old-chap act gone. "I'll wait to talk to *you* in the morning about what the hell kind of stunt you're pulling."

"It's *not* a stunt."

Everett surprised her by removing his cap. He studied her, serious and somber. After a moment, his eyebrows went up in quiet surprise.

"Yeah," he whispered. "I can see that."

All her annoyance at her brother faded when he said those five words. Her uncertainty remained, though.

She continued standing on the front porch even after the two men had gotten in a car and driven down the hill.

Fifteen

"Where's Rill?" Katie asked when she stumbled bleary-eyed into the kitchen the next day and saw her brother sitting at the table reading a newspaper. Katie had glanced down the hallway when she came down the stairs and seen Rill's bedroom door wide-open, so she'd assumed he was up.

Everett set down the paper and took a swig of his coffee. Katie noticed he was wearing the newsboy hat again, a white T-shirt, horrid knee-length sweat shorts, black socks and white Converse tennis shoes. With his tall, lean body and careless elegance, he actually managed to make the ensemble look quirky chic instead of atrocious, which it would have been on any other human on the planet. If Katie thought Everett was trying to be cute on purpose, it would have annoyed her, but she knew the truth. Almost everything Everett did was effortlessly perfect, right down to the fact that he typically couldn't care less about perfection.

On one or two occasions, Katie had been known to snort with the deepest sarcasm when a friend complained of being overshadowed by an older sibling.

"Don't know where he is," Everett said. "When I was leaving for my jog I saw him disappear into the woods."

Katie sighed and padded over to get a cup of much-needed coffee. Autumn was definitely upon them now. Despite the fact that she'd been sure she wouldn't be able to sleep last night, the cool night air flowing through her window had acted like a soporific.

She was a little shocked at how well she'd slept given the tumultuous events of yesterday . . . despite the fact that she and Rill had practically set his bed on fire. Twice.

The memory caused her muscles to clench tight. Another reason she'd thought she wouldn't sleep well was that she thought Rill might come to her bedroom. He hadn't, though. She supposed with Everett in the house, he would find it easier to deny his sexual attraction for her.

"Rill does that a lot, hikes in the woods. I think it helps him to think," she said as she scuffed to the table in her fuzzy pink slippers. "I hope you didn't keep him out too late last night."

Everett gave her a sharp glance. "In case you didn't notice, Rill and I were up long before you. We had one beer, I tried to talk to Rill, and he blew me off. That was about the extent of our wild night out."

"What do you mean he blew you off?" Katie asked cautiously. Rill had seemed so resigned last night, she'd assumed he felt guilty and was planning to atone by confessing his sins to Everett. Rill could be strangely old-fashioned about sex for a Hollywood film director.

"I mean I tried to draw him out, but it was a rerun of when I visited him here last winter. I talk; he grunts a few times and generally avoids looking me in the eye altogether." Everett glanced out the window onto the gray fall day, his expression thoughtful. "Do you get the impression he's extremely pissed at you?"

"Are you kidding? *All the time*," Katie said in a beleaguered manner.

Everett caught her eye. "He seems agitated by you being

here, but I think we're talking about two different things. Sometimes I get the impression I've done something to offend him."

"Have you?"

"Not that I know of," Everett replied with a shrug. "If anything, I've been way too easy on him since Eden died. I tried to help him, he blew me off, and I let him. You did the right thing, you know. Coming out here. Mom thinks so, too."

Katie stared at him, shocked.

"Mom actually told you that?" she squeaked.

"And Dad. Both of them think you have the right idea. Rill's in a bad place. Just because he acted like a complete ass when I was here before didn't give me an excuse to get all self-righteous and bail on him."

"I thought you were going to lecture me on how stupid and impulsive and childish I was being by coming here."

Everett gave her a clumsy pat on the back of her hand. "You got it right, Katie. I'm the one who was wrong."

Knowing that her family wasn't thinking she was a complete dingbat, that she actually "got it right" by following her heart, caused warmth to flood her. Of course . . . they didn't know about the job situation yet—

"The stunt I was talking about last night wasn't coming out here to try and cheer up Rill. I was talking about the fact that you're sleeping with him."

Katie paused with her coffee cup three inches from her mouth. Dread quickly replaced the warmth in her veins. "You didn't lecture Rill about that last night, did you?"

Everett shook his head, his expression sober. "No. I don't think he realized I knew. Christ, Katie. You're not just sleeping with him, are you? You're falling for him."

"I fell for him a long, long time ago," Katie replied gruffly.

Everett closed his eyes and let out a sigh. She guessed from his reaction that, like Rill, her brother had never guessed she had feelings for Rill beyond friendship until this visit. She should give herself credit. Apparently, Everett wasn't the only actor in the family.

"He's in an awful place." Everett sounded exasperated

and worried by her revelation, but it was the tinge of sadness in his tone that made tears spring to her eyes. "He has nothing to give you right now. Rill will only hurt you, Katie."

Katie straightened her spine and took a determined sip of coffee even though she was seeing things through a curtain of tears.

"Katie—"

"I'm not leaving."

Everett looked surprised by her abrupt statement.

"I'm not leaving." Katie whispered her mantra again, meeting Everett's gaze. Several tears spilled down her cheeks, allowing her to see the tinge of awe that settled on her brother's face.

The sound of Rill's step on the back stairs and the door opening made them both start. When Rill walked into the kitchen a few seconds later, Katie's tears were nowhere in evidence. She glanced over her shoulder and attempted a smile. He looked wonderful to her, despite his obvious bad mood. His shoulders appeared even broader than usual beneath a white T-shirt and dark blue, long-sleeved chambray shirt. He'd rolled back the sleeves. Katie's eyes lingered on his strong forearms. His dark hair gleamed with moisture. His blue eyes ran over her from head to pink slippers, but his expression remained stony.

Katie'd sacrifice her life savings for a means to read Rill's mind.

"It started raining, huh?" She stated the obvious in order to break the silence.

"Yeah, a bit," Rill muttered as he reached for a coffee cup.

"It's supposed to clear up later," Everett said. "I heard it on the news on the drive here last night. We should do something fun." Everett wasn't cowed by Rill's dark, burning glance. "It's football weather, and it's Saturday. Let's find a game somewhere. Is there a college nearby?"

"Southern Illinois University, in Carbondale. You and Katie shouldn't have too much of a problem getting tickets. The SIU Salukis aren't exactly powerhouses," Rill stated flatly.

"If you don't want to go to a game, we'll just watch one on the tube. UCLA is at USC today," Everett persisted. All three of them had gone to UCLA for their undergraduate degrees. Eden had as well. Everett and Rill had been huge football fans, and the four of them—Everett, Katie, Rill and Eden—had been to a dozen or more games together, in addition to watching a countless number on television over the years. Eden was fairly shy, but she always was completely herself around the three of them.

Katie realized with a sinking feeling that Everett had forgotten a fourth person was missing when he suggested a repeat of the long-standing tradition of watching a football game together.

"You know where the TV is," Rill said before he turned and walked out of the room. A second later, Katie heard his bedroom door shut.

"Smooth," Katie said to her brother.

"It's *football*," Everett said defensively. "If football isn't safe to mention, what is?"

"Anything associated with Eden is a land mine," Katie said. She glanced toward the hallway, considering. Everett stood suddenly and clapped his hands.

"Come on. You go first in the shower and get dressed. We'll go for a drive, check out the river and the fall foliage."

With a sinking feeling, Katie realized her brother had known she was thinking about going back to Rill's bedroom.

Great.

Now Everett felt like he had to try to save both of them.

The sun had come out at around noon. It shone brightly in Katie's eyes, making her squint as she threw the football to Everett. They'd returned from their drive an hour ago. Katie had made a lunch of salad and grilled cheeses on the seven-grain bread Sherona made for the diner and also— she'd learned last evening—for the co-op. Now that Rill had told her he wasn't sleeping with Sherona, Katie was starting to feel very warmly toward the woman.

She'd knocked on Rill's closed door earlier, asking him if he wanted to join them for lunch, but he'd mumbled he wasn't hungry. Katie had opened her mouth to protest, but then she'd heard the light, clicking sound of fingers on a keyboard.

Wow.

He might be isolating himself from Everett and her, but at least he was writing again. That was a good sign, wasn't it?

She tried to convince herself it was, anyway.

"Go out long," Everett yelled. Katie ran toward the creek in the backyard, waiting for Everett's throw. Something distracted him, however, and he looked toward the side of the house. Rill was walking around the corner. He must have gone out on the porch, heard their voices and walked to the backyard. He'd removed his outer shirt. The white T-shirt skimmed his torso. His hands were tucked in the pockets of his jeans. He paused in the backyard. Katie felt his gaze on her like a palpable touch.

His head jerked back when the football struck his temple.

"Everett," Katie shouted in disbelief. She couldn't believe he'd just beaned Rill that way. It must have hurt. Everett gave a sharp bark of laughter when he saw Rill's rigid expression of disbelief.

"Sorry, mate. I didn't realize you weren't looking."

Rill didn't say anything, but something about his posture set an alarm bell to start ringing in Katie's head. He picked up the ball, stood and stretched back in one fluid motion.

He didn't throw the ball at Everett. He hurled it. Everett caught the missile, even though he wore a stunned look on his face. Rill lunged, racing toward Everett. Jagged, surprised bursts of laughter popped out of Everett's mouth as he started to run. He tossed the ball to Katie as Rill closed in on him.

"Rill, *don't*—" Katie yelled.

But it was too late. Rill grabbed Everett's waist and brought him down in a potentially bone-crunching tackle.

"Are you okay, Everett? What the hell did you do that for, Rill?" Katie demanded breathlessly as she ran up on a pile of close to four hundred pounds of male brawn. Rill's swift, furious glance silenced her. Nobody said anything as Rill rolled off Everett, stood and stalked through the yard, disappearing around the side of the house. Katie looked down at Everett, her mouth gaping open in shock. Everett just gave her an "I told you so" look.

"Why's he so pissed at you?" Katie blurted out.

"I told you. I have no fucking idea," Everett replied, grimacing.

Everett had been right. Rill may act irritated and exasperated with her presence there, but that was *nothing* compared to the explosion of pure fury he'd just shown toward Everett.

"You've got to find out, Everett."

"Mind telling me how? The man's a black box, and I ain't got the key," Everett said darkly as he stood and flipped a layer of grass and dirt off his hip. He winced as he twisted his torso.

"Everett, are you all right?" Katie asked worriedly.

"I'm fine."

"Do you want me to ask him what's wrong?"

"What's wrong is that Rill is a fucking pain in the ass." He noticed Katie's expression. He exhaled and rolled his eyes. "No, you don't need to ask him. I will."

Something caught Katie's attention from the corner of her vision—the sight of Rill's white T-shirt through a slight clearing in the trees. "Why don't you go and ask him now," she told her brother, nodding toward the woods. "He's right there, on that trail. He hasn't gone too far for you to catch up."

Everett put a hand on his ass and grimaced. "You go follow him. I'm too pissed to talk to him right now. I'm going to take a hot shower."

By the time Katie glimpsed Rill's T-shirt in the distance, she was badly winded. She worked out regularly—she took an aerobics class three times a week and a belly-dancing class every Saturday to keep things interesting—but the trail Rill had chosen went at a fairly steep incline.

"Rill! Rill, hold up," she gasped. He heard her the second time and paused on the path. As she approached him, she realized he wasn't even breathing heavily.

He also didn't exactly seem thrilled to see her. She glanced at his stony expression and blazing eyes. Was he still as angry as he had been down there in the yard?

"You walk so fast, I had to run to catch up," she said lamely as she approached. She stopped a few feet away from him and struggled to take a deep draw of cool, clear air. "What . . . was all that . . . about?" she asked between huffs and puffs, waving downhill in the direction of the house. He didn't immediately respond. Katie noticed how tense he seemed, like a coiled spring. "Are you mad at me, as well as Everett?"

"I'm not mad at you."

"Well, what *are* you, then? I can't figure you out, Rill," she panted.

"Come here." He took her hand and led her over to a large rock. He nodded pointedly and she sat. She placed her hands on her thighs and lowered her head, trying to catch her breath.

She went still when Rill reached out and touched the back of her neck. She'd put her hair in a ponytail before she went out into the yard with Everett, but the band had slipped. The weight of it pressed against her nape. He lifted the bunch of hair and Katie felt the delicious cool air tickle her neck. She shivered, her body going on instant high alert, when Rill's forefinger glided over the sweat-dampened skin of her neck.

She looked up slowly.

He stood closer than she'd realized, looking down while she tried to catch her breath. Her head was level with the zipper of his jeans. If she lifted her hands a mere few inches, she'd be touching his thighs. Her mouth fell open when she realized that the fire in his eyes wasn't from anger.

All thoughts of trying to figure out why he was pissed off at Everett melted from her mind when his fingertip trailed deliberately from her neck, brushed her earlobe, traced her jaw and then her mouth. He pushed it slowly between her lips and she closed around him. Their gazes locked. She searched his skin with her tongue and tasted salt.

"Maybe I'm mad at Everett for interrupting this," he said gruffly.

Katie blinked. She hadn't expected him to say that. Maybe he guessed her thought, because he smiled. "I told you now that it's done, I'm not going to be able to stop until this fever does. Did you think I was joking?"

She pulled her head back, dragging her teeth gently against the pad of his finger as he slid out of her mouth. His smile faded and his nostrils flared.

"I thought maybe you'd changed your mind . . . after what I said in the shower," she said.

"It *should* have changed my mind," he replied flatly. "I told myself that about ten thousand times last night. It should have changed my mind to know that I would end up hurting you even more than I'd thought I would. But it's just like I said. I can't stop now. I didn't sleep for a long time last night for wanting you."

"You don't know if I'll be hurt or not, Rill. You have to take a chance." Katie didn't know why she whispered, but for the charged, hushed atmosphere that surrounded them. Beams of sunlight danced across Rill's T-shirt and his face. A robin twittered and trees rustled in the breeze. They might have been the only two humans on the planet, as focused as she was on him. Rill pressed the damp tip of his forefinger against her lower lip.

"This doesn't feel like taking a chance or making a choice. It feels like a compulsion . . . an addiction," he said quietly. His gaze flickered from where it'd been fixed on her mouth to meet her stare. "Did Everett warn you to stay away from me?"

She swallowed. "Not . . . not like that. Not so harshly."

"So he knows," he said grimly. "He did tell you it was unwise to get involved with me, didn't he?"

Katie nodded once hesitantly.

"He's right. I'm no good for you. You deserve better."

She took his hand and kissed a knuckle. "I don't want whatever you think is better," she whispered. She placed her opened hand directly on the bulge below the fly of his jeans. "I want you, Rill."

He said nothing, but she felt the tension that leapt into his body at her touch. She traced the contours of him, the full-ness of his testicles, the shaft of his cock, which rode along his left pant leg. She glanced up and held his gaze before she leaned forward and opened her mouth. He made a low hissing sound when she bit carefully through denim at the thick head of his penis. A thrill went through her when she felt him stiffen beneath her lips. His hand opened and closed on the hair band at her nape. He tugged gently. She moaned as her mouth shifted upward, using her lips to nibble and caress his cock.

"You never did know when to keep your mouth shut, Katie," he said hoarsely.

Sixteen

$\backsim\!\!\!\!\!\!\!\!\!\!\!\!\!\!\sim$

Katie smiled against his penis. She couldn't help it. The edge of desperation in his voice had pleased her. He began to open his button fly with his free hand. Katie lifted her head and helped him. She immediately stuck her hand through the opening of his jeans, eager as a child for candy.

"Let me," he said.

She watched as he merely lowered his jeans an inch or two. He reached inside a pair of white cotton boxer briefs. Before he could pull his cock over the waistband, however, Katie impulsively widened the slit in the boxer briefs. He grunted, but Katie couldn't tell if it was in amusement or arousal. Either way, he followed her lead, allowing her to poke her fingers through the hole and find the tapered, smooth head of his penis. She laced his cock through the slit of cotton. His erection was so thick she had to work the fabric back until the majority of the shaft protruded for her consumption.

It made a decadent sight. His penis was large and firm. The head was heavy enough that it didn't typically stick out at a sharp angle from his body when he was erect. With cloth bunched up around the base, however, it was displayed ideally. Katie took a moment to enjoy the erotic sight— inches and inches of dusky, tumescent flesh. The head made her mouth water. It flared from the straight shaft into a thick rim and then tapered to the tip. She'd already learned how delicious that delineated rim felt beneath her tongue.

He was so beautiful that she looked up at him, blinking in the dappled sunlight. She smiled. His eyelids narrowed on her face. His expression went grim before he tightened his hold on her ponytail and lifted his cock to her mouth. She moaned around his flesh as he slid it along her tongue.

"How can you look at me like that?" he muttered. "You make me burn, Katie."

She was vaguely confused by his accusation until she realized he'd meant her look had been what burned him. If the state of his cock was any indication of his meaning, he'd meant her smile had aroused him. She wanted to show him how much he aroused her, in turn. She made a study of the succulent head with a pressing, stiff tongue. He made a sound of protest when she sucked and popped him out of her mouth at once. His hand tensed at the back of her head. Rill wasn't one to be polite about what he wanted, and she knew that was a good, strong suck, but she had other plans first.

She lifted the shaft of his cock and licked from where he poked out of the cotton all the way to the tip. A ripple of pleasure went through him. Katie sensed his eyes on her as she coaxed those tiny tremors out of him again and again by wetting his cock with her tongue. When he glistened with moisture, and she'd paused to examine a blue, pulsing vein with the tip of her tongue, Rill growled, low and deep, from above her. She hoped it was a warning. He tugged slightly on her ponytail and she lifted her head, blinking in the sunlight.

"Suck," he demanded.

Katie complied happily. She took him as deep as she could on her first draw and put her hand beneath her lips. He moved closer between her spread thighs. She set a brisk pace, bobbing her head over him, jacking the few inches at the base with her hand. From the sounds of Rill's grunts of pleasure, the pace and pressure were working for him. Sunlight warmed her closed eyelids. A bird twittered above her, the song striking her as sweet and refreshing in her overheated state. She entered a sublime, focused moment, her awareness utterly on the sensation of Rill's straining flesh filling her mouth and stretching her clamped lips. The scents of musk and aroused male filled her nose. With every pass of his cock, she worked him deeper and deeper. Her hunger mounted.

Rill cursed from above her. She paused with his cock sunk to midstaff in her mouth. She blinked open her eyelids heavily. He looked down at her with a blazing stare.

"Drop your hand," he said, his voice thick with arousal. Katie reluctantly dropped her hand, still staring up at him, her lips still stretched wide around his cock. "Put both of your hands in your lap," he insisted. Her brow wrinkled slightly in confusion, but she did what he asked. He glanced down to her lap. His lips twitched with amusement, but his eyes flashed with heat. She realized she'd placed both her palms faceup in her lap and wondered why that had both amused and aroused him.

His expression grew grim and determined once again, but his hands were gentle enough when he placed them on either side of her head. He held her steady and began to flex his hips, fucking her mouth with several inches of his cock. It was a little intimidating to give him control over such a delicate procedure. But she trusted Rill, and she thought he realized that as he pinned her with his stare and began to thrust into her more forcefully. It excited her, this surrender of control. She could tell by Rill's intensity and the swelling of his cock that it excited him, as well.

She sucked him as he thrust for all he was worth. Her lips and jaw began to ache, but she didn't care. Her hunger didn't dissipate. It grew. Maybe Rill saw the wild excitement in her eyes because his mouth twisted into an anguished snarl.

"I want you to take it all," he rasped.

Liquid heat seeped from her pussy. Her clit tingled with excitement. When he plunged his cock into her mouth this time, she lifted her chin slightly in his hold and sucked him strongly. The tip of his cock brushed her throat, causing her to flinch, but then he was withdrawing. His cock filled her mouth again. This time the tip entered the opening in her throat. She stilled her gag reflex with effort and drew air in through her nose. Her eyes watered. She opened them into slits. She saw only two inches of unattended shaft beneath her lips. She strained against his hand, but he let out a loud grunt and withdrew with a harsh moan. Her throat ached now along with her lips and jaw, but it was a low-grade pain that added to her excitement.

She felt alive, thrilled . . . downright *raunchy*, in fact. She'd never experienced anything like Rill's demanding, dominant nature. Since she'd never known sexual domination in such a focused form, she'd never known how aroused she'd become at the idea of succumbing to it.

"Are you that hungry for it, baby?" She heard the wonder and the thick lust in his tone.

She looked up at him and nodded as she treated the head of his cock to a hard polishing with her tongue. She could see his chest moving up and down rapidly beneath his T-shirt as he breathed.

"Put your hands behind you on the rock," Rill directed. "Lean back a little bit. That's right." She'd placed her hands behind her on the moss-covered rock. It felt cool beneath her heated flesh. Rill leaned down over her. He lifted his right hiking boot and placed it on the rock. He sunk his cock into her mouth several inches.

Her eyes went wide. He still held her head in his hands. His foot on the rock gave him the leverage he needed to thrust at a slightly downward angle. He must have read her mind.

"Shhhh, I'm not going to let you come to harm, Katie. Just push back with your head if you want me to stop," he said, his gravelly voice resounding from above her. She couldn't meet his gaze in this strange new position. She nodded once in agreement, knowing he'd feel it since he held her head in his hands and his cock was lodged in her mouth. It was intimidating. He was partially crouched over her, his leg bracing him off the rock, his hands holding her head up to his cock. Her hands braced the weight of her upper body.

She was completely at his mercy.

"It's okay," he whispered gruffly. "I've got you. Just try and relax. Ahhh, Jaysus," he mumbled after he began to plunge his cock in and out of her mouth. The leg he used to brace himself flexed as he made free with her. The whole experience felt more intense at the downward angle, more imperative.

"Let me in, Katie," he rasped after a moment.

She breathed through her nose. His cock squeezed into her throat. Tears leaked out of her eyelids, but she experienced pure triumph when her lips touched the fabric of his boxers. A shout ripped out of his lungs. She groaned helplessly at the sensation of his cock swelling. She resisted a wild urge to pull back. His cock began to spasm. He roared and she knew he was coming. Her entire world became the sensation of his hot, teeming cock in her mouth . . . down her throat.

He unblocked her throat after a moment, shooting more semen on her tongue, gasping and cursing. Katie sucked his cock while he continued to climax, eagerly lapping up his emissions.

At first, she thought he'd ejaculated less than he had before until she realized he'd shot the majority into her throat. It reminded her of doing a beer bong once in college . . . no need to swallow. The idea both amused and aroused her for some reason. She pushed up with her hands, his cock still in her mouth and irregular spills of semen still pooling on her tongue. When she leaned forward slightly, he dropped his foot from the rock and straightened, letting Katie straighten as well.

She transferred her hands to his hips. She moved her mouth up and down the shaft of his penis, loving the sound of his ragged breathing above her, reveling in the sensation of his softening flesh. Now she took him much easier. Her throat had been desensitized by his demanding possession, and he wasn't quite as iron hard. She gobbled him up, sliding him into her throat with relative ease, treasuring the little ripples of pleasure she felt in his flesh.

After a moment of this, he called her name in warning at the same moment she felt him swelling again in her mouth.

"Katie, if you keep it up, we're going to do this again."

But they already *were* doing it again, and she thought Rill knew that. She continued without pause. Her mouth hurt, and her throat felt raw, but she was a woman possessed. She slid him out of her mouth until her lips surrounded the thick rim at the base of the head. She sucked while moving her head back. He popped out of her mouth like a pressurized cork. The heavy member bounced.

"Now you've done it," he growled from above her. He fisted his cock and brought it back to her mouth. She glanced up and flashed him a quick, mischievous smile. "I ought to turn you over my knee again," he said, grinning. "But instead, you're going to finish what you started. It felt so damn good, I can't help myself. I want to feel it again."

He pushed his cock between her lips, stretching them.

This time was different, but no less arousing to Katie. He let her suck at him while he watched from above. Every once in a while, he'd talk to her softly.

You have the hottest little mouth.

How come your tongue knows that sweet spot so well?

Aw, God, you're a greedy little thing, aren't you? Greedy and so damn beautiful . . .

Yeah, yeah, right there . . . Katie, Jaysus, that's fucking fantastic.

The gentle wind blew in the trees, and the birds spoke to one another, and Katie listened to Rill's passionate anthem above her. His pleasure was her gift to him. She celebrated her ability to give it. Once again, she lost herself in the moment. She used her hand as well as her mouth, and soon he was as stiff, swollen and delicious as he had been before.

"No . . . no . . . you don't have to again, Katie; it's too much," he grated out when she sucked him hard, tempting him. When she nodded her head once again, and took him deeper, he groaned. She could almost feel the sharpness of his pleasure like a knife scraping gently against an itch that had plagued for days.

This time when he began to climax, she controlled her instinct. She kept him deep. She never swallowed, but she felt him pouring his warm, fragrant essence into her body. It enlivened her, somehow, nourished her; not just his shooting seed, but the knowledge that she could give herself to something so wholly . . . so unselfishly.

That'd been why she'd sucked him off not once, but twice. It'd been an enlightenment, of sorts.

After she'd squeezed out every drop of come he had to give her with that hot little mouth, she released him slowly. The sensation caused one last shiver of pleasure to course through him. Rill blinked dazedly when he felt her press her forehead against his hip and nuzzle him with her nose. His hand opened, releasing her ponytail. He palmed her head and stroked her scalp with his fingertips. She pressed her mouth beneath the bottom of his T-shirt and kissed the skin above his hip bone. A feeling of tenderness swept through him, the strength of it surprising him. Katie was a natural hedonist when it came to sex, but she was also a born snuggler. It amazed him to realize he not only planned to ravish every square inch of her, but he also wanted to feel her supple body pressed against his in lazy moments, to absorb her warmth . . . to hear her laughter.

Guilt swept through him when he recalled how ruthlessly he'd just treated her. Sure, it'd been a fantasy come true, but it was the type of fantasy Rill kept tightly sealed within him. When he'd been younger, he may have more openly demonstrated his dominant nature with experienced women. For Rill, however, those wild nights in bed with females whose names he'd long ago forgotten were on the same par as the nights of wild partying during his younger years. He'd considered them a thing of his past, youthful peccadilloes, something he'd grown out of when he'd married and taken on the responsibilities of adulthood.

Rill knew he wasn't like most men, who fantasized about having a constant parade of beautiful, willing women in his bed. He hadn't wanted that, even though it had been available to him in spades when he'd become a successful film director. If anything, when he'd started taking his career seriously, he'd wanted the opposite of a buffet of easy sex. He'd craved stability. He wanted a smart woman he could respect; a partner with whom he could build a stable, fulfilling life.

Maybe that was just the way of human beings, to always want what they'd never had.

Rill grimaced slightly in self-disgust and puzzlement at the brief thought of treating Eden like he'd just treated Katie. Eden's and his sex life had been decent. It'd been—sufficient. He'd been attracted to Eden's elegant beauty, but he'd never burned for her. Rill had wanted it that way. He wanted to treat his wife with respect, not hold her at the mercy of his potentially rabid sexual appetites.

Since Eden had died, his world had been turned upside down. He no longer understood the man who lived in his skin, the man who cared so deeply about Katie, and yet wanted to restrain her while he face fucked her; the man who demanded that she take his cock in her throat while he came in a rush of ecstasy and blinding need.

Rill distantly realized the birds had stopped singing. Perhaps he'd startled them with his harsh shout of anguished release when he'd climaxed. All was still in the forest but the sounds of their soughing breath.

He caressed Katie's neck and hair in the sylvan silence.

After his breathing had slowed, he put his finger beneath Katie's chin and lifted. Her head fell back. Her green eyes shone as she stared up at him. Her cheeks were flushed pink and were damp with tears. Golden tendrils of hair curled next to her cheek, escapees from the band she wore at her neck.

He touched her lips gently. They'd grown red and puffy from his forceful possession of her mouth. Regret surged through him. So did sadness, because the experience had been so potently addictive, he was sure to want to do it again . . . and again. He couldn't stop himself from wanting Katie, and no half measures would do.

"Thank you," he whispered. Before she had a chance to respond, he touched her swollen lips gently. "Do they hurt?"

She smiled beneath his fingertips. "A little."

"I won't kiss you the way I want to, then," he said before he knelt. Her lips felt warm and soft beneath his kiss. He kept it brief, and he was gentle, but he hoped she felt a small degree of his gratitude in that kiss. She'd given herself so wholly to provide him with ultimate pleasure. He'd taken advantage of her sweetness . . . her generosity . . .

. . . the fact that she'd admitted to having a crush on him.

He'd take advantage of her again. He couldn't seem to stop himself. But he wanted Katie to know that it wasn't just the fact that he was at the lowest point in his life or that he possessed degenerate genes that had made him sacrifice their friendship.

It was her—Katie—who had him spinning in a whirlwind of need.

He lifted his head and straightened, reaching for her hands. He pulled her to a standing position and began to unfasten her jeans.

"Is the rock cold?" he murmured, focused on his task.

"Uh . . . yes," she responded breathlessly.

"Would you rather stand?"

"Rather stand . . . for what?" she asked as he gripped the waistband of her jeans and lowered them over her round ass. The tiny little thong she wore would hardly have gotten in his way, but he lowered it anyway. It struck him that the air was chilly. He was still warm from multiple, boiling orgasms, but Katie was likely getting cold. He didn't want to expose her completely to the cool air if he could prevent it.

"While I make you come," he said as he went to his knees. He grasped her hips and drew her closer, eyeing the triangle of dark gold pubic hair he'd just exposed. He inhaled. A small smile tilted his lips when he caught the delicate, sweet fragrance of her arousal. He glanced up. She looked a little dumbstruck. "You didn't think I was going to leave you hanging after what you just did for me, did you?"

"I . . . I don't know. I'm just a little taken aback by your . . . forthrightness, I guess."

He smiled. Still holding her gaze, he leaned forward and slid his tongue between nectar-sweet labia. He felt her quiver beneath his hands as he gave her clit a firm rubbing. She whimpered softly when he withdrew.

"Jaysus, Katie. You're soaking wet," he rasped in awe, staring up at her. "Did it really turn you on so much? What I just did to you?"

Her puffy lips fell open in surprise. "Yes. Is that bad?"

He winced at the sound of her voice. She sounded like she'd just polished her tonsils with sandpaper.

"Aw, Katie," he whispered, moved by what she'd said and feeling guilty for the discomfort he'd caused her. He responded in the only way he knew how. He leaned forward and covered her with his mouth, eager to make up for his sins.

Because she stood, and because she wore a pair of tight jeans that he'd shoved just beneath her bottom, it was a tight, delicate maneuver. He'd rather have her legs spread wide for his ravishment, but these circumstances provided their own charms. Her jeans created a restraint at her hips. She could only part her legs an inch or two, so Rill focused exclusively on her external sex. He ran his tongue along her labia, gathering honey, carefully avoiding direct stimulation on her clit at first. She moaned and held on to his head. Her cream was delicious; musky, sweet . . . abundant. He pressed his nose between her labia and nuzzled her clit, drowning for a second in her essence. Her fingers tightened in his hair.

He lifted his head and sent his tongue where his nose had just been. He laved her clit briskly until her fingernails scratched his scalp. The tip of his tongue struck again and again, darting between tender folds, beating against that sensitive morsel of flesh like a metronome.

He heard her cries and felt the sting of her tugging at his hair, but he continued his assault on her senses. He held her buttocks in his hands, not allowing her to stray an inch. She cried out sharply when he turned his head and sucked her clit between the seam of his lips. The darting motions of his tongue resumed against her captive clit. He heard the desperation in her raspy voice as she leaned into him and called his name.

Her ass tightened in his palms as she began to shudder in orgasm. He held her tightly to him, continuing to stimulate her while she came. Her knees seemed to weaken, but he gladly took a measure of her weight, loving how it made him experience even more of her pleasure vibrating into his hands. Thoughts of her tight, clamping channel tortured him while he nursed her through her orgasm and the scent of Katie's pleasure surrounded him, an intoxicating perfume.

He couldn't wait to get back inside her.

A feral sense of possession overcame him. If Everett hadn't come and ruined everything, Rill thought, he might have spent the majority of the past night and day with his cock buried in Katie.

Once her trembling had stopped, he lifted his head and moved his hand between her thighs. He grunted in male appreciation when he felt just how soaked she was. He wetted his finger in her creamy lubricant by lightly stimulating the opening of her slit. A postorgasmic shiver coursed through her at his intimate touch.

He withdrew his hand and glanced up to meet her gaze. Her eyelids were half-closed. She looked sex-drugged, dazed . . . indescribably beautiful.

He pushed back one of her bottom cheeks and pressed his lubricated fingertip to her rectum. Her body, which had previously grown warm and supple from orgasm, tautened.

He didn't know why he did it. Or maybe he did. All control had been lost to him. He'd gone feral. He wanted Katie to know it. His nostrils flared as he watched her while he pushed his finger in her ass. She was tight and smooth and so hot he gritted his teeth. He saw a trace of puzzlement shadow her features. Her cheeks flushed pinker.

"Don't look surprised," he whispered. "There's no going back. I'll have all of you, Katie. Eventually."

Her lower lip fell open. A chilly breeze whisked past them and rustled the trees. Katie shivered like the leaves. He leaned forward and placed a kiss on her fragrant mound. She didn't speak, and neither did he, when he withdrew his finger, stood and helped her to pull up her jeans, covering her from the bite of the wind. After he'd straightened his own clothing, he grabbed Katie's hand and made to start back down the hill.

"Rill? You'll talk to Everett, won't you? About what's bothering you?"

He paused and briefly closed his eyes at the mention of Everett's name.

"Rill? What *is* it?" Katie asked, clearly mystified and concerned.

"It's okay," he lied. "I'll talk to him when we get down to the house. Just do me a favor, okay?"

"What?" Katie whispered.

"Don't *you* talk to him, at least for a little bit. If he hears the state of your voice, he'll probably skin me alive. And I can't say I'd blame him."

"Don't be ridiculous." She gave a hoarse laugh. "I'm a thirty-year-old woman."

"And you're Everett's little sister," Rill countered matter-of-factly. He kissed her knuckle, silencing the protest on her tongue. Still holding her hand, he led her down the hill.

Seventeen

Rill stood in the kitchen, listening to the televised football game in the living room and the sound of Katie's feet on the stairs. He'd make it up to her later for his selfishness up there in the woods. For a few seconds, he wished he could join her right that second in the dormer bed.

He didn't really want to *talk* to Everett.

He wanted to beat his face in.

Rill sighed heavily, banking his temper. In truth, he was nowhere near as furious with Everett as he had been last winter when he'd visited. It'd been nothing short of a miracle that he'd managed not to pulverize Everett at some point in his three-day stay in the house.

It was time to lance this wound, once and for all. The fact that it didn't fester anywhere near as much as it had a year and a half ago somehow didn't reassure Rill that much.

What if talking to Everett made everything a hundred times worse? There was always that chance, which was exactly why Rill had chosen a year ago to simmer in a pot of suspicion, confusion and anger versus confront Everett.

Uncertainty had its merits.

Once he knew the truth, it couldn't be taken back. For the first time, though, Rill thought he could handle it. The truth didn't have the potential to scald his consciousness as much as it had in the past.

"Hey," Everett called out when he walked into the dim living room. "We're down by seven points."

"Great," Rill murmured distractedly. "Do you think I could talk to you?"

"Sure," Everett said, looking surprised and a little wary. He wondered if Everett was recalling Rill tackling him in the yard, but he didn't apologize. Everett hit the remote control and the beer commercial winked off.

"Not in here. Can we go out on the porch?"

"Yeah, no problem."

Everett strode ahead of him. "What's up?" he asked Rill once they'd both sat down on the wrought-iron chairs.

Rill opened his mouth to start, but couldn't get the words out. He stared out at the golden fall day moodily.

"Just go ahead and spit it out, Rill. I know you're pissed at me. If my bruised hip isn't proof enough, the fact that you haven't been able to look me straight in the eye for a year and a half now has clued me in. I assumed you were mad at the world, but now I get it. It's me in particular, right?"

Rill didn't deny it, even though what Everett said was only partially true. He wasn't too thrilled with the world in general at the present time, but he'd reserved a special place of distrust for Everett.

For the first time in more than a year, he stared at Everett . . . really tried to *see* him. Everett met his stare steadily, without a trace of guilt. Everett was a good actor, though. One of the best on the planet. Suddenly, the question was there in his throat, burning him. There was no turning back.

"Were you sleeping with Eden?" burst out of his mouth.

For a surreal moment, he wasn't sure he'd actually spoken the words. The question had rolled around in his mind so long now, perhaps he couldn't tell the difference between the real question and the imagined one. Everett's blank expression only increased the sense of unreality.

Finally, Everett blinked his bluish-green eyes as though he tried to bring Rill into focus. "What did you say?"

"You heard me," Rill rasped. "Were you sleeping with Eden? Before she died?"

Everett gave a disbelieving bark of laughter. Rill should have been glad to have seen his sheer incredulity, and he did feel *some* relief. Everett may be a great actor, but he wasn't sure that even Everett Hughes could pull off that genuine of an expression of utter and complete shock.

His friend hadn't betrayed him. Rill's anger and confusion only mounted, though. The idea of Everett sleeping with Eden had been a bitter pill, but at least it was an understandable scenario . . . something he could wrap his mind around.

"*That's* what this is about?" Everett asked. "Jesus, Rill. *No.* The answer is no. Why the hell did you even *ask* me that?"

Rill stared at Katie's Maserati parked in the drive, but he didn't really see it. His mind was filled with the image of the coroner who'd told him the truth a year and a half ago, the day after Eden had been killed.

"She was pregnant. When she died. Eden, I mean," Rill said hoarsely.

The words just hung there; even the crisp, pristine forest air couldn't seem to dissipate the toxicity of them. He didn't look at Everett, but he sensed his deepening incredulity.

"And . . . and . . . from what you just said, I gather it wasn't yours?" Everett asked.

Rill shook his head. "I had told you we'd been fighting."

"Yeah, I remember you mentioning that she was feeling neglected," Everett said after a moment, sounding disoriented. "I knew she wasn't thrilled about you being out of the country again to film *An Elegant Heist.* You always asked her to come and stay with you on location, but she never wanted to. I didn't know things had gotten that bad between you two, though."

Rill's glance flickered over Everett's face. He looked like he'd just been clobbered. Rill sighed heavily and collapsed back in the chair. "That makes two of us who didn't know. I thought things were bad, but nowhere near as bad as Eden must have thought."

Neither of them spoke for a minute. Rill sensed Everett waiting patiently for him to continue.

"We hadn't slept together for close to half a year before she died. She never wanted to. Still, I hadn't given up hope. Not completely. Still hadn't, up to the point I got the phone call about the car wreck."

"Jesus," Everett whispered.

"The coroner told me she was three months pregnant when she died," Rill stated flatly. "When he mentioned it to me, he had all this sadness and compassion in his eyes. He'd assumed it was my child."

They both sat in silence for a moment. Rill suddenly felt exhausted, like he could sleep for a week.

"Why did you think it was me?" Everett asked.

Rill shrugged. "You knew Eden. She was reserved. Shy. She hardly was a social butterfly. If she wasn't at the museum, she was at home in her garden. Her only good friends were you and Katie." He glanced over at Everett. On this side of having asked the question, Rill realized the full impact for the first time of wrongfully suspecting his friend. "I'm sorry," he said truthfully. "The fact of the matter is, I'm glad it wasn't you, but—"

"But *what*?" Everett asked. Rill heard the trace of anger in his voice and, deep down, was glad for it. He deserved Everett's animosity for having judged him all these months without offering him a chance to proclaim his innocence.

"At least if it was you, I could have understood," he said gruffly. "Things were falling apart for Eden and me. If she'd turned to you for comfort, at least it would have made sense to me. She loved you as a friend. You would have treated her decently, at the very least. Better than I did."

"You treated Eden like a queen."

"Apparently she didn't think so. But that's not the point. I hated the idea of you two being together, but like I said, it made sense. I left a hole in her life, and you could have filled it. It's not like every damned woman in the country wouldn't want to be with Everett Hughes."

"That's bullshit, Rill. It's not fair, and you know it. Eden cared about that crap about as much as I do," Everett said bitterly.

Rill closed his eyes.

"Yeah . . . yeah, it is. Unfair," he mused after a moment. "It was wrong for me to assume it was you."

Neither of them spoke in the charged silence that followed. Rill wouldn't have been surprised if Everett left in an offended huff, or punched him, or did just about anything, really. He didn't have the energy to try to explain to him his confusion and his regret and his anger. It wasn't Everett's problem; it was his—Rill's.

Everett sighed heavily. "Jesus fucking Christ," he mumbled. "I wish you would have just asked me a year and a half ago."

"Then I would have been right here a hell of a lot sooner. Maybe I didn't want to have to think about who she was sleeping with if it wasn't you."

Everett started to speak, seemed to see Rill's point, and cursed under his breath.

"I can't believe Eden did that," Everett said.

"Yeah . . . well, she did," Rill replied quietly. "And I'll probably never know what her life was like during the months before she died. I was off doing my own thing. Maybe she had a right to find happiness somewhere else . . . somewhere close by, where she needed it."

"It sucks. No matter what your problems were, she shouldn't have done that. She should have been honest with you, at the very least. There's no justification for it. And what a fucking way to find out. You must have been plowed under," Everett mumbled.

Rill found himself assessing how he really did feel at that moment. What he experienced was no longer the lancing pain of betrayal, just the fading ache of regret. He hadn't realized until recently how much fantasy had gone into his speculations about Eden's last days. He'd likely never know the truth, never know whom her lover had been, whether or not she'd been happy or miserable. Now that he'd confronted Everett, he understood that never knowing the identity of Eden's lover was nowhere near as bad as discovering his suspicions about Everett had been correct. He'd lost Eden as a wife long ago. Her death had been another blow.

Losing his best friend, as well, would have really sucked.

Everett dug his fingers into his eye sockets and shook his head, as though he was trying to clear it. "Damn. I could use a drink."

Everett blinked open his eyes in time to notice Rill's wry glance. He started to laugh.

"I guess you've had a similar desire for the past eighteen months," Everett said between jags of laughter.

"You might say that." Rill chuckled mirthlessly. It felt good to laugh with Everett again. Really good. "Only my need for a drink was about a thousand times stronger."

"Well, Katie's pretty much declared prohibition around here, so—"

Rill sobered when he saw Everett's amusement abruptly fade midsentence.

"Jesus," Everett said.

"What?" He was surprised to see anger reenter Everett's face.

"Damn it, Rill, you'd *better* not be fucking around with Katie to get back at me because you thought I slept with your wife."

"What?" Rill snapped, offended by the unexpected accusation.

Everett pointed at him, eyes blazing. "You just told me you thought I'd been sleeping with your wife . . . that I got her pregnant, for fuck's sake. I have every right to ask you if you've been sleeping with Katie out of some kind of twisted bid for revenge."

He just stared for a second, dumbstruck. "That's ridiculous," he boomed finally. "Katie doesn't have anything to do with this."

"Yeah?" Everett challenged. Rill hadn't even realized

they'd both stood until Everett took an aggressive step toward him. Rill didn't want to fight with Everett—not anymore—but he held his ground. "Well, you'd better make damn sure of that. Katie's fallen for you."

"She *thinks* she has. But—"

"She's fallen for you, Rill. Hard. She's vulnerable right now. If you're taking advantage of her, if you hurt her, you're going to be dealing with me. Not just me. Stanley and Meg, too."

Rill frowned, thinking Everett was fighting dirty by bringing up his parents. He stopped himself from retaliating when he remembered how he'd flattened Everett in the back-yard earlier.

Everett's eyes flashed a dire warning before he stalked off the front porch toward the woods.

Rill just stood there, replaying the past few minutes in his mind. How could it have gone from bad to good to shit again so fast? Everett had a lot of fucking nerve, accusing him of sleeping with Katie for such a mercenary, cold-blooded reason. Sure, he'd suspected Everett of something nearly as bad, but at least he'd never believed that Everett was fucking with Eden to shaft Rill behind his back.

Where did he get off?

There wasn't an ounce of truth in his accusation. Rill would never do something to intentionally hurt Katie.

Would he?

He stood there on the porch alone, playing devil's advo-cate with himself.

No.

You'd never intentionally hurt her, but chances are, you'll hurt her in the end.

He thought of her sitting on that rock and looking up at him with that sublime smile. He recalled—in graphic detail—how she'd given him so much pleasure so unself-ishly . . . how she'd met all his demands, even surpassed them . . . how he'd let her . . .

. . . how he'd loved it.

"Jaysus," he muttered gruffly under his breath. He walked

back into the house. The sound of the shower running penetrated his volatile thoughts.

He didn't know why he did it, for sure. He walked down the hallway in a daze and opened the bathroom door. Warm, humid air struck his face. He could see the shapely shadow of Katie's body behind the ivory shower curtain. She started when he whipped back the curtain. She blinked in surprise.

Rivulets of water ran down smooth planes and curves that Rill knew fit his palms perfectly. He itched to touch her. Her nipples were relaxed and pink, large and succulent from the heat.

"Rill?"

He unglued his eyes from Katie's beautiful breasts and glanced up to her face. He felt like everything had gone into slow motion.

"Do you want to get in with me?" she asked breathlessly.

Hell *yes*, he wanted to get in with her.

"No," he said.

She looked confused, but smiled. "Then what are you doing?"

Good question, Rill thought. What the hell was he doing? Why had he subjected Katie, of all people, to his chaotic state of mind and volatile libido? Better he'd chosen a stranger to work through this—or even a prostitute—than Katie Hughes.

He just stood there on a knife-edge, because despite his thoughts, he experienced a nearly overwhelming desire to put his hands all over her wet, naked body. He longed to carry her out of that bathroom, lay her on his bed and lick every drop of water off her skin. The need to bury himself in her and lose himself in a nirvana of pleasure was so strong, so sharp, it felt like it'd choke him.

"Rill?"

"I just wanted to look at you," he said stupidly. He caught a brief image of her bewildered expression before he flicked the shower curtain shut, depriving himself of the sight of her.

He went into his bedroom and shut the door. His cock

tingled. He lay on his back on the bed and stared up at the ceiling, willing his arousal to cool. His cock only stiffened and swelled, though. He couldn't erase the image of Katie from his mind. What the hell was wrong with him? He'd had two thunderous climaxes barely an hour ago, and here he was, chubbed up and horny for her *again*?

He felt a little desperate when he went over to his desk and jiggled his computer mouse. The screenplay he'd started came up on the screen.

At least he knew now why he'd walked into that bathroom. It'd been a personal challenge. He'd needed to stand in the presence of pure temptation and walk away.

He thought of what Everett had accused him of out on the porch. He saw Katie standing in the shower, warm and supple and naked.

Do you want to get in with me?

He grimaced and sat down in the desk chair. It hadn't been much of a personal triumph, really. It was useless to think he could resist Katie for long. He'd been blaming Everett in his mind for the worst kind of betrayal, but it was Everett who should have chosen a more worthy friend.

His fingers began to fly across the keyboard.

Eighteen

Katie felt like the only cheerful person at a funeral. She made chicken fajitas for dinner, even preparing a home-made salsa from the tomatoes, corn, peppers and fresh cilantro that she'd bought at the co-op. For all her efforts, she might as well have served Rill and Everett cardboard for dinner. Rill barely looked at her, wolfed down his meal, cleaned up his dishes and retreated once again to his bed-room. Everett was nearly as bad, but instead of not looking at her, she'd catch him examining her while she ate like he suspected she'd caught a fatal disease or something.

"Everett, why do you keep looking at me like I'm sick?" Katie hissed after Rill had left the kitchen.

"I'm not looking at you like you're sick."

"You are so. What's going on? Did you and Rill have a fight this afternoon? He's acting very strangely." She glanced down the hallway uncertainly. "Although he is writing again. That's a good thing, isn't it?"

Everett grunted and closed the dishwasher.

"What is *wrong* with you?"

"My hip hurts like hell, if you must know," Everett responded tetchily.

Katie sighed. "I'll get you some Tylenol. I knew it was worse than you were letting on."

If she thought she was going to get anything more that night out of her brother or Rill, she'd been wrong. Everett took his Tylenol and was soon asleep on the couch.

Rill never came out of his bedroom.

Katie stood outside Rill's door for nearly a full minute, undecided about whether she should knock or not. She knew Rill wasn't comfortable with the idea of them having sex. Now that Everett was here, he was only more conflicted about his desire for her. She'd read that conflict like a flashing neon sign on his face when he'd stared at her in the shower earlier.

Well, she wasn't going to beg. She had *some* pride left.

Despite a restless night, she sprang out of bed the next morning at six, excited for her meeting with Monty. It was a crisp, crystal-clear fall morning. Technicolor leaves shivered in the trees and formed a thin carpet on the ground. Neither Rill nor Everett had stirred by the time she left the house at seven thirty.

She picked up the paper sack she'd placed in the passenger seat before she got out of her car and headed for the diner. Barnyard was scratching his ear with his hind leg when she approached the door. His pumping leg paused and he looked up at her with doleful brown eyes.

"Come here, boy," she said softly. He wolfed down the leftover chicken from their dinner last night. He looked up at her soberly as she fastened a flea collar around his neck. "There you go. No more itchy fleas."

The diner was as crowded as Katie had ever seen it and smelled of bacon and maple syrup. Even though Katie was early, Monty was already there, reading his paper and making a good dent in a stack of pancakes. He lifted one shaggy eyebrow when she slid into the booth across from him.

"You came, huh?"

"I said I would, didn't I?" Katie replied loftily. Her attention was on the group of twenty or so people toward the rear of the diner. "Is Olive running a meeting?" Katie asked, nodding toward Olive, who was speaking now while the rest of the group listened.

"Yeah, it's most of the folks from the co-op and the Trading Company. Two big things on their meeting agenda today—the same two big things that are *always* on their agenda," Monty said. He noticed Katie's raised eyebrows and explained further. "One—how to stop that damn gambling boat. Ol' Marcus Stash over there"—he nodded at the weird guy with the buzz cut who worshipped Sherona— "he's going to birth a heifer the day that boat opens. Two— they're trying to figure out a way to get the word out to the world about Food for the Body and Soul. My Olive, she's the one who's always pushing for that."

Even though Monty's voice sounded just as gruff and brusque as usual, Katie felt warmer toward him for saying "my Olive."

She nodded toward the group. "Marcus Stash? What's that man do for a living?"

"Stash used to be an Army Ranger, years back. Real patriot. He's got a piece of land he raises sheep on. That farm's passed down to him from generations of Stashes. Solitary type, Stash is. He used to be okay, but this riverboat business knocked a screw or two loose, if you know what I mean. Or maybe those screws were rattling around in his skull since he returned from the army. I never did completely believe the honorable discharge line of crap he sold people around here."

"If he's so solitary, how come he's always in this diner?" Katie asked, even though she thought she already knew the answer.

"I'm guessing there's something about this diner he likes an awful lot," Monty replied blandly.

Sherona was standing next to Stash, listening to Olive and holding a coffeepot. Stash put a hand on her hip. Sherona jumped slightly and looked over at him. She smiled as she refilled his cup, but Katie decided Marcus Stash's infatuation was unrequited. Maybe Sherona had finally declared Rill a lost cause, but she hadn't transferred her affections to Stash.

Katie beamed at Sherona when she approached the table.

"Hi, Sherona. Nothing for me. Oh, but if you'd get me another loaf of that delicious seven-grain bread, we could sure use it."

"Sure thing. I hope that means Rill is eating a little better."

"I'm trying," Katie said. Maybe she'd been wrong in thinking Sherona had designs on Rill when she'd first come to town, but she didn't think so. She had a sneaking suspicion that if Rill had shown an ounce of interest, Sherona would have been all over him.

Sherona filled Monty's coffee cup and went behind the counter. Stash's face was turned toward Olive, but his eyes followed Sherona as she put Katie's loaf of bread in a paper sack and set it on the counter for Katie. The guy was seriously infatuated.

"So . . . why'd you tell me to come here, Monty? You said it was something I could do to make a difference," Katie said. Her curiosity had been mounting all weekend.

Monty stuffed a forkful of pancake, butter and gooey syrup into his mouth and reached for his wallet. He threw some bills on the table and pointed to the diner door. "Easier just to show you. I'll drive."

"Is this where one of your clients lives?" Katie asked five minutes later when they pulled into a decrepit-looking trailer park. Her confusion and curiosity were rising by the second, but she'd guessed Monty was a "show, don't tell" kind of a guy, so she hadn't badgered him with questions in the car.

"Joe Jones *is* one of my clients, actually. His trailer used to be down by the river. When he sold his land to Miles Fordham, he moved it here," Monty replied before he brought his car to a halt. He glanced over at Katie while she stared out the window at the nearest trailer home. The top of it had started to cave in, so that the roof resembled a flattened letter *M*. At one time, the double-wide had been blue and white, but dirt and time had turned the white a dingy gray. There were about fifteen bags of garbage scattered on the plywood front porch and the tiny front yard.

"Thinking about changing your mind already?" Monty asked nonchalantly.

"Of course not," Katie said, stung. "But I would appreciate you at least telling me what you want me to see here."

"Joe Jones needs help with his taxes."

"What?"

Monty nodded, impervious to her incredulity. "Yeah, believe it or not, a lot of poor people need help filing their taxes. More so than those hotshot movie stars you worked for need assistance with them. At least most of them know how to read and could figure out how to file a return if they weren't too lazy to pay you so you could finagle ways for them to save all that money. Maybe they never told you in that slick Hollywood tax school that every American has to file a tax return if they have income, regardless of whether or not a body has the ability to read, or write or understand just what it is they're agreeing to with an *X* on the dotted line?"

Katie flushed. "Of course I know that. So . . . you want me to do Joe Jones's taxes for him? That's how you said I could make a difference?"

"I figured it couldn't hurt to ask you. Truth is, the community center where I work has just been given a state grant for a financial and tax assistance office. It's muchneeded. Prairie Lakes County has one of the largest rates of illiteracy in the state. You get men like Miles Fordham who come into Vulture's Canyon and start offering people like Joe here a pittance of money for their land, and the need for some sound financial advice for the poor rises exponentially. From what I hear about you, you'd be a good fit for the job. If you haven't already decided it's beneath you, that is."

Katie reached for the car door. It hadn't been what she expected . . . but hell. Why not?

"Let's go," she said.

An hour later, Katie and Monty got back into Monty's car. It'd been a heartbreaking experience, no matter how Katie spun things in her mind. The trailer home had been a hovel, and Joe Jones had been a sweet, broken old man with no front teeth and a proclivity to smile at everything that was said to him, despite the lack of any understanding in his rheumy blue eyes.

She'd come close to tears upon seeing the bill of sale and the amount of money Miles Fordham had paid Jones for his land. True, she didn't know the going rate for land around here, but the casino complex Fordham was building would increase the value of the land a thousandfold, if not more so. He could have at least offered Joe a decent amount for the valuable land, something that could have improved the quality of his life a bit.

Instead, he'd stolen the old man's sole asset right out from under his nose. The fact that it'd all been legal made it no less criminal in Katie's eyes.

She had politely asked Joe if she could assess all his financial records, which he'd brought to her in a cardboard box that was falling apart at the seams.

"Do you want to see my granddaughter's papers, too?" he'd asked eagerly.

Katie had assured him that she'd need only records associated with his own income in order to file a return. She'd gone through every piece of paper in the tattered box while Joe and Monty sipped coffee and talked about the fish they'd caught over the summer. Afterward, Katie had told Joe she'd return on Tuesday afternoon to assist him in filling out the tax form that had never been filed that year. After the sale of the land, the IRS would come knocking when they realized Joe hadn't paid his taxes. Joe had seemed so grateful for her offer that it'd made Katie feel guilty for not being there a year ago to give him the advice he'd sorely required when he sold his land.

She'd seen his bank statements. After he paid his taxes, it'd be a close thing whether or not he had any money to live on. Katie grimly informed Monty of that fact as they drove back to the diner. Monty sighed.

"I had a feeling you were going to tell me that," he said wearily. "Joe's granddaughter has had her fingers in that till ever since Joe got the money, and little Amber's got some highfalutin tastes."

"Joe's granddaughter is Amber Jones? The girl who works for Miles Fordham?"

Monty gave her a knowing look from beneath heavy eyelids. "That's the one," he said.

Katie stared out the window thoughtfully.

"So what do you think? There are lots of folks like Joe Jones all over these woods. Do you want to come by the community center and fill out an application for the job?"

She thought of her life up to now, of her flight across the country, of these beautiful woods . . . and Rill. She thought of the emptiness inside her that she'd finally determined she had to fill, or die trying.

"You know . . . I really would,' she replied softly.

He grunted, and Katie had the impression she'd just passed muster with Montrose Montgomery.

When Katie returned she found both Rill and Everett at the side of the house, splitting logs. She paused for a few minutes and observed them before they became aware of her presence. She sensed by the way they silently worked in tandem—one retrieving the log and placing it, the other chopping, pausing occasionally to mutually gather the split logs and then switch places—that they must have worked through the snarl in their friendship.

Her gaze lingered on the sight of Rill heaving the ax. Even his ass muscles flexed tight before he split the log neatly. The fact that he hadn't come to her bedroom last night once again caused her to ache. How was it possible to miss so greatly something she'd never had until recently? She waited until the ax was resting against the chopping block before she approached.

"Morning, He-Men."

"Where did you go so early in the morning?" Everett asked as he tossed a log on the neatly stacked pile. Rill's gaze raked over her before he met her stare. She tried to ignore the little prickles of excitement his glance evoked, but it was difficult.

"Oh, I was just down at the diner," she replied evasively. She'd tackle telling her family and Rill about her new job if and when everything was certain and settled. It wasn't cowardice. Not really. She just wanted to make sure about things first. It wasn't as if she officially had the job yet, after all.

"So did you bring us something to eat from the diner?" Everett asked single-mindedly.

"No."

Rill cocked his head. "You were down at the diner? On a Sunday morning?"

"Yeah," Katie replied, uncertain about his narrowed gaze. He glanced over her again, and this time she sensed more than heat in his assessment.

"Why are you dressed like that?" Rill asked.

Katie looked down at herself. She hadn't wanted to show up for her meeting with Monty dressed inappropriately, but since she hadn't known why he wanted to meet with her, she hadn't really known what "appropriate" was. She'd chosen a brown skirt, brown leather high-heeled boots, a crisp white shirt with a wide collar and a tailored Burberry jacket.

"You look like you were on a job interview," Rill continued, his dark brows knitted together in puzzlement. His piercing glance seemed to slice right through her discomfort at his astute observation. "You haven't let Olive Fanatoon and her co-op crowd recruit you to their cause, have you?"

"No, I haven't," she bristled. How could he be so attractive and so insufferable at once? "How did you know Olive and those people would be down at the diner?"

He gave a negligible shrug and bent to pick up the ax. "Because Olive has asked me to attend their Sunday meeting practically every weekend since I came to Vulture's Canyon."

Katie forgot her embarrassment. "She does? Why?"

"She seems to think that if I were a spokesperson for their cause—Food for Body and Soul—they might get a lot more publicity."

"Oh, she wants a celebrity spokesperson," Katie murmured. It shouldn't have surprised her, of course. She was used to every charitable organization under the sun vying for celebrity attention, both from her work experience and her private life. As a popular film director, Rill got his share of pleas for endorsements, time and money, although Everett was the one who was besieged constantly. Katie did Everett's taxes, so she knew for a fact how much he gave back to the community and various charitable organizations. Rill gave just as generously, even sponsoring a valuable scholarship program at UCLA in the film department. The scholarships were all done through a trust, so the program had continued since Rill had holed up in Vulture's Canyon. Still, Katie found herself wondering about Olive's pleas for help.

"And you don't want to do it, obviously . . . help out Olive and Food for Body and Soul, I mean?" Katie persisted.

"Obviously," Rill replied.

"Because it might do you some good, to get involved with something," Katie observed, unaffected by his blue-eyed glare.

Everett placed a log upright on the chopping block and stepped back. Rill let the ax fly. The log split like it'd been struck by lightning.

"*Okay*," Katie said, rolling her eyes. "I get the message."

"You've already got him whiskey-free and eating fresh fruits and vegetables, Katie," Everett said, his mouth quirked in a little grin. "Best give yourself another week to turn him into Mother Teresa."

Katie gave her brother a sarcastic glance and turned to go. "I'll be a good little woman, then, and go make you He-Men omelets . . . keeping my mouth shut the whole time, of course."

Rill spoke with her back turned. "Everett's leaving in a little while."

"What?" Katie asked, spinning around. "You just got here."

Her brother shrugged. "Lawson called," he said, referring to his agent. "I need to get back. Besides, I saw what I came here to see."

"You did?" Katie blurted out before she could stop herself.

Everett shrugged and gave first her, then Rill, a dubious glance. "Rill doesn't seem determined to do himself in anymore, and that was my main worry. As for the rest of what's happening in Vulture's Canyon, I haven't got any control over it, so I'd rather not hang around and see anything that'll make me nuts."

Rill gave her a sideways glance. *God*, she wished she knew what was going on inside that brain of his. She blushed for some stupid reason, mumbled under her breath about the omelets and hurried into the house.

After they'd eaten a brunch of omelets and whole-wheat toast, Everett went to pack. Rill helped her clean up in the kitchen. The whole time, Katie sensed he wanted to ask her more questions about what she'd been doing in town this morning. She'd prepared herself for it, but she had no safe response for what he did end up saying.

"Katie." She turned from the sink and looked at him. He was leaning against the counter, his arms crossed beneath his chest, looking rugged and handsome in jeans, hiking boots and a cobalt-blue long-sleeved cotton shirt that set off the color of his eyes. She had to admit, these woods agreed with him. As long as he wasn't drinking himself to death in them, anyway.

"I think you should go with Everett."

She turned around and started putting the plates away in the cupboard, rattling them together loudly to stop the ringing of Rill's words in her ears. She paused and turned around in surprise when she felt Rill's hand on her arm. He stood close. She could take a lot of crap from Rill, but she couldn't stand the expression of compassion in his eyes at that moment.

She jerked her arm out of his hold.

"Are you kicking me out?"

"No," he said. "But Everett reminded me of something yesterday. I care about you, Katie. I've told you what I'm capable of right now." His blue eyes flickered down over her. "I've showed you. I *want* to be able to offer you more. I just don't think I can right now."

Katie glanced down so he wouldn't see her hurt. "I'm a grown woman. There are no guarantees when it comes to relationships," she whispered. She swallowed thickly when she felt one hand on her shoulder and the other cupped her cheek, urging her to look at him. She tilted her chin up in desperate determination. "And don't even *think* about telling me that we don't have a relationship, Rill Pierce, or I swear, I'll clobber you."

He closed his eyes and inhaled through his nose, as though trying to gather his patience. Everett came into the kitchen carrying his suitcase, and Katie broke away from Rill's touch.

They escorted Everett onto the front porch to bid him good-bye. Despite her frazzled state, after what Rill had just said, she smiled when the two men shook hands and then hugged.

"Don't do anything stupid," Everett mumbled before he clapped Rill on the back and withdrew.

"Little late for that advice." Rill attempted a smile, but Katie saw the tension in his whiskered jaw.

"Tell Mom and Dad that I'm fine," Katie instructed when Everett squeezed her in a bear hug. "Tell them I've been eating fantastic and breathing smog-free air and that you've never seen me so healthy."

"I'll tell them you're where you want to be," Everett said as he leaned back and studied her face. "That's the truth, right?"

"Yes," Katie whispered.

Everett nodded. "Well, that'll have to satisfy us, then."

"Call me when you get home," Katie said.

Everett tipped his newsboy hat and grinned as he went down the stairs. "Don't be a stranger," he told Rill.

"Yeah. I'll try," Rill replied, and Katie had the impression he really meant it. After Everett had gotten in his rental car and driven down the hill, Katie gave him a sideways glance.

"So . . . what happened between you two yesterday?"

"What do you mean?" Rill asked as he touched her shoulder, urging her into the house in front of him.

"You and Everett must have had it out over something. You don't look like you want to tackle him anymore."

"Yeah . . . well, we had a talk."

"Did you tell him why you were mad at him?"

"Yeah, I did. And he told me why he was pissed at me. And then we got over it."

His swift smile caused a swooping sensation in her belly. Katie examined him in the sunlit kitchen. Clearly, he wasn't going to tell her the details of what'd happened between Everett and him.

"Hmmm, funny how men can do that," she murmured. It struck her that they were all alone in the old, silent house. She thought Rill would try to resume the conversation they were having before Everett left, but the way he was staring at her mouth didn't seem to fit with that topic. In fact, it called vividly to mind what had happened in the woods yesterday.

"Yeah. Funny," Rill said, but Katie couldn't recall to what he was agreeing.

"Rill . . ." she began, taking a step toward him, but he stepped back, his trance seemingly broken.

"I found some tools out in the shed. I'm going to fix some of those busted posts on the porch railing."

"Okay," Katie said dubiously, watching him walk away. She closed her eyes at the sound of the front porch door slamming shut.

"We are *not* going back to playing that old game, Rill Pierce," she muttered under her breath.

But if she wanted that to be true, she was going to have to be a lot more active about seducing Rill to the obvious.

Nineteen

Rill felt good and tired by the time he reentered the house later that afternoon. After he'd fixed the posts on the porch, he'd found half a dozen things to do around the property. He must have been in a deep depression, never to have felt the urge to pick up a hammer or a pair of pliers. Rill had always liked doing manual labor, sometimes even pitching in on carpentry on movie sets when an extra pair of hands was needed and they were on a tight filming schedule. His uncles had taught him how to be handy with tools. Ray and William Pierce—Rill was named after a combination of his uncles' names—had learned how to be fine carpenters in prison. Too bad learning a decent trade had never dissuaded his uncles from gambling, womanizing, stealing and scamming.

Never kept them out of jail, either.

Rill set his newfound toolbox on the front porch and hesitated before entering the house. He knew what was going to happen when he went in there . . . what he'd been avoiding ever since Everett had accused him of possibly having twisted reasons for having sex with Katie.

After twenty-four hours of thinking about the matter, Rill came to the definite conclusion he didn't possess any twisted reasons for lusting after Katie. Not unless one considered feral horniness as a twisted motivation, which it may very well be, to the degree he was taking it.

Everett's accusation may have made him think twice about what he was doing, but his spurt of morality was already wearing thin as he worked around the house and thought of Katie in there, alone.

In the distance, he heard music and the sound of bells tinkling. Katie walked into the kitchen wearing some kind of flowy magenta skirt that rode low on her hips and fell to her calves. She was barefoot and Rill could see ten perfect toes tipped in pink polish. Around her right ankle, she wore a gold anklet adorned with what looked like tiny bells. She wore a top—of sorts—that tied between her breasts and fell in loose sleeves around her wrists. Her belly and curving hips were left bare. She'd pulled her long, waving hair back in the front, but the back of it fell around her shoulders. There was a slight sheen of perspiration on her face and in the valley of her breasts.

His already translucent moral conscience vanished into a puff of vapor. She looked like something that ought to be illegal.

His cock agreed wholeheartedly.

He glanced up from where he'd been gawking at the luscious curves of her breasts in the little bra-like top she wore when he heard a clear, precise ringing sound. Katie stared at him with a friendly smile and one arched eyebrow. He realized dazedly that the sound he'd heard had been Katie attempting to draw his attention off her breasts by tapping the little metal cymbals she wore on two of her fingers.

"Hi," she greeted him. "I was just working out."

"In *that*?" Rill asked in a choked voice, nodding at the sexy little gypsy costume she was almost wearing.

"Yeah. I have lots of belly-dancing costumes. It makes the workouts more fun."

"Don't tell me you go out in public like that," Rill muttered.

Yeah, he was a guy, and yeah, he definitely had his uncles' genes, because his gaze had returned to her body. He realized that the eight-inch-wide panel of her skirt that encircled her hips and crotch was made of magenta see-through mesh. He could see a minuscule pair of black panties beneath it.

"Sure, I wear this one at dance class. I do have one number that I've never worn to class, though. Never worn period." She walked toward him. More like sashayed. Why hadn't he ever noticed before what a sexy walk Katie possessed? Her hips moved in a fluid, tight roll. Rill blinked when he heard the ring of the bells on her ankle and glanced up curving hips gloved in pale gold skin. When he finally got to her face, he saw her light green eyes shining with merriment and mischief.

"Would you like it if I put it on?"

"What?" Rill asked stupidly.

"The costume I mentioned. The one I don't wear in public. I could show you the routine I learned in my last class. It'll only take me a minute to change."

"Katie—"

She took another step, close enough that Rill became hyperaware of the short distance between the tips of her breasts covered in the scanty little top and his rib cage.

"Do you want to know something, Rill?" she asked quietly. "You are far, far too uptight about sex. I have to admit, I'm stunned about it. Could this be the same man who had Citizens for Morality picketing his last film in five states?"

His nostrils flared and he caught her scent: flowers and sweet sweat and just a hint of something Rill immediately identified with sex. Or his cock did.

"I'm not uptight. I'm trying to rein myself in. There's a difference."

A curious expression crossed her beautiful, flushed face. "So if I were someone else, someone different from your friend, you wouldn't be so uptight?"

"If you were someone else, I wouldn't feel the need to be."

She blinked, and he realized too late how harsh he'd sounded. She licked her lower lip in an anxious gesture. He resisted an urge to pick her up and ravish her on top of the kitchen counter.

"But you like sex . . . right?" she asked.

"Sometimes, I think, too much."

Her brow crinkled. "But you never seemed to have a . . . a . . . problem with it. You were never a typical Hollywood player, screwing around and getting caught and blaming everything on a sex addiction. You were always so faithful to Eden." Her cheeks flushed a shade deeper of pink, and Rill wondered what she was thinking. "That's what it's about, isn't it, Rill? You're fighting against wanting to have sex with me because you were so happy with Eden?"

He couldn't stand to see that flash of uncertainty in her eyes. If there was one person on this planet who never should doubt herself, it was Katie Hughes. "This hasn't got anything to do with Eden," he said firmly. "It's got everything to do with you. And me."

For a few seconds, she didn't speak, just looked up at him with pink lips parted. Her springtime eyes became lambent. "So let me dance for you, then. There's no one here but us. And you told me we couldn't stop it, now that it's started."

"You do like to play with fire, Katie."

Her radiant smile made something lurch in his chest. She grabbed his hand and pulled him into the living room, the bells on her ankle tinkling rapidly. She pushed him down on the sofa and turned up the music.

"I'll be right back," she told him, sounding like she was barely repressing her excitement.

"Katie," he called before she could scurry out of the room. She froze and glanced back.

"Hurry up," he said quietly. She smiled.

He sat there alone listening to Middle Eastern music and getting more aroused by the second. In order to try to bring himself under control, he detailed in his mind all the work he'd done around the house that day: fixing and varnishing the seat for the tree swing in the backyard, cutting back an overgrown bush that was obscuring a window, reattaching fallen gutters, mending the porch posts—

Where the hell was Katie?

He got up and stoked the failing fire in the hearth. That didn't help distract him, either. He kept pausing, tilting his ear, hyperalert for the sound of Katie's footfalls on the stairs. He finally returned to his seat on the couch.

Had he ever been this anticipatory for a woman? It'd turned him on more than he'd expected to see her in that skimpy costume. He smiled. Damn little gypsy, turning him inside out every chance she got.

What was she doing up in that bedroom, sewing a damn costume from scratch?

She came down the stairs so quietly that he wasn't aware she was close until he heard the muted ring of the tiny bells. He glanced over toward the entryway, expecting her to charge into the room in her typical fashion. Instead, he saw an extended leg through sheer, light green fabric. His gaze ran greedily over a taut calf and a shapely thigh. He craned his head, looking for the rest of her around the entryway. When she didn't spring into the room, he called her name.

She pirouetted into the room, a vision of graceful long limbs, green veils and shining gold. She knelt before him, her eyes downcast. He stared at her, stunned by her beauty and her very un-Katie-like pose.

She glanced up timidly, and he caught the glint of humor and heat in her gaze. She'd lined her eyes artfully in black kohl and the lids shimmered with a golden-green shade. The effect was striking. She wore a gold collar, and some kind of ornament had been woven through her hair. It looked like golden coins. They shimmered next to the equally shiny tendrils of her hair. Beneath layers of wispy green veils, he saw the teasing hint of more gold.

"If it would please you, then your slave-girl will dance for you, Master," she whispered breathily.

He chuckled softly. *This*, he liked. "Oh, it would please me."

She smiled before she assumed her sober, slave-girl act.

And *what* an act, Rill thought in growing wonder as she rose and began to move in a subtle dance to the music. She was typically such a whirlwind; it mesmerized him to the core to watch her move with such fluid control. At first, he could only glimpse her limbs and rolling hips through the veils. It surprised him how arousing it was, to catch only a hint of a shapely calf and dainty, pointed foot or the tight, circular motions of round hips. She seduced him with her eyes as much as her gliding body, watching him with shining orbs of light green over the edge of a sheer veil. Rill had never been made love to by a woman's eyes before that moment.

The tempo of the music increased. The beat throbbed in his ears and blood pounded into his cock, and he couldn't move . . . he couldn't blink, he was so greedy for the vision that spun and danced before him.

The veil she twirled around her torso artfully slithered to the floor and somehow the one draped around her upper body was in her hands. He sat up straighter when he caught a glimpse of her smooth belly. The curves of her hips made his palms itch to touch her, and the way she moved them . . . sometimes slow and beguiling, like she was drawing some kind of invisible circles with her pussy, and increasingly as the music grew more frantic, with tight, precise little gyrations that had Rill sweating uncontrollably.

The second veil she flung away with a wilder, hedonistic gesture, and she danced before him with her torso nearly naked with the exception of a tiny, metallic gold bikini top with little chains that hung in a swaying fringe at the bottom. Her control continued to amaze him as she moved supplely to the music, faster now, beginning to look precisely like the whirlwind he accused her of being, albeit a tightly coiled, controlled one. The metal fringe beneath her full, plump breasts shimmied and shivered as she moved. The bells on her ankle tinkled in rhythm with the music . . .

. . . and if he couldn't put his hands on her luscious, gyrating hips or bury his face in the erotic expanse of her belly very, very soon, he was going to go mad.

The music built to a crescendo. Perhaps she saw the manic gleam in his eyes because she pulled on a fastener as she spun and the skirt she wore fell around her ankles. Beneath it she wore a tiny gold metallic thong. She spun, her arms outstretched, her long hair flying around her hips. Rill was the one who grew dizzy, though . . . dazed with lust and need.

He called her name sharply.

The pulchritudinous whirlwind before him suddenly halted as the last note of music sounded. She fell before him on her knees, her head bent. For a moment he just stared at the erotic image she made, her long hair falling before her, leaving her nearly naked back bare, her ribs expanding and contracting as she tried to catch her breath.

"Katie," he said.

She didn't move from her subservient pose, but she looked up slowly.

"You're the most beautiful thing I've ever seen in my life."

Her eyebrows went up quickly in an amused expression, but she didn't smile. "I'm glad that I pleased you," she said soberly. "How may I please you next? Your wish is my command."

It was on the tip of his tongue to tell her to stop her foolishness. She really was playing with fire. He didn't want to demean the gift she gave him, though—such a priceless gift. His cock throbbed uncomfortably in his jeans, though, refusing to be silenced. He lowered his hand to his crotch and saw Katie follow his action with her eyes.

"It seems this is the master of me, at the moment," he spoke quietly. "So I suppose it's the master of both of us."

She glanced up at his face, her eyes shining with excitement. Her head bent once again. "Would you like me to remove your boots?"

"Yes," he replied. He watched her as she unlaced his hiking boots and pulled them off. Afterward, she removed his socks. He shivered at the sensation of her lightly touching his heels with her fingertips.

"Stand up, Katie," he said when she'd finished.

He knew she was playing a part when she came to her feet gracefully and her head remained lowered, but she was still playing *him* perfectly. It would have never occurred to him that she'd take to the role of a submissive so perfectly.

"Turn around," he said gruffly. "Stand still, so I can look at you."

She followed his command without pause. Her hair was still mostly in front of her shoulders, but a few curling tendrils were falling down back and tickled the tops of her buttocks. Her ass was a sweet, plump, edible confection. Her legs were long for her height and perfectly proportioned. He stood behind her and removed his jeans and underwear, then, pausing to remove a condom from his wallet, sat back down on the couch.

"Now face me again," he murmured.

Her gaze immediately dropped to his lap. He couldn't help but smile.

"Are you sure you want to do this?" he asked quietly.

She nodded, causing the gold coins in her hair to clink subtly.

"Yes. I want to please you, Master."

"Then get one of your veils and bring it to me."

"Yes, Master."

Maybe it was his imagination, but he no longer sensed the laughter in her gaze. She suddenly seemed as solemn and earnest as the part she'd been playing. She was a magician, he swore.

"Turn around," he murmured when she brought him a pale green veil. He twisted the fluid fabric in his hands, liking the sensual feel of it on his knuckles, his gaze glued to Katie's ass. "Now move all of your hair behind your shoulders and place your wrists at the small of your back."

When she'd done as he asked, he tied her wrists together with the twisted fabric.

"Now turn around and get on your knees," he whispered gruffly. He parted his thighs and she moved between them. With her hair no longer covering her like a silken veil, her breasts were exposed. He took a moment to appreciate the sight of them—firm, curving flesh and capped with nipples that had already stiffened in arousal. He lowered his hands and cradled both breasts softly, wondering at the silkiness of her skin and the responsiveness of her nipples. His erection jerked in arousal, thumping against the hem of his shirt. He glanced up at Katie's face and saw she stared at his cock. He fisted it and began to stroke himself slowly.

"Look at me, Katie," he said. Her gaze flickered up to meet his. "You have a gorgeous body and a beautiful face, but do you want to know what had me about ready to explode in my jeans while I watched you dance?"

She shook her head once.

"Your eyes."

A smile flickered across her lips.

"I want you to suck on me, but I want to see your eyes."

She nodded. He held his cock at an angle where she could lean down and he could still see her eyes. She watched him as she slid the tip into her mouth and he was surrounded by her humid heat. Her lips held him in a viselike grip. Their gazes held as she laved him with her tongue, applying a stiff pressure with the tip at the slit.

He winced in pleasure.

He put his hand on the back of her head and eased her down over the rim onto the staff. Her eyes glistened like fire-lit jewels as she looked up at him. It was a wickedly potent combination, to feel her polishing the sweet spot beneath the head of his dick with a stiffened tongue and see her staring up at him with so much trust.

He didn't deserve her trust. But he was so greedy, seeing the evidence of it aroused him exponentially anyway.

So did this little game she was playing about master and slave-girl. Given his past, Rill didn't typically encourage sex play that might bring out what he considered to be the worst in him.

Her tongue teased his cock like a flicking hummingbird and then gave him a deep massage on his sweet spot. All thoughts about what was the "worst" in him were forgotten. He was just a man who had been exposed to the elemental feminine flame.

His fingers tightened in her golden hair.

"Suck it good and hard. Ahhh." He grimaced when she immediately did what he asked. Her cheeks hollowed out as she inhaled him deeper. It felt like a damp, warm, gentle vacuum tugging at his cock. He instinctively twitched his hand on her head and she slid him farther into her mouth, then out an inch and down again.

It was sublime. His head fell back on the couch cushion for a few seconds, but he found he couldn't stop looking at her. She continued to bounce her head up and down, mid-staff on his cock, moving only an inch or so. He was stunned at the way she kept him in such a tight vacuum as she moved.

"I'm going to spank your ass pink for knowing how to suck cock the way you do," he said as he watched her. "And then I'm going to thank you for it in ways you'll never forget."

He smiled when he saw her eyes widen. He pushed down on her head and she took another inch of his cock, her strong suction making him grimace in pleasure.

"Aw, Katie. You kill me," he whispered, but he meant the opposite. He felt as if her dance, and her eyes, and her sweet mouth—everything about her—was bringing him back to the world of the living. He watched her through narrowed eyelids as she sucked him deeper and her head began to bob exuberantly over his lap. Her lips butted against his hand where he fisted the base of his cock. He was overwhelmed with a need to let her take him to paradise again like she had in the woods yesterday.

But his need to make her feel the same way overpowered even that blinding lust.

She made a sound of protest when he tugged on her hair and his cock popped out of her mouth. He resisted an urge to slip it back between her lips, to plunge into her mouth and throat until his entire body erupted in fire. Why did he feel this mixed urge to protect her, cherish her, and yet also to take everything she offered, use her for his pleasure . . . slake his monstrous lust in Katie's supple, willing flesh?

"Stand up, Katie," he whispered as he stroked his damp, steely cock, unsuccessfully trying to tame the animal in him. He smiled when he noticed the mulish expression on her full lips. "You said you would do whatever I pleased, isn't that right?"

Her stubborn expression faded. Her golden eyebrows arched with peaked interest. He recalled he'd restrained her wrists behind her back and helped her to rise with his hands on her shoulders.

After he'd rolled on the condom, she gave him a secret smile.

"Now turn around," Rill ordered. She complied. He slid a finger beneath the waistband of the tiny, sequined thong she wore. He felt her go still beneath his touch. He moved aside the ends of the knot he'd made on the veil. Her ass looked like a plump, ripe piece of sex fruit. "I'm not so sure it's wise for a slave-girl to wear quite such indecent little thongs around."

"I thought my costume would please you, Master," he heard her say as he drew the golden thong down to her thighs. He grasped a firm buttock and molded it into his palm.

"Your ass pleases me," he stated bluntly.

Her long hair swished around her hips when she glanced over her shoulder. He smiled at her briefly before he forced himself to look stern. "It pleases me so much I'm going to have to spank it."

"Oh," she said, the whites of her eyes showing. "Okay."

His smile broke out again. Katie was too adorable to censor it.

"Bend over," he instructed, his eyes glued to hers. She bent at the waist, her movements striking him as always as supple and fluid.

He more caressed than spanked her. He enjoyed the sensation of her firm flesh beneath his hand, whether he was swatting it or shaping a buttock in his palm. Her ass looked so succulent in the fire-lit room he leaned forward and bit tenderly. She moaned softly at his action, and Rill knew for a fact at that moment he wouldn't be able to play this game much longer.

Her position was awkward, bending over with her hands

tied behind her back, so he released the knot of the veil and pushed her thong down around her ankles.

"You can put your hands on your knees to support yourself. Spread your thighs. Bend over a little farther. No, farther, baby. Arch your back and send your tailbone up in the air. Let me see your pussy."

When she was positioned the way he wanted, he came down on his knees behind her. He parted her pink ass cheeks and gazed hungrily at her exposed treasures. Her pussy was glossy and flushed with arousal. The sight of the blood-swollen, tiny, erect bundle of flesh that slightly protruded from her labia and the puckered, closed bud of her asshole made his cock pop in the air. His need for her was sharp and nearly untenable, but the anticipation was sweet . . . *so* sweet.

He leaned down and lowered his nose to within an inch of her pussy. Her unique scent filled his nostrils. He heard her soft cry of anticipation. He used his thumb and forefinger to slightly widen the moist slit. And with no further ado, he lowered his head and slid his tongue in deeply to taste her. It was like plunging into a tube of warmed sex honey.

He tongued her until her cries became increasingly desperate. He grasped her buttocks in his hand and pushed them back farther. His tongue slid between her labia and found her clit. He pressed with his lips and applied a firm suction while he stroked the nerve-packed flesh. She cried out in pleasure and jerked in his hands. Her hips dipped as she came, making it hard for him to continue his stimulations.

"Awww, baby," he murmured regretfully when he heard the edge of anguish in her cry as he withdrew. He considered forcing her back into the position so that he could nurse her through her orgasm, but his cock plagued him with acute arousal. Eating Katie's pussy did something to him on a chemical level.

It turned him into a madman.

He sat back on the couch and grasped her hips, pulling her toward him.

"Get down on my cock," he instructed. He hadn't meant

to sound so terse, but he could tell by her small whimpers and tense muscles she was uncomfortable from her interrupted climax. He held up his cock while Katie placed her hands on his knees, bracing herself. He found her slit and arrowed his penis into her.

He groaned in pleasure at the sensation of being enfolded by her tight heat. She whined and pumped her hips, wild to seat him in her. Her frantic need and actions were so arousing that Rill popped her bottom with his palm. He pulled her down on him until her bottom smacked against his pelvis and lower belly.

"It's okay, Katie. Hold still," he ordered. She sat in his lap, his cock skewering her, and wiggled and moaned. A drop of sweat rolled between his ribs and down his belly, he restrained himself so greatly. He reached around her and massaged her clit briskly. "Go on, baby. Come for me."

He felt her shudder. Her scream sounded like it'd been waiting in her throat and leapt out at his touch. He cursed under his breath when he felt a rush of heat around his cock and the tiny convulsions of her vaginal walls squeezing him. He bit his lower lip as he continued to stimulate her, this time until her spasms waned.

She sat in his lap, her back to him, her head forward, panting heavily. He removed his finger from her clit and ran his hand beneath her hair, stroking her back.

"Okay?" he asked hoarsely.

She caught her breath and nodded, moving her curls over his knuckles.

"Good, because I want you to fuck me now."

He saw her head come up at his words.

"Go on, Katie. It's not going to take much," he assured her in a choked voice.

She firmed her hands on his knees and straightened her thighs, rising over him. He growled between a clamped jaw. He gripped her hips and jerked her back along the shaft of his cock. As soon as her ass smacked back into his lap, she was straightening again, and he was yanking her right back where he wanted her. The friction was optimal. Delicious.

He went a little berserk in those taut moments as Katie's bottom bounced in his lap and her pussy rode his cock until he was seeing double.

He'd been amazed by her strength many times before, and he had good reason to think it again as she fucked him for all she was worth. The clear, tinkling sound of the bells on her ankle rang in his ears, seeming to add to the franticness of their mating. In some distant part of his brain he guessed what a workout it was for her, the way she was flexing and straightening like she was doing squats at the gym at some unholy rate. He should have let her slow down, but he was too greedy.

"My thighs are burning so bad," she moaned at some point during the frenzy.

"I'm at the vinegar strokes, Katie," he roared. "Don't you *dare* stop now."

Her ass smacked in his lap two more times. He held her down and wrapped his arms around her ribs. He pressed his face into her back and shut his eyes as he detonated inside her. Pleasure ripped through his consciousness. He lost track of time for a moment as his body shuddered helplessly and wave after wave of orgasm flooded his senses. He held on to Katie like she was a life preserver and he was being tossed and tumbled in a sea of bliss.

He blinked his eyes open dazedly to the sensation of Katie whimpering softly and trying to move in his lap, but he held her against him fast.

"I'm sorry, baby," he whispered. He burrowed his fingers between creamy labia and played her clit with the ridge of his finger. He helped her shift on his cock, giving her the pressure she required. When she started to come, he moved aside her hair and pressed his face against the skin of her back.

He experienced her shudders of pleasure as though they were his own.

When she quieted, he carefully lifted her off his cock and turned her. The compactness of her body struck him anew, the delicacy of her rib cage, the sublime loveliness of her face. He murmured to her quietly. She put her arms around his neck when he stood. He carried her back to his bedroom and laid her on the bed. She called his name when he turned to go and dispose of the condom.

"I'm sleeping here with you tonight, Rill."

He paused and glanced back at her. She watched him from beneath heavy eyelids. She still wore the gold sequined bra from her belly-dance costume. Her abdomen moved up and down as she tried to catch her breath. The dim light from the hallway showed him that her pubic hair glistened with moisture. Even though he was completely sated . . . utterly satisfied . . . he knew it wouldn't be long before he wanted her again. He couldn't seem to stop this incessant hunger.

"Yeah, you are," he replied gruffly. "Just don't plan on sleeping for a while. Okay?"

A small smile flickered across her lips. "Okay, Rill," she whispered.

Despite what she'd said and the gleam in her green eyes, she was fast asleep by the time he returned to the room. He shut out the hall light and rolled her against him while he pried the sheet and comforter from beneath her body. He crawled over her inert form and lay on his side, pulling her back against his chest. She murmured unintelligibly when he tucked the covers around her and then poked his hand between them. He tossed the golden bra onto the floor a few seconds later. His palm found a bare breast and cradled it.

He lay there, feeling Katie's even breath beneath his hand, feeling her heartbeat slow. He strangely felt both content and energized at once. The tantalizing vision of Katie's dance played behind his closed eyelids. The screenplay he'd been working on seemed to call out to him from his computer across the room. He shaped Katie's breast to his palm softly, planning to get up any second to work for a while.

It surprised him that instead of getting up, he fell into a deep sleep for hours with Katie held fast in his arms.

Twenty

He scowled the next morning when he opened his eyes
to a sunlit room and realized he was alone in the bed. It jarred
him. He'd become too quickly accustomed to the feeling of
Katie snuggled in the curve of his body like a pea in a pod,
not to mention how addicting it was to begin to make love
to her countless times during the night. They'd gotten up
after it'd turned dark and made a quick meal of rice and
Asian-style vegetables, then taken their dinners back to bed.

Rill hadn't been able to keep his hands off Katie. It surprised him that he'd gotten any of the food into his stomach,
he'd been so busy exploring every patch of skin on her body
with his fingertips and searching mouth.

"Katie?" he called as he grabbed a pair of jeans and
pulled them on. No one answered his call. He found one of
her signature pink notes in the kitchen and smiled.

*Morning, Sleepyhead. I'm off to take Errol to his rehab
appointment. There's orange juice and homemade
bread and honey from the co-op for toast. I should be
back at around noon.*

P.S. One of my bells from my anklet popped off! Let me know if you find it. Katie

He shook his head. Who knew where that bell was after the workout they'd given it last night? He'd taken such a liking to the clear, sweet sound of them as they made love repeatedly that he hadn't let Katie take off the anklet. He'd become conditioned, just like Pavlov's famous dog, during those carnal hours. He'd probably get a boner every time he heard a bell ringing in the future.

He snorted at the thought and went about the business of getting himself coffee and breakfast, grinning like an idiot the whole time. Katie's absence disappointed him, but it was probably for the best. If she were here, he'd have trouble focusing on his writing, and he found that was precisely what he wanted to do: write. Experiencing the old, familiar drive to get a new project down on paper felt terrific. There were times in the past year and a half he seriously doubted he'd ever feel the urge again.

Besides, with Katie absent, it was easier to avoid the question of just what it was he'd started with her.

"One day at a time," he muttered to himself as he headed back toward his bedroom. Despite growing enthusiasm to write, he ended up spending fifteen minutes looking under the bed and stripping the sheets, looking for Katie's bell. Once he'd found it, he took a shower and wandered out into the yard, where he tested the dryness of the varnished tree-swing seat. He reattached the seat to the ropes that hung from the old oak tree, went back into the house and began to write in earnest.

Four hours later, he blinked and glanced up from his computer screen when he heard a sound he couldn't quite identify. He rose slowly from the makeshift desk he'd created for himself and looked out the window.

He smiled at what he saw. The sound he'd heard had been the noise the ropes made rubbing against the thick tree branch.

For a minute or two, he watched Katie as she soared through the air on the swing, her booted feet pumping and her long hair flying out behind her. She looked like an earth-bound angel, striving to take flight.

Something about the thought struck a chord of memory in him. His brow crinkled as he tried to bring the recollection into focus. Nothing clear came back to him, but he found himself getting aroused for some reason.

Really aroused.

Not that he should have been surprised by that. He was watching Katie, after all.

He grabbed something from his bedside table and headed out of the house.

"You didn't tell me you fixed it!" Katie called to him excitedly when he walked around the side of the house to the backyard.

"You never gave me time to come up for air last night. I didn't have an opportunity," he said. He came to a standstill and watched her.

"Why are you frowning like that?" Katie asked as she tucked her feet back and began to let the tree swing slow to a halt.

"What?" Rill asked. The shadow of the elusive memory had flitted once again in his consciousness as he looked at Katie's face. He walked toward her. "Sorry. I'm just preoccupied."

"Were you writing?" she asked him brightly. Her green eyes shone. She seemed to glow with happiness as she half stood, half sat, her legs straightened, her boots on the ground, her bottom on the seat of the swing and the ropes in her hands. She wore a multicolored gypsy skirt that looked as if it could have passed for the bottom of one of her belly-dance costumes (except this one didn't include a sheer panel) along with an ivory sweater. She looked a picture with the brightly colored woods as her backdrop. He approached her and reached for a golden curl that had fallen on her cheek.

"Yeah," he said as he tried to push back the coiling tendril, but ended up stroking her ear instead. "How was Errol's rehab?"

"He's coming along. He never complains," Katie murmured. He wondered distractedly if her voice had gone hushed because of his touch on her skin. "Dave thinks he'll need at least four weeks of therapy, three days a week."

"Who's Dave?"

"Errol's physical therapist."

"You have a tiny ear," he observed.

"It hears just fine."

He smiled and leaned down to examine it with his lips. Her floral scent filled his nose. She placed her hands on his ribs. He bit gently at the delicate shell of her ear and felt her shiver.

"It seems to feel just fine, too," he said through a smile.

He pressed his mouth to her neck in order to better feel her soft laughter. Her hands came up to caress his shoulders.

"I'm not so sure you'd laugh if you knew what I planned to do to you," he told her quietly. "You have to be taught there are consequences for distracting me every opportunity you get, Katie Hughes." She pulled her head back in order to see his face. Her eyebrows went up in a mixture of puzzlement and interest when he looked back at her soberly.

"Consequences?"

He nodded.

"What kind of consequences?"

"Get undressed, and I'll show you."

"Take off my clothes? Out here in the yard?"

"There's no one around," he said evenly. "And the sun is nice and warm."

She considered him for a moment. Rill knew she wouldn't back down from a challenge. Not Katie.

He hid a smile when she stepped away from the swing and whipped her sweater over her head, revealing a sheer white bra. He jerked his gaze off the vision of pink nipples straining against see-through fabric.

"No. Leave on the bra," he said when she started to remove it.

She smirked and unfastened her skirt. She kicked it onto the grass when it fell around her ankles. The boots she wore were the high-heeled ones she'd had on yesterday when she'd

looked so dressed up. They turned him on about as much
as the other pair she wore.

"Leave the boots on, too," Rill ordered gruffly. "Get rid
of the panties. They'll definitely just be in the way."

She whipped the panties down her thighs. His breath
caught when she stood before him, wearing nothing but
sunshine-gilded skin, leather boots, a peek-a-boo bra and a
smile that warranted a good spanking.

"You better be careful, Rill," Katie warned. Her mischievous gaze lowered to where his erection pressed against the
front of his jeans. "You're starting to make me think you
missed me."

He picked up the seat of the swing. "I'm going to show
you how much."

"Hey!" she called out in surprise when he suddenly threw
the seat of the swing over the thick branch of the tree that
held it. "What are you doing?"

Rill caught the seat and tossed it over the branch again.
"When I hung it yesterday, I hung it at a height for swinging." He caught the seat in his hands before it flew straight
into his cock. "For what I have in mind, it needed to be up
a bit higher." He pushed back the varnished wood plank
with one hand and glanced pointedly at it.

"Have a seat, Katie."

Katie's smile faded. Heat simmered between her thighs.
She'd caught the hint of amusement in Rill's voice, but the
sudden hard gleam in his blue eyes sobered her.

Aroused her.

She walked toward him cautiously and took the seat he
proffered her.

"What's got you so worked up?" she asked. The wooden
seat felt warm beneath her thighs and ass.

"I'd written two complete scenes before I looked out the
window and saw you," he said as he grasped the sides of the
wooden plank. He pulled her toward him and continued in
a mild tone. "I wanted to write another scene. It was right

there, in my mind. Good stuff. Brilliant, even." Katie opened her thighs and hugged his hips with her knees. He pressed the edge of the swing against the tops of his thighs and— Katie couldn't help but notice—along the ridge of his erection. "But instead, I looked into the yard and saw you on this swing, and all those brilliant ideas were gone in a puff of smoke."

"I'm sorry," she said, actually meaning it. He hadn't written in so long, after all.

"Are you?" he murmured. She blinked, realizing she'd been staring at his mouth, which was just inches away from her own. The sun warmed her naked skin, creating a thick, sweet torpor in her flesh. A delicious feeling of anticipation prickled beneath her skin and created a tingling feeling in her clit. She scooted forward on the smooth, warm wood and pressed her opened pussy against Rill's hard crotch.

"I am," she whispered. "I'll make it up to you. You can ravish me, if you'd like."

His dark brows rose. "I *would* like. But you don't have to give permission. I would have taken what I wanted anyway."

His head swooped down. His kiss was hard and demanding, stealing her breath. She experienced the strength of his hunger in that kiss. It felt like an assault on her senses. The sun felt warm and gentle on her skin, but inside, Katie's temperature quickly rose to a low boil. He flexed his arms and rubbed her pussy against his straining cock. He groaned, deep and rough, and released his hold on the swing.

Katie cried out in surprise and gripped the ropes as she flew backward a few feet. Rill walked forward and caught the seat on the swing, stilling it. He stepped back and inspected her. She'd been about to speak, but when she saw the expression on his face as he stared at her lap, the words faded.

"Spread your thighs wide, Katie," he said quietly.

She opened her legs until her outer thighs touched the ropes attached to the swing. She felt the sun-warmed air tickle her sensitive, exposed flesh, but it was nothing compared to Rill's gaze. His stare made her burn.

"Look at you. Like a flower opening to the sun," he murmured, looking mesmerized. "Lean back in the swing a little."

She did as he asked, watching him with bated breath as he grasped her hips in his palms, his gaze still fixed on her pussy. He placed one hand on her lower belly just above her mons. She whimpered when he trailed his fingers lightly through her pubic hair. Then he was separating her labia, parting her for his gaze, exposing all her secrets. She stared in rising awe at his face as he gazed at her.

It was the most intimate experience she'd ever had in her life, so intimate, in fact, that she wasn't at all sure she'd ever previously known the meaning of the word.

After a pregnant moment, Rill blinked, as though he were coming back to himself.

"Sit up, Katie," he said in a hoarse voice as he reached in his back pocket. She leaned forward and watched in rising excitement as Rill unbuttoned his jeans. He peeled off his shirt and tossed it into the yard. He was still wearing boots, however, and he didn't appear to be in a mood to take the time to unlace them and get them off his feet. Instead, he pushed his jeans and underwear down around his muscular thighs. The sound of the paper tearing on the condom package sounded unusually loud in the still yard.

Once he'd rolled the condom on, he moved hastily. He held her breasts in his hands and used his fingers to push the nipples into further pronouncement.

"Like sex candy, I swear," he muttered before he lowered his head and sucked on a nipple through the sheer fabric. Katie cried out at the jolt of pleasure that stabbed through her. His mouth on her nipple felt so good she leaned forward slightly and ground her pelvis down onto the hard swing, stimulating her pussy. Her ass tingled with excitement as well. Then Rill's mouth was moving, and he was kissing her ribs and opening his mouth against the sensitive skin at the sides of her body, testing her with his tongue. Thrills of excitement coursed through her. He went to his knees. Katie held on to the ropes and gazed up blindly at the sun-drenched blue sky and moaned as he examined her skin with his lips and tongue and teeth.

It felt sublime. She'd waited for him for so long . . . and who knew how long these precious days would last?

Her hand dropped to her lap when Rill stood. Katie realized only then that she'd lowered it to tangle her fingers through his hair as he'd moved his mouth over her belly and hips. The side of her waist throbbed pleasantly where his teeth had gently abraded her flesh. He took the hand in her lap and placed it on the rope of the swing.

"Don't remove your hands from the ropes unless I tell you to. Do you understand?"

Katie nodded dazedly.

A small smile flickered across his lips. "Good. Scoot forward in the swing. Put your pussy right at the edge of it."

She eagerly did what he asked. His cock looked ready and enormous with need. She longed to feel it inside her, rubbing and firing deep, secret flesh. He surprised her by going to his knees again.

"Legs wide," he ordered.

She parted her thighs as wide as they would go. He pushed the swing toward his face and, without any preamble, slid his tongue against her clit.

Katie cried out as pleasure shot through her flesh. He placed his hands on her hips, controlling her movement with the swing. As he stimulated her clit, he subtly pressed her against his tongue. The swing made the whole process breathtakingly efficient. He manipulated her with hands and mouth until Katie became desperate. He pushed her forward against his stiffened tongue, then let her sway back ever so slightly, easing the delicious pressure while his tongue played in the folds of her sex. It was like she'd been placed on some kind of roller track that he used to torment her. Instead of his mouth and tongue altering pressures, he controlled her pleasure with the swing, pressing her tight against his stabbing tongue, moving her back until it became a teasing flicker against her hungry clit, then back close while he applied an eye-crossing suction.

She began to beg in a breathless chant. Nothing existed
but the white-hot, burning need at her core and Rill's ruthless
tongue. She barely noticed when he moved his hand, her
pleasure was so acute. He continued to tongue her clit as his
finger found her slit. Katie jerked in the swing when he penetrated her pussy. She was so close to the edge, she shook.
His probing finger was giving her just the extra jolt she needed
to explode, so she keened in protest when he withdrew.

He lifted his head from her lap and looked at her face.
"Lean back in the swing. Farther. Give me your ass."

Katie followed his terse instructions without thought,
rolling back onto her lower spine while she held on tight to
the ropes of the swing. He continued to watch her as he
pushed his lubricated finger against her rectum. A cry leaked
past her lips as he slid into her to the knuckle. Her clit
twanged in painful arousal when he began to move his finger
in and out of her ass while he studied her reaction.

"You're so hot. So tight," he said in a gravelly voice. She
bit her lip hard to stop from moaning. A tear leaked out of
her eye and skittered down her cheek.

"Don't cry," he said softly. "I can't stop, Katie."

"No," she agreed through choppy breaths. She was too
close to rapture to explain that she hadn't been crying
because she didn't like what he was doing to her. Once
again, the intense intimacy of the moment had nearly overwhelmed her.

He embraced her with one arm around her hips and pushed
her toward his lowered head. Katie sighed when he buried his
face in her lap, his tongue finding her clit unerringly. He shifted
her slightly in the swing, increasing the pressure of his burrowing tongue and the finger thrusting into her ass.

She hung onto the ropes of the swing for dear life as she
came. He continued to stimulate her as she climaxed, so that
she existed in a sunshine- and pleasure-infused world for
an untold period of time. Then she felt the swing lurch as
he stood and his voice was near her ear.

"You have had your pleasure, beautiful. Now I'll take
mine."

Katie blinked open her eyes dazedly. Rill stood in front of her, one hand at the back of the swing, the other fisting his cock, his eyes trained on her spread pussy. He stepped back and watched himself push the flaring tip of his cock into her slit. She moaned, feeling him stretch her tissues. He felt hard and unrelenting against her sated, sensitive flesh. He flexed his hips, gentle but firm.

"Take me, Katie," he whispered.

His lips fell open and she gasped as the shaft of his cock slid into her. His hands transferred to the sides of the seat of the swing. He began to rock her back and forth an inch in either direction on the swing, working his cock into her pussy. She moaned. His nostrils flared as he watched her face.

"I like having you at my mercy," he said.

She whimpered as he slid another inch deeper and her pussy clamped around the steely pillar of warm flesh. She was at his mercy, all right, with her thighs spread wide and Rill in complete control of her movements as she perched on the swing. She craved full possession, but she was unable to push her hips without risking falling off the seat. She had no choice but to be patient and accept Rill's pace.

"Look at my cock in you, Katie."

She glanced down. For a taut, sensual moment, they both watched as Rill pulled and pushed on the swing and his cock burrowed its way into her body. When he moved the swing back several inches and his cock was exposed to the sunlight, she saw how the thin condom glistened with her juices.

"Your pussy is pulling on me," Rill grated out through a tight jaw. "I swear, Katie, you always try me."

She opened her mouth to tell him she didn't mean to, but he tightened his hold on the seat and flexed his arms. She swung forward. His pelvis smacked against her spread thighs with a brisk *whap*. Katie cried out sharply at the sensation of suddenly being filled by a hard, teeming cock. Rill growled in his throat, deep and low. He moved the swing in a tiny, subtle circling motion, grounding her pussy against his balls.

"Oh, *yeah*," he muttered gutturally. "This is going to be so good."

He spread his legs slightly, planting his feet. He eased the muscle tension in his arms and the swing swung back. Her pussy slid along his cock. He pulled on the swing and Katie flew forward, swallowing him into her body and smacking against Rill's pelvis and thighs.

The swing made the whole process almost mechanized in its efficiency. He stood unmoving, his ass and thigh muscles clenched tight, his gaze glued to the image of his cock pounding into her body in short, forceful thrusts. He fucked her hard. His shoulder, pectoral and abdomen muscles looked rigid with strain. His biceps swelled as he used them to control their mating.

The precision and intensity of the whole process, the obvious relish he took from watching his cock plunging in and out of her, should have embarrassed her. He was completely using her body for his pleasure, utterly focused on finding bliss in her flesh.

Instead, it aroused her to see Rill so lost in the moment, so infused with need that he became the essence of pure, driving desire.

A low, desperate whine began to vibrate her throat. The friction was almost brutal, it was so precise. His arms quickened the pace. Loud, staccato slapping noises of skin against skin blended with Rill's grunts of pleasure and the paradoxical sounds of peaceful birdsong from the trees.

His breath came in jagged puffs. A sheen of perspiration shone on his chest and flat abdomen. Katie wanted to touch him so bad. She ached, wanting to ease him in his crisis of anguished ecstasy.

She strained to find her own release from this blissful torment.

"Harder," she whispered between pants.

Her eyes popped wide when he growled menacingly and complied. She hadn't really thought he could be any more forceful in his possession, but she'd been wrong. She had a fleeting image of Rill's snarl as his pleasure crested, and then her right cheek was pressed against a pectoral muscle that had grown hard as stone as he held her against his body. His roar of release vibrated up from his chest to her face. His cock swelled, then lurched inside her body, the sensation so intense it made her grimace in a mixture of pain and pleasure.

She felt him twitching deep inside her as he ejaculated. She clamped her eyes shut, overwhelmed with the intensity of the moment . . . slain by the feeling of harboring the man she loved deep within her while he surrendered himself to her.

Her fear of how fleeting, how impermanent the feeling was made her relish it . . . cling to it with a wild desperation.

After several moments, his rigid hold on the swing slackened. She cried out when she swung away from him and their physical connection was broken.

He stepped forward and caught her as she swung back toward him. He brought her against him with one arm around her waist.

"Shhhh," he murmured, his lips against her neck. His hand moved between her thighs. Sunlight warmed her forehead and her body sang beneath his touch. He kissed her parted lips when she shuddered in climax a moment later, swallowing her sharp cries of pleasure.

"You make me crazy, Katie," he said as they clung together and her muscles turned to soft, heated mush.

She ran her sensitive lips against his whiskered jaw and spoke next to his neck.

"And you make me sane."

Twenty-one

A week and a half later Katie pulled into the drive in front of the Mitchell place, only to see that Rill's car was gone, but another sat in its place. She heaved a sigh of disappointment. She'd been looking forward to seeing Rill after a long day of running Errol to rehab and meeting with the director of the county community center. She'd been offered the job Monty had mentioned. While Katie was still flush from her success, Jane Sacks, the director, had surprised her by immediately sending her on her first assignment.

And *what* an assignment. She'd gotten lost in the wooded hills searching for a woman most of the locals knew merely as the chinchilla lady. The chinchilla lady, whose real name was Lila Raschamack, lived all alone on a chinchilla farm, which she'd inherited from her husband.

The chinchilla lady had welcomed Katie to her ramshackle farm with a soggy cigar hanging from her mouth and a loaded shotgun in her hands.

Fortunately, Katie was used to dealing with crazy old coots; she'd had her share of them in visiting Hollywood mansions. Movie stars were nearly as idiosyncratic and loony as the people of Vulture's Canyon.

She'd eventually been able to convince the gun-toting Lila that she'd been sent by the county to help her with the compliance audit the federal government had sent her for the sale of some of her chinchillas last year to a furrier. After some investigation of the circumstances, Katie thought she could make a good case to the IRS given the costs associated with raising the livestock. Lila had been so pleased with the news, she'd offered Katie one of her cigars and took her out into her backyard to show her the spectacular vista of the sun setting in the deep canyon.

Katie had turned down the cigar, but she'd been strangely pleased by the offer. That and the blessed fresh air she'd been able to inhale after leaving the revolting-smelling barn where Lila kept the chinchillas.

Miles Fordham got out of his car and started across the parking space toward her Maserati. *What is he doing here?* Katie thought sourly. She wasn't in the mood for another tour of Miles's dynasty. She thought she could still smell the sickening, intense musk exuded by the squirrel-like little creatures emanating from her sweater. She couldn't get into the shower fast enough to wash her hair.

Before Miles could reach her car, she snatched up the bag from the passenger seat and stuffed it into her purse. She'd had to make a special run to the pharmacy this morning while Errol was doing his rehab.

"Where've you been hiding yourself?" Miles asked when she got out of her car and slammed the door.

"Just now? Oh, I was dodging bullets at a rodent farm. What are you up to?"

He laughed as though she'd just told a joke. He had a harried, distracted air about him, despite his mirth. Katie also noticed the usually perfect wave in his hair looked disheveled.

"Something wrong, Miles?" Katie asked as she started to walk toward the front steps.

"It's the damn terrorists living in these woods."

Katie came to a halt, scattering gravel beneath her boots. "Terrorists?"

"May as well be," Miles commented, throwing her a dark look. "They took a couple shots through my living room window and vandalized the hotel and riverboat construction site last night. Set back our schedule by weeks. It's nothing I can't work past, though. These stupid hill people aren't going to stop me or the opening of the riverboat." He seemed to recover from his bout of bitterness. "It's a nice evening. Thought you might like to join me at the club for dinner?"

"Sorry, no," Katie said in a friendly manner. She flung her bag over her shoulder and started for the house. "I've got a scalding shower in my future and then I'm going to make some salmon linguini."

"Sounds delicious."

"I'm making it for Rill," Katie said point-blank as she paused on the stairs.

Miles's eyebrows went up in understanding. "Oh, I see. That's the way of it, is it?"

"Yeah. It is."

Miles's scowl transformed into a smile. He shrugged good-naturedly. "Kind of hard to be a sore loser when you look so happy, Katie. You be sure to come find me if Pierce treats you badly, now."

Katie laughed despite the glimmer of anxiety that went through her at Miles's words.

Rill had been nothing but wonderful toward her for the past eleven days. He smiled so regularly Katie had almost forgotten his depressive gloom. He'd become so active in sprucing up the Mitchell place, Katie hardly recognized the old house.

He spent at least six hours every day in front of his computer, writing. Sometimes she'd wake up in the middle of the night and see him at his desk, his fingers moving rapidly over the keyboard. She liked to watch him as he worked, but eventually she'd call his name. He'd turn and give her a smile, his air adorably distracted at first. Then his eyes would narrow as he focused on her and he'd rise and join her in bed.

They didn't seem capable of keeping their hands off each other. They teased each other and talked of inane, lover-like things. They ate excellent, healthy meals. Katie was inspired by all the good food offered at the co-op.

Rill refused to let her read his screenplay, saying she could look at it when he'd made the final decision of whether—in his words, accent included—it was *shite* or not.

He never spoke of Eden, and Katie was so ecstatic in their newfound relationship, reveling in the experience of being with the man with whom she'd fallen so deeply in love, she kept quiet on that topic as well. They'd joined in a silent pact not to bring up anything associated with Eden, and the knowledge of her own collusion in that little conspiracy rankled at Katie . . . especially when she considered what she'd just shoved inside her bag. She'd come to terms with her relationship with Rill with regard to Eden. She sensed that Eden would have wanted what was best for Rill, that she'd want him to get on with the business of living, and that included loving. Her collusion in the silence wasn't because *she* was uncomfortable. She was just worried *Rill* thought the topic of Eden was too inflammatory to broach.

"Rill isn't going to treat me badly," Katie told Miles with more confidence than she felt.

"You know how these Hollywood types are."

"I know better than most people," she countered swiftly.

"Well, I can't argue with that," Miles said with a shrug that signified it was her own grave she was digging. "If you won't come out on a date with me, can I at least ask a favor as a friend?"

"What?" Katie asked. She didn't consider herself a friend of Miles. In fact, her dislike of him had grown regularly as she'd completed Joe Jones's tax return last week. Still, she couldn't help but be curious about what he'd ask her.

"Would you mind looking over a few things for me, business-wise? I have some questions I need answered, and the gaming commission is running my lawyers in circles up in Springfield. A representative from the gaming commission is going to be here soon to make a site visit, and I need to make sure all my ducks are in a row."

Katie started to make a polite refusal when something occurred to her. Going over Joe Jones's bank statements—and inadvertently, some of his daughter Amber's—had pricked Katie's curiosity in regard to Miles and some potentially shady dealings at the Forest River Country Club. It would probably be a mistake—her curiosity had certainly gotten her into trouble in the past—but the thought of Joe Jones with nearly nothing to his name but that disintegrating old mobile home got the better of her.

"Sure, Miles. I'll give you a couple hours, if you think it'll help."

"You're a godsend, Katie."

They agreed on a time and a place to meet the following morning. Katie was in a hot shower, scouring all traces of chinchilla-musk residue from her skin and hair within two minutes of Miles walking away.

She thought of telling Rill tonight about taking the job at the community center as she showered. Nervousness flickered in her belly at the prospect. He wouldn't mind, would he?

Would he be insulted? Would he patronize her?

The fact of that matter was, taking on a job implied a state of permanence to her and Rill's relationship that she wasn't sure was at all justified.

But the nervousness she experienced when she thought of telling Rill about her new job was nothing in comparison to what she felt when she reached into her purse ten minutes later and drew out what was in the bag from the pharmacy.

"Rill's going to kill me."

Her fingers felt rubbery with rising anxiety as she opened the box of the early home-pregnancy test.

Twenty-two

꩜

Rill had bought an antenna for the old television set and was finishing setting it up when Katie walked into the living room.

"Well, I'll be damned," Katie murmured. "It's a *color* TV."

Rill chuckled and fiddled with the channel dial. When he stood and Katie neared, he noticed her expression.

"You okay?" he asked as he came down on the couch next to her. "You've seemed kind of out of it this evening."

"No, I'm fine. It's just . . ."

"What?"

"We just figured out that old TV set shows color and you picked a black-and-white movie," she said bemusedly.

Rill laughed. Katie had always cracked him up, ever since he'd first known her. He was glad to know that giving free rein to his monumental lust for her hadn't diminished his appreciation of her humor.

He reached for her and pulled her against him. He buried his nose in fragrant gold waves. "It's Hitchcock. You know I never pass on Hitchcock. Besides, I wasn't really planning on spending much time watching TV," he informed her. "Seems like I haven't seen you in ages."

"It was just this morning," she murmured as she stroked his shoulders and kissed his ear. His cock appreciated not only her actions but her delicious, clean scent. She'd just taken a shower when he'd come home earlier and she'd greeted him in the kitchen. Her long hair had been damp and she'd been wearing a soft-looking yellow and white short nightgown and robe. Her skin had been dewy-looking and her green eyes shone. He'd scowled when she'd casually mentioned Miles Fordham had been there earlier, nosing around.

The guy was a fucking nuisance.

Rill had wanted to haul Katie off to bed instantly, but he couldn't without giving away his true identity as an asshole caveman since she'd made such a nice meal for them.

She'd seemed distracted during dinner. Her preoccupation didn't have anything to do with Fordham, did it? Surely not. Katie wasn't stupid. She'd sidestepped his question about what was bothering her, but he really wanted to ask her about it again, and he would . . . if she stopped kissing him, that was.

He picked up the end of a tendril and squashed a fat curl between his fingers. "Thanks for the dinner. You're going to spoil me, you know."

"Have you ever been spoiled before?" Katie asked as she continued to kiss his ear and make him shiver.

"Never."

"I refuse to believe that."

"I'm too contrary to be spoiled."

"You've got that straight," she murmured wryly.

She shifted her focus to his face, where she began to rain little kisses on his eyelids and cheeks. Her lips felt warm and soft when she finally landed on his mouth. For a few delicious seconds, he kissed her back, molding her lips to his languorously. Kissing Katie was like a sensual gateway drug . . . heady, intoxicating . . . making him crave the next high making love to her would give him.

He groaned when she pressed her breasts against his chest. He steeled his restraint, something that was starting to be nearly impossible to do when it came to Katie. He became a rabid animal when he was in her presence.

She looked miffed when he put his hands on her shoulders and pushed her back so he could see her face.

"Something wrong?" he said gruffly.

"What makes you ask that?"

He shrugged. "I told you. You've seemed out of it all evening. Did something happen today?"

He saw her swallow. "Not much. I got lost in the woods. A woman who raises chinchillas nearly shot me."

His eyes widened in amazement. "You ran into the chinchilla lady?"

Katie nodded.

"Getting fed up with Vulture's Canyon?"

"No," she replied quickly. "In fact, this place is starting to grow on me. Are . . . are you? Getting fed up, I mean?"

He picked up another curl and rubbed it between his fingers. His cock buzzed pleasantly at the sensual sensation. He wanted to bury himself in the wild mess of Katie's hair.

"I'm not feeling any need to go anywhere at the moment." He met her eyes. "But I do wish you'd tell me whatever it is you're hiding, Katie."

Her mouth dropped open.

"What do you mean?" she squawked.

"You're hiding something," he said levelly. He rolled his eyes when she looked outraged. "Unless Errol moves at the rate of an inchworm, I seriously doubt his rehab appointments last for most of the day. You're gone all the time. I'm not upset about it; I'm just curious. What the hell are you doing during the day? I mean . . . this is Vulture's Canyon. What *is* there to do?"

She just stared at him openmouthed. He could almost hear her mind churning out the excuses.

"Katie," he warned softly.

"Oh, all right. I've found a job."

"What?"

"A *job*. You know, the thing you do to get money and pay the bills. Not all of us are multimillionaire film directors." She threw him a dark glance, but he wasn't buying her wounded act.

"Explain, Katie."

She sat back and began to fidget with one of the couch pillows. He was confused by the way she wouldn't look at him. *Jaysus.* What had Katie gone and done this time?

"I . . . I took a job with the county working as a financial advisor for people in need." She glanced at him nervously from beneath long lashes. "You know . . . like, helping people who can't read file their taxes or giving financial information to people who are considering a land sale or something and can't afford legal advice." When he didn't say anything because he was so busy trying to figure out why she was so anxious, she continued. "Monty told me about the job. They had just gotten a grant from the state to start the service. There are a lot of people in this county who are illiterate, or who might be pushed into doing something stupid thanks to coming into contact with people like Miles Fordham. It's a much-needed service," she added defensively.

"I agree," he replied, taken aback by her fierceness. "It sounds like the perfect job for you."

She gawked at him.

"What?" he asked.

"You . . . you think it sounds like the perfect job for me?" she asked shakily.

He shrugged, becoming more bewildered by the moment. "Yeah. It's a perfect fit. You can use your education, and you always wanted to do stuff for people in need. All those Junior League events you planned for different charities—"

"I hated the Junior League," she mumbled, although she didn't seem much aware of what she was saying. She looked transfixed as she stared at him.

"Yeah. You never fit very well with all those other girls. But you always wanted to help people, so—" Air popped out of his lungs when Katie threw herself against him.

"What the . . . What's this all about?" he asked, his confusion rising to concern when Katie started to kiss his jaw, cheeks and lips feverishly and he felt the dampness of her tears on his skin.

"I love you, Rill Pierce," she whispered in a pressured hiss before she covered his mouth. His mind churned with questions. He patted her back in a bid for her attention but with increasing feebleness as his blood started to boil. Kissing Katie was pure delight, but having Katie kiss him was like being hit by a Mack truck of lust.

His arms closed around her and he submerged himself in her heat. He muttered a protest a moment later when she broke the kiss.

"I thought you'd laugh at me."

It took him a second to process her meaning as he tried to make the difficult mental segue from horny beast to rational man.

"Why would I laugh? Do you *want* the job?"

"I really, really do," she said.

"Well, that's great, then. Congratulations for getting it." Something occurred to him. "Does this relate at all to why you were tangling with the chinchilla lady this afternoon?"

She nodded. Her smile was infectious.

"And . . . and you're not upset that I took a job? In general, I mean," she added, giving him a meaningful look that took him a moment to interpret. His smile faded. He paused before answering, trying to quiet his bout of horniness, because this was important. He chose his words with care.

"I don't have any claim on your life, Katie," he said gruffly. When he saw her face fall, he cradled the side of her head. Her solemn expression tore at him. "Don't misunderstand me. I'm just saying that the reasons I came to Vulture's Canyon are a world away from the reasons you did."

"I came here for you," she whispered.

"In part you did. I know that, and I'm grateful. Have I told you that? Well, I am. But you came here for yourself, too. You hated your job. I'm beginning to think you disliked your whole life." She sniffed, and Rill used his thumb to wipe away a tear from her cheek. "You came here to find yourself, Katie. Me? I came here to get away from myself."

A spasm of emotion flickered in her face.

"So when I say I don't have a claim on your life, I just mean I don't have any say in how you plan your future. Because I think that's what you're doing here, Katie. You're carving out a future for yourself, and it's going to be *great*. How could it not be, when you have so much to offer the world?" He grimaced when she sobbed softly.

This wasn't going how he planned at all.

"Aw, Katie," he murmured regretfully when more tears spilled around his thumb. "I came to this old town and existed like a festering sore up on this hill. You came and lit up the place like a beacon. It's not wise for you to worry about what I think of your plans, not when your future is so bright, not when you have so much to give."

"You're *not* a festering sore," she snapped between sniffs.

Rill suppressed a sigh of relief. Having her pissed at him was a damn sight better than seeing her looking so sad and lost. He couldn't stand that. He smiled and dried off the last of her tears with his fingers.

"Thanks to you, I'm not quite so bad. At least I don't smell like a rancid wound anymore."

She gave him a forbidding glance for his levity. "You smelled more like a distillery when I arrived. Festering wound, my butt; no variety of infection could have existed in the midst of all that alcohol. Just inhaling your breath was enough to make me tipsy," she told him testily.

"Thank God," he muttered under his breath. "I don't know what to do if you're not grouchy."

She bit her lip and took a deep breath. His admiration for her grew as he saw her master her emotions. "Don't worry," she grumbled. "I'm not asking you to make a life-long commitment to me just because I decided to take a job in this godforsaken place."

He put his fingers beneath her chin and tilted up her face. "I can make you one promise. I will always care about you,

Katie. Always." He pressed his thumb to her plump lower lip when it trembled.

"There's something else," he admitted. "Now that you're in my blood, I have a feeling I'm never going to be free of you."

He leaned forward and kissed her. A powerful emotion rose in him as she softened beneath his mouth. He didn't recognize it, and since the feeling coincided with the experience of his cock stiffening into a lead pipe, he assumed it was blinding lust. He'd grown used to having it happen constantly in Katie's presence, although he had to admit, the feeling seemed to have grown exponentially tonight.

"You know what I'd like?" he asked Katie against her damp lips after a minute or two of slaking his monumental thirst on her mouth.

"Let me guess," she whispered between soft pants. "You want to tie me up and have me go down on you one or a couple dozen times."

He grinned. "You do come up with the good ideas."

"That's what I'm paid for," she said, her arch look assuring him she was all for forgetting what he'd just said about not having any hold on her future.

"A couple dozen times?" he mused.

"Are you suggesting I'm not good enough?"

"I'm suggesting *no one* is good enough, even if you traveled back in time and looked me up as a seventeen-year-old. I have to admit, though," he added under his breath, his gaze fixed to her mouth, "if anyone could make a decent run at it, it'd be you, Katie. No, that's not what I had in mind, though, as appealing as the idea is. I think I'm in the mood to watch a black-and-white Hitchcock movie on our color TV."

She rolled her eyes. "You may not be seventeen, but you're not eighty-five, either, Rill."

He smiled and reached for the hems of her robe and nightgown. Beneath the two layers, she was wearing a tiny scrap of silk. He wondered for the thousandth time in the past several weeks why Katie even bothered with underwear. He settled her with her back against his chest and slipped his fingers beneath her panties.

"You're right. I'm thirty-six," he spoke next to her ear. "Which is the perfect age for dissecting a classic movie and making you come one or a couple dozen times."

"Oh," Katie gasped in understanding.

Twenty-three

❧

"Again," Rill whispered in her ear. The man was insufferable. He'd just made her come three times as they snuggled there on the couch, and he had the nerve to order her to climax again. Given the magic evoked by his fingers, she'd probably be complying very quickly.

She was so hot she was melting. Her cheeks burned and the soles of her feet tingled from sustained arousal. Perspiration beaded between her breasts. He'd gathered her wrists in one hand and held them next to her waist, preventing her from doing anything but stare blindly at the television screen and gush in orgasm. She couldn't touch, but she could see the magnificent erection that pressed against his jeans. It was driving her crazy not to touch him.

She twisted around and tried to see his face. She made a disgusted sound when she saw that his eyes were glued to the TV.

"Are you actually *watching* that damn movie?" she accused.

"Sure," he replied, even as he strummed his fingers and the sound of wet flesh agitating wet flesh entered her ears.

She was soaked. It was a little humiliating to hear the evidence of her flagrant arousal and to burn beneath Rill's hand when he sat there and did a mental film critique of *Rebecca*. He glanced down and noticed her irritation. His gaze held.

"It's helping me keep my cool. When I see your face while you're coming, it drives me nuts," he muttered. "I can't control myself."

"Oh," she said, ensnared by the vision of the TV screen flickering in his blue eyes. She gasped as he began stirring in the juices of her pussy more stringently. He made a sound of dissatisfaction and removed his God-given hand.

"Hey—" she protested. He jerked her panties down her legs. When she'd kicked free of them, he pulled her into his lap. His hold on her wrists remained, but at least now she could feel his hard, strong thighs and the stiff column of his cock against her bare ass. He spoke directly next to her ear as his hand settled between her legs again.

"I want to make you hot and bothered enough to scream, because as soon as this movie is over, I'm going to take you back in the bedroom and put my cock in your ass," he whispered roughly. "Shhhh, Katie," he growled. His tone surprised her. It sounded rough and hard. He wasn't as unaffected as she'd thought when she'd glanced at his face a moment ago. He was edgy with arousal. "I'm going to release your hands, but I want you to keep them where they are, or I'm going to spank your ass before I fuck it. Do you understand?"

"Yes," she muttered as she shifted her bottom in his lap and groaned at his continued relentless clitoral stimulation. What he'd said had sent her into a fever pitch. She'd wondered when he was going to ass-fuck her several times over the past few weeks, mostly because he often pushed his finger in her rectum when she was all hot and bothered and alluded to the fact that he would. She wanted it, too, although she'd never desired it with another man, always pulling back when it was suggested. With other men, the raw intimacy of the act seemed repulsive.

With Rill, the idea made her feel horny as hell.

Rill released her wrists and slid his free hand between their bodies. He palmed an ass cheek and pressed up on her, grinding her pussy against the stroking hand between her thighs. She whimpered in excitement. He'd sandwiched her between both of his hands, playing her pussy with ideal pressure. Her muscles grew tight with arousal.

"Are you going to come for me again, Shine?" he rasped in her ear before he kissed her there.

Her hips made subtle little bucking motions against his diddling finger. "Oh, *yes.*"

"And are you going to take my cock in your ass?"

She rolled her head on his chest as the sizzling burn at her clit rose to the flash point. "Yes, yes," she groaned. "Every inch." She reached for him mindlessly, stroking the tip of his cock where it strained beneath his jeans. She felt him leap at her touch.

The next thing she knew, her ascent toward rapture came to a rude halt and Rill was scooping her into his arms and striding out of the living room.

"Movie's over," he muttered.

A potent mixture of wariness and excitement surged through Katie's veins as Rill flew down the hallway to his bedroom. He set her on the bed and began to remove her robe and nightgown. The cool air struck her nipples and made them tingle and tighten. Then again, Rill's blazing eyes might have been responsible for that. She could see them by the light filtering into the room from the hallway. His facial features were rigid with arousal as he undressed, his movements rapid and forceful.

Maybe it wasn't wise for her to undertake such an intimate act with him. What he'd said out there in the living room had hurt. But he'd said things that had given her hope, as well. Or maybe she was just an eternal optimist.

Maybe she was just an idiot.

At least the pregnancy test had come back negative. Or at least she *thought* it had. When she heard Rill come into the house earlier, she'd wrapped up the kit and thrown it in the bottom of the garbage can, too anxious to read the nitty-gritty details of the directions to accurately interpret the test.

It'd been foolish to buy the test anyway. Surely it was too early to tell anything. She'd get her period any day now.

Which was a *good* thing. Especially since Rill had made that comment about not having any claim on her future.

Rill stood before her, naked and aroused. She unglued her gaze from his swollen cock when she realized he hesitated.

"Maybe I should have come first before trying this," he said.

Katie scooted to the edge of the bed and reached for his erection, happy to bring him off after all those times he'd made her come. Rill grabbed her wrist. She looked up at his face.

"I said maybe I should have." He pulled her up to a standing position next to him. "It's too late now, Katie."

"Okay," she agreed.

His hand rose to caress a breast. He shook his head regretfully.

"You give yourself too trustingly, Katie. Do you know how turned on I am?"

She glanced down at his engorged penis. "I have a pretty good idea."

"I come from a family of lecherous, selfish wastrels. Did I ever tell you that?"

Her mouth dropped open. She giggled. She couldn't help it. He seemed so serious. When his expression didn't break, she sobered.

"Rill, you're hardly a lecher." She thrust her breasts out so that his caressing hand was filled with flesh. He immediately molded her to his palm. "Maybe you're way up there on the bell curve of horniness, but in a good way, not an ick one."

His nostrils flared slightly as he gazed down at her. "Well, like I said. It's too late now. Bend over the bed, Katie."

She turned and did what he said. She licked her lower lip

nervously, thoughts of their first, impulsive tryst while she held that very same position flooding her mind. A moan leaked past her lips when she felt Rill open his hand on a bottom cheek. He rubbed her and shaped her buttock to his palm before he lifted. A long finger reached, finding her slit.

He made a choked sound at the evidence of her abundant arousal. His hand moved and he popped the cheek with his palm.

"Hey," Katie mumbled in surprise. It hadn't really hurt—it never did when Rill spanked her—but it made her ass prickle and tingle. That sensation inevitably made its way to her pussy. As aroused as she already was, it didn't take long for that burn to transfer tonight.

"I told you I'd spank you if you didn't keep your hands to yourself," he murmured behind her. Katie noticed how thick his accent was before he spanked her again. It was one of the reasons she'd started to become so horny at the warning of a spanking. She liked how much it aroused Rill.

Pop. His hand smacked against her ass again. He stepped closer and Katie's eyes sprung wide. She felt his cock brush against the skin of her ass. She twisted her head around, eager to see him. The next thing she knew, however, his hand was pressing down gently on the back of her head.

"Put your forehead on the mattress, Katie. I've told you what your eyes do to me."

Katie lowered slowly, pressing her forehead to the mattress. Her bottom stuck up farther in the air in this new position. She thought Rill must have noticed, because she felt his cock leap against her ass before he stepped back and resumed her spanking.

Her ass began to burn under Rill's hand. When he thought she'd had enough, he'd paused and rubbed her in circular motions that struck her as lascivious and exciting.

He held up one buttock and smacked her several times low, near her pussy. Then he gathered both cheeks in his palms and lifted. She felt her wet tissues stretch and cool air lick at her pussy.

"Spread your thighs more, Katie." She trembled because

his breath had struck her bottom. He was bending down . . . looking at her. She parted her thighs and waited on a razor's edge in the silent seconds that followed while he inspected her.

"You make my mouth water."

Katie blinked. She'd barely understood him, his voice had been so thick with arousal and Irishness. Her heart began hammering double time when he released her and she heard him rustling behind her.

"Rill?" she asked anxiously, barely managing to keep her forehead on the mattress, her curiosity was so great.

His hand was back, stroking her tingling bottom.

"Don't worry. I'm not going to try it yet. I'm just going to play with you a little more." He rubbed her bottom again before he landed a spank. He palmed the cheek and spread it back. This time, she had a very strong feeling he wasn't staring at her pussy. She jumped when she felt him press his finger to her rectum.

"Shhhh, just my finger," he soothed. "I've done this to you before."

Yes and no, Katie thought as he penetrated her ass. He hadn't ever used bottled lubricant when he'd done it before, just eased into her with the help of her own juices.

He hadn't ever told her in the past his cock would follow.

She moaned as he began to move his finger in and out of her, his progress made slippery and easy with the lubricant. Still, Katie felt the friction. She moaned as her clit began to sizzle.

"Feel good?" Rill asked.

"Yes," Katie admitted. She was glad her face was hidden so he couldn't see her blush. It was too intimate to put into words, what he was doing to her, what he was making her feel.

"It's going to be a hell of a tight ride," he mumbled as he fingered her with more force. Katie began to pump her hips against the pressure of his hand. "You like this, lovely?"

"Uh-huh," Katie gasped. "Does that make me a lecher, like the rest of your family?"

She couldn't quite tell, because he smacked her bottom

with his left hand at the same moment, but she thought she'd heard him laugh. He paused in his thrusting. Katie stilled when she felt a stream of the cool, silky liquid hit her ass.

"I'm going to put another finger in you," Rill said behind her. "I'm sorry I don't have anything better to prepare you. Tell me if it hurts. Push back against my fingertips; that'll help. There you go." He rubbed an ass cheek soothingly as he penetrated her and she gasped.

She began to moan as he fingered her. It didn't hurt, but the pressure created an indirect friction on her pussy. Nerve endings she'd never known existed began to throb and burn, millions of them seeming to beg for Rill's stimulation. She bit her lip to keep from wailing in arousal.

That keen of pleasure broke loose when Rill used his left hand to rub her clit while he continued to probe her ass.

"Ahhhhh," Katie wailed.

"Okay, okay," Rill murmured as he withdrew his fingers.

Okay? What did he mean it was *okay*? Katie wondered dazedly as blood roared in her ears. She'd been on the verge of coming yet again, and he'd deprived her!

"Rill, what the—"

"Get on the bed, Katie, on your hands and knees," he interrupted.

Katie scrambled onto the bed. She glanced over her shoulder and froze. Oh no. What had she gotten herself into this time?

Rill stood at the side of the bed and was rubbing lubricant over his cock. He glanced up at her from beneath lowered brows when it glistened from cock head to balls.

"Katie?" he asked slowly.

"Yeah?" she asked in a wavering voice.

"You've done this before, right?"

She bit her lower lip, trying to decide how to answer.

He cursed bitterly under his breath. She never had been very good at misleading someone. He sat down on the bed.

"Lay on your side," he ordered.

"But—"

"Kai-tie," he said in an exasperated tone.

Katie rolled over on her side, her bottom facing him. He came down behind her, his chest to her back. "You're not going to stop because I've never done it before, are you?" she asked shrilly. "Because there has to be a first time for—"

She stopped rambling when Rill parted her bottom cheeks and she felt his erection slide into the crack of her ass, feeling like a slick, hot poker.

"I told you it's too late now," Rill muttered. "You're going to get it in the ass, all right. It should go easier on you this way. And there's less chance I'll lose control in this position." Her eyes popped wide when she felt the slippery head of his penis probe her rectum. She was so eager to show him that she wasn't afraid that she pushed back forcefully. Pain jolted through her, the concentrated force of it making her gasp.

Rill grunted and popped an ass cheek with his palm.

"If you don't take it easy, Katie, I'm going to drill this hot little ass of yours and then find something to paddle it with. *Do you feel that?*" he grated out furiously. Katie didn't have to guess what he meant. The first three inches of his cock throbbed in her ass. "That's a stick of dynamite, angel. Quit playing with what you don't understand."

"All right, all right," Katie mumbled aggrievedly.

Rill grunted as though he was in pain, which she supposed he was, in a way. "Does it still hurt?" he asked in a choked voice.

"No," Katie whispered, which was true. The sharp jolt of pain had almost immediately dissipated. Now her entire consciousness was focused on the sensation of having a very large cock lodged in her ass.

She heard Rill swallow behind her. "Okay," he began, his tone making her think of a character in an action-adventure movie who was gathering the troops before battle. "We're going to take this nice and easy. I'm going to move slowly, but tell me if it—"

"Oh, go on, Rill, will you?"

He exhaled in obvious frustration and began to pump his hips. They both let out guttural groans at once. Even though he had to apply a firm pressure to make any headway, the lubricant did its job.

It was excruciating, Katie decided. He was taking his sweet time, holding her hip and thrusting back and forth, back and forth . . . no more than an inch each way. But with each pass, he sank deeper. The pressure felt intense where he stroked her, but it was causing nerve endings in both close and distant places in her body to throb with arousal. She moaned uncontrollably and he paused.

"Katie?"

"Yes?" she replied in a muffled voice.

"Are you . . . are you pinching your nipple?" he rasped. She blinked open her eyes and glanced down.

"Uh . . . yeah," she mumbled in surprise. She hadn't realized she had been, but it was imperative to get some friction on some of the burning places in her body.

"Jaysus." His fingers clutched at the flesh of her hip. Katie yelped in both excitement and slight discomfort when he thrust several inches farther into her. He paused, panting behind her. Feeling him throbbing in such an intimate place caused a fireworks show to start shooting off in her clit. As if Rill sensed the finale inside her body, he rasped behind her.

"Show me how you make yourself come, Katie. *Show me*," he added roughly. Katie moved her hand between her thighs. She started to moan as Rill pistoned his cock in and out of her, still with short, electrical strokes, but more quickly now and with more force.

"There's something I didn't tell you out there in the living room," he grated out behind her as his cock burrowed farther and farther into her body, and Katie tried to stop keening in order to better hear him. "I don't want that fuckin' Miles Fordham nosing around you anymore."

"Ahhhh . . . huh?" Katie managed, curiosity barely penetrating her excitement. The stimulation of her fingers on her clit combined with anal penetration was sending her out into sexual orbit. When she finally came, it was going to be the mother of all orgasms. Rill didn't protest this time when she began to bob her ass in counterstrokes to his thrusts.

His grip on her tightened, and Katie was held immobile for his possession. Her cry was obliterated by the sound of Rill's harsh groan when his pelvis struck her buttocks. Katie forgot to move her fingers on her clit at the sensation of his full balls pressed tightly against her and his breath hitting her ear in jagged pants. He paused for a second, and for the first time, Katie experienced a moment of trepidation. It was like the moment before a powerful storm breaks.

Rill finally moved his head and spoke quietly next to her ear. "I don't want that fuck Fordham nosing around you. I don't want *anyone* nosing around you but me. I want people to know you're mine, Katie. I wish I could mark you. . . ." He slid his cock out of her and back, his pelvis smacking against her ass. Whatever he was going to say was forgotten as they were both swept up in the incendiary moment.

Katie clutched at the bedding with her free hand. His groans of anguished arousal as they crashed together tore at her for some reason. His powerful possession scored her, but she could tell he held back in consideration for her. She wanted him to lose himself. The fact that he leashed himself made her hurt . . . and love him more.

"Come, Katie," he said, emphasizing his demand by driving his cock into her ass and smacking against her buttocks.

Katie tipped over the edge. Orgasm slammed into her like a tidal wave, shaking her entire body. Distantly she was aware of Rill's harsh grunt of triumph.

He began to thrust more forcefully as she shuddered in pleasure, racing to follow her into the climactic fires.

Her eyes sprung wide when their skin smacked together and he held her tight against him. She gritted her teeth at the sensation of his cock swelling in such a tight place. His harsh growl sounded a little ominous right next to her ear. It escalated to an agonized shout as he exploded. After a moment, he flexed his hips and thrust in and out of her with tight, forceful strokes. He continued to groan while he emptied himself inside her body.

After a moment, he slowed. He dropped his forehead against the side of her head. Katie loved the feeling of his harsh breath in her ear. She closed her eyes, feeling soothed by the way their bodies slowed in unison, their breaths evening in tandem, the tension leaking away from their ecstasy-scored muscles, leaving them limp and satiated.

"Are you all right?" he asked after several minutes.

"Yes," she whispered.

"I couldn't help myself, there at the end. I never knew a woman could get so hot."

She turned her head and tried to see his face in the dim light.

"I didn't want you to hold back."

His nostrils flared slightly as he stared back at her. He stroked her from hip to waist. "You shouldn't say things like that, Katie," he said, his tone as gentle as his touch.

"Why?"

"Because now I'll have to have you again," he said.

Katie raised her lips to receive his kiss.

Twenty-four

Rill woke up the next morning to find Katie gone. He wondered where she was. She'd told him that aside from her drop-in on the chinchilla lady yesterday, she wasn't due to report into the community center for official duty until next week. His disappointment in her absence was slightly assuaged by the pink note he found stuck to the counter in the kitchen.

I ran into town to pick up a couple necessities. I'll have a surprise for you when I get back!

Katie

He had become used to Katie being gone in the morning when he woke up, but this morning his disappointment was sharper than it had ever been. He found himself anticipating her return so much he had trouble concentrating enough to write. Every time he recalled the sober, sad expression on her face when he'd said he had no hold over her last night, a stab of pain went through him. It'd been like seeing a gray

cloud fall over her summertime eyes. That was how he felt
sometimes—like a pall on her effervescent spirit.

He'd just been stating the truth, though.

Hadn't he?

All he knew was that he was looking forward to making
her smile today . . . looking forward to it a lot. He stood up
from his desk and found the bell that had fallen off during
their lovemaking the other night. He was in the process of
reattaching it to the ankle chain when he heard her car in
the front drive.

Katie's surprise ended up being a dozen brightly colored
chrysanthemums, their pots dropping soil all over the soft
red leather of her Maserati. She used to be fastidious about
that car, but it seemed Vulture's Canyon was having an effect
on Katie in more ways than one.

She greeted him with a kiss that reminded him of sunshine and sex and he wasn't sure what else. He was just
getting into the groove of delving deeper into her mouth to
discover that elusive mystery when Katie broke their kiss
and informed him she needed to pee.

"I'll be right back, I promise," she said over her shoulder
as she jogged toward the house. "Is there a spade in the shed
I could plant the mums with? I was thinking they'd look so
pretty right in front of the porch."

She'd scurried away and still hadn't come out of the house
a half an hour later. Rill had gone out to the shed and found
some rusty gardening tools. He planted three of the colorful
flowers himself before he'd started to wonder what was
keeping Katie. Upon inspecting what he'd done so far, he
decided he was glad he'd fixed the porch posts. The old
house looked a picture nestled there amid the fall foliage of
the forest, the colorful yellow, dark red and orange flowers
flaming against the backdrop of white paint.

He went inside to wash the dirt from his hands. When
he shut off the water, he heard Katie's voice in the distance.
He couldn't make out what she was saying, but something about her tone made him dry off his hands and move

cautiously down the dim hallway. He paused a few feet outside the bathroom.

"Well, when is she coming back, Everett?" Katie demanded in a muffled voice. Rill had the impression she was agitated, but trying to keep her voice volume low. "No, *no* . . . She's not answering her cell phone. I've tried a half a dozen times. Can you run over to Mrs. Addison's and get her? Its two freaking blocks away, Everett. I don't care about yours and dad's damn tee time. I need to talk to Mom!" she cried out after a pause, her voice shaking. "No . . . no, I don't want to tell you or Dad—"

Rill's alarm had been growing by the moment. Jaysus, was this all because of what he'd said to her yesterday? She must have been far more upset than he'd thought. He was such a worthless piece of shit. When he heard a sob emanating from the bathroom, he flung open the bathroom door.

Katie spun around at the sound of the door hitting the jamb with force. Tears wet her unusually pale cheeks. She dropped what she held in her hand. It hit the tile floor with a clicking sound. He glanced down, stared and then looked back up at Katie's face in rising confusion.

"What are you doing with *that*?" he asked bluntly, pointing at what was undoubtedly a home-pregnancy test on the tile floor. His quick glance at the sink confirmed his suspicion when he saw the packaging for the test and the instruction sheet spread out on the counter.

Her cell phone had fallen away from her ear. Her lips were open, but she seemed incapable of speech as she gawked at him. Everett made up for her temporary muteness by shouting into the phone. Rill could hear him even through the ringing noise that had started up in his ears.

"Katie? *Katie?* Answer me. Is that Rill? What's going on?"

Everett's tiny, distant voice pierced his vibrating brain. "What's going on?" Rill repeated, unable to come up with anything original on his own.

Katie's mouth moved, but nothing came out at first. "I . . . I . . ."

"*What's going on, Katie?* Why are you taking a pregnancy test?" Rill boomed.

"Because . . . because I thought I might be pregnant. I'm way late for my period," Katie said tremulously, her eyes glued to Rill's face.

"*What?*" he heard Everett bellow on the phone.

"Shut up, Everett," Rill said loudly. He lunged across the room and picked up the piece of plastic. His heart seized temporarily. When it resumed, it felt like it'd leapt up and lodged itself between his ears. He looked up at Katie.

"This . . . this is a positive sign, isn't it?"

Katie nodded. For an untold period of time, they just stared at each other. He became distantly aware of how glaring the bathroom light was and how the silence seemed to roar in his ears.

"WHAT'S GOING ON?" Everett shouted, breaking the blank trance on Katie's pale, tearstained face. Rill blinked and gently unclenched Katie's fingers from her clutch on the cell phone.

"Everett?"

"Rill? Tell me what's—"

"Everything's okay. We'll call you back."

Rill ignored Everett's loud protest and hung up the phone, then turned it off. He grabbed Katie's hand, which was still hovering uselessly in a frozen position near her chest, and led her out of the bathroom. When they reached the living room, he urged her to sit down on the couch.

"Do you want some water or anything?" he asked once he'd sat down next to her.

She shook her head. He couldn't decipher her expression.

"Are you . . . are you going to be sick?" he asked dubiously after a moment.

"Quite possibly," she whispered.

He cursed under his breath and put his arms around her. He leaned back, taking her with him. A spasm shook her, and the sounds of her soft sobbing reached his ears. Even though she cried, he was relieved to feel the tension in her muscles began to ease.

"Shhh," he whispered as he stroked her upper arm and back with a hand that felt like it'd gone partially numb. "It's going to be okay, Katie. Everything will be okay." His tongue felt as rubbery as his hand, but he continued anyway, desperate to soothe that flattened expression he'd seen on her face in the bathroom a minute ago.

"I didn't mean for it to happen. It was the last thing I expected. I thought . . . maybe I was . . . but that seemed so unlikely . . . and the test yesterday came back inconclusive, so I wasn't sure. Then today . . . this test said . . . Do you think it could be wrong?" Katie rambled wetly against his chest.

"My understanding is that false positives are pretty rare. We'll make an appointment at the doctor, though, just to make sure," he said as he continued to stroke her.

She lifted her head and peered at him through teary eyes.

"I can't believe you're being so sweet about this. I thought you'd be furious."

He cupped her jaw with his hand. "How can you think that? I told you I'd always care about you, Katie. Why in the hell would I be mad at you because you're pregnant?"

A fresh wave of tears spilled from her eyes.

"Do you want to keep the baby?" he asked her gently.

"God, yes," she whispered.

He nodded. "We'll take good care of you, then. Everything is going to be okay."

She nodded and gave him a watery smile. He tried to smile back, but his facial muscles didn't seem to cooperate. Instead, he concentrated on trying to dry her cheeks with his thumb.

"Katie?"

"Yes?"

"Do you want to tell me who the father is? If you don't, I'll understand."

"What do you mean?" she asked slowly.

"The father . . . of the baby."

He blinked in surprise when she straightened with a jerking motion. His embracing arms fell down around her hips.

"You're the father, Rill."

He knew he'd done the wrong thing immediately when he laughed. Anger sparked in Katie's eyes.

"May I ask what you find so funny?" she asked stiffly.

He forced all the humor out of his face, suddenly realizing he was laughing as he maneuvered around a minefield. "It's just . . . I've used protection every time we were together, Katie. I was careful. Even if there had been a mistake, we've barely been having intercourse for two weeks. I mean . . . I know these tests are supposed to detect things early, but Jaysus . . . *this* early? I don't think so."

"Oh, you don't think so, huh?"

He just stared at her for a moment, doing the math in his mind repeatedly, but no matter how he worked the numbers, it didn't make any sense.

"You can't be serious, Katie."

She pushed off his chest roughly and stood. "You saw that little 'plus' sign as clearly as I did. How much more serious can it be?" she asked in a high-pitched voice.

"So there was no one else?"

"No."

"No one in California, before you came to Vulture's Canyon? Wouldn't that make more sense, timing-wise, than you thinking the father was *me*?"

She crossed her arms under her breasts. "Either it's you, or I'm the latest candidate for immaculate conception."

"But—"

"It's all pretty clear-cut," she bit out. She paused when she saw his face and seemed to reconsider. "Look . . . I know what's confusing you. I can explain—"

"I think I might have an idea of what's going on," he interrupted.

"Really?"

He nodded grimly. "You're upset about what I said last night."

Her mouth dropped open. Understanding began to dawn slowly on her face.

"That's what you think? That I'm saying you're the one who got me pregnant because I'm trying to get the commitment out of you that you weren't willing to give last night?" she asked shrilly.

"No," he said as he stood. He put out his hand to touch her, but Katie backed away from him like she thought he suddenly had gone rabid. "I just meant that you're probably still upset about what I said. On top of that, you find out about the pregnancy, and . . ."

"I go so mad out of my love for you that I make up a lie in order to trap you, saying you were the one to get me pregnant?" she finished for him.

"No, I just mean that under the stress of the moment, your mind might have leapt to what you *wanted* the truth to be instead of the logical answer."

"No, my mind leapt to the *truth*. Period." More drops skittered down her face, but her tone and her stiff posture told him that unlike the earlier ones, these tears were of the outraged variety.

"Katie . . ." His mind grasped for the right words, but he felt himself sinking. "Didn't you hear what I was saying before you brought this up? I don't care if the baby isn't mine. I'm going to be here for you either way, if that's what you want."

Her eyes seemed to overtake half her face.

"Let me guess. You want to be there for me as a *friend*?"

He fell back on the couch, feeling utterly slain. *Jaysus.* Talk about being clobbered. What had happened to the golden, peaceful morning, to the pleasant, growing anticipation of seeing Katie walk through that front door? He'd wanted to make her smile, and now look at what he was doing.

He put his forehead in his hand. "Just tell me what it is you want me to say, Katie. If you want me to say the baby is mine, I will. God knows I deserve it. I'm the one who has taken advantage of you." He grimaced when he recalled the extent of how much he'd taken advantage of her sweetness . . . how much he'd reveled in it. "I'm the one who has been drowning my sorrows in these woods. When the alcohol wouldn't do it anymore, I became addicted to you."

"That's what this is all about?" He looked up, alarmed by the fact that her voice had gone flat and hollow. He'd much prefer it being so high with fury that it was about to pass out of human hearing range.

"What do you mean?" he asked slowly.

"You've been thinking all this time that making love to me was the equivalent of getting trashed on whiskey? You consider me to be . . . what? . . . the drug that helps you forget Eden?"

"*No*. That's not what I meant, Katie. You keep misunderstanding me. I meant that—"

"I don't think I'm misunderstanding," she interrupted, letting her arms fall. She suddenly looked small standing there, no longer swelled up with her anger. "I even offered it to you, didn't I? I said it'd be better if you fucked me blind instead of drinking yourself into a grave. I just hadn't realized you were taking the idea of trading a bottle of whiskey in for me so literally."

"Katie, that's a hell of a thing to say," he said, launching himself off the couch and stepping toward her. She backed away. He froze in the middle of the living room when he registered the small, sad smile on her face.

"Why should you be so averse to hearing the truth? You've been so good about saying it for the past month." She held up a hand, silencing him when he started to launch into a heated defense. "Firstly, I'm not a liar, Rill. So here are a couple more truths for you, while we're at it. If I'm pregnant, you're the father. Not in my fantasy world. In reality. Secondly, I've changed my mind. I'm done being the drug that'll mask your grief for another woman. I hid a bottle of whiskey in the corner of the bottom cabinet. Have at it."

Rill just stood there in the living room for three solid minutes after Katie stalked out of the room, wondering what the hell had just hit him.

Twenty-five

Katie spent far more time the following morning over at Miles Fordham's offices looking through his accounts than she'd originally planned. She was back to avoiding Rill again. At first, she was so mad at him she wanted to spit. Slowly, she'd started to calm down, but it'd taken a good part of the night, which she'd spent alone up in the dormer bedroom.

A small part of her—a teeny-tiny part that began to grow with every hour—felt sorry for him. He didn't remember seeing her on her first night in Vulture's Canyon, let alone recall having unprotected sex with her. To discover she was pregnant and have her tell him he was responsible must have confused the holy hell out of him. She'd been willing to calmly try to explain things to him before he'd started to say all that crap about claiming to be the father because he deserved it for seducing her. Then he'd gone on and said that thing about her fantasizing he'd been the one to get her pregnant because she was under so much stress.

Honestly. He didn't deserve a shred of her pity.

Still, she felt a good deal more prepared to tell Rill the

truth about the night she'd gotten pregnant as she left Miles's office the following day. She turned down Miles's hopeful offer of lunch and headed up the hill, ready to have it out with Rill.

She found him easily enough, for once. He stepped onto the front porch when she pulled up into the parking space at the end of the drive. She studied him for a few seconds through the windshield. His hands were in the pockets of his jeans. He wore the blue chambray shirt she favored because it brought out the color of his eyes. His expression was sober as he waited for her.

"Hey," she said noncommittally as she walked up the steps.

"Where've you been?" he asked gruffly, his gaze running over her.

"Miles Fordham's office." When she saw his expression stiffen, she sighed. "He asked me to look over a few things for him, and I agreed. I had my reasons for doing it," she said when his expression remained rigid. "And it had nothing to do with my burning lust for Miles Fordham. You were right. The guy's a weasel."

She saw him swallow. He seemed partially mollified, but she still sensed the tension in him.

"Will you sit down?" he asked, nodding at the porch chairs.

Katie went over to a wrought-iron chair and plopped into a seat. She watched him as he sat down next to her.

"There's something I need to tell you. Something you need to know," he said. "You keep talking like I was dying up on this hill because Eden was killed in that wreck. You were partially right—I loved Eden. Maybe not as much as I'd conjured up in my head, but still. She was a big part of my life, once. But you're also wrong about how I felt about her."

"What?" Katie asked, sitting forward slowly. It had been the last thing she'd expected him to do in that tense moment, to start talking about the verboten topic of Eden. She stared at him, riveted. He closed his eyes briefly. Katie had a flash of intuition and suddenly knew how difficult this conversation was for Rill.

"We hadn't been getting along for more than about a year before she died—Eden and I."

"Really?" Katie asked in a quavering voice. "But I thought . . . She never said . . . You never said."

"She never spoke to you about our marriage being in trouble?" Rill asked her, his manner calm.

Katie shook her head. "No. I had no idea you two were anything but happy in your marriage."

Rill searched her face. After a moment, he nodded. "It was, in the beginning. Happy, I mean. Or at least I thought it was. When she died, the coroner told me she was three months pregnant. It wasn't my baby, Katie. We hadn't slept together in over half a year."

Katie just stared at him, her mouth partially open. The sound of the blood rushing in her veins segued from a dull throb to a roar in her ears.

"Eden was pregnant?" she whispered incredulously. "Who was the father?"

Heat burned in her cheeks when she realized what she'd just said. Rill had just asked her the same question last night. A wave of dizziness struck her.

Holy shit. Rill's surprising news was bad in more ways than the obvious, she realized with a rising sense of dread.

"I don't know," Rill replied. "I was shocked when the coroner told me. You knew Eden. She didn't socialize much, let alone go out with men. Her coworkers were mostly women."

Katie blinked. The image of the fury in Rill's face before he'd tackled Everett in the backyard flashed into her mind's eye. "Jesus. You thought . . . *Everett*?"

He glanced away, looking vaguely ashamed of himself.

"You did," she said huskily. It made so much sense now. Everything. Rill's anger at Everett, his deep depression up here on this hill, his dislike of the world . . . his willingness to sacrifice everything.

"Nothing made sense to you after she died . . . after you found out she'd been unfaithful, did it?"

"I guess not," he said after a moment.

"You stopped believing in yourself when you realized you couldn't believe in Eden anymore. She meant that much to you," she said quietly.

His mouth tightened, but he didn't speak.

"I know how much you put her on a pedestal. I'm sorry, Rill." She saw him swallow thickly. "She didn't deserve to be idolized," Katie burst out heatedly. She flushed when Rill glanced at her sharply, but her flash of fury at Eden was difficult to withhold. It was anger at what Eden had done to Rill, true, but she also experienced a sense of betrayal over the fact that Eden had never confessed this secret part of her life to her—Katie. "She *didn't* deserve it. Not if she was screwing around on you."

He gave her a wry glance. "Shit happens, Katie. People fall out of love all the time. I obviously wasn't making her very happy. She must have thought my work was more important to me than her. I'm not so sure she was wrong, if my actions were any indication of how I felt."

Katie made a disgusted sound under her breath. Eden should have been talking to Rill if she was that upset with him . . . suggested they go to therapy . . . or asked for a divorce, if she was *that* unhappy. She shouldn't have been off fucking some other guy behind his back.

"Who was it?" Katie asked irrepressibly. "The guy she was having an affair with, I mean."

He shrugged. "I don't know. Truth? It used to consume me, that question. I don't think about it that much anymore."

"No?" Katie asked him in a hushed, shaking voice. "Not . . . not even after you saw that pregnancy test last night and I told you that you were the one responsible for it? How could you *not* have thought of Eden being pregnant with another man's child when I told you that last night?"

The air seemed to thicken in the silence that followed. Rill pinned her steadily with his stare, his eyes shining with something she strongly suspected was pity. For some reason, she knew what he was going to say next. She fought the rising dread like she would her worst enemy.

"I'm *not* leaving, Rill," she blurted out of a constricting throat.

"I *am*, Katie," he said quietly. "Not for long," he added when a tear fell down her cheek. "I'll be back in a week or two. I promise. There's somewhere I have to go."

Katie didn't say anything. She couldn't. He was leaving for good. She just knew it. This was the day she'd been dreading since she first came to Vulture's Canyon.

"Katie," he said firmly. She forced herself to look at him. "I've made an appointment for you with an ob-gyn clinic in Carbondale. I called around and got several references for the best doctor. I wrote down the date and time on a notepad in the kitchen. I called Olive Fanatoon and she says she'll go with you to the appointment."

She swallowed and just stared at him, unseeing. It was the same when he reached out and cupped her jaw. She was too numb to really feel it.

"Katie?"

"Yes?"

"I'm going to be here for you during your pregnancy. I promise you that. I'm not abandoning you. I just . . . just have to go somewhere. I need to figure something out, and when I have, I'll be back. I'll be back," he repeated with emphasis.

"Okay," she said through leaden lips.

She sensed him studying her in the silence that followed. "You'll go for the appointment? With Olive?"

Katie nodded. There was a buzzing in her ears. Everything had gone fuzzy . . . surreal.

"Are you okay, Katie?" he asked, his forehead creasing with anxiety.

"I'm fine." She tried to smile.

Rill'd disappeared into these woods in a bout of hurt and confusion nineteen months ago. The shock of Katie telling him she was pregnant and accusing him of being the father when he couldn't even recall the deed would likely send him off on another anguished escape.

Hell, given what he'd just told her about Eden, she

could hardly blame him for coming up short in the trust department.

Of all the fucking bad timing. Only something this unlikely could happen to her.

"I'll be back, Shine," he whispered, his thumb wiping away a tear.

Katie nodded, even though she couldn't allow herself to believe a word he was saying. If she let herself, it'd hurt too much when he didn't return.

Twenty-six

Rill didn't exactly know how his mother would react when she saw him. He'd stopped trying to reach out to her twelve years ago. Fiona Pierce had never tried to contact him, not once since he'd moved stateside for university when he was nineteen years old.

Rill always had the idea growing up that his mother didn't know what to do with him . . . didn't know how to relate to a son. She knew precisely how to relate to men, and men seemed to know exactly how to relate to Fiona. Women tended to both despise and be enthralled by her. Fiona had that effect on people—like a queen who'd flipped off the world and become a whore because it made her laugh to consider the irony of the concept.

Fiona certainly knew how to treat her brothers—Ray and William—with a harsh tongue and a healthy dose of disdain.

Despite the fact that he'd long ago given up trying to have a relationship with his mom, he still felt a sense of sharp anticipation as he closed the kissing gate behind him and made his way across the broken stone of the sidewalk. A few chickens strutted up to him, obviously used to being fed by a human hand. He'd learned from the bartender—Mick—at the Regal Lion Pub in downtown Malacnoic that his mother's latest place of residence had changed a few years back. Rill hadn't been surprised. Fiona made a habit of changing residences at the same rate she changed lovers.

He knew her instantly when she opened the front door at his knock, although he could tell by her blank expression she didn't recognize him. Her long, dark hair didn't show a sign of gray, and Rill realized distantly she must color it. Maybe she had since he was a child. For all he knew, she'd been born a redhead.

Her hair may still look lustrous, but her face showed signs of wear and age. Wrinkles deepened around her eyes when she peered up at him.

He knew he resembled his mother. Almost every person in Malacnoic had said it at one time or another. Dark with blue eyes and a confidence people seemed to feel he had no right to, as a bastard child, even if they did admire that characteristic.

You're the spitting image of your mam, aren't you?

The townspeople had never said it joyfully, like they might other children—but rather sadly or suspiciously, like a person might say the devil's spawn resembled its father.

Fiona gave a dry, crackling laugh when she recognized him. Apparently, his mom still hadn't broken her pack-and-a-half-a-day habit. He could smell the scent of stale cigarette smoke coming off the too-tight cotton dress she wore.

"Lord, I thought you were the guy here to fix my oven for a few seconds. I was wondering when Fitzgerald got so tall. Come on in, then," she told Rill briskly, waving him inside the house as though he were a neighbor she saw every day of her life. Rill followed her down a dark hallway that smelled strongly of cigarette smoke to a sunny kitchen. She sat down at the dented, pockmarked oak table and picked up a lit cigarette. Smoke wafted through the air as she waved at the ancient AGA oven.

"That's the broken oven I was talking about, there. Been driving me mental, that thing. Patrick finally went and called Fitzgerald, the repairman, when he didn't get his dinner on time for the fourth day in a row, lazy sod," Fiona said fondly before she took a long draw on her cigarette. "What brings you here, then? I'd heard on the television you'd gone mad after that prissy wife of yours died."

"Do I look mad?" Rill countered quietly.

Fiona shrugged. She studied him as she smoked, clearly undecided on her answer . . . or uncaring, most likely.

Rill inhaled slowly, resisted his typical inclination to say something foul to his mother and storm out of the house in a fury. On the flight across the Atlantic, he'd ritualistically prepared himself for her typical coldness. He'd come here with a purpose and he wasn't going to stay here long.

He wasn't a child anymore. He wasn't a masochist, either.

He glanced around the stark, serviceable kitchen. "You live with a man named Patrick, then? This is his house?"

"That's right."

"You have everything you need?" Rill asked, already knowing what her answer would be. Hadn't he offered to give her money over the years, given her the opportunity not to prostitute herself to these men? She'd just laughed at him with that deep, raspy voice he supposed some men found attractive.

You're *not going to take care of me, Rilly. Not a chance.*

"Do I look like I need anything?" she asked him.

He glanced at her. Her figure was still full and voluptuous, but she was going to fat. Truth be told, she didn't look well. There was a gray cast to her skin that alarmed him . . . hurt him to see, because he knew there was nothing he could do about it.

Nothing.

He steeled himself against the onrush of sympathy he felt for her. He knew what would happen if he expressed it, knew it deep inside his bones. She'd insult him if he communicated his concern, send him into a fury so that he forgot for days, or months, or years why he'd ever felt an ounce of compassion for Fiona Pierce.

"I came here to ask you who my father was," he stated starkly.

She paused in the action of inhaling her cigarette. Her sharp blue eyes flew to meet his gaze. She slowly pulled the cigarette away from her mouth.

"Lord, you're not going back to that, are you? I haven't heard you sing that old tune since you were sixteen years old," she said, smoke curling around her smile as she spoke.

"Tell me, Ma. What've you got to lose by telling me?"

"He's dead. What've you got to gain by knowing?"

"Some peace of mind," Rill grated out. "I want to know. I want to know who he was. Who're you to deprive me?"

"I'm your ma."

"Don't make me laugh."

It was Fiona who laughed after a moment, though, low and rough.

"Do you want some tea, then?" she said after she'd recovered from her bout of mirth at Rill's expense.

"No," he bit out.

"Whiskey? I'd heard you'd developed a taste for it."

He stood, his chair scraping loudly against the tile floor. She shook her head, a smile still lingering around her full lips.

"You won't find any answers here, Rill. You and I were always as different as north and south."

He wanted to snarl at her that he'd tried to meet her halfway for his entire childhood and most of his adult life, but she'd been too busy wallowing in her selfishness. How many times had he waited for her as a small child outside a closed bedroom door when she'd told him she'd take him to the park, or promised him she'd take him into town for a festival or a friend's party?

But Fiona had always had better things to do with her time, was always willing to do them with men who were frightening strangers to a child. As he'd gotten older, he'd learned to treat his mother's men with a coldness that he'd soon realized they found as intimidating as his mother's dark, volatile moods.

By the time he'd reached eleven years old, he'd given up the childhood fantasy that each man his mother molded her body against and kissed might be his absent father.

He wanted to tell her she was a coldhearted bitch who had sacrificed her only child to her carnal appetites and laziness.

But what was the point? He continued, determined to finish this mission.

"I also came to tell you I'm going to have a baby. It's your loss you never knew the mother, Katie. She's a light I reckon you and I never deserved. One thing's for certain: I won't be showing up here with your grandchild. I won't be showing up on your doorstep ever again. If you call, if you *try*, Ma, that's another thing entirely."

He walked out of the house and didn't look back. Fiona wouldn't be waiting for the backward glance. Rill knew that for a fact.

He'd said what he needed to say to Fiona Pierce.

Rill had spent most of his life being embarrassed by his namesakes, William and Ray Pierce. The fact his uncles had just been sent to prison for gambling and soliciting prostitutes had been the main reason he'd made the final decision to film some scenes in Malacnoic four years ago.

But this visit wouldn't be complete until he'd sat across a table from William and Ray Pierce. Micky the bartender had informed him the pair was currently out of prison, so Rill knew exactly where to find them that evening. William didn't go anywhere without Ray, and vice versa. They even managed to organize it so that they were conveniently arrested together for similar crimes.

Tonight he was looking forward to seeing his uncles again for some reason. Maybe it was just because after his visit with Fiona he didn't think any family visit could get much worse.

He waited in a dark corner of the Regal Lion, keeping a

low profile and sipping his Guinness sparingly. Round about seven o'clock, the dim, musty pub began to bustle. He recognized his uncle Ray as he walked through the front door—tall, dark-haired, the remnants of great handsomeness still clinging to his worn visage. Rill stood. The movement caught Ray's eye.

"Well, if it ain't my long-lost nephew," Ray bellowed so that most of the people in the noisy pub paused and gaped at Rill. Ray turned and spoke to a tall, wiry man who had just walked into the pub and who looked remarkably like Ray despite his stooped posture and graying hair. "Look 'a there, William. You see him, too, don't you? It's our nephew, Rilly, looking rich as a prince . . . rich enough to keep our cups full tonight, at any rate. Howsitgoin' boy?" Ray boomed as he accepted Rill's outstretched hand and pulled him toward him for a clumsy hug.

"Well, blow me raw, it is Rill!" said William Pierce, squinting. He joined his brother by giving Rill a hardy hug. "What brings you to this feeble town, then? Come to see your worthless ma, I'm thinking. Come to drown your sorrows now that you have, eh?" William said with a sly look in his blue eyes.

"It's good to see you both. Have a seat, and I'll buy you a pint," Rill offered, waving at the wooden bench on the opposite side of him. He was eager to disappear back into the shadowed corner booth. Every eye in the pub seemed to be on Rill and his uncles.

"Margie, send us over a pint, eh?" Ray called to the busty waitress at the bar. "Look at her, will ya?" Ray leaned confidentially toward Rill and spoke in a low voice. "Ought to be shot for cutting her hair off like that. She was a good-looking woman. If it weren't for those fun bags she's got"—Ray cupped his hands in front of his chest—"I'd think Margie was a fucking man."

"You didn't seem to have any problems with her two nights ago, back there behind the bar after the pub closed," William said drolly. "Sounded to me like your pipe was finding the lady parts just fine."

Both men roared.

"I haven't had her yet," William muttered between jags of laughter. "So don't mind me when I tell her I think her haircut is a bag o' swag."

Rill couldn't help but grin as his uncles tried to calm their hilarity. Their expressions were sober and innocent as choirboys by the time Margie brought them their pints.

"That new haircut is real elegant, Margie. Makes you look a picture. That's my nephew there, and he ain't got nothing I don't," William assured her as the waitress eyed Rill and gave him a flirtatious smile. "Mine's just the vintage version, that's all."

Margie rolled her eyes and walked away, putting an extra twitch in her ass. William took a long drink of his Guinness and smacked his lips appreciatively, his gaze glued to Margie's rear view.

"She wants me bad," William declared.

"Aw, shut it," Ray said. "Our nephew is here. We've got better things to discuss than the frickin' party your prick is throwing." William's expression looked doubtful, but he joined in the conversation jovially, anyway. William and Ray Pierce may be loudmouthed wastrels, but unlike their sister, Fiona, neither possessed a mean bone in his body.

They caught up over the next hour, his uncles becoming more expansive in their speech with each successive pint Rill bought them.

"You never told us why you came back to this bloody town," Ray said a while later. "Did you visit Fiona?"

"Yah, I did. Came to ask her again who my dad was."

"Aw, well, that couldn't have gone well. Fiona always kept a tight clamp on her mouth about that topic even if she was loose with everything else she had to offer," Ray said.

"You know," William said significantly after he took a deep draw on his Guinness. "I have a theory on that and all. Want to hear it?"

"Sure," Rill replied casually.

"I think your dad was that bloody vicar."

Ray snorted. "You're busting at the seams with it, William."

"My dad was a vicar," Rill repeatedly dryly.

"No, no . . . hear me out," William defended, scowling at his brother. "I figure Fiona'd have to be ashamed of what she'd done, for her to keep her mouth shut about it all these years. Angus Rourke, that was his name. Big, strapping man, like you, Rill. Preached his bit in Dublin. Fiona used to visit our cousin Dina in town and the two of 'em would coo over what was under the vicar's church robes. Knowing Fiona, she found out for herself firsthand."

"Is Rourke still alive?" Rill asked. He'd heard many theories on the identity of the man who had fathered him, and this particular claim was an unheard one.

"Nah, died ten years back in a plane wreck. You'd think he would have had better relations with his employer," William said, pointing upward.

"You know," Ray said, wagging his finger at Rill. "Maybe he's onto something."

"You really think so?" Rill asked, amused.

"It'd sure explain why you were always so uptight, Rilly. Never chasing after the sallies even when they was practically lying in the path in front of you with their legs spread wide. Maybe it's because you've got some vicar genes in you."

William snorted with laughter.

Rill tilted his head as he studied his uncle. Here was something odd. Rill'd had his share of girlfriends in his teenage years. "You really think that? That I'm uptight?"

"Sure, I do." Ray nodded his head sagely. "You don't think I called you a prince when I saw you just because you're so blessed tall and look as though you got plenty of coin in your pocket, do you?" Ray took a swallow of beer and seemed to consider. "Course, you wouldn't need vicar genes to make you a gentleman with the ladies. Not when you had Fiona for a ma."

"Or us for uncles," William said.

For a second, both men studied their Guinnesses soberly.

They broke out in simultaneous laughter, William slapping the wood table for emphasis.

Rill chuckled along with them. His uncles would never change, but Rill was okay with that for the first time. He opened his mouth to ask more questions about the vicar, but stopped himself at the last moment. Would it really do him any good? He'd never really know one way or another who his father was. Even if he ever succeeded in locating the dead vicar's family, it wasn't as if they'd be thrilled with his allegations their relative had been screwing one of his parishioners.

No, it was time Rill gave up on discovering that mystery from his past. He had a future to consider now.

"Are you going to be making another movie in Malacnoic, then? Seeing as we're not in the lockup at the moment, William and I could play ourselves," Ray suggested later.

William's blue eyes sparked with annoyance. "I'll be having a word with you about that last film you made here in town, Rilly."

"What do you mean?" Rill asked.

"What were you thinking, letting that foine-looking man play Ray when you got that fellow with the face like a bag o' dead rats playing my part!"

Ray gave an evil chuckle, clearly liking the topic a great deal more than his brother. "He's got to play it like real life, ain't that so, Rill? That guy—Everett Hughes, right? Perfect casting for me. I was much blonder when I was younger, and that's a fact."

William snorted derisively. "You're a fuckin' dose, you are, Ray. I think you're mixin' yourself up with that fleabitten golden retriever we had as boys, old Tom."

Rill laughed. "I don't know what you're talking about. What makes you think I'd written the parts with you two in mind?"

Both of his uncles gaped at him.

"Well, it *was* us, or at least it would have been, if you'd gotten someone like that Colin Farrell to play me instead of that hatchet-faced git. Everyone in Malacnoic says it was us," William explained patiently.

"Well, there you have it, then," Rill said, grinning. It hadn't occurred to him until he sat there with his uncles that he really *had* written them—at least partially—into the characters. Not just the ones from the film they spoke of, either. There were aspects of his wily, fun-loving uncles in a lot of his characters.

The realization shocked him a little. He hadn't really envisioned that anything about Ray and William Pierce was worthwhile, aside from the fact that they'd taught him how to use a hammer. Moviegoers and critics usually liked his quirky male characters, but it just hadn't penetrated his awareness until now just how much of Ray and William were in them . . . how much his uncles were in *him*—Rill.

Not just the reprobate parts, either. There were great things about Ray and William—their charm, their irrepressible humor, the fact that they greeted every new day like it was their best friend, even when they woke up in a prison cell.

Perhaps they weren't the best role models for a boy, but William and Ray were the only thing Rill had ever had. They'd do, he supposed.

Another thing struck him. Katie would love his uncles. The three of them would laugh together until tears leaked out of their eyes. He found himself looking forward to introducing her to the pair someday.

He bought himself a second Guinness and leaned back, relaxing for the first time since he'd made the decision to take a trip to Malacnoic. Maybe he *would* make another film here.

He and his uncles talked until late, and in the morning, Rill knew it was time to leave.

He'd done a little soul searching since he'd gotten on that plane in St. Louis; he'd done a lot of thinking. Now that it was done, he wondered if he hadn't needed to somehow sew Katie into the fabric of his past, weave his future together with his history.

Or maybe he'd needed to return to better make sense of everything that had come after Malacnoic . . . why he'd needed to put Eden on such an impossibly high pedestal . . . why it had crushed him to learn she was flawed and only human . . . why he was so disturbed by his insatiable need for Katie . . .

. . . how it was that he could have fallen in love with Katie Hughes and not even known it.

The tiny, grimy town of Malacnoic, the impenetrable barriers behind his mother's eyes, the joy in his uncles' laughter, a vague, elusive memory of an angel falling on his doorstep—he'd found some answers in those things. He'd put together the puzzle, and even if there were some missing pieces, Rill could make out the picture.

It was time to start living again.

It was time to go home to Katie.

Twenty-seven

The week after Rill left Vulture's Canyon, Katie had her first obstetrics appointment. The doctor confirmed what she already knew. Katie was four and a half weeks pregnant. She already had accepted that fact—one, because of the pregnancy test, and two, because it was the exact sort of ludicrous thing that would happen only to her.

It wasn't all darkness and self-pity, though. She spent extra hours at the community center, decorating her new office and poring over resources, trying to figure out the best way to service her clients. The best training was just to visit people in their homes, however, get to know them where they were most comfortable. Fortunately, she was typically received with a great deal more hospitality than the chinchilla lady had shown her on that first day.

Last Thursday evening, she'd walked into the empty diner and called out to Sherona, who popped up from behind the counter.

"Will you be upset if I adopt Barnyard?" she asked Sherona.

Sherona set some napkins on the counter. "I'd love it, if

you're completely confident you can give him a permanent home."

"I can. I'm not going to be leaving Vulture's Canyon anytime soon. Besides, I'm going to have a baby. I figure I need the practice, taking care of something else."

Sherona nodded and offered her congratulations on her pregnancy. Katie had come to admire the woman's unflappability. "You want some newspapers to set down in the seats of your car for when you take Barnyard?" Sherona asked.

"Nah. The car will survive some dirt. I've got a nice bath ready for him up at the house."

Barnyard hadn't thought the bath was so nice. Katie had never seen the basset hound move so energetically until she'd attempted to scrub him clean. Barnyard tipped over the little tin tub she'd found in the shed three times before she'd wrestled him down long enough to scour years of dirt off him. Katie hoped the dog had forgiven her by the time she set a diced-up skirt steak in front of him as he sat on the kitchen floor, damp and smelling of her favorite shampoo.

He'd glanced up at her with doleful brown eyes before he'd stood to eat. Katie saw his tail wag for the first time in her life. His entire butt swayed along with it as he sloppily ate his meal.

Her pregnancy started to feel a little more real to her, even though her new doctor had informed her that the baby didn't even measure an eighth of an inch in length at that point. Olive Fanatoon had been a godsend, as the mother of three grown children. Olive was generous with her time in answering Katie's questions and with her sympathy when, on one occasion, Katie had burst into tears seemingly out of nowhere.

Well, perhaps it wasn't completely out of nowhere, as she had sobbed Rill's name repeatedly the entire time.

Stupid hormones.

When she'd first seen the positive sign on the home-pregnancy test, Katie had wanted nothing more than to talk to her mother. Bawl to her, more like it. Since then, she'd decided not to tell her parents about the pregnancy until she reached the end of her second month, just to be on the safe side. No reason to get them worried. They'd be thrilled for her, as long as she was happy.

Katie figured she'd have to polish up on her acting skills for that particular role.

She had told Everett, however, feeling like she had to, seeing as how her brother had heard what was happening in the bathroom the day she took the pregnancy test and Rill burst in on her. Everett had been extremely quiet when she told him the details of her pregnancy, but then moaned miserably when she told him about Rill's reaction.

"Christ Almighty, Katie. What do you mean he doesn't remember getting you pregnant?" Everett had demanded when they'd spoken on the phone earlier today.

"I mean he was stone drunk. And I'm not giving you any more details about it, either. It's none of your business."

"I'm not much in a mood for feeling sorry for Rill, seeing as how he got my sister pregnant and took off," Everett grumbled, "but I can see how it might have floored him. I don't suppose he told you about Eden?"

"Yeah," Katie had replied flatly. "How she was pregnant when she died, and it wasn't his baby."

"Of all the fucking things—"

"Yeah, I see the dark irony of it all. Trust me, I'm drowning in it."

She'd regretted saying that when Everett said he was booking a flight to St. Louis the next day. She'd scolded him out of it, saying she had her new job to attend to, and assuring him Olive and Barnyard were there for support. She told him he could fly out with her parents once she told them about the baby, if he wanted.

Katie figured she'd need a good dose of moral support at about that point, living alone on top of that hill and wondering where Rill was . . . what he was doing . . . whom he was with.

She kept dreaming about him incessantly; Rill holding her fast in his arms, his male laughter filling up the whole house, the moment when his amused expression turned hot as he looked at her. The dreams were so realistic, she'd wake up in the morning and experience her loneliness like a slap to the face. She knew she should have washed the sheets, or slept in the dormer bedroom, but she couldn't resist lying in his bed at night, his pillow pressed against her belly and face, his scent filling her nose.

He'd tried to call her twice that Katie was aware of, but cell phone coverage in the hills was spotty and unreliable. She hadn't gotten his brief messages until hours after the call was actually placed.

He hadn't called for two days now, and Katie was beginning to get jittery with anxiety over that fact. She couldn't allow herself to believe he was going to return, but she couldn't seem to stop hoping, either, and she knew how unhealthy that was. When she realized the state she was putting herself into late Saturday afternoon as she paced around with her cell phone sitting on the kitchen table like a time bomb she couldn't deactivate, Katie resolved to go into town and eat at the diner. One of Sherona's meals would put her straight.

"Come on, Barnyard," she told the dog, who had been soberly watching as she walked back and forth. He skipped in front of her, sliding on the kitchen floor before he hit the wood of the hallway.

She determinedly left her cell phone behind in the house and opened the passenger door for Barnyard to clamor into her Maserati on scrambling, stubby legs.

Barnyard turned in an anxious circle and whined when he reached the front of the diner, unwilling to plant his bottom in his usual spot. His sad eyes tore at Katie when he looked up at her.

Was he worried she was going to leave him there again?

"Would you rather wait in the car, Barnyard?" she asked him quietly.

He whimpered and Katie headed for the car. He followed her. She opened the windows, letting in a cool fall breeze, and left a more content-looking Barnyard behind.

Katie waved at several people she knew when she entered the diner. Errol was sitting in his usual booth when she arrived, but he immediately got up and hobbled toward her on his crutches, sitting beside her at the counter.

"Want something to eat, Errol?" Katie asked as she nodded a greeting at Sherona, who was at a booth giving Marcus Stash his change. Monty was talking to a man Katie had recently met named Nick Brown, who did beautiful oil paintings of the local forest and hills and sold them at the Dyer Creek Trading Company. She'd decided she wanted to buy one for the empty space above the mantel at the Mitchell place, but she hadn't told Nick yet.

Marcus Stash looked tense as he glared at the back of Miles Fordham's head. Miles was having a serious discussion with a man wearing a business suit, although he did keep glancing in Katie's direction.

"Already ate," Errol told her placidly. "Meat loaf, mashed potatoes, green beans and corn on the cob."

"Yum. Maybe I'll have that," Katie said, peering at the menu. The bells on the door jangled as Marcus Stash charged out of the diner.

"What can I get you, Katie?" Sherona asked when she bustled behind the counter. Katie made her order.

"How you feeling? Any morning sickness?" Sherona asked under her breath while Errol studied his model plane.

"A little, but nothing some soda and crackers doesn't settle. I hear it might get worse," Katie replied. She noticed Sherona seemed unusually distracted.

"Something wrong, Sherona?" Katie asked.

Sherona rolled her eyes. "I know it sounds stupid, but I keep thinking I left on my coffeepot at home. Derek has football practice, so I couldn't call and have him check. It's been driving me nuts all afternoon."

"Why don't you go home and check? I'll look out for things around here," Katie volunteered.

Sherona shook her head at first, but then glanced around the diner, which was fairly empty. At that moment, Miles Fordham checked his watch and stood up from the booth.

He left the suited man behind to finish his coffee, waved at Katie and hurried out the door.

"Are you sure, Katie? It'll take me five minutes, tops. The only thing you might have to do is fill a coffee cup or two until I get back," Sherona said.

Katie hopped down from her barstool. "No problem. Go on." She shooed Sherona off. Sherona removed her apron and hurried into the back room toward the rear entrance.

Errol looked uncomfortable at the image of Katie behind the counter tying Sherona's apron around her jeans. Errol liked his world unchanging and orderly. "It's just for a little bit, Errol. Sherona will be back in a flash." She gave him a smile before she picked up a newly brewed pot of coffee and headed toward the man in the business suit.

"Another cup for you?" she asked the man. She glanced around at the sound of the bells and saw Derek Legion enter the diner. His hair was damp and his face was flushed. He carried a blue-and-white football helmet under his arm. He seemed surprised to see Katie holding a coffeepot, but he returned her wave before he went to talk to Errol.

"Don't mind if I do," the man said, setting his cup in the saucer. "I have the red-eye out of St. Louis, so I've got some time to kill. Gorgeous country you have around here. Don't see anything like this upstate."

"You from the Chicago area?" Katie asked.

"Springfield. The name's Harlan. George Harlan." The man paused to shake Katie's hand.

"Katie Hughes. I don't suppose you have anything to do with the gaming commission?" Katie asked, although she already knew the answer after spending time in Miles's office last week.

"That's right. Here to make our final inspection. That riverboat complex is going to provide lots of jobs for this little community," Harlan said with a smile. "With the coal mine fixing to cut back its output and cut jobs, the boat will be a gift to Vulture's Canyon."

"Maybe," Katie said, smiling. "If Fordham planned to give the jobs to locals, anyway."

"What do you mean?" Harlan asked, his expression sobering.

She paused and looked around at the sound of the bells jangling loudly. Someone wearing a dark brown puffy coat was in the process of locking the front door.

"Hey!" she called out, miffed.

Marcus Stash turned around. He pointed a gun in Katie's and George Harlan's direction.

"Everybody does exactly what I say, and chances are you won't get hurt," Stash yelled. His manic gaze landed on Katie. For a second, he looked as confused as Errol had seeing Katie standing in for Sherona. He recovered instantly.

"Everybody into the back room. Now!" he bellowed.

Katie walked toward the counter. Derek Legion looked pale with shock, but Errol seemed only mildly perturbed.

"Come on, Errol . . . Derek. Let's go to the back room," she said, trying to keep her voice even.

She figured it was best to just go along with Marcus Stash. The brown coat he wore was open. She'd seen enough dynamite strapped to his torso to put tiny Vulture's Canyon, Illinois, on the map in a very big way.

Twenty-eight

⁓⧉⧉⧉⁓

Rill's time clock was warped from two overseas trips within the span of eight days. He'd left Malacnoic before sunrise on the night after he'd seen his uncles and got on the first flight out of Dublin to the States. He couldn't sleep on the flight in his growing anticipation to see Katie. His excitement had festered when he'd been stuck at LaGuardia for a two-hour layover.

Finally, he was home, gritty-eyed and tired, but energized, too—buzzing to see Katie again. He had a lot to talk to her about. A lot. He'd been trying to call her ever since he reached stateside, but much to his disappointment, she wasn't answering. One thing was for certain: with Katie being pregnant he was going to have to do something about the spotty phone service on the top of that hill.

He'd finally reached the Mitchell place, only to see that Katie's car was gone. His heart had dropped down to the vicinity of his navel. What if she'd gone away for good? She'd said she'd be okay when he left last week, but he'd suspected she was more hurt by his sudden trip plans than she let on. He should have told her more details about where he was going . . . about *why* he was going.

But truth be told, Rill hadn't possessed a clear-cut reason for returning to Malacnoic. He felt like a fool as he considered trying to explain his actions to her. He'd known only in some vague way that if he wanted to move on with his life, the trip was necessary.

Learning of Katie's pregnancy had galvanized him somehow.

He stormed into the house, feeling a small measure of relief when he saw all of Katie's toiletries in the bathroom and her cell phone sitting on the kitchen table. He was back in the car within a minute of arriving, headed back toward town.

By the time he reached Vulture's Canyon, the sun had dipped behind the western tree line, casting Main Street in long shadows. He saw Katie's Maserati parked across the street from the diner and pulled into an empty spot with haste. He paused when he saw the eager face looking back at him.

"Barnyard?" he said, feeling disoriented by the sight of the dog who was the usual sentinel of the diner sitting in Katie's Maserati's passenger seat. He looked unusually clean and sleek. Something about the way Barnyard wiggled made him think the dog was wagging its tail like crazy.

Confused as he was by the unexpected image, his heart started to roll against his ribs and he had to smile at himself. *Katie was here.* He was like a fifteen-year-old about to encounter his first crush.

No, that wasn't right. He'd never in his life felt like he did in those moments before he prepared to claim Katie. He'd never questioned the restraints he put on himself when it came to her before, because they'd been part of the air he breathed. Fact was, Rill had never really trusted himself before when it came to sex and love.

He hadn't had much in the way of role models.

His distrust of his sexual nature and his embarrassment and denial of his family had been what had made him put

Eden on some kind of unrealistic pedestal of womanhood. It'd been what had made him pull up short with Katie, leaving him unsure he could offer her anything substantial, especially when she deserved everything . . . the best.

In the end, it'd been Katie who had taught him that intense sexual need could be a genuine outlet for love. Maybe it was obvious to everyone else on the planet, but Rill guessed he was a slow learner.

He lunged out of his car, his gaze glued on the diner. He hauled up short in his energetic pursuit when he heard a woman's muffled yell.

"Rill!"

Rill paused in the middle of the deserted street and watched in mounting puzzlement and concern as a cop car screeched to a halt twenty feet away. Sherona Legion practically fell out of the passenger door, she was in such a hurry to reach him.

"Marcus Stash has gone mad," she said as she ran toward him. "He's got a gun and he strapped enough dynamite on him to blow up half the block. He's got a bunch of them in the diner!"

Sherona's speech was so pressured and fast, Rill could hardly make her out. Sheriff Mulligan talking loudly on his radio while he sat in the driver's seat with the door open didn't help matters, either, especially when Rill heard the words "hostage situation."

"Slow it down, Sherona," Rill said as she drew up to him. He put his hands on her upper arms, trying to brace her.

She panted and swallowed, obviously trying to staunch her rising fear. "He says if that man from the gaming commission—George Harlan—doesn't refuse a recommendation for Miles Fordham to get a gambling license, he'll shoot him and then blow up the place. He's taken some hostages. He told me he's strapped enough dynamite on him to blow up half the block. He put Monty on the phone, and Monty verified that everything Stash said was true."

Rill just stared at Sherona's pale face for a stretched moment. Her dark eyes were wild with anxiety.

"Is Katie in there?" he asked slowly.

A strange sensation like a burning chill went through him when Sherona nodded her head.

"She told me she'd look out for the diner while I ran home to check if my coffeepot was off. Rill . . . my little brother is in there, too. His friends said he walked in there just minutes before Marcus called me." Sherona's voice shook. "I can't believe this is happening. Why is Marcus doing this?"

"It's like you said. He's gone a bit mad, I suppose," Rill said, his gaze running over the ancient storefronts that lined the street. "How long have they been in there?"

"Marcus just called me on my cell phone not much more than five minutes ago. He told me to call Mulligan, and then have Mulligan call him back. I was lucky enough to catch Sheriff Mulligan while he was here in Vulture's Canyon. Then I saw a couple of Derek's friends walking home from practice, and that's when they told me Derek had gone to the diner instead of home after practice. Derek *must* be in there."

Rill tried to focus on Sherona's face, but it was difficult with his mind churning through a thousand thoughts a second.

Katie was in there with a madman. What the hell would he do if something happened to her?

He acknowledged the icy blade of fear that seemed to have lodged in his chest and then he pushed it to the periphery of his consciousness.

"Okay, so let me get this straight. You ran to your house to check on your coffeepot and asked Katie to watch over the diner. Who else was in there?"

Sherona shut her eyes as though she were trying to see a film clip in her head. "Monty was there with Nick Brown. Errol was sitting next to Katie. Miles Fordham was having dinner with that man from the gaming commission that Marcus says he'll shoot, George Harlan, but then Miles left right before I did. I have no idea if anyone left while I was gone."

"And then Derek went in, you think?"

A single tear skipped down her cheek when she nodded.

"Did you say that Marcus Stash called you? Not the police directly?"

"No, he called me while I was still at my house. He wanted me to call Mulligan and have Mulligan call him. He seemed angry that I was there instead of at the diner."

Rill noticed Sheriff Mulligan—a squat, balding, middle-aged man—coming to join them in the distance and spoke quietly under his breath.

"Stash has a bit of a thing for you, doesn't he?"

"Yes," Sherona admitted reluctantly.

"He didn't realize you weren't in the diner. He must have been disappointed."

Sherona looked at him with glazed shock, but Rill didn't explain as Mulligan approached. Rill had met the sheriff on only two or three occasions and wasn't a huge fan. Mulligan disliked Rill in return, and Rill had never done anything to alter that opinion. He'd never much cared about the local sheriff's opinion one way or another, but he'd made his own character assessment of the man. Mulligan wasn't that bright and he must have known it on some level, because he bulldozed over people who even hinted at challenging his authority.

"What are you doing here, Pierce?" Mulligan blustered.

"My fiancée is in there," Rill said levelly. Sherona glanced at him in surprise, but he continued. "She's pregnant. I suggest you call Stash immediately and try to encourage him to release Katie Hughes and Derek Legion. Stash considers himself a hero . . . a patriot, not a murderer of women and children. You can start negotiating with him for the release of the others following that."

Mulligan blinked, obviously shocked that Rill had the nerve to issue such concise instructions.

"This isn't a movie set, Pierce. What *I* suggest is that you leave this to me. We have local backups and hostage negotiators on the way from St. Louis."

"Who knows how long they'll take to get here?" Rill asked. "Besides, you aren't taking Stash's character into account. He *hates* outsiders. That's one of the reasons he's doing what he's doing, because he doesn't want outsiders polluting Vulture's Canyon. You'd be much better off negotiating with him now, before the others get here. Federal agents from the city will just make Stash more paranoid."

Rill knew he'd gone too far when Mulligan shoved a fat finger at him. "You need to keep your mouth shut. You're not the expert here; I am."

Fury and helplessness boiled near the eruption point in Rill's chest. "Neither one of us are experts, you idiot. Don't tell me you've ever handled a hostage situation before. The fact of the matter is, though, you *do* have some pull with Stash because you *are* the local authority. He knows you. He asked Sherona to call you. *You*," Rill repeated loudly. "Would you pick up the fuckin' phone and at least try? What could it hurt, and you'll more than likely save a couple lives with just a few dozen words?"

Mulligan's face turned beet red. "I will do no such thing. I'm waiting for the hostage negotiators to handle this, as will you! I'm ordering you to vacate this area and move a full block away. This is a restricted area. You, too, Sherona."

"But, Rodney, Derek is in there," Sherona pleaded.

"That building may blow at any second," Mulligan said, his face getting redder. "I can't have civilians standing around here." He gave Rill a venomous glare. "Or ordering me around. Now, get out of here!"

Rill had to stop himself from causing bodily harm to the sheriff when Sherona's knees wilted under her at his mention of the diner blowing up. Instead, he steadied Sherona in his arms and led her down the sidewalk.

When they reached the steps in front of the now-closed Vulture's Canyon Savings and Loan, Rill eased Sherona down on the stone steps. In the distance, a couple men wandered out of the tavern and Rill caught phrases like "go on home" and "restricted area" as Mulligan shouted at them.

"He's an idiot," Sherona said numbly.

"Are any of his deputies any better?" Rill asked hopefully.

Sherona just shook her head, her gaze glued to the diner as though she thought she could retract her little brother by staring at it hard enough.

"Rill, what did you mean earlier, when you said Stash must have been disappointed I wasn't in the diner? Are you suggesting he's pulling this crazy stunt for me?"

Rill gave her a quick glance before he went back to studying the strip of buildings across the street. "He had to get your attention somehow . . . show you how powerful he was. It wasn't as if you were giving him the time of day otherwise."

"You can't really believe that."

"Not entirely, no, but it wouldn't surprise me a bit if his obsession with you played a part in all this shit," Rill replied distractedly. He nodded across the street. "These storefronts are relatively new, even if the structure is ancient. Sometimes when you have old buildings like this, they're divided in different ways over the years. Any chance the diner is connected to the vacant space next to it, or the Trading Company?"

"Yes," Sherona said so quickly he blinked. She seemed to come out of her trance and sat up straighter. "The Trading Company and the diner share a common coal room—where they used to keep the coals to run the furnaces."

"What's the layout of the coal room, exactly, in relation to the diner?" Rill asked. He'd helped Sherona on a couple of occasions load supplies into the back room. He listened carefully while she described the interior structure of the buildings in relation to the diner storage room. It seemed that the coal room was attached to the large pantry in her storage room.

"Does Stash know about the coal room?"

"I can't imagine why he would," Sherona replied.

"I'm going to go tell Mulligan. It could be key information for them to have," Rill said, standing. He paused when he saw that two more police cars had pulled up in the street, cherry lights flashing. A cop wearing a light brown uniform charged out of the driver's seat and ran around Mulligan's car, only to jolt backward and barely catch himself from falling on his ass when he ran straight into Mulligan's opening car door. Mulligan began shouting at the dazed deputy.

"Oh, my God, Rill, what's going to happen to Derek and Katie and the others?" Sherona murmured behind him, obviously watching the same thing he was. She sounded desperate, and Rill understood why. It was a little like realizing Barney Fife had been put in charge of your most valuable treasure.

Rill cast a grim look over his shoulder. "It's going to be okay, Sherona."

He headed toward Mulligan and his bumbling crew, wishing he really believed what he'd said. Mulligan immediately started ranting at him to leave the "restricted area" or face arrest when Rill approached. He was trying his hardest not to lose his temper and find an opening to give the information about the coal room when he glanced down the street and saw Sherona was missing from the steps.

"Now, are you going to get out of here, Pierce, or should I get out my handcuffs? I've had just about enough of your interference."

Out of the corner of his eye, he saw movement. Sherona had just run behind the long strip of ancient storefronts that lined Main Street.

"Shit," Rill muttered under his breath.

"*That's it*. You're under arrest for interfering with an officer of the law," Mulligan shouted.

Rill looked down at the sheriff in mixed outrage and disbelief and staggered backward. He suddenly turned and jogged down the street.

"Set foot inside this restricted area again and I'll arrest you for sure, Pierce," Mulligan shouted.

Rill hardly heard him. He reached the end of the street and glanced around, wondering if any of the police were watching him. All three men were on their radios, receivers held up to their mouths, jabbering rapidly, each absorbed in his separate communications.

Rill ran across the street at top speed, wondering if he'd be too late to stop Sherona from doing something stupid.

Twenty-nine

"Do I really *have* to tie up Errol?" Katie asked Marcus Stash. "You know he'd be much better if he could look at one of his airplanes while we sit back here in this storeroom, Marcus."

Stash seemed undecided and beleaguered by her request, but eventually barked out an order for her to tie Errol up and be quiet. Rill had always told her she wouldn't know how to shut her mouth even if her life depended on it.

Katie found out for certain that was true on the day Marcus Stash went crazy.

"Why don't you let Derek go, Marcus?" she reasoned as Stash tied her hands behind her back once she'd restrained her fellow hostages. He'd checked to make sure she'd tied the others tight. She'd thought to fight Stash when he put down his gun to restrain her, but at the last second, he told her he'd shoot Errol if she so much as moved a muscle while he did it. He set down the gun much closer to him than her, so Katie couldn't justify anything rash with Errol's life at stake. Still, she continued with the only weapon she had.

Her mouth.

"You can't have meant for Derek to be caught up in this. Sherona wouldn't like it. You wouldn't want a kid to get hurt in all this, would you?"

Stash's blondish-brown hair seemed to stand straight up from rising agitation versus a crew cut. A sheen of sweat shone on his ruddy features.

"All right, I'll think about it, okay? Just . . . give me some peace for a minute, will you?" he barked.

"Sure," Katie said as she immediately began to work her nimble wrists around in the knot. Nobody tied her hands up aside from Rill, she thought irritably.

She glanced around, taking in the details of her surroundings. The fluorescent lights made everything seem surreally bright. She sat next to Errol and a sack of potatoes. The back door was at the end of a short hallway to the right of her. An enormous pantry entrance was to her right, as well, but in her vision, whereas the rear exit wasn't. The door to the pantry was partially opened, and she saw shelves filled with cartons and cans of food. Stash had taken Errol's crutches from him and leaned them against the wall next to the pantry.

Katie watched, trying to contain her terror, as Stash placed the switch box for the dynamite on a crate. The green light at the top of the box that flickered on and off struck Katie as very ominous. It was strange and awful to consider what it would be like to die in an explosion. She'd never see her parents, or Everett . . . or Rill again.

She'd never see her and Rill's baby. Period.

The possibility seemed too untenable to think about, so Katie squashed the idea down until it was a distant nightmare.

Stash began to pace in front of the hostages' feet. Once, he slinked out to the front of the diner, obviously checking what was happening on the street through the front windows.

She glanced down the line of people who had been tied up. Derek Legion seemed calm enough, his expression a mixture of fear and outrage. Katie got the impression he wanted to football-tackle Marcus. Monty looked precisely as he always did, observing the proceedings with an aloof, wry interest. Katie thought if his hands were untied and he had a newspaper, he could have made himself quite content while being held hostage. Errol was growing increasingly antsy in his restraints, but seemed more anxious about being tied up than afraid of what Stash threatened. Nick Brown looked frightened and shocked, but not as much as George Harlan.

Harlan had heard what Marcus Stash said on the phone earlier with Sherona about being shot unless he refused the gambling license to Fordham. Apparently it hadn't occurred to Harlan that all he had to do was lie to Stash.

People tended to get a bit discombobulated when they heard they were the target of a madman's bullet.

"We need to try to keep him talking . . . encourage him to let Derek go first, then Errol," Katie whispered at them.

She looked around anxiously at the sound of Stash reentering the storeroom.

"It's going to be okay, Errol," Katie murmured, feeling Errol squirm around beside her "Calm down. I'm right here with you."

"Why doesn't that idiot sheriff call?" Stash mumbled under his breath after what seemed like an eternity to Katie, but probably was no more than twenty minutes.

"Maybe you should call Sherona back," Katie suggested.

Stash's head snapped around when she spoke. She couldn't help but recoil at his glance. He looked rabid.

"You could ask her again to have the sheriff call," Katie said tentatively. "She may not have understood you before . . . out of shock, you know? Maybe you could let her know, since you'll be calling her anyway, that you plan on letting Derek go. I know you want the world to know that the gambling boat would be a very bad thing for Vulture's Canyon, Marcus, and I think Sherona would agree with you, don't you?"

Stash's feral expression shifted at the sound of Sherona's name.

"She'd agree," he muttered. "We always talked about how much she hated the idea of that gambling boat. Vulture's Canyon is about nature, and the clean air, and *privacy*, not some damn playground for rich people who want to party and drink and tear up this forest."

Katie nodded sympathetically. "But I'd imagine Sherona's in a state right now, thinking about her little brother being in here, you know . . . with all that." She glanced sadly at the dynamite strapped to Stash's heaving torso. "Don't you think it'd be best to call her and let her know you're going to let Derek out the back door?"

Stash seemed undecided between his tough-guy-Rambo role and his adorer-of-Sherona role. He seemed to deflate slightly and he nodded his head.

"Yeah, I'll do that."

"That's the courageous thing to do, Marcus," Katie assured as Marcus withdrew his cell phone. She increased her efforts to get her hands free as he started to dial. When she noticed Monty looking at her, she nodded her head toward Stash, indicating he should distract him while she tried to break free.

"Do you really think this will work, Stash?" Monty asked evenly. "The only thing that's going to maybe happen is we all get blown up, and we're all on *your* side. Nothing you've done will stop the riverboat from coming."

Katie rolled her eyes in exasperation when Marcus stopped, giving Monty a crazed glare.

"What about Sherona?" Katie prodded, trying to turn his attention back to releasing Derek.

Stash glanced down at his phone. "No service."

Shit, Katie thought. *Damn these hills.* She glanced over at Monty, who raised his eyebrows in a "now what?" gesture. Katie winced in pain as she almost got her wrist through one of the rope loops.

"You know, Marcus, I wish I would have known how important it was to you to keep that gambling boat out of the area. I really do. I could have helped you," Katie blurted out. From the corner of her vision, she saw Monty give her an incredulous look.

"You? Help me? Some fancy girl from California? What could you have helped me with?" Stash asked belligerently.

He started to pace again, his gun in one hand and cell phone in the other.

"I may be an outsider, but I have some insider information that I think could have made a difference in Mr. Harlan's decision."

"Well, go on; spill it, then. Harlan's right there. We're all listening," Stash said bitterly, obviously not believing a word she said.

Katie glanced to her left and saw four pale, sweat-glazed faces staring at her. Errol was too busy twisting around and looking uncomfortable to notice her.

"It's just that I have proof that Miles Fordham is involved in offering prostitution services to the men who come to his club."

Marcus Stash abruptly stopped pacing. Even Errol quit his squirming for a few seconds.

"It's true," Katie said after a pregnant pause. "I saw some records at Fordham's office that proved what I'd suspected, once and for all. I wouldn't have been able to pull it all together if I hadn't been asked by Monty and my new job with the county to help Joe Jones file a tax return. He insisted on showing me his daughter Amber's financial records as well. On our first visit to Joe's trailer, Monty had alluded to the fact that Amber had been taking her share of Joe's money from the sale of his land. So when Joe offered Amber's records the second time, I figured it wouldn't hurt to try to find out what was happening to all of Joe's money. Anyway, that was where I first saw for a fact that Amber Jones was being paid by Miles Fordham to spend time with certain men. Amber kept pretty good records of all the men she slept with, including all her paid checks from Miles. I believe, given what I saw at Miles's offices, that there are two other ladies besides Amber Jones that Miles has been paying to entertain his customers. I would imagine he plans something on a much larger scale when he opens the new casino, though."

Katie appealed to George Harlan. "Maybe I don't know everything about your line of business, Mr. Harlan, but I assume it would make a difference, in the state's final decision, to know that Miles Fordham has been involved in prostitution? It was my understanding that gaming commissions tended to steer clear of folks dabbling in the sex trade."

Monty gave her a small, sly smile in the distance, but George Harlan just looked confused.

"Well, of course . . . of course if something like that could be proved by legal means, that would be one thing—the gaming commission is highly cautious about screening applicants for past crimes—most especially for prostitution—but—"

"Oh, it can be proven. Trust me," Katie interrupted Harlan before he dug them all a deeper grave by not playing along with her scheme.

"How?" Stash asked.

"I made copies of the records," Katie lied. She met Stash's beady-eyed stare, forcing herself not to blink. It was imperative that he believe her. "I don't like that sleazebag Fordham any more than you do."

Stash resumed his agitated pacing. Katie swallowed through an achy throat and jerked one hand out of the rope. *Bingo.*

"I think she's on to something, Stash," Monty said, his voice lending a calm, sure note to the proceedings. "Maybe you ought to end this thing before someone gets hurt. We can stop Fordham through legal means."

Katie was busy getting her other wrist free, her gaze fixed on Stash to make sure he didn't notice her shoulders twitching around, when movement occurred at the corner of her vision.

She gasped so loudly that everyone in the room stared at her.

"Ouch!" she wailed, jerking her gaze to her lap. *"Leg cramp."*

She glanced up covertly from under a lowered brow and saw Stash resume his pacing.

"It'll never work. Fordham and all his fancy lawyers—he'll slime his way right through the courts," Stash mumbled.

"Not necessarily," George Harlan said nervously. Katie

had the impression Monty had just elbowed him hard, trying to knock some sense into the government official. As Harlan began to elucidate how a claim and subsequent proof that Fordham had been involved in prostitution would damage his bid for a gambling license irreparably, Katie glanced toward the pantry cautiously.

She really *hadn't* been hallucinating.

Rill stood in the opening of the entrance to the pantry, the partially closed door blocking him from Stash's view. She saw another person standing behind him and recognized the auburn color of Sherona's hair.

Rill held his finger up to his lips. She couldn't believe she was staring at Rill . . . in a pantry . . . in a back room . . . in Vulture's Canyon . . .

. . . when she'd suspected he wasn't ever going to return.

He did something that looked too realistic to be a dream. He pointed in Stash's direction through the door. Then he held his hand up and mimicked holding a switch down, and then jerking his thumb upward.

Katie nodded her head, understanding what he meant.

Maybe they were just a couple idiots from Hollywood, but both of them had been well educated from movie plots about a "dead man's switch." Stash wasn't going to detonate the dynamite if somebody clobbered him and he released a button in his unconscious state, blowing them all to oblivion. He wasn't carrying the radio-operated switch. It needed to be activated or deactivated manually.

She couldn't take her eyes off Rill, and was glad Stash seemed so intent on listening to George Harlan. For some odd reason, Rill's right cheek and forehead were smudged with black cinder. Was it a disguise?

Katie glanced nervously to a pacing Stash and back to Rill, letting him know with her eyes where Stash was in the room. But she needn't have worried because Stash started talking, giving away his location.

"You can't guarantee me, or anyone in Vulture's Canyon, that Fordham wouldn't wiggle his way past the legal obstacles, Harlan. You don't know Fordham. He's the devil."

Katie's eyes went wide and her heart lodged in her throat when Rill reached out of the pantry—quick as a snake at the strike—and snagged one of Errol's crutches. It suddenly struck her what Rill was going to do.

Terror sliced through her when she thought of Stash's gun . . . the dynamite. All Stash had to do was run eight feet, pick up that switch, flip it and POW.

All of them were dead. It somehow seemed a thousand times worse when she considered that Rill would die in the explosion with them.

Rill edged up right next to the opening of the door, his expression intent as he listened to Stash talking. Katie realized with rising anxiety he was waiting for the sound of Stash's voice so he could tell the moment when he turned his back to Rill.

"If I had some solid proof, it'd be one thing. But I can't take that chance. I've got to stop Fordham. He's taking away my rights as a citizen," Stash ranted. "I'm the last line of defense Vulture's Canyon has." He seemed to be gaining momentum as he listened to himself talk. Katie watched in a misery of anticipation as Stash pivoted and turned away from Rill. "I've got to stop that son of a bitch before he ruins—"

Thwack.

Rill had lunged out of the pantry and swung the thick part of the crutch at the back of Stash's head like a baseball bat. Katie recalled the way he'd chopped logs with one clean, powerful blow. He had a similar effect on a human being, she realized through a haze of shock.

Marcus Stash fell to the floor like he was a robot that had suddenly had its battery yanked. His gun slid all the way across the wood floor where it disappeared down the back hall. Sherona went after it and returned to the storeroom. She trained the weapon on the fallen Stash. Katie was impressed by how confidently she handled the gun.

"Where is it?" Rill asked Katie, and she knew he meant the switch box.

"There." Katie nodded toward the crate behind him.

They all breathed a collective sigh of relief when Rill

flipped a switch and the light on the mechanical box blinked out.

Katie jumped up from her sitting position like she was on springs. She flew at Rill, who caught her against him after a surprised *umph* at the impact of her body hitting his.

"You okay, Katie?"

His low, lyrical voice vibrated next to her ear.

"I'm fine. I thought you weren't going to come back." She lifted her head.

"I told you I was coming back, Shine. I'm back for good."

"For good?" Katie asked breathlessly, worried she was misinterpreting the message broadcast in his blue eyes.

Rill nodded and pulled her closer to him. He spoke quietly near her lips, so that no one else could hear. It didn't appear to matter, as the other hostages were talking among themselves excitedly.

"I've been thinking—what do you say we get some work done on the house? The baby will need a new room," he said.

"And the exterior needs painting," Katie whispered breathlessly as his mouth brushed against hers. "I adopted Barnyard."

"Yeah, I saw," he said before his head sank, and Katie forgot about gun-wielding maniacs and house decoration.

Rill had come back.

He'd come back.

"Do you suppose you two could untie us before you get on with your happily-ever-after?"

Katie leaned back from Rill's kiss, grinning at the sound of Monty's wry question.

Thirty

It was past midnight and Rill's muscles began to grow heavy with exhaustion. He'd slept for only a few hours last night, eager as he'd been to get back to Katie. He'd wanted to snatch her and take her away to the privacy of the hilltop house once Stash had been revived and arrested, but Mulligan had kept all of them at the diner, taking their statements.

The diner had filled with Vulture's Canyon citizens as the night progressed, each of them being harangued by Sheriff Mulligan for their presence and told to go home. Most of them, like Olive Fanatoon, had just ignored him, and cuddled up to their previously endangered loved ones, refusing to let go. The federal agents, who had arrived about a half hour after the crisis was over, became flat-eyed and dangerous when Mulligan approached them.

Several of the agents started to dig into Sherona's award-winning pies with relish. A manic sort of party atmosphere prevailed as the townspeople celebrated the hostages' narrow escape and speculated on Marcus Stash's character and motives.

When Rill had heard Katie give her statement about trying to get Stash to believe her story about Fordham being involved in prostitution, he'd been amazed at her courage.

Now they were finally home. Rill noticed Barnyard was growing as heavy-eyed as him as the dog stretched in front of the fire on his belly.

Katie walked into the living room, saying her good-byes to her mother on her cell phone. Rill's fatigue seemed to vanish as he watched her. They'd talked a lot in the past few hours, filled each other in on facts and details of the past week plus, but they hadn't really touched . . . hadn't really communed save for that pressured, emotional exchange in the storeroom of the diner.

Katie had changed while he'd been in the shower—he had gotten filthy as he'd chased Sherona across the cinders in the coal room. She'd been so determined in trying to confront Stash and save Derek, Rill had finally come to the conclusion he had no choice but to help her. If he kept arguing with her, Stash would have heard them, and all hell would have broken loose.

Katie had changed into one of the gypsy skirts he'd come to like so much because they suited her lithe figure and effervescent spirit. She wore her hair loose. Golden curls swayed around her hips.

He put out his arm and she lowered down next to him on the couch. His fingers burrowed through silken waves.

She gave Rill a secret sort of smile before she said her last good-bye to her mom and disconnected the phone. That small smile lingered on her lips as she set aside the phone, spellbinding him.

He reached for her.

"Did you tell your mother you were pregnant?" Rill asked against her damp lips a while later. He'd spent the last several minutes trying to discover the mystery of that smile with his searching tongue. All he'd succeeded in doing was to grow hot and hard for her, ready to move on to the next thrill he knew he'd find in Katie's soft flesh. But he could wait, and the delay would be delicious as well.

A lifetime stretched before him like a golden, sun-kissed beach, as long as Katie was in his arms.

"No, I just wanted to call her and Dad and tell them we were safe. Mom says she'll call Everett. Stash's arrest probably won't get to the Los Angeles news—it all was pretty low-key there at the end, thanks to you—but the local news trucks came to the diner, and who knows what Dad might see on CNN or something."

He filled his fist with soft curls and leaned down to inhale the scent at Katie's neck. Both sensations made his cock purr in appreciation.

"So you haven't told your parents about the baby?"

"No," she said softly. "Only Everett. I thought it was best, you know?"

He glanced at her questioningly.

"Because I might still lose it, at these early stages," she said.

Rill leaned away so he could focus on her better. "Did the doctor tell you that? Is something wrong?"

"No, there's nothing wrong," she said, pulling him back toward her and pressing her breasts against his ribs. "It's just customary to wait, to be as sure as possible, that's all."

"You're not going to lose the baby."

Her eyebrows arched up. "What makes you say that with such confidence?"

"Because it's a Pierce, and Pierces are known for their stubbornness."

"It's not a Pierce yet."

He smiled at her subtle challenge.

"It's been a Pierce since day one," he said. "And if you're talking about the legalities of the matter, we'll resolve that as soon as I can talk you into marrying me."

Her playful smile froze and then faded. He cradled her jaw with his hand.

"What are you shocked about?" he asked. "The fact that I remember the night we made the baby? Or the fact that I just asked you to marry me?"

"Both, I guess," she whispered. "You . . . you *remember*? That first night?"

"Not like I should, no," he admitted with a grimace. "And until I went back to Malacnoic, I don't think I *could* have remembered it. But after a while . . . I knew. I remembered some things."

"What do you mean?"

He shrugged, feeling a little sheepish at having to explain his vulnerabilities and blind spots.

"I remembered what you said, the evening I found you in the bathroom with the pregnancy test. You mentioned something about how drunk you'd found me . . . how you'd almost got tipsy inhaling my breath," he said quietly, meeting her eyes. "I hadn't gotten really shit-faced since you came here, Katie. Or *ever*, in front of you. You and I both know I was never a big drinker before Eden died. Or at least I hadn't been drunk around *you*. Not until that night when you came to Vulture's Canyon."

He closed his eyes and inhaled, trying to gather his thoughts.

"Rill? Are you all right?" she prodded.

He shook his head. "Yeah. It's just . . . It's hard."

"What's hard?" Katie whispered, her expression both confused and compassionate.

"To admit you made a huge mistake by marrying the woman you married. To admit that I forced Eden into the role of a saint because I was so afraid of my nature . . . afraid of being like my mother."

"And your uncles?" Katie asked.

"Yeah, I used to feel that way. I don't anymore, though. I'm glad I saw Ray and William again. I hadn't realized how much a part of me they are. They're both pieces of work, and they might be in prison for some petty crime the next time we go to Malacnoic, but I'd like you to meet them."

She smiled. "I'd like that. But I still don't understand what you meant, when you said you don't think you could have remembered anything about that first night I came here until you went to Malacnoic."

"I wanted you so much on that first night. *That's* what I remember, in a general kind of way, not with any detail. I guess it was the whiskey doing its thing, but I don't remember ever wanting another person like I wanted you that night. And . . . and it wasn't a new feeling, either. I'd become so fucking good at pushing down my needs over the years . . . pushing down my desires." He met Katie's stare, wishing he could will her to understand the complexity of what had happened to him on that night when she'd shown up on his doorstep. "But suddenly you were there, Katie, and I was weak . . . weaker than I'd ever been in my life. All of it rose up in me. All the need. I had to have you. I *did* have you. After that, I struggled every second of every day and night while you were in this house, trying to forget how I'd let myself drown in all that need even while I was obsessed with the idea of giving in to it again.

"When I went back and saw my mother, I realized how different she and I are. It's like she said—we're as different as north and south. I always told myself we were different. But deep down inside, I was worried I could become like her . . . that I could be addicted to sex . . . totally focused on myself . . . unable to really care or feel for another human being."

"You're not even remotely like that," Katie exclaimed, looking miffed.

He chuckled and brought her closer. He kissed her nose. "I love you, Katie. For saying that and so much more," he whispered before he settled his mouth on her lips. She broke their kiss a while later and rubbed their lips together while she spoke.

"Rill?"

"Yes?"

"Does this mean you wanted me . . . even . . . even years ago?"

"I don't know when it started," he admitted. "All I know is that night when you showed up here like an angel on my doorstep, it all rushed out of me. The strength of it makes me think I must have loved you, in different ways, since the first time I saw you, Katie. Only a fire that's been tamped down for so long can grow so wild."

"You didn't even recognize me. I thought it was maybe because my hair was darker."

He gave a sharp bark of laughter.

"What?" she asked.

"I recognized you, Shine. I may not have wanted to, but I did. What do you think this has all been about? What do you think I've been trying to tell you?"

When he saw her lips parted in wonder, he sank his head. Their kiss magnified in hunger even as they fed off each other, until they both were moaning in need.

"I want to have you like I did on that first night. I want to try and remember. Will you show me?" he asked huskily as he plucked at her lips.

"Yes. Yes," she whispered. To his surprise, she whisked her top over her head and removed her bra. He stared appreciatively at her tender, firm breasts, but her smile snagged his attention. She took his hand and led him down the lit hallway to his bedroom, the sight of her curls swishing subtly against the bare skin of her back and hips mesmerizing him.

He plastered himself against her when she paused next to the bed, wild to feel her pressed against him.

"What happened next?" he whispered hoarsely as he stood behind her. He leaned down and kissed her neck.

"This," Katie replied. She turned her head and craned up for him. Kissing her was like drowning in the deepest well of pleasure.

He bent his knees and pressed his aching cock against her bottom. "Aw, Jaysus. I have to have you now, Katie."

"Yes."

When she went to place her hands at the edge of the bed, he stopped her abruptly.

"Like that? From behind? The first time?" Regret lanced through him. "Aw, Katie. I'm sorry."

She looked radiant when she glanced around and shook her head. "I'm not, Rill. I'm not."

His need boiled to the surface as he watched her bend over the bed. She really was a miracle, the way she always offered all of herself to him, never holding back an ounce.

A moment later, he held his cock in his hand and arrowed it into her warm, narrow cleft, gritting his teeth at the ecstasy of feeling her grip him like a velvet, milking fist.

"Let me in, Katie," he demanded on an anguished moan. "I've waited for this for so damn long."

A while later, they lay together on their sides on the bed, Katie nestled in the curve of his body, both of them drowsy, but highly aware of each other, tired, but unwilling to slide separately into the world of dreams.

"It's a shame that stuff you told Marcus Stash about Fordham paying Amber Jones and those other girls to sleep with his customers was a lie. It'd be nice to be rid of the jerk," Rill murmured.

"I thought you were the guy who didn't care about this town or its occupants," Katie said, turning in his arms to see his face.

Rill shrugged. "I *was* that guy." He picked up one of her curls and squished it between his fingers before he brushed it against his chin thoughtfully. "Things change, though. I'm thinking I'll go and have a talk with Olive Fanatoon about Food for Body and Soul."

Katie twisted around farther in surprise. "Are you going to be the spokesperson for the charity, like she's been asking you to be?"

"I'm thinking about it," he murmured in such a nonchalant way that Katie knew he'd already decided to do just that. "I'll be writing, and eventually directing again. I'll be doing my share of traveling. But I want Vulture's Canyon to be more than a base of operations. I want it to be a home. Our home. I don't want to shut myself off from the town, like I had been doing."

She shifted so that they were face-to-face and kissed him hard. "I'm so happy to hear you say you plan on working again. But why are you thinking about volunteering to be the spokesperson for Food for Body and Soul?"

"It'll help out Vulture's Canyon, won't it?" he asked, as

though the answer was obvious. "I want our baby to grow up in a nice town with some good values."

"Hmmm," she mused as she pressed her breasts against his chest and studied him. "In that case, I should tell you that I didn't entirely make up what I told Marcus Stash about Miles Fordham."

Rill lifted his eyebrows and stared at her with interest.

"I was actually planning to sell my Maserati, buy a pickup truck—it'd be great for hauling supplies up and down the hill—and using the leftover money to hire a private investigator to collect all the details of Fordham's crimes." She laughed softly when Rill's expression turned incredulous. "Everything I said was true—the evidence is all there; I just didn't have an opportunity to make copies or anything, like I claimed I did. I want Vulture's Canyon to stay a nice town, too."

She laughed harder when Rill grasped her shoulders and rolled until she was beneath him. The light from the hallway gleamed in his eyes as he looked down at her.

"How did this town ever survive without you? How did I?" Her laughter faded when she sensed his intensity. "You're not selling that Maserati."

"It doesn't belong here, Rill. Not in Vulture's Canyon."

"It belongs, because you belong," he said simply. "You can have a whole fleet of pickup trucks if you want them, but . . . don't sell the Maserati. I think we can swing a private investigator without proceeds from its sale."

"I . . . I don't know. We can talk about it," she whispered.

She was so focused on the image of Rill's hungry eyes on her mouth and his lowering head, she didn't know what else to say. In that moment, Katie, who had formerly lived in a backdrop of fantasy, facade and make-believe, saw her world coalesce into glorious reality.

Rill's mouth seized hers in a quick, fierce kiss before he paused and spoke next to her lips.

"It's going to be the healthiest thing I've ever done in my life, becoming addicted to you."

TURN THE PAGE FOR A PEEK AT
BETH KERY'S NOVEL

Sweet Restraint

COMING TO BERKLEY SENSATION IN
MASS MARKET IN DECEMBER 2013!

The man sitting in the driver's seat of the car parked in an abandoned parking lot near the Cal-Sag Channel was a keg of dynamite about to blow. In fact, Randall Moody had come here on this cold January Chicago night to ensure that he did. He wanted to be the one to toss the igniting match in his own good time, however, and he didn't want to be anywhere near the explosion when it occurred.

He cautiously tapped twice on the car window.

"What the hell? How'd you find me?" Huey Mays asked after he'd peered through the window and unlocked the car door. Moody got into the passenger seat. His nose wrinkled in distaste.

"Smells like a distillery in here." He glared repressively at Mays when he saw the other man had drawn his gun when he heard the knocking on the window, but didn't tell him to put it away. He planned on Huey using that gun sometime soon, after all. Huey'd need it handy.

Moody shivered uncontrollably for a moment, cursing his aching joints and aging body. Dammit, Huey Mays's life was about to come to an end. What he wouldn't give to have

his younger, more virile body, even though Mays had
wasted much of his health on alcohol, drugs and multiple
daily doses of rich, fatty foods. Moody was pushing sixty
but he worked out at his health club vigilantly and was fastidious about what he drank and ate. He considered aging
a weakness, but what he despised even more was Huey's
lack of discipline and tendency to wallow in his carnal
nature.

"One of the patrolmen saw your car out here," Moody
replied, his tone smooth and warm, carrying no hint of
the bitter resentment he felt. There was no reason to elabo-
rate further. Mays knew as well as anyone Moody had
one of the best information networks in the city. If something significant was going down in Chicago, chances
are Randall Moody knew about it. Thirty-five years in the
Chicago Police Department and carefully established con-
tacts in both government and the underworld had seen
to that.

"I'm glad you're here," Huey muttered. His hands moved
nervously along his thighs as he wiped the sweat off his
palms, but Moody was glad to see he merely placed his gun
in his lap instead of putting it away. "You've gotta help me
get out of this mess. The feds are breathing down my back
to name names, you know."

"I told you they would. I also told you why it wouldn't
be in your best interest to do so," Moody said calmly.

"They say it'll reduce my sentence to almost nothing."

"Almost nothing? Your best scenario—*best*, mind you—
would be five years in federal lockup. Might as well say an
eternity when it comes to you, Huey. Have you thought about
what that'd be like? No cocktail available every time you
get nervous. No cocaine to give you a nice jolt." Moody
slowly removed his leather gloves and stacked them neatly
on his black cashmere overcoat. He inspected his well-
manicured nails. "And, of course . . . you'll be on the receiv-
ing end instead of the instigator in the type of sex you
prefer—"

"There's not a chance in hell!" Huey shouted. His eyes

looked bloodshot and wild. Moody was pleased to see he looked like a man who stood right on the edge.

"And the fact of the matter remains, Huey. Any benefit you receive from pointing fingers will be very short-lived. It's time you took responsibility for your own actions."

"Nothing?" Huey entreated gruffly. "There's nothing you can do for me?"

"Your fate is in your own hands, I'm afraid," Moody said, his gaze flickering down to the gun in Huey's lap.

"I should have gotten rid of Shane Dominic years ago."

"When the time is right, Dominic will be taken care of, I assure you of that."

"Or better yet, we should have just whacked *her* back then."

"Your wife is a lovely woman. We aren't such monsters that we kill something so delicate and rare," Moody remonstrated.

"Better you would have married the bitch, then." Huey's smile resembled a snarl as he stared blankly out the front window, obviously picturing something much more pleasant in his mind than the black winter's night. "I got her good, though. Both her and that asshole Dominic."

Moody shook his head sadly and reached for the handle on the passenger door. "This is your chance, Huey, to show your wife she married a strong man, a disciplined man. Do yourself a favor and take advantage of the opportunity while you still possess not only your freedom and your honor, but your manhood. Don't let Shane Dominic take *that* away from you as well."

Moody patted Huey's knee in a gesture of paternal encouragement before he exited the car.

Shane Dominic noticed Clarissa's sharp brown eyes on him in the reflection of the mirror on the antique armoire and coat tree. He dropped his hand from where he'd been pressing his fingertips to his scalding eyelids and caught her in his arms as she spun around.

"You know how horny this dress makes me," he murmured next to her neck. "You wore it to the City Club dinner
last fall. I could barely string two words together during my
speech because I kept thinking about getting you into bed
and stripping you out of it."

Clarissa's laughter vibrated into his lips as he pressed
them to her throat.

"That was last fall, Dom. What about tonight?"

His fingers found the zipper on the sexy burgundy cocktail dress and lowered it. "Tonight I can't wait for bed. I'm
going to have to take you right here in the hallway, I think."

He smiled when he felt her shiver beneath his marauding
mouth. Her fingers delved into his hair, urging him down to
the breast that he'd just revealed by sweeping aside the clinging fabric of her bra. He paused, however, and grabbed her
wrist. When he pushed it behind her it forced her back into
an arch. She moaned as he inspected her small, pink-tipped
breast. He blew on it softly.

"You're such a tease, Dom," she mumbled. But she
arched higher for him, pushing her nipple closer to his
mouth.

He chuckled before he licked her nipple lightly. "You're
the one who teased me all night by wearing this dress. Now
you're going to have to pay for it."

"I can't wait," she whispered.

He glanced up at her. His eyes chose that unfortunate
moment to burn and water. He clenched his eyelids shut for
a brief second to get relief.

"Do you want to know what I think?" Clarissa asked.

"What?" he mumbled, not really paying attention. He
lowered his head to Clarissa's beading nipple, his entire
attention focused on the sensation of every tiny bump rolling
across his tongue. Single-minded, that's how Clarissa always
described him.

She moaned in pleasure, so it surprised him when she
jerked at his hair with the hand he wasn't restraining behind
her back. He glanced up at her.

"I think you're trying to change the subject. I think you're exhausted, that's what I think. You've worked nonstop this week on that corrupt cop investigation only to have another speaking engagement tonight at the Magellan Club. You're burning the wick at both ends, Dom. Why do you feel you have to hide your fatigue from me?"

"I don't feel the need to hide anything from you, Clarissa," he assured her before he bent his head again to attend to a tight nipple.

She snorted.

Shane regretfully straightened to his full height. He didn't need to be an expert on human behavior to know that she wasn't going to allow him to make love to her until she said whatever was on her mind.

"If you refer to my work, you know I can't tell you much beyond what the press releases about any bureau investigations," he said as he removed his overcoat and hung it on the entryway armoire. The jacket to his tuxedo followed.

"Give me a break, Dom. You know that's not what I'm talking about."

He hid a grimace when he saw the expression of stark annoyance on her face. He'd let the familiar phrase out of his mouth before he'd had time to censor himself. But worse, he'd apparently delivered the line in that brusque manner that never failed to push his fiancée's red button of irritation.

Don't you dare use that Special-Agent-in-Charge tone with me. *Christ, no wonder they say you've got a heart of stone, Dom.*

Clarissa's past accusation echoed in his head as he gently pulled the fabric of her dress back into place on her shoulder.

She had a right to be pissed at him. He'd barely spoken with her in a week and a half, he realized guiltily. Robert Elliot, the United States attorney for the northern district of Illinois, had just handed him those much-sought-after arrest warrants four nights ago, designated for several cops in the Chicago Police Department.

But no matter how good his reasons for doing so, Clarissa wasn't likely to appreciate him ignoring her for the past ten days only to have him maul her the second he had her to himself.

He led her into his book-lined study and sat her down on the leather couch.

"I know I haven't been able to see you much this week. Tell you what," he said softly. "Let me go and get out of this monkey suit. I'll make us a drink and we'll talk."

Her dark eyes swam with tears as she looked up at him. Clarissa was one of the smartest and most successful financial analysts on LaSalle Street. She didn't cry easily.

"We're going to be married in two months, Dom. Why can't you even admit to me that you're exhausted? Can't you show even a shred of vulnerability in front of your future wife?"

He smiled. "You want me to tell you that I'm exhausted? Okay. I'm about ready to fall flat on my face. I've probably slept a total of eight hours in the past week and my eyeballs feel like they're going to burn through my eyelids. My vision is so blurry that I told the president of the Magellan Club that he needn't bother with getting me a drink from the bar because another gentleman was already getting me one."

"What's so terrible about that?"

"That other *gentleman* was his wife."

Clarissa's lips twitched with humor. "You didn't."

Shane shrugged sheepishly.

"You also told the superintendent of police that you were going to give a nice Liverpool kiss to the next man who ribbed you about being named the 'Sexiest Man in Chicago' by *Chicago* magazine. I didn't understand that you were threatening him until John McNamara explained to me that a Liverpool kiss was a street-fighting technique—a brutal head-to-head blow."

"That threat counts for women, too," Shane said with a mock somber expression. Clarissa grinned.

"Maybe you should have threatened someone besides the superintendent of police, considering the fact that more than half the city sees you as being responsible for taking away their trust in the Chicago Police Department."

Shane's eyebrows went up at that. "Operation Serve and Protect exists for the sole purpose of returning the public's trust in the CPD. Jake Moriarity knows that. That's why he's backed the FBI's investigations of CPD corruption one hundred percent."

"Are you sure that's the only motivation behind your mania for this investigation?"

Shane paused in the process of untying his bow tie. "*Mania*? That's a bit harsh."

Clarissa didn't break their stare.

"This case falls directly under several FBI directives for investigation. Christ, we've uncovered the largest organized theft ring in known history, one that crosses multiple state lines and is run by public officials. What other motivation do we need?"

Clarissa looked vaguely uncomfortable at the question but she didn't look away, nonetheless. "Well . . . there *are* those insinuations that Channel Six News made about your connections to the Vasquez family."

Shane rolled his eyes. "I know a quarter of the cops and most of the detectives on the CPD. I not only have worked with dozens of Chicago cops, I call many of them friends . . . *including* Joey Vasquez."

"But how many of those cops did you attend elementary school with like you did Joey Vasquez?" Clarissa persisted. "And . . . and that news report said Huey Mays's wife is Joey Vasquez's sister and that you've known her for ages . . ."

She trailed off but continued to study his face hungrily.

Shane froze before he jerked the bow tie off his neck, the sliding silk making a hissing sound. "I *knew* Laura Vasquez, Clarissa. I haven't spoken to her in over a dozen years. What's your point?"

Clarissa exhaled slowly. "I don't know what my point is. You've just seemed so obsessed with this case."

"You tell me I'm always single-minded about whatever's on my plate."

"You are. You have a one-track mind, Dom." She shook her head and laughed softly when he lifted an eyebrow and lowered his gaze to her still erect nipple pressing against thin fabric.

"They showed a picture of her, you know," Clarissa said, laughter still clinging to her lips. "On the news. Laura Mays, I mean. She's extremely beautiful."

"Is *that* what this is about?"

"Maybe. I don't know." Her expression turned a little sheepish. "Of *course* you have good reason to be obsessed with this case. Some of the things those cops were doing . . ." She shook her head in mixed disbelief and disgust as she removed a clip at the back of her head. Her dark blonde hair fell around her shoulders. "I mean, using the police department's resources to steal from innocent people, severely beating some of those innocent people, three of them nearly to death in the process, extorting untold amounts of cash from drug dealers and other criminals . . . it boggles the mind, to be honest. They were nothing more than a vicious organized gang operating out of the offices of the CPD.

"*Hello?* Dom? Where'd you go?" Clarissa asked a few seconds later.

Shane blinked, realizing that once again he'd been lost in his thoughts.

Lost in this case.

Why Clarissa put up with his late hours and divided attention was beyond him. She was even good enough not to hold over his head the fact that he'd postponed their wedding—not once, but twice now—every time they got in a spat. He'd been starting to experience those old, familiar doubts about marrying her yet again, and he knew as well as anyone what a jerk that made him.

"I don't deserve you, Clarissa," Shane muttered, wishing for the thousandth time that he could rid himself of these uncertainties. Surely it was just the longtime bachelor in him getting the jitters?

But at the same time he couldn't help but think that if Clarissa was truly the woman for him, there wasn't a chance in hell thoughts of her would so rarely cross his mind for ten days in a row, no matter *how* compelling his work was.

The sultry expression she wore as she looked up at him went a long way toward erasing his doubts for the time being. His eyelids narrowed as he watched her lean forward and plant a kiss on the root of his cock. Despite his fatigue he felt himself stir with arousal.

"You're right. You don't deserve me. I have to admit one thing though. *Chicago* magazine was dead-on. You're downright edible in this tux, Dom."

"Is that a promise?"

She arched her golden eyebrows. "Why don't you go and get comfortable and pour us a drink. Then we'll decide if you're in the mood to sleep or fuck."

"I know what I'm in the mood for, and it's not sleeping. I owe you after this week, Clarissa," he murmured as he pressed his thumb to her lower lip.

"We'll see if you're up for it."

"Oh, I'm *up* for it all right," he assured her.

The sound of Clarissa's appreciative laughter followed him out of the den. He grinned. She really was an amazing woman. She'd just thrown down the gauntlet, knowing full well that he never walked away from a challenge. He may be tired as hell but it was the exhaustion that came after a bloody battle. Some lusty sex would be the perfect way to celebrate his triumph.

Not to mention make him forget his doubts in regard to marriage.

He wasn't a young man anymore. He needed to settle down. So what if he wasn't necessarily eager to rush home to see Clarissa at the end of a workday? He'd just have to try harder to be considerate, that's all. She was a fine woman. He enjoyed her company. There weren't a lot of smart, independent women out there who could meet his needs sexually, but once they were behind bedroom doors, Clarissa submitted very sweetly to him.

Still . . . those doubts lingered.

Thirteen and a half years, for Christ's sake. How lame could he be to carry a torch for a woman for so long? Not just any woman, either. A woman who clearly didn't want him.

A woman he obviously shouldn't want.

Clarissa was standing directly in front of the television set when he returned a few minutes later wearing pajama bottoms and carrying two brandy snifters. He was used to her occasionally switching on CNN business news for any recent headlines, but he was a little surprised that her attention remained fixed on the screen when he came up beside her.

"Oh no, Dom," she whispered.

"What?" he asked

"Look . . ."

His gaze shot to the television screen. It showed a handsome man with dark hair graying at the temples dressed in an expensive, immaculately tailored gray suit exiting the doors of the Dirksen Federal Building. Shane knew the footage had been taken two days ago, just after Huey Mays had been released after posting bail.

A feeling of profound hatred swelled in Shane's chest, the magnitude of it shocking him a little. It must have been the unexpectedness of the image that had taken him off guard.

"Yeah, that's Huey Mays. They'll be running the story about the arrest of a captain of the organized crime division running the most extensive jewel, fur and rare coin theft ring in history from the offices of the Chicago Police Department for quite a while," he muttered with grim satisfaction.

"That's not the story they're running," Clarissa said as she looked up at him anxiously. She took the drink that he offered her without seeming to be aware of what she was doing. "Or at least that's only part of it. The story is that Huey Mays shot himself earlier this evening. He was just pronounced dead at Northwestern Memorial a half hour ago, Dom."

Shane slowed his car on Erie Street next to the entrance of Northwestern Memorial Hospital. He spotted one of his nemeses, Blaine Howard, a reporter for Channel Eight News, dashing toward the doors leading to the east side of the massive building, his cameraman huffing and puffing to keep up with his long-legged sprint.

In Shane's experience the only characteristic that exceeded Howard's ignorance was his arrogance. It wasn't a pretty combination. But if there was one thing Blaine could do it was smell blood.

Shane recognized her immediately when she exited the glass doors and jogged down the sidewalk. A bevy of reporters and cameramen followed several feet behind her, shouting questions and clicking off photo after photo. Shane saw the trace of panic in her rigid features as they closed in on her.

He knew how much she hated crowds. When they were teenagers, her brother Joey had slacked off on studying for his entrance exams to Whitney Young Magnet High School and had had to attend St. Ignatius instead. So when Laura had started at Whitney as a freshman and Shane had been a senior, he'd taken Joey's kid sister under his wing. He'd coached her in order to get her through a required public-speaking class. She was a bright student and a brilliant artist, but she was reserved. Not shy necessarily.

The public arena just wasn't Laura's domain.

Or at least it hadn't been when he'd known her, when innocence still clung to her like morning dew to an exquisite, unopened rose. Things were different now, of course. Huey Mays had seen to that. Huey and whoever else he'd granted rights to the use of his stunning wife's body.

To his stunning slave's body.

There were a lot of things an officer of the law learned from electronic surveillance that he'd rather not hear. In Laura's case they'd been things Shane would have paid any price to permanently erase from his memory banks.

She abruptly broke free and sprinted ahead of the pursuing reporters and photographers. He pulled up a few feet in front of her as she ran down Erie Street and slammed on the brakes.

"Get in," he barked through the lowered window.

She pulled up short, her eyes widening when she saw him. She hesitated.

"Get in the damn car, Laura. They'll be all over you in a second."

Once she'd made her decision she moved fleetly. He stomped on the accelerator the second she'd slammed the door. One of the members of the rushing media slapped the back of his car in frustration as it took off down the street.

For almost a minute neither of them spoke as he merged onto Lake Shore Drive south. It struck him as surreal to be driving a car with Laura Vasquez in the passenger seat. This morning he'd never have guessed in a million years that this was how his day would end.

"You shouldn't have done that, Shane. One of them might have seen your license plate and figured out that I was just picked up by the special agent in charge of the FBI's Chicago offices—the same man who was responsible for Huey's arrest."

"*Huey* was responsible for his arrest, Laura."

His stern tone might have been an attempt to neutralize the effect her low, husky voice had on his body. She was one of three people on the face of the earth who actually called him by his given name—his mother and father being the other two. He hadn't heard it coming off her tongue for more than a dozen years now.

He glanced over at her, taking in the clean, harmonious curves and angles of her profile against the lights of the city, a flawless diamond set among glittering rhinestones. She appeared calm and untouched by his provocative statement.

How did she really feel about her husband's death? He forced his stare back to the road.

As usual it was impossible to plumb her depths. She was the one person he'd ever encountered who represented incontrovertible truth that his ability to judge another human being's character was grievously flawed. His peers would say that was Shane's expertise—the ability to comprehend people's motivations, to predict how they'd act given a certain set of circumstances.

The fact that his feelings toward Laura were such a stark discrepancy of what they *should* be given reality bugged the shit out of him. It'd been like a burr under his skin for thirteen and a half years, a wound that just wouldn't heal no matter how he tried to forget her and move on with his life.

"So what if they do realize it was me?" he muttered. "I'll say that I picked you up for questioning."

"Is that really what you're doing?"

For a brief second their eyes met in the shadows. "Questioning you has never gotten me anywhere in the past, has it, Laura?"

She looked like she was about to say something but then she stopped herself. Her face looked set and pale—the most beautiful mask he'd ever seen in his life. He resisted an urge to pull the car over and shake her until she showed him something. Her rage. Her sadness. Her passion.

Anything but this cold indifference.

"Where are you taking me?"

He blinked at the mundane question in the midst of such a charged moment. Charged for *him*, anyway.

"I don't know. Where do you want to go?"

"So you're really not taking me in for questioning?"

He cast a hard look in her direction. "Didn't the police question you?"

"Yes. At the hospital. They said they'd be contacting me in the morning to clarify a few other things. I received the news that Huey had passed away as they were questioning me . . ."

He didn't say anything for a few seconds when she trailed off. Huey Mays's unexpected death by suicide pissed him off so much that he'd practically been blind with rage for a few seconds as he stood there in front of his television set forty-five minutes ago.

Oily little weasel to the finish, wriggling free of the snare he'd caught himself in like the coward that he was. Shane seethed.

Mays had been the linchpin to the FBI's continued investigations into corruption at the CPD. The man was slimier than the stuff that got stuck to the bottom of your shoe in a

sleazy dive's john. Except Mays was worse because he was
handsome enough to appear on the front of a men's magazine and just as slick as the glossy cover.

Shane suspected that Mays would have spilled names to
save his own neck, and his instinct was rarely wrong in such
matters. He had hoped that he'd sing one name loud and
clear—that of the current chief of the Organized Crime
Division of the CPD, Randall Moody.

"Did they tell you that Huey left a note?" he asked Laura.
He'd spoken to the commander in charge of the precinct
where Huey's body had been found and knew the basic
details of the case.

"Yes," she replied.

He took in her unruffled composure. Shane sighed,
ineffectively venting an almost fourteen-year-long frustration at the sight.

"His body will still be examined by one of the Bureau's
agents at the crime lab, but as long as everything checks out
with their report and the note is genuine, there won't be a
formal investigation. It'll be ruled a clear-cut case of suicide.
Picking you up on the street just now wasn't official business. It was a spur of the moment thing," he mumbled after
a few seconds when he saw her smooth brow wrinkle in
puzzlement. "I saw the media charging you. I spend half my
life escaping from those jackals."

A small smile tilted her full lips. "Still saving me from
the bad guys, Shane?"

"That would require you *allowing* me to save you,
wouldn't it? You've swum way too deep now, sweetheart,"
he snarled.

He paused when he noticed the glaze of shock in her wide
eyes. He inhaled slowly and fixed his stare on the road.
Jesus, what the hell was wrong with him?

"I'm sorry. You didn't deserve that. Not tonight." He felt
her gaze on him, making his skin prickle, but she didn't
speak for several moments. Finally she cleared her throat.

"I suppose they would have told you that he . . . he did it
in his car?" she asked. "Another police officer found him.

Huey had parked in a deserted area near the Cal-Sag Channel. The police officer thought the car had been abandoned and went to investigate. Huey was still alive but unconscious. He never woke up."

"Who was the officer?"

"Josh Hannigan, from the Sixth Precinct."

"Do you know him?"

Laura shook her head.

He peered at her suspiciously through the darkness. Laura came from a family of cops. Her uncle Derrick—her guardian—had been a twice-decorated sergeant. Her older brother, Joey, was a vice detective.

And, of course, her husband had been a cop—though Huey'd made a mockery of the title. Now it looked as if Joey might be entangled in the whole affair as well.

And Laura sat in the midst of it all, silent and inexplicable. Who was she protecting with her aloofness? Her husband? Joey?

Herself?

He blinked to clear the blurriness from his sleep-deprived eyes and took stock of his surroundings. He realized he'd been driving south on Lake Shore Drive without a clue as to where he was going. He got over into the right lane and narrowly made the closest exit.

Joey Vasquez might be a person of interest in the CPD theft ring case, but he also was an important part of Shane's history and Laura's only living immediate family. Joey and he hadn't seen much of each other since Shane had returned to his hometown, this time to head up the Chicago offices of the FBI. Still, he knew that Joey lived in Hyde Park. He ducked his head and tried to make out the street sign as he passed to get his bearings.

"You shouldn't be alone right now. I'll take you over to Joey's," he muttered.

"No, not to Joey's. Take me to my house, please."

"*Laura*, you just—"

"Joey is out of town," she interrupted calmly. She noticed his skeptical glance. "I'm telling the truth, Shane. He and

Shelly took a van-load of kids to Springfield for the high
school girls state volleyball championship. Carlotta is playing in the finals."

"Carlotta can*not* be in high school," Shane proclaimed
flatly, referring to Joey's daughter.

His gaze caught and stuck on the tantalizing image of
Laura's small, wistful smile. "She's a junior at Marie Curie
High School."

Shane shook his head. You could ignore your advancing
age as much as you wanted, but the next generation refused
to allow you to remain secure in your denial.

"You're thirty-four years old," he said as he drove down
the silent, dimly lit city street.

"Since November," Laura replied in a hushed voice.

It took him a half a minute to realize that she was crying.
She never made a sound as she stared straight ahead, the
tears clinging like ice crystals against her smooth cheek.